Outer London
Step by Step

ff

faber and faber

LONDON · BOSTON

First published in 1986 by
Faber and Faber Limited
3 Queen Square London WC1N 3AU

Photoset by Parker Typesetting Service, Leicester
Printed in Great Britain by
The Bath Press Ltd, Bath
All rights reserved

British Library Cataloguing in Publication Data
Turner, Christopher
Outer London Step by Step.
1. London (England)—Description—
1981—Guide-books
I. Title
914.21'704858   DA679
ISBN 0-571-138987-6

Contents

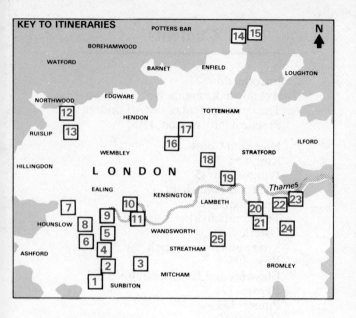

KEY TO ITINERARIES

Introduction

This book has been written to complement *London Step by Step* which explores the central area of London. A similar format has been adopted, whereby the visitor is treated as someone who, without precise guidance, will get lost and confused.

Complete directions are given for reaching and leaving an area by public transport from central London. Having arrived, the visitor is led, literally step by step, around the exterior and, when permitted, the interior of each location. Every point of interest is referred to precisely as it is reached and directions are then given for continuing.

The twenty-five areas are generally described throughout the book from the west to the east of the capital so that visitors can appreciate more easily how they may be linked. Although the most important sights are included, there are, of course, some locations of interest that have been omitted as *Outer London Step by Step* is a guide book rather than a gazetteer.

Whether on a guided tour or a 'do it yourself' visit, this book will add immeasurably to the appreciation of London's rich heritage that lies outside its centre. Not only strangers, but also local residents will find much of its contents a revelation.

Christopher Turner

Acknowledgements

For their kindness and help I should like to thank the numerous librarians, architects, press officers, church officers, clerks, hoteliers and curators who have advised on and checked the contents of this book. A tremendous amount of valuable time was given by the following in particular: the London Visitor and Convention Bureau; the Historic Buildings and Monuments Commission; the Superintendent of Hampton Court; the archivists of Harrow School; the Victoria and Albert Museum; and the National Maritime Museum.

The Buildings of England series and the *London Encyclopaedia* were especially useful sources of information.

The development of outer London

It is difficult to comprehend that within living memory most of the outer London boroughs were widely separated, semi-rural towns and villages. Towards the end of the nineteenth century, Sherlock Holmes was able to refer, even to Chiswick, as being 'in the country'.

No other western European city has spread as extensively from its ancient core as London has. Fortunately, English conservatism and sentimentality have managed to preserve the essence of many of these towns and villages so that they retain much of their individuality and charm.

England's security first became established when the Norman Conquest had been assimilated, and the nobility were leaving the protection of the walled City for unfortified Thames-side mansions as early as the twelfth century. Royal palaces were established on the river also, but even further from the City, at Richmond and Greenwich. When the monasteries were dissolved, the Crown appropriated their vast estates and sold most of them for private development. Greater London's population quadrupled during the remainder of the sixteenth century but, as there was insufficient employment, wages fell and poverty became widespread. Alarmed by this, successive monarchs forbade the construction of new houses within varying distances from the City walls but the tide could not be turned.

Dockyards, and their attendant warehouses, swallowed up much of the banks of the Thames, east of London Bridge, and by the nineteenth century this area had become one vast slum. It has never fully recovered, and this is the chief reason why most of outer London's areas of greatest interest to visitors lie to the west. A notable exception, of course, is Greenwich, which, because of its great royal estates, has remained an oasis of outstanding beauty.

The prime cause of London's tremendous expansion during the last hundred years was, of course, improved communications. New roads and bridges had been built, but it was the opening, in 1863, of the Metropolitan Railway, followed by the first underground tube train in 1890, that led to the real breakthrough.

Property developers moved in, and Londoners were only too happy to purchase the cheap houses which initially followed the convenient railway lines. It should be borne in mind that London was, until quite recently, one of the world's most polluted cities with yellow killer smog a regular visitor. Escape to what was then healthier countryside was, therefore, a great attraction.

Although little genuine country survives in Greater London, many ancient towns, most of which are featured in this book, retain great parks, heaths, village greens or a sylvan riverside which provide a pleasing sense of timeless rurality. Here, the ancient core of the town or village may frequently be identified by Georgian houses clustered around the parish church.

No other city can claim so much of interest lying immediately around its centre. Thanks to the continuity of the monarchy and England's stability, many of the ancient royal estates, private mansions and scholastic establishments that surround the capital have survived. Hampton Court, Greenwich, Kew Gardens and Syon House are unmatched elsewhere in the British Isles, let alone central London.

Although Georgian architecture dominates most of the towns featured in this book, examples of the Gothic style survive in many of their parish churches and some timber-framed houses have miraculously survived, especially on the periphery. The great buildings, of course, exhibit a wider variety of styles and the area is particularly rich in examples of late Perpendicular Gothic, English Renaissance and English Baroque. Architectural styles, correlated with some of the examples featured in this book, are detailed on page 258, followed by a glossary of architectural terms.

Much of importance has been lost due to indifference, but England has now become extremely preservationist and most buildings with any pretence to architectural importance are well cared for and protected. Almost as important, modern building has at last taken a turn for the better with the advent in the 1980s of the more sympathetic Post-Modernist style, whereby traditional English materials such as brick and tiles are employed. The redevelopment of London's old dockland is proceeding apace and it is confidently predicted that by the turn of the century this derelict eyesore will have become a tourist attraction.

Practical information

Accommodation
It is assumed that most visitors to outer London areas will already have arranged accommodation, generally in or near the city centre. However, a stay in, for example, Richmond makes it possible to explore these centres at a more leisurely pace. The National Information Centre at Victoria Station (730 3488) will be able to provide assistance.

Transport
The Underground
The quickest and easiest way to travel around London is by Underground – 'the Tube'. Unfortunately, the service stops completely around midnight.

Fares are priced on a zonal basis. A seven-day all-zones Travelcard, allowing unlimited travel on Underground and bus systems within London, will certainly prove economical to the visitor wishing to make trips to outer London, especially if journeys are to be made on consecutive days. Twelve of the areas detailed in this book can be reached directly by Underground. The Travelcard can be obtained from any Underground station and some newsagents on production of a passport-size photograph.

Buses
Although London's double-decker buses provide good views, services are unreliable and, of course, much slower than the Underground or trains. Unfortunately, there is sometimes no alternative public transport in the outer London areas, in which case they are indispensable. Most central London services end at around 23.30 – even earlier than the Underground.

When boarding a bus at a request stop – indicated by a red sign with 'Request' in white letters – hail the bus by extending an arm. Similarly, when alighting at a request stop, ring the bell once, well in advance. Bus fares, also based on zones, are cheaper than the Underground for very short journeys but no change of route can be made without incurring an extra charge.

Check the current situation regarding Travelcards, etc., and obtain free bus and Underground plans at any of the following Underground stations: Heathrow Central, Euston, Kings Cross, Piccadilly Circus, Oxford Circus, St James's Park and Victoria, or ring London Transport Information (222 1234).

Taxis
These are generally, but not always, black vehicles which, if they are free, display an illuminated 'For Hire' notice above the windscreen. A standard additional charge is levied on Saturday and Sunday and daily between 20.00 and 06.00. Minicabs are cheaper for longer journeys but must be hired in advance as they

cannot, by law, be hailed in the street. Their fares are not metered and must be negotiated first.

Waterways
The Thames, once London's 'High Street', now has no public transport but there are excursions from the piers at Westminster, Charing Cross and the Tower to Greenwich and the Thames Barrier, throughout the year. From Easter to October, excursions also run to Kew, Richmond and Hampton Court. For details telephone LTB riverboat information service 730 4812, or the piers direct as follows: Westminster Pier for Greenwich and the Thames Barrier 930 4097; for Kew, Richmond and Hampton Court 930 8294. Charing Cross Pier for Greenwich 709 9697.

Trains and coaches
British Rail Travel Centre, 4–12 Regent Street (personal callers only), or by telephone 928 5100.

Victoria Coach Station 164 Buckingham Palace Road 730 0202.

Opening times
Specific opening times for locations featured in the book are given in the text. The following list indicates customary opening times in general.

Public buildings
Most close during bank holidays. When an entry charge is made, admission is usually refused 30 or even 45 minutes before closing time. Few open before 14.00 on Sunday.

Banks
Monday to Friday 09.30–15.30. A few also open Saturday 09.30–12.00.

Licensed drinking hours
Public houses generally open in outer London areas Monday to Saturday 10.00–14.30 and 18.00–23.00. However in areas near the centre times may be 11.00–15.00 and 17.30–23.00. On Sundays, Good Friday, Easter Sunday and Christmas Day opening hours throughout London are as elsewhere in England, 12.00–14.00 and 19.00–22.30. Licensed restaurants are usually permitted to serve drinks, with meals, up to an hour later than public houses. Hotels may serve residents and their guests at any time. Other exceptions to the general rule include trains, boats, aeroplanes, private clubs and sports and entertainment venues.

Churches
Most are open daily 10.00–16.00. However, Sunday services and baptisms and Saturday weddings are limits to sightseeing.

Post Offices
Monday to Friday 09.00–17.30, Saturday 09.30–13.00. Many have machines outside for the purchase of stamps at any time.

Restaurants
Most take orders between 12.30–14.30 and 19.00–23.00. Some
fast food outlets will provide meals throughout the afternoon.
Luxury restaurants may close Saturday lunchtimes and Sunday.

Shops
The majority open Monday to Saturday 09.00–17.30 without a
midday break. Many food stores, however, have longer opening
hours – particularly those run by Asians. In some London areas
further from the centre shops close on one weekday afternoon,
generally Wednesday or Thursday. It is expected that the
regulations forbidding the opening of shops on Sunday will be
repealed during 1986 and many will then open on that day.

On Sundays alcoholic drinks may only be sold during licensing
hours.

Postage
Stamps are generally obtainable only at post offices but some
large hotels and postcard shops also supply them. All mail to
Europe travels by air automatically. Within the United Kingdom
there are two classes of postage, first and second. Second class is
guaranteed to be slower.

Telephones
Telephone calls, made within the British Isles, are amongst the
most expensive in the world (in spite of huge profits). There are
three time scales – very, very expensive, Monday to Friday 09.00–
13.00; very expensive, Monday–Friday 08.00–09.00 and 13.00–
18.00 and expensive, Monday to Friday 18.00–08.00 and all day
Saturday and Sunday. Unlike some countries, local calls are never
free nor is time unlimited. Calls made via operators, rather than
dialled direct, are even more expensive, and if the call is made
from a hotel room the hotel will charge a supplement. Public
telephone booths in the street are generally painted red. They
may contain telephone directories, but as many booths are
vandalized these are frequently damaged or missing. Numbers
required may be obtained, free of charge, by dialling 142 for
addresses in London or 192 for those outside. Operators will
advise on overseas dialling – call 100. The free emergency number
for Police, Ambulance or Fire is 999. Most pubs, restaurants,
hotels and British Rail stations provide public telephones. Ensure
that a good supply of 10p pieces is to hand.

Churches/chapels
In all churches and chapels, unless stated otherwise, the altar is at
the east end – a great help in orientation.

Roman numerals

Many monuments are inscribed with dates given in Roman numerals and the following conversions may be helpful:

1=I, 2=II, 3=III, 4=IV, 5=V, 6=VI, 7=VII, 8=VIII, 9=IX, 10=X,
11=XI, 12=XII, 13=XIII, 14=XIV, 15=XV, 16=XVI, 17=XVII, 18=XVIII, 19=XIX,
20=XX, 30=XXX, 40=XL, 50=L, 60=LX, 70=LXX, 80=LXXX, 90=XC, 100=C,
200=CC, 300=CCC, 400=CD, 500=D, 600=DC, 700=DCC, 800=DCCC, 900=CM, 1000=M,
1500=MD, 1900=MCM, 2000=MM

Toilet facilities

Public toilets in London are better maintained than in most cities. Some now charge for entry, but those in large hotels, pubs and stores are, of course, free. No tipping is necessary. There are always facilities at mainline railway stations, but few on the Underground.

Public holidays

In England these are known as bank holidays and are as follows: 1 January, Good Friday, Easter Monday, the first and last Mondays in May, the last Monday in August, Christmas Day and Boxing Day (26 December). Practically everything closes.

Tourist information services

The National Information Centre run by the London Visitor and Convention Bureau is at Victoria Station (730 3488) and opens daily. Other LTB centres are at: Heathrow Airport; Harrods, Knightsbridge (fourth floor); Selfridges, Oxford Street (ground floor); and the Tower of London (April–October). The City of London Information Centre is located at St Paul's Churchyard (606 3030).

Daily events in London are listed in *The Times* newspaper – particularly those attended by members of the royal family. Details can also obtained by telephone 246 8041 (Teletourist). London's weather forecasts are available from 246 8091.

Hampton Court

The Tudor part of the palace, with its Great Hall, Chapel Royal and lofty chimney stacks, represents the finest royal building of its period to survive in England. It still evokes Henry VIII and his wives; five of the six lived here at some time. Of at least equal importance architecturally is the section designed by Sir Christopher Wren, which is effectively the greatest Baroque royal palace in the British Isles.

Timing Monday to Saturday is preferable, with an early morning start advisable. Allow at least half a day to see everything. The only interiors open throughout the year are the State Rooms, Renaissance Paintings Gallery and the 'Tudor' Tennis Court. The remainder generally close from October to March.

Suggested connection Continue to Syon Park, which may be reached directly by bus from Hampton Court Green.

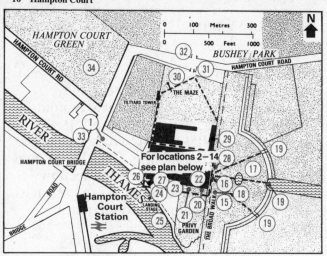

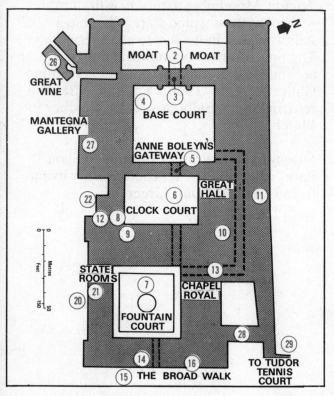

Locations
1 Trophy Gates
2 Moat and bridge
3 Great Gatehouse
4 Base Court
5 'Anne Boleyn's' Gateway
6 Clock Court
7 Fountain Court
8 The Building of Hampton
   Court Exhibition
9 State Rooms
10 Wine Cellar
11 Great Kitchens
12 Renaissance Picture Gallery
   and Wolsey Rooms
13 Chapel Royal Entranceway
14 King's Private Apartments
15 Broad Walk
16 East Facade of Wren's Building
17 Fountain Garden
18 East Grounds
19 Tijou Screen
20 South Facade of Wren's
   Building
21 Upper Orangery
22 South Facade of the Tudor
   Building
23 Knot Garden
24 Pond Garden
25 Banqueting House
26 Vinery
27 Lower Orangery
   (Mantegna Cartoons)
28 Old Close Tennis Court
29 'Tudor' Tennis Court
30 Maze
31 Lion Gate
32 Bushy Park
33 The Mitre
34 Hampton Court Green

Start *Hampton Court Station (BR) from Waterloo Station (BR). Exit and cross the bridge ahead. At the entrance to the second path R are the Trophy Gates.*

Alternatively, Hampton Court may be approached by river from Richmond Pier (30 minutes) or Westminster Pier (3 hours). If the tide is unfavourable the boat can take up to two hours longer from Richmond, so check first (940 2244). From Hampton Court Landing Stage turn L and continue to the first path R. This leads to the bridge over Hampton Court's moat (the Trophy Gates are seen later).

The main courtyards and grounds are open daily, 08.00–dusk. Admission free. Interiors are open April–September Monday–Saturday 09.30–18.00, Sunday 11.00–18.00. The State Rooms, Renaissance Paintings Gallery and 'Tudor' Tennis Court are also open October–March, Monday–Saturday 09.30–17.00, Sunday 14.00–17.00. Admission charge to the most important interiors.

Hampton Court Palace was first built in the Tudor period and then partially rebuilt almost two hundred years later. This is why it combines, unusually, both Tudor and Baroque styles. The western sections of the complex were commissioned by Thomas Wolsey as a manor house but soon extended by Henry VIII to become a royal palace. Adjoining this to the east are the state apartments built for William III and Mary II by *Wren*.

Wolsey, the son of an Ipswich butcher, was appointed Archbishop of York in 1515. In the same year he leased the manor of Hampton from the Knights of St John and the construction of Hampton Court began. The master mason was *John Lebons*. Within three years, Wolsey, now Henry VIII's favourite, had become Lord Chancellor, Cardinal and Papal Legate. He was the King's richest and most powerful subject and resided in a manor house more splendid than any of England's royal palaces.

Sensing Henry's envy, Wolsey fearfully assigned Hampton Court to the King in 1525, but was magnanimously allowed to remain in residence. In spite of tireless efforts, Wolsey failed to obtain the Pope's approval for Henry's divorce from Catherine of Aragon and for this failure was stripped of all his titles except that of Archbishop of York. He retired to York in 1530, but later that year Henry arrested him for high treason. Wolsey, however, was a sick man and died at Leicester on his way to London for trial and virtually certain execution.

Henry now occupied Hampton Court, carrying out major alterations between 1529 and 1538, and thereby creating the most sumptuous palace that England has ever known. It was the birthplace of his only son, later Edward VI.

During the Commonwealth, Hampton Court, together with its contents, remained relatively unscathed as it was appropriated by Oliver Cromwell for his personal use.

Following the accession of William and Mary in 1689, buildings to accommodate new royal apartments were designed, in the then current Classical style, by *Wren*. They replaced most of Henry VIII's State Apartments and it was planned to rebuild all of Hampton Court, except for the Great Hall, in similar style. This project was abandoned, however, and much of the old palace remains: England never did have its rival to Versailles.

Many rooms in the palace were converted to 'grace and favour' homes in the 18C and they still serve this purpose.

The State Rooms were opened to the public by Queen Victoria in 1838.

| Location 1 | **TROPHY GATES** |

These were designed for William III to provide the main entrance to the palace, but the trophies and Coat of Arms were added by George II.

Enter Outer Green Court. Proceed ahead to the moat and bridge passing the old barracks L.

| Location 2 | **MOAT AND BRIDGE** |

The moat was filled and its bridge buried by Charles II. They were rediscovered in 1910. Henry VIII had built the bridge to replace an earlier structure.

Its parapets have been renewed. The Queen's (or King's) Beasts, flanking the bridge, are replacements carved in 1950.

Cross the bridge to the Great Gatehouse.

| Location 3 | **GREAT GATEHOUSE** |

This was built for Wolsey and was originally two storeys higher and surmounted by cupolas and weather-vanes. The structure was shortened and remodelled in 1772 and refaced in the 19C.

The roundels of Roman emperors by *Maiano*, c.1521, were brought from Windsor. They may be those which originally decorated the Holbein Gate at Whitehall Palace.

On the oriel window are the arms of Henry VIII (renewed).

Flanking the Gatehouse range are two projecting wings, which were extended later. The stone weasels on their battlements are original although much restored.

Oak doors to the Gatehouse are Tudor but its vault was renewed in 1882.

●➡ *Pass through to Base Court.*

Location 4	**BASE COURT**

On this side of the Gatehouse the arms of Henry VIII, above the arch, have also been renewed.

Both turrets bear the arms of Elizabeth I.

All the buildings in this court are from Wolsey's period and formed an extension to Clock Court that lies further east. Henry VIII's Great Hall appears in the background ahead L.

●➡ *Continue eastward to 'Anne Boleyn's' Gateway.*

Location 5	**'ANNE BOLEYN'S' GATEWAY**

This was built by Wolsey but is named after Henry's second queen probably because it was embellished during Anne's brief reign.

The 18C bell turret houses one bell dating from 1480.

The clock, made in 1799, was brought from St James's Palace in 1835 to replace the west face of the Astronomical Clock which was lost during restoration.

Above the arch are the arms of Henry VIII.

The two roundels of Roman emperors are part of a set of eight made for Hampton Court by *Giovanni da Maiano* in 1521. The others are seen later. They are an early example of Italian Renaissance work in England.

Beneath the arch, on two small bosses, the 'H' and 'A' monograms (Henry VIII and Anne Boleyn) in the ceiling, were restored with the vaulting in 1882.

●➡ *Pass through the gateway to Clock Court.*

Location 6	**CLOCK COURT**

On the other side of Anne Boleyn's Gateway is the east face of the Astronomical Clock which was made, in England, by the Frenchman *Nicholas Oursian* in 1540. Its mechanism was renewed in 1879. The dial, 7ft 10in in diameter, indicates the hour, day, month, moon phase and time of high water at London Bridge. The last information was most important when the main approach to Hampton Court was by water. In the centre the sun is depicted revolving around the earth, as it was believed to in the 16C.

Above the arch are Wolsey's arms in 16C Italian terracotta work, incorporating his cardinal's hat. The arms were defaced by Henry VIII but have been restored.

Two further roundels by *Maiano* are seen.

It is believed that Wolsey began his manor house on part of the site of this court and much of the west side, with Anne Boleyn's Gateway, dates from this period. He later extended this range southward.

Henry's Great Hall L occupies all of the north side. It was built by *John Moulton* in 1534 and incorporates the site of Wolsey's original more modest hall. The bay window may have been re-used from that building.

Behind *Wren's* 17C colonnade, on the south side, are the Building of Hampton Court Exhibition and Renaissance Picture Galleries. Return later to visit them. These rooms occupy the second of the south ranges built by Wolsey when the courtyard was extended southward. Paving in front of the colonnade indicates the line of the earlier range.

The east facade ahead was remodelled for George II by *Kent* in 1732. It is an early example of Neo-Gothic work which was insisted on, allegedly by Prime Minister Walpole, to harmonize with the remainder of the court. The range was remodelled further in 1844.

The George II Gateway is embellished with more roundels. Originally a high building stood here with private suites on three floors. These became the royal apartments until Henry built more extensive accommodation further east. Some of the Tudor fabric remains.

➤ Pass through the gateway towards Fountain Court. Wren's Queen's Stairway is seen L but may not be entered at this point.

| Location 7 | **FOUNTAIN COURT** |

The contrast between Wren's Classical court, completed in 1694, and those seen previously comes as a surprise. It was planned as the core of William and Mary's new palace and is built on the site of the slightly smaller Cloister Green Court which Henry had added to Wolsey's building to accommodate his royal apartments.

The State Apartments and Queen's Private Apartments are on the first floor. Above and below them were the apartments of the staff, courtiers and guests.

The ground floor of the south range housed the King's Private Apartments.

Surrounds to the circular windows were carved by *Cibber*.

➤ Proceed ahead to the barrier and then return to Clock Court L. (Do not exit to the grounds at this point as re-entry from the east side is prohibited due to security checks.) Enter the Building of Hampton Court Exhibition from Clock Court's colonnade.

| Location 8 | **BUILDING OF HAMPTON COURT EXHIBITION** |

Open April–September. Admission free.

The recently enlarged exhibition describes the evolution of Hampton Court.

➤ Exit L and proceed to the ticket office for entry

*tickets to the State Rooms and Renaissance Picture
Galleries. Return along the colonnade to the
entrance to the State Rooms in the south-east
corner.*

| Location 9 | **STATE ROOMS** |

*Open daily.
Admission charge.
NB: retain the ticket
for admission to the
King's Private
Apartments and the
Banqueting House.*

On Mary's death in 1694 the sorrowing William
immediately halted all work and interior
decoration did not commence until 1699. William
died in 1702, with only the King's Apartments
and Queen's Gallery completed. Most of the
Queen's Apartments were eventually decorated
for Queen Anne but some later work dates from
the reigns of George I and George II.

Great craftsmen who worked on the apartments
included carver *Gibbons*, ironsmith *Tijou*,
painter *Verrio* (he died at Hampton Court in
1707), and later designers *Vanbrugh* and *Kent*.
Some of the furnishings and paintings remain in
their original positions.

At present, the rooms are seen in almost
precisely reverse chronological order. Visited
first are the King's State Apartments, on the
south side, in the order that courtiers would have
proceeded. The King's private rooms are situated
below on the ground floor and may be seen later.
The Queen's State Apartments, on the east and
north sides, are then entered in reverse order to
the original approach. Her private rooms are on
the same floor adjacent to these facing Fountain
Court. Before all the Queen's rooms have been
seen, a brief detour is made to part of the Tudor
section via the Cartoon Gallery. Finally, the
major surviving Tudor buildings are entered.

The name of each State Room is written in gold
above its exit door.

As the most important rooms, together with their
contents, are described on display panels and the
paintings are titled, only a selection will be
described in this book.

King's Staircase. Completed after William's
death. The balustrade is by *Tijou* and the wall
paintings are by *Verrio*.

King's Guardroom. Yeomen of the Guard
originally stood on duty here. Over 3000 pieces of
arms are displayed, all as originally arranged in
the 17C.

King's First Presence Chamber. The chair is 17C
but a replacement.

Only the carving above the door is by *Gibbons*.

••• *Proceed through the* **King's Second Presence
Chamber**.

King's Audience Chamber. This chair is 17C, but
also a replacement; the decorated sections of the
pier glasses (mirrors) are original.

King's Drawing Room. The overmantel is by
Gibbons.

King William III's State Bedchamber. The ceiling
was painted by *Verrio*.

The state bed, chairs and stools are original.

A rare 17C close stool (commode) retains its original upholstery.

Tapestries are from the 16C Abraham series; the remainder are seen later.

The cornice by *Gibbons* is judged some of his finest work.

King's Dressing Room. William III generally slept here, rather than in the more public State Bedchamber.

The ceiling is by *Verrio*.

The furniture is not original to the room.

•➡ *Proceed through the* **King's Writing Closet**.

Queen Mary's Closet. This room was never, of course, used by Queen Mary but at one time the walls were hung with her needlework.

Queen's Gallery. This was designed as an art gallery to display the Mantegna cartoons which now hang in the Lower Orangery, seen later. It was the last room to be completed before William's death.

The cornice and doorcases are by *Gibbons*.

Tapestries from the Alexander series are Flemish, made in the 18C to designs of *Lebrun* executed in 1662. They were probably fitted here for George I.

The fireplace, judged outstanding, was brought from the King's Bedchamber in 1701. It was carved by *John Nost*.

Queen's Bedchamber. This room was decorated and furnished for the Prince and Princess of Wales (later George II and Queen Caroline).

The ceiling, painted by *Thornhill* in 1715, had been whitewashed over but is now restored.

The bed retains part of its rare 18C upholstery.

The chairs and stools were made in 1716.

Queen's Drawing Room. This room was decorated for Queen Anne by *Verrio* in 1705.

Comprehensive views of the Baroque *patte d'oie* (goose-foot) layout of the east grounds are obtained from the windows.

Queen's Audience Chamber. This chamber was decorated for George II when Prince of Wales.

One of the 16C tapestries from the Abraham series is hung, the remainder are in the Great Hall, seen later.

The chandelier was made in 1707 to commemorate the union of England and Scotland.

Public Dining Room. This was decorated as a music room by *Vanbrugh c.*1718 for George II but it eventually became a dining room where the king would occasionally eat in public.

The cornice and arms of George I on the chimney-piece are by *Gibbons*.

Prince of Wales's Suite. This suite of three rooms was decorated for Queen Anne by *Vanbrugh* but first used in 1716 by George II when Prince of Wales.

In the last room of this suite, the bedroom, Charlotte's bed, *c.*1778, has been fitted with new covers which incorporate the original embroidery.

The **Queen's Private Apartments** consist of a series of small panelled rooms.

•➤ *Pass the* **Prince of Wales's Staircase**.

George II's Private Chamber. The flock wallpaper, *c.*1730, is original to the room.

Cartoon Gallery. The gallery, by *Wren* 1699, lies behind the King's State Apartments. It was planned for the display of seven cartoons, painted by *Raphael* in 1516, part of a series of ten illustrating the lives of St Peter and St Paul. These were produced as designs for tapestries commissioned for the Vatican's Sistine Chapel. Charles I purchased the cartoons for Hampton Court but they are now displayed in the Victoria and Albert Museum. The 17C Mortlake tapestries that now hang in this gallery were copied from the cartoons.

All the carving, including the chimney-piece, is by *Gibbons*.

Communication Gallery. This gallery linked the King's and Queen's State Apartments.

The 17C portraits by *Lely* are of ladies from Charles II's Court. They originally hung at Windsor Castle and are still known as 'The Windsor Beauties'.

•➤ *At the end of the gallery a door L leads to some Tudor rooms.*

Wolsey's Closet. The panels were painted in the 16C over 15C work, presumably brought from elsewhere.

On the original 16C ceiling is painted Wolsey's motto 'Dominus Michi Adjutor' (The Lord is my helper). The 16C linenfold panelling was fitted here in 1886.

Cumberland Suite. This series of rooms was briefly occupied by a son of George II, the Duke of Cumberland, 'Butcher Cumberland of Culloden'. Some of the wall fabric is Tudor but the interior was completely remodelled for George II by *Kent* in 1732.

Windows and one ceiling are in the Neo-Gothic style.

•➤ *Return to Wren's building and turn L.*

Queen's Staircase. The balustrade is by *Tijou* and most of the walls and ceiling were painted by *Kent*. The 'Apollo' wall painting of 1628 is by *Honthorst*.

•➤ *Turn immediately R.*

Queen's Guard Chamber. On the walls are hung the 18C paintings known as 'The Hampton Court Beauties' by *Kneller*.

Queen's Presence Chamber. Decorated for George I by *Vanbrugh*, most of the carving is by *Gibbons*.

The furniture comes from Windsor Castle and was made for Queen Anne in 1714.

•● *Return to the Queen's Staircase, turn R and enter the most important Tudor section of the palace.*

Haunted Gallery. This gallery, redecorated in the 18C, linked the Chapel Royal with Wolsey's state apartments. It is reputedly haunted by Catherine Howard, Henry VIII's fifth wife, who was executed for adultery. Under arrest, it is alleged that she escaped from her room and ran along this corridor screaming for Henry, who was at prayer in the chapel nearby.

•● *The door R leads to the gallery of the Chapel Royal.*

Holyday Closets. On either side of the Royal Pew are two pews used by the king and queen, known as the Holyday Closets.

The first entered has a Tudor ceiling, much restored.

Royal Pew. This pew was redecorated for Queen Anne by *Wren* in 1711 and the ceiling painted by *Thornhill*. From here the interior of the Chapel Royal, not open to visitors, may be viewed.

Chapel Royal. Although the chapel was built for Wolsey, little survives internally from his period. The timber-vaulted ceiling was added for Henry VIII in 1536 and redecorated in the 19C by *Pugin* who added the stars to the design.

Much of the chapel was remodelled by *Wren* early in the 18C.

The wooden reredos is by *Gibbons*; the painting above this is by *Thornhill*.

Wren's replacement windows were in their turn replaced in the 19C to match the originals.

•● *Return to the Haunted Gallery which continues R. Continue through the first room.*

Great Watching Chamber. This was built for Henry VIII in 1536 as a guard room and is all that remains of his state apartments.

The panelled ceiling was restored in the 19C. Some of its bosses incorporate the arms of Henry and his third wife, Jane Seymour.

The early 16C Flemish tapestries were probably purchased by Wolsey.

The bay window has been renewed.

All the stained glass in this chamber is 19C.

The entrance with double doors to the hall was added in the 19C.

●➡ *Enter the hall and proceed directly to the first door R, this leads to the Horn Room.*

Horn Room. From here, food was served to the high table.

Original oak steps still lead directly to the kitchen and cellars below.

The ceiling was initially painted.

●➡ *Return to the hall.*

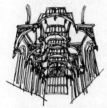

Great Hall. The Great Hall, 1554, replaced Wolsey's original hall and was Henry VIII's most important addition to Hampton Court. Leading members of the household feasted at a high table set on the raised dais but the king generally dined within his private apartments. Others ate at common tables set along the side walls.

Incorporated in the hammerbeam roof by *Nedeham* are the monograms and badges of Anne Boleyn and Jane Seymour.

The design of its hanging pendants reflects a Renaissance influence.

Originally an open hearth stood in the centre of the hall and smoke escaped from its fire through a vent in the roof, since filled in.

The Abraham tapestries are Flemish, made in 1540. They are threaded with gold and silver.

At the far end of the hall, above an oak screen, the minstrels' gallery, although basically Tudor, has been much restored.

The screen is original and was built to obscure the servants' passage.

●➡ *Exit to the foot of the stairs R and pass through Anne Boleyn's Gateway. Take the first path R keeping to the east side of Base Court. Continue through the arch in the north-east corner ahead. Proceed R along North Cloister (a dark passage). Enter the fourth door R.*

Location 10	**WINE CELLAR**

The vaulting is of plastered brickwork. In Tudor times all the wine drunk at Hampton Court was imported although the beer was brewed on the premises. Modern casks illustrate the stillages, a typical Tudor arrangement.

●➡ *Exit L. First R is the entrance to Service Place and the kitchens.*

Location 11	**GREAT KITCHENS**

These are the most extensive examples of Tudor kitchens to survive and were in use until the 18C. Food cooked here on open fires was passed through hatches into Serving Place and thence up the stairs to the Horn Room. It was then taken to the high table in the Great Hall and the royal apartments.

The first kitchen entered was built for Wolsey but most of the utensils exhibited are 18C.

The next two kitchens were added by Henry in 1529 to serve the common tables in the Great Hall. Originally they formed one room but were subdivided in the 17C. Their ceilings were lowered *c.*1840.

The third room was converted into an apartment in the 19C and some fittings from this period have been retained, e.g. the range with its boiler.

➥ Exit from the kitchens and proceed ahead keeping to the west side of Base Court. Return L through the Anne Boleyn Gateway to Clock Court. The entrance to the Renaissance Picture Gallery and Wolsey Rooms is beneath the colonnade. From The King's Staircase, proceed along the ground floor passage, known as Stone Hall, to the Beauty Staircase. Alternatively, proceed ahead from Clock Court to Fountain Court and the Chapel Royal entranceway (Location 13).

Location 12	**RENAISSANCE PICTURE GALLERY AND WOLSEY ROOMS**
Open daily. *Admission charge.*	**Beauty Staircase.** The staircase was named from the paintings of 'The Windsor Beauties' by *Lely* which formerly hung in the king's adjacent private dining room but are now in the Communication Gallery previously described.

➥ Ascend the stairs and enter the Tudor building.

The first two rooms were remodelled in the 18C and again in the 20C.

Tapestries are 17C Italian.

Wolsey Rooms. These rooms were most probably occupied by guests or senior household members, but possibly by Wolsey himself. The two rooms R were originally one but sub-divided in the 17C.

The 16C linenfold panelling is original.

In the second room are remnants of a stone Tudor doorway in the corner.

➥ Return to the central room.

This has a 16C ribbed ceiling, recently restored. Its design was influenced by the Renaissance.

The fourth room also has a restored 16C ceiling which incorporates Wolsey's badge.

The windows in this room are 18C.

➥ Cross the lobby.

Renaissance Picture Gallery. Renaissance paintings on wood from the royal collection are displayed. These rooms were probably once occupied by an important member of the Court. They were mainly refitted in the 17C but some fragments of Tudor doorways and panelling remain.

Beyond are two rooms which have been decorated as a Victorian 'grace and favour' residence.

➥ Return along the corridor and descend the

*Elizabethan spiral staircase. Exit R and proceed
from Clock Court to Fountain Court. Turn
immediately L and proceed beneath the arch.
Enter the door R to the Chapel Road.*

| Location 13 | **CHAPEL ROYAL ENTRANCEWAY** |

*The chapel is only
open for services.*

Above the door are the arms of Henry VIII and
Catherine Parr, his sixth wife, who outlived him.

The interior has already been described as seen
from the Royal Pew.

➡ *Return to Fountain Court. On the east side is
the vestibule with the entrance R to the King's
Private Apartments. Do not exit yet from this
vestibule into the grounds.*

| Location 14 | **KING'S PRIVATE APARTMENTS** |

*Open April-
September.
Admission by ticket
for the State
Apartments.*

This suite is connected with the King's State
Apartments above, by a private staircase. The
long Cartoon Gallery on the first floor left no
space for the king's private rooms to run, like the
queen's, adjacent to the State Apartments.

Little is known about their use or furnishing and
William III probably only ever occupied a few of
them. They were remodelled in the 19C to form
grace and favour residences.

Some of the furniture in the rooms is
contemporary with William III's reign. Paintings
from the Royal Collection, together with ancient
prints of Hampton Court, are displayed.

➡ *Exit from the Apartments and return to the
vestibule.*

The three iron screens R are by *Tijou*.

➡ *Exit to the east grounds.*

| Location 15 | **BROAD WALK** |

This gravel path, running north to south (L to R),
was laid out by *Wise*, *c*.1700, to separate the
Fountain Garden and Privy Garden.

| Location 16 | **EAST FACADE OF WREN'S BUILDING** |

The low height of the ground floor was designed
so that the asthmatic William would not have to
climb too many stairs.

Portland stone carvings by *Cibber* include the
central 'Hercules' pediment.

| Location 17 | **FOUNTAIN GARDEN** |

This parterre with yew trees immediately fronts
the east facade. It is a restoration of the formal
garden originally laid out as a *patte d'oie* (goose-
foot) pattern for William III by *Loudon* and
Wise. Initially, there were thirteen fountains but
only a pool remains.

The statues are 19C.

➡ *Continue eastward along any path to the semi-
circular canal.*

Location 18	**EAST GROUNDS**

These grounds were laid out for Charles II by *Mollet* in the Classical Baroque style, pre-dating all of Wren's work at Hampton Court.

The Long Water, when completed, almost reached the palace but it was shortened later to form William's Fountain Garden.

The iron gates to the three avenues are by *Tijou*.

The semi-circular canal around the lime trees was added for Queen Anne.

━━ Proceed to the south-east corner of Wren's building. The gate R leads to the south grounds. Immediately L is the Privy Garden.

This garden was also laid out as a parterre in 1701 but has been much altered.

━━ Follow the central alley, known as Queen Mary's Bower, through the garden towards the river and proceed to the end.

Location 19	**TIJOU SCREEN**

These twelve wrought iron panels, judged some of Tijou's finest work, were brought here from the Fountain Garden in 1701.

━━ Return to the south facade.

Location 20	**SOUTH FACADE OF WREN'S BUILDING**

Carved to form the stone centrepiece above the window are the names, in Latin, of William and Mary.

Below this, the cherubs and royal coats of arms are by *Cibber*.

Originally the blind circular windows were decorated with paintings by *Laguerre*.

━━ Pass through the central gates and proceed to the entrance to the Upper Orangery.

Location 21	**UPPER ORANGERY**
Open April-September.	When built, orange trees were kept here in the winter and the building has recently been restored as an orangery.

━━ Exit R to the end of the terrace and pass through the gate.

Location 22	**SOUTH FACADE OF THE TUDOR BUILDING**

Immediately R, the bay window, adjoining Wren's buildings, displays 'ER 1568' on its stone work. This denotes rebuilding in the reign of Elizabeth I.

The octagonal turret, L, is Tudor and the Wolsey Rooms are situated on the first floor behind and to the right of it.

The decorative lead cupola has been restored.

| Location 23 | **KNOT GARDEN** |

This small area in front of the Elizabethan bay was planted in 1924 in the manner of a 16C garden.

| Location 24 | **POND GARDEN** |

On the L is the Old Pond Garden.

▪● Follow the path to the Banqueting House at the river end.

| Location 25 | **BANQUETING HOUSE** |

Open April–September. Admission charge or included with State Apartments ticket.

A Tudor garden tower was converted, or probably completely rebuilt, for William by *Wren* in 1700 to accommodate summer banquets.

▪● Enter the building.

Paintings are by *Verrio* and the door, mirror surround and window cases were carved by *Gibbons*.

▪● Return northward towards the south facade of the Tudor building. Turn L.

Immediately L is the New Pond Garden. This was planted in 1925 following the 17C style.

▪● Return again towards the south facade of the Tudor building. Turn L to the Vinery.

| Location 26 | **VINERY** |

The Great Vine was planted in 1768. Grapes are still produced in late summer and may be purchased. A record crop in 1985 yielded 840 lb. The girth of the trunk is 78 in.

▪● Exit L and proceed to the Lower Orangery.

| Location 27 | **LOWER ORANGERY** |

Open April–September. Admission charge.

Nine late 15C cartoons by *Mantegna* illustrate 'The Triumph of Caesar'. These were purchased by Charles I and are the world's oldest known paintings on canvas. All except one have been restored. They were originally displayed in the Queen's Gallery.

▪● Exit L and return to the east facade of Wren's building. Continue to the end. Immediately L are the remains of the palace's Tudor east facade.

| Location 28 | **OLD CLOSE TENNIS COURT** |

Not open.

This building is buttressed and lies behind the garden wall. Added by Henry VIII, *c.* 1530, it was remodelled in the late 17C, and converted to lodgings.

▪● Continue ahead. Enter the first gate L.

| Location 29 | **'TUDOR' TENNIS COURT** |

Open daily.
Admission free.

This tennis court is not Tudor but was built *c.*1625, and later altered for Charles II.

The windows are 18C.

'Real' tennis, the predecessor of lawn tennis, is still played and matches may be viewed.

●● Exit L. Proceed to the first gate L. Take the first path R and proceed ahead. Take the second path L towards the Maze.

| Location 30 | **MAZE** |

Open March–
October. Admission
charge.

This was laid out in its present triangular shape in 1714, replacing an earlier circular version planned for William III as part of a formal garden known as The Wilderness.

●● Exit L. First L Lion Gate.

| Location 31 | **LION GATE** |

The gate was built for Queen Anne as the north entrance to the palace grounds. Its design incorporates her cypher.

●● Exit from the grounds and cross the road ahead.

| Location 32 | **BUSHY PARK** |

Although not part of Hampton Court grounds, the park with its chestnut avenue seen through the gates was planned by *Wren* as a grand approach to his projected, but never to be built, Classical north facade of the palace.

The Diana Fountain by *Fanelli*, seen in the distance, was brought here from the Privy Garden in 1713.

Deer roam the park which may be driven through.

*●● Return through the Lion Gate to the Hampton Court grounds. The second path R passes the Maze. Continue ahead towards the **tiltyard tower**.*

This is the only remaining example of the four towers which stood at the corners of Henry's tiltyard, where knights jousted.

●● Follow the path L past the tower and continue ahead towards the palace. The path R leads to the Trophy Gates. Exit and cross the road.

●● Alternatively, turn L and cross the bridge to Hampton Court Station (BR).

| Location 33 | **THE MITRE** |

The 17C Mitre Hotel faces the palace. Its facade was remodelled early in the 19C and little of interest survives internally.

●● Proceed northward to Hampton Court Green first L. Follow its south side.

Location 34   **HAMPTON COURT GREEN**

Palace Gate House is mid 18C.

The Green is early 18C with a later bay.

The Old Court House *Wren c.*1706 (?). Occupied by Wren from 1706 until his death in 1723. It was his official residence as Surveyor General. The upper floor and bay window are later additions.

Faraday House. Michael Faraday, discoverer of electricity, retired here from 1858 until his death in 1867.

Take the first drive L signposted 'TMYC'. Proceed to the end L.

King's Stone Cottage. The weather-boarded 18C house is topped with a weathervane.

Above the drainpipe is George III's monogram.

Return along the drive L.

Tudor Royal Mews. This long range with arches encompasses a cobbled courtyard. Here the royal horses were stabled. It was built in 1538 and extended in 1570. Much remodelling followed.

Exit R. If continuing to Syon (page 99) take bus 267 from the south side of Hampton Court Green to Busch Corner, London Road, Isleworth. Cross the road to Crowther of Syon Lodge.

Alternatively, cross Hampton Court Bridge to Hampton Court Station (BR).

Alternatively, follow the towpath to the landing stage for boats to Richmond and London.

Kingston

Kingston is the ancient coronation town of the Saxon kings, some of whom may have lived nearby. The stone on which they are believed to have been crowned still exists, but the church where the ceremony was probably held has long vanished. However, in spite of external appearances, the parish church of All Saints, which probably stands on its site, is medieval and of great interest. Kingston also boasts a picturesque market place and splendid new riverside walk. Bentalls, its famous department store, is one of the largest in the country.

Timing Monday to Saturday are preferable as the weekday market adds to the liveliness of the town and Bentalls may then be visited.

Suggested connection Precede with Ham and Petersham.

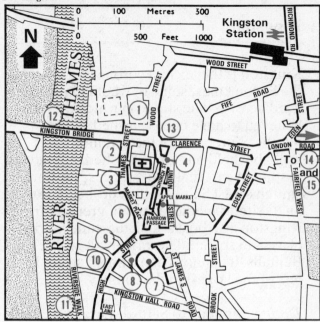

1 All Saints
2 Thames Street
3 Market Place (north side)
4 Church Street
5 Apple Market
6 Market Place (except north side)
7 Guildhall
8 Coronation Stone
9 Clattern Bridge
10 High Street
11 Riverside Walk
12 Kingston Bridge
13 Bentalls
14 Cleaves Almshouses
15 Lovekyn Chapel

Start *Kingston Station (BR) from Waterloo Station (BR). Leave the station by the exit ahead (R). Cross Wood St and proceed ahead, Fife Rd. R Clarence St. Cross Clarence St to All Saints and proceed to its chancel at the east end.*

Alternatively, continue from Ham and Petersham, as indicated on page 64.

Location 1	**ALL SAINTS**
Clarence Street	The Victorian flint cladding of All Saints disguises a splendid medieval church, a fact easily appreciated immediately the interior is entered. It is likely that a predecessor of the present building was the coronation church of many of the Saxon kings.

A Saxon and in turn a Norman church stood on the site of the present All Saints. Little certain is known about them. King Egbert of Wessex held his Great Council of 828 at Kingston and the Saxon church may have been its venue. It has even been surmised that Egbert built the church expressly for this event. The same building probably housed the coronation ceremonies of seven Saxon kings which are known to have taken place at Kingston, beginning with Edward the Elder, son of Alfred the Great, in 902 and ending with Ethelred II 'The Unready' in 978.

Nothing survives of this building, which was probably destroyed by the Danes during their raids in 1009.

Gilbert, the Norman Sheriff of Surrey, built a larger church c.1130 and presented it to the priory that he had recently founded nearby at Merton. Part of its fabric survives, encased in the present walls, and some Norman stonework is visible internally. Unfortunately, the last known example of 12C detailing at All Saints, a Romanesque portal discovered at the west end in the 19C, was, although photographed, almost immediately destroyed.

The present **chancel** dates from the mid 15C when it was rebuilt and enlarged by the addition of north and south chapels.

Tracery in the east window is 19C.

Perpendicular tracery in the chancel's north window is original 15C work and survived only because the Victorians had blocked it.

Flint cladding of the chancel, and the rest of the body of the church, was added in 1866.

The stone-built north **vestry** was added in the mid 15C.

Both **transepts** were probably rebuilt in the late 14C but enlarged in the 19C.

The **nave** was rebult, this time with aisles, c.1370. The aisle windows were altered and clerestory windows added by *Brandon* in 1866.

All the buildings clinging to the north side of the nave are 19C additions.

A tall wooden spire which had been added to All Saints **tower**, probably in the 13C, was struck by lightning in 1445. The tower, with a new spire, was completely rebuilt in 1515, but storm damage in 1703 necessitated the reconstruction of its upper section. This time, the architect *Yeomans* used brick rather than stone and omitted a spire.

The tower's 18C work was completely refaced in 1973 but its 16C lower section of stone survives.

●● Enter the church from the west porch.

The **nave** roof was rebuilt c.1855.

Old tombstones in the churchyard were used to form the new floor in 1973.

Rebuilding of the nave commenced c.1370 but probably took several years to complete as the north aisle pillars are more slender than the south aisle's. They are also positioned differently, aligning with the outside of the tower's north piers, whereas the south pillars align with the centres of the tower's south piers. For this reason the centre of the nave does not coincide with the centre of the crossing.

*●● Turn L and proceed to the **north aisle**.*

The roofs of both aisles were rebuilt in 1721. Above the north door is the monument to Philip Meadows by *Flaxman* 1795.

•● *Continue ahead to the* **crossing.**

Although the four piers that support the tower are believed to be Norman, they are encased in 13C stonework, the oldest visible structural element within the church.

The east and west crossing arches were heightened by *Pearson* in 1883 and the roof of the crossing was raised, part of several steps taken to improve visibility for the congregation – a three-decker pulpit was lowered, box pews removed and galleries dismantled.

The sanctuary, with its high altar, was brought to its present position in the crossing from the east end of the chancel in 1979.

•● *Turn L and enter the* **north transept.**

This transept now serves as an extension to the vestry.

Behind the door ahead R, which leads to the tower staircase, is a 13C piscina, indicating that this transept was once a chapel.

Stone casing of the staircase wall is 13C work.

Two original lancet windows are visible at upper level.

•● *Proceed ahead to the* **Holy Trinity Chapel.**

The fraternity of the Holy Trinity was formed at Kingston in 1477 by Robert Bardsey. It evolved from the Shipmen's Guild, important to the town in medieval times, as Kingston was then a major river port.

The recessed tomb on the north wall L is probably that of the chapel's leading benefactor, Robert Mylam, d.1498.

Immediately R of this tomb is the lower section of a 13C arch, indicating that an earlier room preceded the 15C vicar's vestry which now lies on the other side of it.

The colours which hang here, and elsewhere in the church, are those of the East Surrey Regiment, which adopted this as their memorial chapel. The Regiment no longer exists as such.

A 15C tomb lies R of the altar.

R of this is a piscina of the same period.

•● *Pass through the modern screen to the* **chancel.**

Immediately R, the 18C beadle's pew has recently been restored. Carvings surmounting the two front panels are possibly remnants from the church's medieval rood screen.

When the sanctuary was relocated in 1979 the chancel became the retrochoir. Its 15C wagon roof was decorated by *Comper* in 1949.

Immediately L, in the chancel's north wall, is the 14C doorway to the vicar's vestry.

Above the arch to the vestry are monuments to M. Snelling, d.1633, with some Carolean strapwork.

A similar monument commemorates Francis Wilkinson, d.1681.

◆● Proceed southward and continue through the arch to the Baptistry in **St James's Chapel** *(the chancel's south aisle).*

This was built as a chantry chapel in 1459 and retains part of its original wagon roof.

The three arcade pillars were constructed when the chapel was lengthened in 1549.

Two mid-15C brasses on the stone table, L of the font, came from the tomb of Robert and Joanna Skerne. Joanna was an illegitimate daughter of Edward III; her mother was Alice Perrers.

The font is dated 1669 but its stem is of later date.

Displayed on a wooden pedestal, next to the penultimate arcade column, is the stone shaft of a Saxon cross. Its sides are carved with an interlaced pattern, much faded. This once stood in the churchyard.

In the south-east corner R is the tomb of Sir Anthony Benn, d.1618, by *Janssen*. He was a Recorder of London and is dressed in his legal gown. There is no relationship with the 20C Rt Hon. Anthony Wedgwood Benn, MP.

A 15C niche R probably accommodated the Easter Sepulchre.

Above this is the monument to Anthony Fane, d.1643.

The monument to Richard Lant, d.1682, is on the south wall, L of the arch to the south transept.

◆● Proceed to the **south chapel.**

This is known as the 'Vicar's Burial Ground' as many of Kingston's vicars have been interred beneath its floor.

The 14C east window originally formed the west window of St Mary's Chapel which was once linked with the church. St Mary's Chapel, built in Saxon times, served as a Lady Chapel to the church and the coronation ceremonies may have taken place there. It was demolished following a major structural collapse in 1729 when a sexton was killed.

Two monuments commemorate separate Henry Davidsons, one, d.1781, by *Reghert* and the other, d.1827, by *Ternouth.*

◆● Proceed to the crossing's south-east pier.

A late-15C memorial brass to Katherine Hertcombe is attached to the east side of this pier. The effigy of her husband, John, has been lost.

On the same pier's north side, a 17C brass records the death, in infancy, of all ten children of Edward Staunton, vicar of Kingston, 'ten children in one grave a dreadful sight'.

● Proceed to the **south transept.**

On the west side of this pillar is a restored painting of a bishop, c.1400, believed to represent St Blaise. This is all that remains of the many brightly coloured paintings that once decorated the church. St Blaise, martyred in the 4C, was allegedly tortured with iron combs used for gathering wool. The figure is depicted holding one and the saint was, therefore, adopted as the patron saint of woollen drapers, who had a large guild in Kingston in medieval times.

Within the transept, on the south side of the tower's south-west pier, is a statue of Louisa Theodosia, Countess of Liverpool, and wife of the early 19C prime minister, Lord Liverpool. It is the work of *Sir Francis Chantry* and one of his few free-standing works.

● Proceed westward along the **south aisle.**

The most easterly column, seen first, is of noticeably greater diameter than the others and the only one to have no base.

On the south wall, between the two most westerly windows, a small stone commemorates John Heyton, d.1584. He was Sergeant of the Larder to Mary I and Elizabeth I.

At the west end of this aisle, on the south wall, is a monument to Elizabeth Bate, d.1607.

Norman stones, with axe marks, survive where the final south aisle column joins the west wall of the church. They were probably salvaged from the Norman building and re-used.

● Exit from the church L.

In the southern section of the churchyard, brass plates and stones mark the position of St Mary's Chapel. It foundations were excavated in 1926.

● Return to the west porch. Turn L and continue ahead to Thames St R. Remain on the east side.

Location 2	**THAMES STREET**

Nos 16–18 are late 17C with later fronts. The half-timbering is fake.
Nos 30–32 are Tudor Revival of 1922 and reminiscent of Chester.

● Return southward and cross to the building R on the King's Passage corner (BBBS).

Facing Market Place is **No 1 Thames Street**. Although plastered, this house is late 16C and timber framed. Immediately south of the building is King's Passage and from here the restored, weather-boarded side of the house is visible.

● Return northward to No 14 Market Place on the east corner of Thames St.

Location 3	**MARKET PLACE (NORTH SIDE)**
Market held Monday-Saturday; closes Wednesday p.m.	Kingston's market place forms, without doubt, the most picturesque town centre to be found in any of the London suburbs. Perversely, however, many of the quaint 'old' buildings are fake,

whereas much genuine half-timbering is concealed by later brickwork or rendering. The approach from the south is more spectacular and seen later.

No 14 is a late-16C timber-framed building. Upright posts were carved to form Classical pilasters in the 18C.

•• Continue eastward to Nos 15–16 adjoining.

Nos 15–16, 'Next', for long the property of Boots, changed ownership in 1985. It was built in 1909, in a highly decorative style, embellished with patriotic statues and motifs.

The section, east of the first two gables, is an extension of 1929 designed in matching style.

•• Continue ahead to No 23 on the Church St corner.

No 23 was built in the 17C as a large timber-framed residence. It was altered in the 18C but has been mostly rebuilt as a replica after a fire in 1973. The building extends into Church Street.

•• Cross to No 2 Church St, immediately opposite.

Location 4	**CHURCH STREET**

Although this is one of Kingston's oldest streets, little now apparently predates the 19C.

No 2, built in the 17C as the Old Crown, was recently converted to shops. Its 18C brick front conceals half-timbering.

•• Turn R and continue ahead following Apple Market to the corner of Harrow Passage (first R).

Location 5	**APPLE MARKET**

This narrow passage, with even narrower interconnecting alleyways, retains a medieval feeling although, like Church Street, little predates the 19C.

An exception is the corner building, **No 9**, formerly the Harrow Inn, as above its modern shop front half timbering, *c.*1530, survives.

•• Continue along Harrow Passage and return to Market Place.

Location 6	**MARKET PLACE (EXCEPT NORTH SIDE)**

No 42. Although, as inscribed, the building was first constructed in 1422, it was completely rebuilt precisely five hundred years later.

•• Proceed to the Market House in the centre of Market Place.

Market House *Hennan Snr* 1840. Kingston town hall occupied this important position for centuries until the new Guildhall was completed. The present building's yellow brickwork has since been painted.

On the south side is a statue of Queen Anne by *Bird*, 1706.

●● Proceed south of the market stalls.

The **Shrubsole Memorial** fountain is by
Williamson 1882.

*●● Cross to the **Army and Navy Store** on the west
side of Market Place. Enter the store and proceed
two-thirds of the way through, following the
wall L.*

Within this modern store is a rare, mid-17C
staircase taken from the Castle Inn that
previously stood on the site. It incorporates
pierced panels, some of which appear to be
original though others may have been added
later.

●● Exit from the store R.

The **Druid's Head** inn is 17C but has an early-18C
front. Internally, a mid-17C staircase, with
decorative plasterwork above the stair-well,
survives.

The **Griffin Hotel** has an early-19C facade.

*●● Continue southward to High St and cross to
the Guildhall on the south side.*

Location 7

GUILDHALL *M. Webb 1935*

*Members' room open
when not in use.
Admission free.*

This Neo-Classical building was extended in
1968.

Of chief interest is the Members' Room where
the end wall has been lined with 16C linenfold
panelling. This was saved from the Elizabethan
town hall which had stood in Market Place on the
site of the present Market House.

Above the arch are the arms of Elizabeth I.

*●● Exit from the Guildhall L to the green where,
behind railings, stands the Coronation Stone.*

Location 8

CORONATION STONE

Seven Saxon kings were reputedly crowned on
this piece of Greywether sandstone. It formerly
stood in St Mary's Chapel, but since that
building's demolition in 1729 it has occupied
several sites in Kingston. The stone was brought
to its present position in 1936.

On the base are inscribed the names of seven
kings and their coronation dates: Edward-the-
Elder, 900; Athelstan, 925; Edmund, 940; Edred,
946; Edwy, 956; Edward-the-Martyr, 975 and
Ethelred-the-Unready, 979. A coin of each reign,
presented by the British Museum, is inserted
below the name of the respective king.

The railings protecting the stone were made in
1850 and incorporate Saxon themes.

*●● Cross to the west side of High St and proceed
through the gate, following the short path north of
the bridge.*

Location 9	**CLATTERN BRIDGE**

This bridge crosses the narrow Hogsmill River. Some of its late-12C stone arches survive on the west side but these can only be viewed from the short path. Unfortunately, a council employee mistakenly believes that it is his duty, from time to time, to lock the gate to the path. Frequent complaints have yet to change the situation.

First referred to in 1293, the bridge was, until the 19C, only eight feet wide, but frequent eastward extensions have since taken place. Its name, once Clattering Brygge, is believed to derive from the clattering noise of horses' hooves.

●● Proceed southward along High St.

Location 10	**HIGH STREET**

No 17, on the east side, with a venetian window and pediment, is typically mid 18C. Bays were restored in 1982.

On the west side, **No 52**, **Amari House**, was built *c*.1730. Its entrance was moved to the south side soon after it was built, the road probably proving too busy even then for any transport to pull up with ease. A north wing was added later.

The rear of the house has an unusual combination of weather-boarding, pilasters, pediments, and a lunette window.

●● Cross High St and proceed R to the East Lane corner (first L).

No 37 was built as two properties in 1458, but much of the building was reconstructed in 1982 following partial collapse.

Nos 39–41 were built as one house, probably in the late 15C.

●● Cross High St and follow the path immediately ahead to the riverside walk.

Location 11	**RIVERSIDE WALK**

Most of this walk, west of the town, is a recent development and follows the closure of timber yards and some light industries. The walk is planned to be continued without a break to Kingston Bridge but until this is done a brief return to High Street must, unfortunately, be made.

●● Continue ahead to the Riverside Centre almost at the end of the path. Turn R and proceed to Ram Passage that runs immediately L of the Ram inn. L High St. Continue to Market Place. Follow the passage L just before the Bradford and Bingley Building Society building and proceed to the next section of the riverside walk R.

Completely new pubs and restaurants line this part of the riverside walk. Some provide excellent views of the river and Hampton Court Park opposite. They are good examples of the current Post-Modernist style with neat brickwork, bays and Romanesque arches.

•• Continue ahead to Kingston Bridge.

Location 12	**KINGSTON BRIDGE** *Lapidge 1828*

A bridge has been recorded at this point since the 13C. The present structure is built of brick faced with Portland stone and was widened in 1914.

•• At the bridge ascend the slope R to Clarence St R. Cross to the main building of Bentalls store on the Wood St corner ahead.

Location 13	**BENTALLS** *M. Webb 1935*

Designed by the architect of Kingston's Guildhall, the same style – a blown up late Wren derivation – has been employed, perhaps in deference to Wren's work across the river at Hampton Court.

The department store, one of England's largest, has since been greatly extended and possesses a separate garage and removals department. It might be compared with an out-of-London Selfridges. Many visitors are attracted to Kingston, particularly on Saturdays, just to visit Bentalls.

•• Leave Bentalls by the Clarence St exit. L Clarence St. Continue ahead to London Rd remaining on the north side.

Nos 43–47 London Rd are late 18C.

Location 14	**CLEAVES ALMSHOUSES** *1668*
49–71 London Road	Six almshouses were built on either side of the pedimented centre.

The coat of arms on the pediment was carved by *Joshua Marshall*, assistant to *Grinling Gibbons*.

•• Continue ahead to the Queen Elizabeth Rd corner (first L). On the east side is the Lovekyn Chapel.

Location 15	**LOVEKYN CHAPEL**
London Road	The chapel, dedicated to St Mary Magdalene,

*Open Monday–
Friday 09.00–17.00.
Closed during school
holidays. Admission
free*

was founded by master butcher Edward Lovekyn in 1309. It has been recorded that he presented the meat for Edward II's coronation feast at Westminster Hall and the grateful King arranged for permission to be given to Lovekyn to build the chapel for his chantry. John Lovekyn, a Lord Mayor of London, partly rebuilt the chapel in 1352. Elizabeth I granted the chapel to Kingston Grammar School in 1561 and it still belongs to the school, now serving as the woodworking department. Restoration took place in 1886.

The building is constructed of chalk bricks faced with stone.

•• Enter the chapel.

Some blocked windows with original tracery survive.

The function of the two recesses is uncertain.

At the east end, the king's head corbel may depict Edward II.

●➤ *Exit R London Rd. Second R Eden St and Kingston Station (BR).*

Wimbledon

Famed throughout the world for its annual tennis championships, Wimbledon has much more to offer the visitor. Part of its parish church, St Mary-the-Virgin, is medieval and several important monuments are displayed.

The south-east corner of the thousand-acre Wimbledon Common protrudes into Wimbledon 'Village' and fine period houses survive along its south and west sides. Wimbledon's Lawn Tennis Museum permits visitors a view of the famous Centre Court.

Timing The Wimbledon Lawn Tennis Museum is closed Sunday morning and Monday. Southside House may be entered October–February, Tuesday, Thursday and Friday afternoons.

Suggested connection Precede with Barnes.

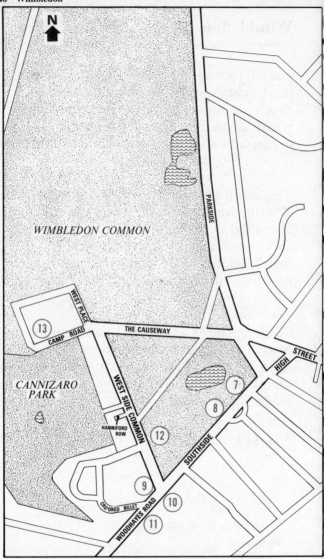

Locations

1 Church Road
2 St Mary-the-Virgin
3 Old Rectory House
4 Arthur Road
5 Wimbledon Lawn Tennis
   Museum
6 High Street

7 Wimbledon Common
8 South Side Common
9 Crooked Billet
10 Southside House
11 Woodhayes Road
12 West Side Common
13 William Wilberforce School

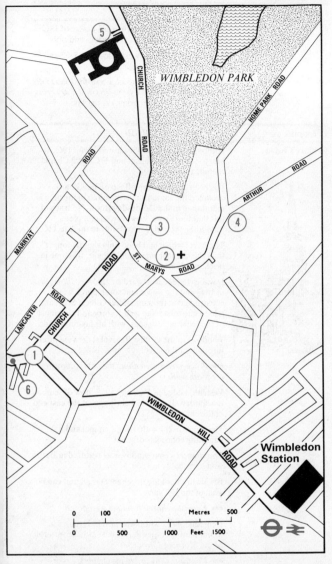

Start *From Wimbledon Station, District Line, or BR from Waterloo Station exit R Wimbledon Hill Rd which becomes High St. Ninth R Church Rd. Proceed to Walnut Tree Cottages (first L).*

Alternatively, from the station cross Wimbledon Hill Rd and take bus 80 or 93 northward to Church Rd.

Alternatively, continue from Barnes as indicated on page 130.

Location 1	**CHURCH ROAD**

Walnut Tree Cottages form a cul-de-sac of 18C cottages. Bow windows are modern additions.

Further north, on the west side, **Nos 45–53** and **55** are early 19C.

•➤ Third R St Mary's Road. Cross the road to the parish church of St Mary-the-Virgin. (If dry cross the field to cut off the corner.) Enter the churchyard.

Location 2	**ST MARY-THE-VIRGIN**

St Mary's Road

Although the bulk of the church is mid 19C, St Mary's medieval chancel and 17C Cecil Chapel remain at the east end.

It is probable that a small Saxon building occupied the same site, as a church in the area is mentioned in the Domesday Book. No trace of this building exists, however, as complete rebuilding took place, probably in the late 13C.

The nave, which had been only slightly longer than the chancel, was again rebuilt, this time in brick, in 1786.

It was extended westward by *George Gilbert Scott* in 1843 and the tower and south porch were constructed at the same time. Gilbert Scott also added buttresses and a clerestory and clad most of the building, as usual, with his favoured flint.

Windows in the Gothic Revival style were fitted throughout the nave.

•➤ Proceed eastward along the path, following the south wall.

Vestries, added in 1920 and 1955, now obscure the south wall of the Cecil Chapel at the east end of the church.

The fabric of the walls of this chapel and the adjoining chancel is original.

The **chancel**'s east window was restored in Bath stone, probably in 1860.

Brickwork flanking the chancel is all that can be seen of the 18C nave.

•➤ Enter the church from the west porch.

Immediately L, within the porch, is the monument to James Perry, d.1821, a proprietor of the *Morning Chronicle*.

*•➤ Continue eastward to the **chancel**.*

No furnishings in St Mary's pre-date the mid-19C.

The late-13C(?) chancel is the most ancient part of the church. Its floor tiling and seating date from the restoration of 1860. At this time the old rafters were exposed and decorated.

There are traces of a blocked doorway in the north wall.

In the north wall, at low level, is the oldest memorial in St Mary's, an Elizabethan tablet

c.1540 commemorating Philip, d.1462, and
Margaret Lewston.

☛ *Proceed through the arch R to the* **Cecil Chapel**.

The Cecil Chapel was added to the church *c*.1628
by Sir Edward Cecil, Lord Wimbledon, as a
family mausoleum. This could not originally be
approached from the church but had its own
external entrance.

An arch was formed in the north wall, linking it
with the chancel, probably in 1860. Its west wall
was demolished in 1920 to provide a link with the
newly built Warrior Chapel.

The large window in the south wall possesses the
most important stained glass in the church. In its
light L are the 16C arms of Lord Wimbledon's
father, Sir Thomas Cecil, Earl of Essex. This was
one of three cartouches that made up an earlier
east window of the chancel.

The knight on the 15C section R carries a shield
bearing the arms of St George. This is part of an
earlier window from the north side of the
chancel.

Four small windows at upper level survive in the
chapel. There were originally six, representing
the two wives and four daughters of Lord
Wimbledon. The other two were removed to the
Warrior Chapel from the west wall when this was
demolished.

The altar tomb of Lord Wimbledon, d.1628,
stands in the centre of the chapel.

Suspended from the ceiling is a viscount's
coronet.

☛ *Proceed westward through the modern oak
screen to the* **Warrior Chapel**.

This chapel was built in 1920 as a First World
War memorial and replaced the vestry of 1860.

Its north wall originally formed the external
south wall of the chancel and here, at low level, is
an early 14C 'leper' window, discovered in 1920.
This was not originally quite so low; the floor has
since been raised 21 ins. Its purpose is uncertain.
Those with contagious diseases may have
observed services from here, or the window may
have served as a lynchnoscope, whereby light
from within the church might scare demons from
the graveyard.

Opposite, in the south wall, are the two small
17C windows removed from the west wall of the
Cecil Chapel.

☛ *Exit from the church R and proceed to the
north side of the churchyard. From here can be
gained the best view of Old Rectory House that lies
behind the wall. (The house cannot be viewed
from the road.)*

Location 3	**OLD RECTORY HOUSE** *c.1500*

Not open.

This became the country residence of William Cecil, later Lord Burghley, in 1549. It originally comprised one range with twin stair turrets but was extended in 1846 and later. The original chapel, with some Perpendicular features, survives. Some external Tudor brickwork is visible.

➧ Turn R and continue to the east side of the churchyard.

The pyramidal monument commemorates Gerard de Visnie, d.1797.

➧ Continue clockwise around the church. At the vestry, on the south side, follow the path L and pass through the gate. Continue ahead to Arthur Rd L.

Location 4	**ARTHUR ROAD**

No 19, The Artesian Well, is a domed octagon, dated 1731. It was built for the Duchess of Marlborough, in connection with her manor house, Wimbledon Park House, and enclosed a well, originally only 40 ft deep. A new artesian well, 563 ft deep, was sunk in 1798 for Earl Spencer, who had commissioned a mansion known as Well House from *Holland* in 1802 (demolished 1949). Much of the estate provided land for the All England Tennis Club that lies further north. The well has been filled and the building was converted to a private house in 1975.

➧ Return southward to the St Mary's Rd junction R.

The Gothic style corner building was constructed as a lodge to Wimbledon Park House early in the 19C. Nothing survives of the house itself which stood east of the lodge.

➧ To view the Wimbledon Lawn Tennis Museum (Location 5) continue westward along St Mary's Rd. First R Church Rd. (It is a ten-minute walk and there is no bus service.) Pass the main entrance and enter the club premises first L.

➧ Alternatively, from St Mary's Rd L Church Rd. Continue to the end. R High St.

Location 5	**WIMBLEDON LAWN TENNIS MUSEUM**

All England Lawn Tennis and Croquet Club, Church Road, Wimbledon (946 6131).

Open Tuesday–Saturday 11.00–17.00. Sunday 14.00–17.00. Many films are available for viewing in the cinema and visitors may be able to see items of specific

The Wimbledon Lawn Tennis Championships are the world's oldest and still regarded as the most important. This museum adjoins the famous Centre Court which is seen during the visit. 'Wimbledon Fortnight' takes place annually during the last week in June and the first in July. It is sponsored by the All England Lawn Tennis and Croquet Club which was founded, initially for playing croquet only, at Worple Road, Wimbledon, in 1868. The first men's tennis championship was played there in 1877. A move was made to the present site in 1922 when most of the existing buildings were constructed.

interest by telephoning the museum in advance.

During the Championships only spectators already within the grounds are admitted to the museum.

The air-conditioned museum was completely redesigned in 1985. Four main sections cover 'The Story of Tennis', 'Visit to the Centre Court', 'Birth of a New Game' and the cinema (20–50 minute programmes). Numerous facts about the club and the game of lawn tennis are provided, for instance, twelve tonnes of strawberries are now consumed during the fortnight of the Championships.

●▬ *Exit from the club R Church Rd. Continue to the end. R High St. Remain on the north side.*

●▬ *Alternatively and preferably telephone for a taxi from the museum, as the uphill walk can be tiring.*

Location 6	**HIGH STREET**

Not open.

Much of the thoroughfare is now lined with 19C buildings but some earlier houses survive.

On the south side, immediately before the Fisherman's Wharf restaurant is **No 35**, 1760.

Opposite, on the north side, **Eagle House** was built in 1613 for Robert Bell, founder of the East India Company. Later the house was occupied by the Marquess of Bath and Pitt's Foreign Minister, William Granville. In the early 19C the building, then Nelson House, was used as a school, but in 1860 it again reverted to private occupation, and was re-named Eagle House by its new owner, Dr Huntingford, due to the stone eagle that still surmounts the central gable. Restoration in 1887 included the complete rebuilding of the central section.

Most of the external brickwork has now been rendered.

On the west side is an extension followed by outbuildings – all early-18C work.

Some original ceilings and the hall overmantel survive, together with the dining room's panelling of 1730. The building has been converted to offices.

●▬ *Continue westward.*

The **Rose and Crown** is a much altered late-17C tavern. Authors Leigh Hunt and Swinburne were once *habitués*.

●▬ *From the Rose and Crown cross the road immediately ahead and follow High Street which curves southward at this point.*

On the east side, **No 38** is early 18C.

No 41 displays stone lions in its front garden which were brought from the late 18C Wimbledon Villa that once stood on the common's south side, seen later.

No 44, **Claremont House**, is late 17C with a later doorway.

➥ Continue ahead to South Side Common which borders the south-east corner of part of Wimbledon Common.

| Location 7 | **WIMBLEDON COMMON** |

The common comprises more than 1000 acres of heath and birch woods. It was protected in perpetuity by Act of Parliament in 1871 following attempts to develop it by the Spencer family, Lords of the Manor.

The common's famous windmill, which stands further north, was erected in 1818 and rebuilt in 1893, when it was heightened and the base reduced in size.

There are two ponds on the common.

Wimbledon Common merges with Putney Heath at its northern extremity.

➥ Continue westward following South Side Common.

| Location 8 | **SOUTH SIDE COMMON** |

No 6, **Lauriston Cottage**, is the 18C converted stable block of Lauriston House, now demolished but once the residence of the slavery abolitionist William Wilberforce.

No 7, **South Lodge**, was built in 1840.

No 12, **Rushmore**, was originally built in the 18C as a farmhouse.

*➥ Continue to **King's College School**.*

The school's Junior's department was transferred to this early 19C building from Strand, central London, in 1897. The westward extension with its great hall was added by *Bannister Fletcher* in 1899.

➥ Continue ahead to Woodhayes Road. Cross the small green to Crooked Billet (the short street that runs parallel).

| Location 9 | **CROOKED BILLET** |

The **Hand in Hand** tavern was built in the late 17C but its porch and east extension are modern.

➥ Continue southward.

Another attractive pub soon follows, the **Crooked Billet**, 18C with a 19C north extension.

➥ Proceed to Woodhayes Rd. Cross immediately to Southside House, on the east side.

| Location 10 | **SOUTHSIDE HOUSE** |

School Teachers Cultural Foundation, Woodhayes Road, London SW19.

Open for guided tours October–February Tuesday, Thursday and Friday 14.00– 17.00. Admission free.

Axel Munthe, physician and writer, lived here for a short time.

The facade of the house, built in 1687, was altered when the building was extended in 1776.

➥ Continue westward.

Location 11	**WOODHAYES ROAD**

No 6, Gothick Cottage, dated 1763, was extended *c.*1890. Author Captain Marryat lived here briefly.

Opposite, on the west side, **Nos 1** and **2** are 18C.

•➡ Return eastward to Wimbledon Common. First L West Side Common.

Location 12	**WEST SIDE COMMON**

Chester House *c.*1670 is now a training centre for Barclays Bank. In the 18C it was owned by the radical politician John Horne Tooke who built a mausoleum for himself in the rear garden. This still survives but Tooke was refused permission to rest there and he was eventually buried in the churchyard of Ealing parish church.

The extension is modern.

No 6, West Side House, is a mid-18C mansion that was occupied early in the 19C by Lord Chancellor Lyndhurst. It has now been converted to flats.

The old stable block survives on the north side.

Nos 14–19 Hanniford Row form a cul-de-sac of cottages built in 1770.

Cannizaro House, built in the 18C, became, early in the 19C, the residence of the Duke of Cannizaro. The house was enlarged late in the 19C

Its grounds, now **Cannizaro Park**, which lie to the rear, are open to the public.

•➡ First L enter Cannizaro Park.

The park, with its many rare trees, affords a good view of the rear of Cannizaro House.

•➡ Return to West Side Common L.

Stamford House, dated 1720, has been converted to flats. Its modern porch and pebble-dash rendering are unsympathetic.

The Keir, 1789, now stuccoed, has similarly been converted to flats.

•➡ First L Camp Rd.

Location 13	**WILLIAM WILBERFORCE SCHOOL** *1761*
Camp Rd.	This, the 'Round School', was built for fifty poor children and included accommodation for the headmaster. It was extended in 1834, and again later in the 19C. The school closed in 1965 but was restored and extended by the polygonal wing in 1976.

•➡ Return to West Side Common L. First L West Place.

West Place comprises early 19C cottages.

•● *Return to West Side Common R. First L The Causeway leads to High St R. Continue ahead to Wimbledon Station (BR), District Line.*

•● *Alternatively, bus 80 or 93 southbound from High St to Wimbledon Station.*

Ham and Petersham

Although close to London, Ham and Petersham are genuine villages with real fields grazed by real cows. Petersham, 'England's grandest village', is outstanding due to its quantity of great period mansions. Unfortunately, most of them line the main road from Richmond to Kingston which bisects the village. Escape riverwards brings some relief. North of Ham Common lies Ham House which is open to the public and uniquely retains most of its 17C décor and furnishings. This may, alternatively, be visited by ferry from Twickenham if preferred.

Timing Ham House does not open before 11.00 and closes Monday.

Suggested connections Precede with Richmond. Continue to Kingston.

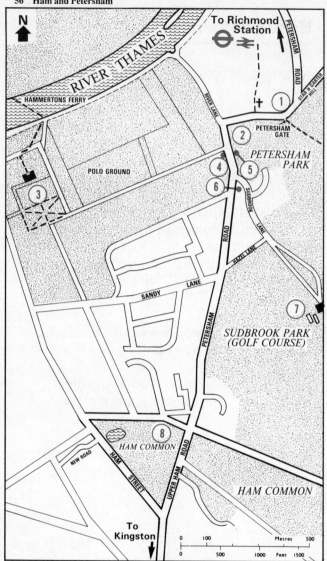

N

To Richmond
Station

RIVER THAMES

HAMMERTONS FERRY

POLO GROUND

PETERSHAM ROAD

STAR & GARTER HILL

PETERSHAM GATE

① ✝

②

③

④

⑤ PETERSHAM PARK

⑥

RIVER LANE

SUDBROOK LANE

HAZEL LANE

⑦ SUDBROOK PARK (GOLF COURSE)

PETERSHAM ROAD

SANDY LANE

⑧

HAM COMMON

NEW ROAD

HAM STREET

UPPER HAM ROAD

HAM COMMON

To
Kingston

| 0 | 100 | | Metres | 500 |
| 0 | | 500 | 1000 | 1500 Feet |

Locations

1 St Peter
2 Petersham Village
3 Ham House and Gardens
4 Ham House Gatehouse
5 Lodges of Old Petersham Park
6 Sudbrook Lane
7 Sudbrook Park
8 Ham Common

Start *Richmond Station (BR), District Line. Exit from the station and take bus 65 or 71 southward to the Petersham Gate of Richmond Park (request stop). From the bus stop cross the road, turn L and continue southward passing the Dysart Arms.*

Alternatively, continue from Richmond as indicated on page 80.

*Noteworthy 18C houses passed R are **Park Gate** and **Church House**.*

Follow the first path R to St Peter's Church. Ahead is the entrance to Church House. (The key to St Peter's may be obtained here if the church is locked.)

Location 1	**ST PETER**

Petersham Road

Although small, St Peter's, with its box pews and galleries, is a rare example of an English village church that retains its early 19C internal appearance.

The original Saxon church was rebuilt *c.*1266 and part of its chancel survives. George Vancouver, discoverer of Canada's Vancouver Island, is commemorated in the church and buried in the churchyard. The parents of Queen Elizabeth The Queen Mother, the Earl and Countess of Strathmore, were married at St Peter's in 1881.

The lower part of the **tower** was built in 1505 and the upper part in the 17C. Surmounting this is a lantern, added in 1790.

Immediately L of the tower is the **north transept**, built in the 17C, but with its upper part *c.*1790.

Much rebuilding took place following Second World War bomb damage.

The **south transept** R was also built in the 17C but mostly rebuilt in 1840 when it was enlarged.

•● *Proceed clockwise to the chancel that protrudes on the east side.*

The north wall of the **chancel** is 13C and retains the only lancet window (blocked) in the church.

Some 17C brickwork remains at the base of the south transept's east wall.

Alongside the south wall, towards the east end of the churchyard, is the tomb of Captain George Vancouver.

•● *Continue to the west porch, built in 1840, and enter the church.*

Displayed, immediately R, is a beadle's uniform.

The short **nave**, rebuilt in 1805, is virtually the crossing of the church and does not extend west of the tower.

Immediately ahead is the font, dated 1740.

The west music gallery, above the entrance, was built in 1838. Other galleries were erected in 1840.

A beadle's staff is displayed L of the entrance.

North of this is George Vancouver's wall plaque, 1798.

The box pews are late 18C and rare surviving examples.

The pulpit, against the east wall of the north transept, was made in 1796.

Above the chancel arch are the arms of George III, acquired in 1810.

Against the north wall of the **sanctuary** is the monument to George Cole, d.1624, and his wife and grandson.

Below the altar, in the Dysart vault, lies the Duchess of Lauderdale, 17C owner of nearby Ham House.

The reading desk, R of the chancel, is believed to be part of a late-18C three-decker pulpit.

•● Return to Petersham Rd R. Remain on the west side.

Location 2	**PETERSHAM VILLAGE**

Petersham, with its outstanding period mansions, astonishingly remains a village, surrounded by fields and parkland, and has been described as England's grandest. Unfortunately, it is bisected by the main road between Richmond and Kingston, a daunting ribbon of noise, pollution and danger.

No 141, late 17C, retains rare examples of casement windows unconverted to sash.

No 143, **Petersham House**, *c.*1674, has an early 19C top storey and porch.

Opposite, on the east side, is **Montrose House** *c.*1670; for many years the residence of entertainer Tommy Steele. The house was enlarged and embellished early in the 18C.

Its main gates, on the corner ahead, are outstanding.

Rutland Lodge, on the west side, by *Jenner* (?) *c.*1660 was converted to flats following a fire in 1967. Its upper storey was added later, above the original carved eaves.

•● First R River Lane. Cross to the south side.

The **Manor House** is early 18C with a later porch.

Glen Cottage, next door, was occupied by George Vancouver from 1795 until his death in 1798.

Petersham Lodge, *c.*1740, has been remodelled and stuccoed.

•● Continue ahead towards the river. Follow the path L to Ham House (Location 3) NB: sections of the path are impassable when there is a flood tide. Almost opposite the Hammerton Ferry landing stage, a short path L crosses a stream. Immediately R is a gap in the fence. The path leads to Ham House. It is important not to miss this, otherwise a detour of half a mile is necessary to reach the house from the west side.

•● Alternatively, if Ham House is not being visited, return to Petersham Road R and continue to Location 4.

Location 3	**HAM HOUSE AND GARDENS**

(940 1950)

The grounds are open daily 10.00–18.00. Admission free.

This Jacobean house, although much altered, retains, uniquely for the period, most of its original furnishings. The interior provides a greater insight into fashionable 17C life than any other house in the country.

Ham House is open Tuesday–Sunday 11.00–17.00. Admission charge.

Ham House was built for Sir Thomas Vavasour in 1610 to an 'H' plan that followed the usual Elizabethan and Jacobean pattern. William Murray, Earl of Dysart, leased the house *c.*1626 and purchased the property in 1637. He then rearranged much of the interior. His daughter, Elizabeth, Countess of Dysart, married Sir Lyonel Tollemache *c.*1647and inherited the house *c.*1654. After Tollemache's death Elizabeth married the Earl of Lauderdale, Charles II's Secretary of State for Scotland and they began major alterations in 1672.

The north front originally possessed a more vertical and picturesque appearance than it does now. There was a central bay above the doorway and the two existing three-storey loggias were surmounted by turrets with ogee (onion-shaped) caps and weather vanes in the manner of Charlton House near Greenwich. All this was removed by the Lauderdales, who preferred the then fashionable Classical style. To help achieve this, Classical busts were added to the forecourt walls.

Greater alterations were made on the south side (seen later) by the Lauderdales but the only major external alterations to Ham House after this were the rebuilding of the bays on both fronts and the usual conversion of most windows from casement to sash in the mid 18C.

The forecourt was originally enclosed by a north wall immediately fronted by a jetty. This wall was demolished *c.*1800 and its busts fixed to the north facade of the house.

The statue of a river god, in Coade stone, is based on a work by *Bacon c.*1784.

•● *Proceed anti-clockwise to view the south facade. Passed R are lodges and outbuildings.*

Wishing to increase their accommodation, the Lauderdales added a series of rooms on both floors between, and on either side of, the two south wings, *William Samwell*, 1674. This almost doubled the size of the house but of course destroyed the original 'H' plan.

The gardens of Ham House were laid out in the 17C and have been partly restored to their formal style.

•● *Return to the north facade and enter the house by the main door facing the forecourt.*

The initials of Sir Thomas Vavasour, and the date, 1610, are inscribed on the door.

As the house is operated by the Victoria and Albert Museum, which does not approve of labelling, every room will be named and its major contents described. Paintings are generally titled.

The house was privately owned by the Tollemache family until 1948 when it was presented, with its contents, to the nation and this unusual continuity of ownership, combined with a long period of storage, is why almost all of the furnishings original to the house survive. A few additional items of furniture have been provided by the V & A.

Much of the internal workmanship is Dutch, including some inset paintings by *Van de Velde, the Younger.*

Great Hall. When built, this formed the eastern half of the horizontal bar in the 'H' plan as, originally, there were no rooms on the south side. It was enlarged by Murray *c.*1637.

Most of the ceiling was removed in the late 17C to increase the height of the hall by combining it with the dining room above. The dining room ceiling of 1636 survived.

Windows in the south wall were filled when rooms were added south of the hall.

Carved figures of Mars and Minerva over the fireplace were allegedly modelled on Murray and his wife.

• Exit from the south-west corner.

Marble Dining Room. This was the first of the domestic rooms to be added by the Lauderdales. It was named 'Marble' from the original black and white marble floor which was replaced by the present decorative wooden floor in the mid 18C.

The wall covering is 17C gilt leather.

• Exit from the south-west corner.

Duke's Dining Room. The wall hangings are a reproduction of the 17C originals.

Duchess's Bedchamber. Originally, the Duke occupied this bedchamber but he later exchanged rooms with the Duchess.

The bed and its covers are modern reproductions of 18C originals.

Above the door are more sea paintings by *Van de Velde the Younger.*

Duke's Closet. Damask wall coverings reproduce the 17C colour scheme.

• Return to the Marble Dining Room and exit from the south-east corner.

Withdrawing Room. Furnishings are *c.*1675.

• Exit from the south-east corner.

Yellow Bedchamber. This room, part of the original house, was Lady Dysart's bedchamber before the extension was built. It became Lord Lauderdale's bedchamber *c.*1677 when he exchanged with her.

• Exit from the south-west corner.

White Closet. The closet was retained by the Duchess after the exchange of bedchambers.

The ceiling painting is by *Verrio.*

The Duchess's Private Closet. This closet was also retained by the Duchess following the exchange; the arrangement could hardly have been convenient.

➤ Return to the Great Hall.

Chapel. Created in the north-east bay by the Lauderdales, the chapel retains its original rare altar hangings.

➤ Exit ahead.

Inner Hall. Furniture displayed here is mid-18C.

Great Staircase. Added to the house for Murray, c.1637, the staircase has a balustrade of carved and pierced panels and is an early example of its type.

The ceiling's plasterwork is contemporary with the staircase.

➤ Ascend to the top of the stairs L.

Lady Maynard's Chamber. The room was occupied by Lady Maynard, the Duchess's sister, from 1679 to 1682. The oak frieze is Jacobean reproduction, carved early in the 19C.

Most furniture is 19C.

➤ Exit from the south-east corner.

Lady Maynard's Dressing Room. This was also occupied by Lady Maynard.

➤ Return to Lady Maynard's Chamber and exit from the north side. Proceed ahead.

Museum Room. Originally a bedroom, textiles are displayed.

➤ Exit from the south-west corner.

Cabinet of Miniatures. This was once a servants' room. Miniatures displayed include 'Elizabeth I' by *Hilliard*.

Exhibited in a case is a lock of hair allegedly cut from the Earl of Essex's head, immediately preceding his execution in 1601.

➤ Exit from the south side.

Round Gallery. Before most of the floor was removed early in the 18C, this served as the Great Dining Room. It forms the first of the State Rooms which were created to impress important guests.

The ceiling and frieze were plastered for Murray c.1637.

Paintings are by *Cleyn, Kneller* and *Lely*.

➤ Exit from the north-west corner.

North Drawing Room. The woodwork, plaster ceiling and frieze were made for Murray c.1637.

Its 17C armchairs retain their original silk covers.

Inset paintings are by *Cleyn*.

• *Exit from the north side.*

Green Closet. Miniature paintings were originally displayed here.

The modern reproduction wall hangings simulate the room's appearance after 1670.

The paintings on the ceiling and its cove are by *Cleyn*.

Long Gallery. This formed part of the original house but was redecorated for Murray in 1639.

Many of the portraits are by *Lely*.

• *Exit from the south-west corner.*

Library Closet. Displayed are plans for a Whitehall Palace by *Inigo Jones* that never materialized.

Library. This, together with its closet, was added by the Lauderdales, thus extending Ham House to the west *c.*1674.

The library steps are *c.*1740.

• *Return to the Long Gallery. Exit ahead from the south-east corner.*

Antechamber to the Queen's Bedchamber. This was one of the three rooms added between the south front wings by the Lauderdales. It was then known as the Green Drawing Room. The furniture is late 17C.

• *Exit from the south-east corner.*

Queen's Bedchamber. The room was prepared for a visit by Catherine of Braganza, Charles II's consort. It was remodelled *c.*1740 and converted to a drawing room; tapestries were then hung.

Queen's Closet. Although small, this is the most sumptuous of all the rooms. Its oval ceiling panel was probably painted by *Verrio*.

The scagliola (imitation marble) fireplace is an early English example.

• *Return through the State Rooms to the Long Gallery. Exit from the west side to the Round Gallery and descend the stairs. Exit from Ham House and proceed through the north entrance gate. Follow the path R and turn R passing the east side of Ham House. The path bears L.*

Passed L are the **Ham House Polo Grounds**.

The German School, **Deutsche Schule** designed by German architects in 1972, is passed next. It stands in the grounds of **Douglas House** *c.*1700, which overlooks the path further south.

The old stable block of the house follows (now part of the school).

• *Continue to the gatehouse ahead.*

Location 4	**HAM HOUSE GATEHOUSE** *1898*
Petersham Road	The gatehouse was built, with due deference to the 17C Ham House, in mock Jacobean style. It is now divided into two private residences.

• *Cross Petersham Rd to Farm House opposite.*

| Location 5 | **LODGES OF OLD PETERSHAM PARK** *17C* |

Petersham Road

Farm House, and **No 190** Petersham Road which faces it, are genuine early-17C buildings. The two properties were originally the lodges to Petersham Park (also called Petersham Lodge). Petersham Park was a mansion built in the 17C but rebuilt in the 18C by *Lord Burlington* for William Stanhope, first Viscount Petersham. The house was demolished early in the 19C and its extensive grounds incorporated with Richmond Park.

●● Turn R and proceed southward. Where Petersham Rd curves R continue ahead following Sudbrook Lane.

| Location 6 | **SUDBROOK LANE** |

Sudbrook Cottage and **Box Cottage** on the east side are early 18C.

Gort Lodge, opposite, is also early 18C. It was built as one residence, with **Gort House** which lies behind, fronting Petersham Rd.

Harrington Lodge was built *c.*1700.

Mullion, opposite, is a Georgian residence.

●● Continue to the archway at the end of Sudbrook Lane and follow the path through the golf course to Sudbrook Park.

| Location 7 | **SUDBROOK PARK** *Gibbs 1726* |

Richmond Golf Club (940 1463)

Grudgingly open to visitors (although a statutory requirement) to view the Cube Room, one afternoon each month. Telephone to ascertain the date.

The house, now the clubhouse of Richmond Golf Club, is a rare example of a private residence by *Gibbs*. It is basically designed to a Palladian plan but its detailing is Baroque.

The main elevation has been completely altered by the later addition of a portico.

●● Enter the hall immediately. Directly behind this is the **Cube Room.**

The Cube Room is one of Gibbs's most Baroque interiors; few in the London area match its flamboyance.

●● Exit from the house and return to Sudbrook Lane. Immediately L is Hazel Lane. Continue to the end. L Petersham Rd. Take bus 65 southbound to Ham Common (north side) to avoid a ten minute walk of little interest. From the bus stop return northward. First L Ham Common north side.

| Location 8 | **HAM COMMON** |

This triangular section surrounded by houses is often regarded as the extent of Ham Common; the common in fact continues eastward from the Petersham Road and that section is three times larger.

The north and west sides of this triangular section are of greater architectural interest.

Hardwick House is late 18C.

St Michael's Convent now occupies Orford Hall, an early 18C residence with later wings.

Two 17C lodges, now private houses, once flanked the south entrance to Ham House.

Selby House is 18C.

•➡ *Turn L and follow Ham Street which, for this stretch, forms the west side of Ham Common.*

Endsleigh Lodge, *c.*1800, has wings with typical Adamesque fans above their windows.

Little House and, after New Road, **Glebe Cottage** and **Gordon House** are 18C.

Forbes House is a good Georgian fake, built in 1936.

Langham House is 18C.

Cassel Hospital now occupies Cassel House, built in the early 19C.

•➡ *At Upper Ham Rd turn L and take bus 65 northward to Richmond Station (BR), District Line.*

•➡ *Alternatively, if continuing to Kingston (page 33) cross the road, turn R and take bus 65 southward to Kingston Station. From the bus stop cross Eden St. Turn L. First R Wood St. Immediately ahead Fife Rd. R Clarence St. Cross Clarence St to All Saints Church. (Sections of Bentalls store will have been passed, the main building is entered later.)*

Richmond

Richmond possesses some of the finest Queen Anne and early Georgian domestic properties in England. Remnants of the great Tudor royal palace survive, facing its green. While an important part of the riverside will be under redevelopment for some years, its path still provides what is probably the most attractive stretch along the Thames in the vicinity of London. From the top of Richmond Hill can be gained the famous view of the sylvan Thames curving towards old Twickenham. Immediately south of the hill are the 2000 acres of Richmond Park, by far the largest of all the London boroughs' royal parks.

Timing Any day is suitable as there are no great buildings to be entered. Fine weather would be a great advantage.

Suggested connections To explore Richmond thoroughly will occupy most of a day but it could be preceded by a brief visit to Kew Gardens or continued with Ham and Petersham.

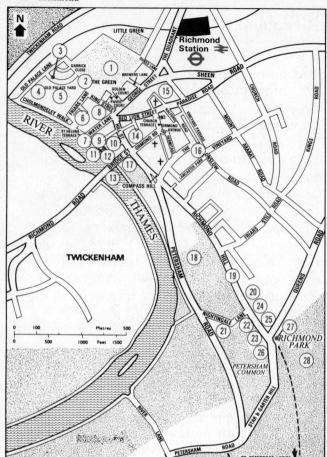

Locations

Start *Richmond Station (BR), District Line. Exit from the station and cross The Quadrant immediately L. Take the footpath first R through the Oriel House archway. First L cross the railway bridge to Little Green.*

Location 1	**RICHMOND GREEN**

Richmond Green is regarded by many as the finest in the country as it is bounded, on two sides, by outstanding examples of five centuries of building styles. Unfortunately, houses on the east side have almost all been converted to offices.

The green once faced Richmond Palace and was a knights' jousting ground. Following the Civil War, the palace fell into disrepair and Richmond was briefly abandoned by the Court. Royalty returned to the area in the late 17C when William III purchased what was later to become Ormond Lodge in the old Deer Park, and Richmond Green become, once again, a fashionable address. As at Kew Green, cricket is played here in the summer. The south and east sides are of prime architectural interest.

Immediately R is Little Green, once waste land, granted by Charles II for bowling.

Richmond Theatre *Matcham*, 1899, faces Little Green. It retains a late Victorian interior.

•➡ *Continue southward along the east side of the green to the Duke's Lane corner. On the corner is No 1, The Green.*

No 1 was built early in the 17C but has been much altered. By tradition, it was the residence of Simon Bardolph, friend of William Shakespeare, who reputedly stayed with him during his visits to Richmond Palace. Bardolph is buried in the parish church.

No 3, Gothic House, was also built in the early 17C. Its facade has been renewed in Neo-Gothic style. Then follows **No 4**, early 18C and **No 5** early 19C.

No 6 was completed recently, in Post-Modernist style, for architects *Darbourne & Darke*, of course by themselves.

No 7 is early 18C with Victorian additions.

No 8 and **9** are mid 18C.

Nos 10–12 are early 18C. All have fine eaves and **No 11, Queen House,** and **No 12** also possess exceptional porches.

•➡ *L Brewers Lane.*

Brewers Lane has Richmond's largest concentration of antique shops.

•➡ *Return to The Green L.*

Nos 15, 16, 17, 22 and **23** are early 18C.

•➡ *Pass the entrance to Golden Court (of little interest) and continue ahead to Paved Court.*

Paved Court. Many late 17C properties survive in what is Richmond Green's most attractive alleyway. Demolition was proposed in the 1960s but a letter sent to the *Richmond and*

Twickenham Times by the author of this book instigated a campaign by conservationists which proved successful.

No 1, at the far end R, retains an early 19C bow window.

•• Return to Richmond Green L and proceed westward.

Nos 31 and **32** are early 18C.

•• The east side again turns southward and is called Old Palace Terrace.

Old Palace Terrace 1692. An early example of a speculative development.

•• Cross the road immediately ahead to the south side of the Green.

Oak House *c.*1769. This is believed to have been built by *Robert Taylor*, who had previously designed Asgill House on the riverside, Richmond's most distinguished villa (Location 4).

•• Turn R and proceed westward.

Old Palace Place. This was built in the Tudor period but remodelled *c.*1700. A 16C wall painting survives internally.

Old Friars 1687. The cellars of this house were built *c.*1500 and survive from an earlier building which stood on the site. A rear extension R was built *c.*1740, possibly as a music or assembly room.

•• Proceed to Friars Lane, first L.

Friars Lane. This divided the Convent of the Observant Friars, a monastery established by Henry VII *c.*1500, from Richmond Palace. No trace of its buildings remains.

No 44, Tudor House and **Tudor Place.** These two houses were originally built in the 18C as one dwelling. Side porches are later additions.

Maids of Honour Row 1724. This terrace of four houses was built by the future George II to accommodate the maids of honour serving his wife, Caroline of Anspach, Princess of Wales, who then lived at Ormond Lodge in Old Deer Park.

•• Continue past the Old Palace and the Palace Gatehouse, both remnants of Richmond Palace which is described later (Location 2).

The Old Court House. The bow window was added early in the 19C to this early-18C house.

Wentworth House. Also built in the 18C, it was originally identical to the Old Court House but was remodelled by *Laxton c.*1858.

•• Pass Garrick Close (the site of an earlier Richmond theatre) and cross to the corner house on the west side of the green.

The Virginals 1813. This was built as Cedar Grove on the site of the palace bakehouse.

Pembroke Villas. On the west side of the green,

these were built *c.* 1850 on the site of Pembroke House and its grounds.

●➡ *Return towards the old gateway to Richmond Palace. Immediately L, facing the Green, are two adjoining houses, the Old Palace and Palace Gatehouse.*

Location 2	**RICHMOND PALACE**
Richmond Green	All that survives of the great Tudor palace are its gateway and some brickwork forming the walls of adjacent buildings, now private houses.

Richmond Palace was built on the site of three earlier royal residences, the first being the 12C Shene manor house which Henry I acquired in 1125. Edward III died there in 1377; Anne of Bohemia, Richard II's first consort, also died at the palace, of the plague, in 1394, and the King, deranged by grief, immediately demolished most of the building. A new Shene Palace was begun by Henry V but not completed until 1462. This burnt down in 1497.

Henry VII, in a rare burst of extravagance, then commissioned, on the 10-acre site, the largest, and at the time most magnificent, of all the Tudor royal palaces. Henry had previously been Duke of Richmond (Yorkshire) and he renamed the palace Richmond. He died there in 1509. After assigning Hampton Court to Henry VIII in 1529, Wolsey was given permission to reside at the palace. Richmond was particularly favoured by Elizabeth I, who also died here in 1603. Prince Henry, the eldest son of James I, lived at Richmond until his premature and unexplained death, which prevented him from inheriting the throne. His brother, Charles I, stayed at Richmond during the plague year of 1625, but following the Civil War, Oliver Cromwell stripped the palace of all its finery and demolished the most important buildings. Charles II preferred Windsor, and although his mother, Henrietta Maria, lodged at Richmond she did not like it and soon moved to Greenwich. James II's children lived at the palace during their infancy and its restoration by Wren was planned. With the King's departure, however, the scheme was abandoned and royalty finally left Richmond Palace.

The Old Palace and Palace Gatehouse. The joint north facades of these two houses once formed part of the external wall of the palace. Much remodelling has taken place, including the 18C addition to Palace Gatehouse of its large bay.

●➡ *Proceed to the gateway.*

Gateway. Above the large arch are the arms, renewed, of Henry VII. It had been implausibly alleged that Elizabeth I died in the small room above the arch.

●➡ *Proceed through the gateway to Old Palace Yard. Immediately L is the west facade of Palace Gatehouse.*

The stair turret is believed to be original.

A link between Palace Gatehouse and the
Wardrobe was built in the 17C.

The Wardrobe. In this building were originally
stored the palace's furnishings and hangings.
Although now converted to provide three
houses, much of the brickwork is original.

Clearly visible are Tudor arches, bricked in,
probably in the 17C.

The west (garden) facade of this range was
completely remodelled in Classical style, *c.*1708,
allegedly by *Wren*. This can only be seen on the
rare occasions when the gardens are open to
visitors in support of charities.

Old Palace Yard was the outer courtyard of the
palace. Two further courtyards lay ahead
between this point and the river. Trumpeter's
House in the south-east corner occupies the site
of the Middle Gateway, through which visitors
passed to the Middle Court.

Trumpeter's House (north facade) 1701. Some of
the fabric is Tudor and may have belonged to the
Middle Gateway. There is no evidence that Wren
worked on the house as has been alleged. The
residence was originally known as Trumpeting
House, from two stone trumpeters that decorated
the facade. Austrian Chancellor Metternich lived
here in 1848, and the house later became the
residence of radio pioneer Marconi. The building
was restored and converted to flats in 1952. Its
south facade is seen later.

●● *Continue westward. Second L Old Palace
Lane.*

Location 3	**OLD PALACE LANE**

This terrace of small cottages was built *c.*1810.

The White Swan inn, towards the river end,
possesses a beamed interior and a rear patio for
summer drinking.

●● *Exit R to the river. L Cholmondeley Walk.
Asgill House overlooks the river immediately L.*

Location 4	**ASGILL HOUSE** *R. Taylor 1758*

Cholmondeley Walk

*Open by appointment
but only to ratepayers
of Richmond-upon-
Thames.*

This Palladian villa was built in stone for Sir
Charles Asgill, Lord Mayor of London and a
friend of the architect. It occupies the site of the
old palace brewhouse that stood outside the
walls. The house, the most outstanding example
of *Sir Robert Taylor's* work near London, was
restored in 1969.

●● *Continue ahead.*

In the south-east corner of the grounds is an 18C
castellated summerhouse. Seen in the middle
distance L is the south facade of Trumpeter's
House.

Location 5	**TRUMPETER'S HOUSE SOUTH FACADE** 1701

Trumpeter's House north facade has already
been seen. This, the river front is more
impressive.

The portico was added *c*.1722.

Both end pavilions were built in the mid 18C.

The lawn occupies the site of the private royal apartments of Richmond Palace that overlooked the river.

➦ *Continue ahead.*

Passed L are two mid-18C houses (**Nos 2** and **1** Cholmondeley Walk) with flood defences.

Location 6	**ST HELENA TERRACE c.**1835

The terrace, approached by steps, was built with private boat houses below. Its name commemorates the island where Napoleon was exiled.

Location 7	**WHITE CROSS INN c.**1840
Cholmondeley Walk	The top storey was added in 1865.

From the river bar, a window provides a good view of Richmond Bridge. Below this window, surprisingly, is the fireplace. Its flue turns to one side before ascending.

➦ *Exit L. Proceed to Water Lane (first L).*

Location 8	**WATER LANE**

Laid out in the mid 17C, this was known as Town Lane until 1712.

On the east side are 18C and 19C warehouses, converted to flats in 1985.

Most paving stones are of granite and were laid to support the loads deposited by watermen.

➦ *Continue ahead.*

Location 9	**RIVERSIDE, WATER LANE TO RICHMOND BRIDGE**

The large area bounded by Water Lane, the river, Bridge St and Hill St, has been neglected for many years due to planning disputes. It is being developed to provide offices, flats and shops. A few of the original facades are to be retained or reproduced.

➦ *Proceed ahead.*

Location 10	**OLD TOWN HALL** *Ancell 1893*

This lies to the north, and faces Hill St. Second World War bombing destroyed its 'Renaissance' gables which were not renewed. The facade is to be preserved.

➦ *Continue ahead. Heron House L is of five brick bays.*

Location 11	**HERON HOUSE** *1693*

Built on the site of the royal mews, Heron House became, *c*.1806, the residence of Lady Hamilton and her daughter (by Nelson), Horatia. Some carved timbers discovered in the roof may have come from the Tudor Palace. The building was converted in 1858 to form part of the Royal (later

Palm Court) Hotel. Its last occupants were homeless mothers and their children who 'squatted' there in the late 1970s.

The external shell of this building and the adjacent 18C facade of the old Palm Court Hotel are to be retained.

●● *Continue ahead to the Tower House which overlooks Richmond Bridge.*

Location 12	**TOWER HOUSE** *Laxton 1858*

With its distinguished Italianate tower, the house was restored in 1968 after conservationists had battled to save it from demolition.

Location 13	**RICHMOND BRIDGE** *Paine* and *Course 1777*

London's oldest remaining bridge is also judged its finest. The bridge, of Portland stone, replaced a horse ferry and was paid for by a toll. It was sensitively widened in 1937, and the addition in paler stone can be seen from beneath.

●● *Ascend the steps first L on the north side of the bridge. L Bridge St. First R Hill St. First L Ormond Rd.*

●● *Alternatively, to shorten the itinerary, continue ahead beneath the bridge (Location 17).*

Location 14	**ORMOND ROAD**

Immediately R is the early-18C Ormond Terrace. The front of **No 7** was remodelled in the late 18C.

Ormond House is also early 18C, but the doorway was replaced early in the 19C.

●● *Continue ahead to Ormond Avenue (first L).*

The Rosary and **The Hollies** were both built by *Rawlins c.*1700 as back-to-back houses.

●● *Cross the road and continue ahead.*

The **Vicarage** was built in the early 19C, its porch is later.

●● *First L Church Terrace.*

Although built in 1797, the **Bethlehem Chapel** was remodelled early in the 19C.

●● *Cross the road and continue northward.*

Hermitage House was built *c.*1730 as was **Church Terrace** which follows immediately. The terrace is much altered.

●● *Cross Paradise Rd and follow the path to St Mary Magdalen's.*

Location 15	**ST MARY MAGDALEN**
Paradise Road	St Mary Magdalen is renowned for its outstanding monuments.

This, the parish church of Richmond, is first recorded in 1211. It probably stood on the present site but no trace of that building remains. St Mary's was rebuilt in 1487 and its tower survives.

Tower. When completed *c.*1507, the tower is believed to have had only two stages, the third was probably added in 1624. It was entirely refaced with flint and stone in 1904.

The clock was added in 1812 but its dial is older (date unknown).

➥ Proceed to the west entrance.

Both brick buildings, on either side of the entrance, providing porches, were added in 1864; stairs once led from them to the north and south galleries.

The entrance doorway is original.

➥ Turn L and proceed clockwise around the church.

Nave north facade. A north aisle was added to the nave in 1699 but this disappeared when the nave was entirely rebuilt in 1750.

The present central window was formed in 1864. It replaced a north porch, which had been the main entrance. The brick cornice was added at the same time.

Against the wall is the obelisk commemorating Sir Mathew Decker by *Scheemakers*, 1759.

➥ Continue clockwise passing the **vestry,** **chancel** *and* **south chapels.**

This eastern section was built by *Bodley* in 1904 when the small Tudor chancel was demolished.

➥ Continue to the south facade of the nave.

Nave south facade. An aisle was added to this side of the nave in 1617. Like the later aisle, on the north side, it also disappeared when the nave was rebuilt in 1750. Unlike the north facade, there was no porch, instead there was a pediment above the central windows.

➥ Enter from the west door in the tower.

Nave. The arch leading from the entrance porch to the nave is Tudor. No other part of the interior of the church pre-dates the rebuilding of 1750.

The roof was constructed by *A. W. Blomfield* in 1866.

Above the entrance are the royal arms.

➥ Turn L.

On the west wall above the door is the monument to *John Bentley,* d. 1660, and his family by *Burman* (?). It has been damaged and rearranged.

Below R is the monument to Shakespearian actor Edmund Kean by *Loft*, 1759. This originally stood outside the church which is the reason for its dilapidated condition.

Towards the east end of the aisle, between the last two windows, is the monument to Robert Delafosse, d.1819, by *Flaxman*.

In the corner, before the organ, is the brass commemorating Robert Cotton, d.1591 (?). He was employed in the royal household of Mary I and Elizabeth I. It is the oldest monument in the church.

Above is the monument to Simon Bardolph, d.1654. He is believed to have been a friend of Shakespeare's and it is said that No 1 Richmond Green was his residence. Shakespeare used the name Bardolph for characters in *Henry V* and *The Merry Wives of Windsor*.

The organ by *Knight,* 1769, has been much rebuilt. It was transferred to its present position in the vestry from the west gallery in 1907. There were three galleries in the 18C; all have been removed.

The pulpit, L of the sanctuary, is believed to be late 17C.

•▪ Proceed to the south aisle.

The font has an 18C bowl, but its stem is modern.

Between the second and third windows from the east is the monument to the Hon Barbara Lowther, d.1805, by *Flaxman*.

•▪ Continue to the south-west corner.

A floor plaque marks the burial place, in the vault below, of Edmund Kean.

The monument to Major George Bean by *Bacon the Younger* commemorates an officer who was killed at the Battle of Waterloo in 1815.

Just before the exit L is the monument to Viscount Brounckner, d.1687, whom Pepys described as 'a pestilent rogue, an atheist that would have sold his king and country for 6d (3p) almost.'

•▪ Exit from the church L and return to Paradise Rd L. Second R Halford Rd. Ahead, where the road bends, is Halford House.

No 27, **Halford House**, was built in 1700. Its short eastward extension was added in 1745. The remainder of the street although mid-Victorian is basically Classical in style.

•▪ L The Vineyard. At the Vineyard Passage corner (first L) is Vineyard House.

Location 16	**THE VINEYARD**

This is one of the most picturesquely varied streets in the London area. It includes houses from the late 17C to the early 19C – some very grand – together with 19C almshouses and a Catholic church. Surprisingly, some light industry still survives. A vineyard probably stood here although none is recorded.

Vineyard House, early 18C, has a projecting wing to its garden. The doorway is late 18C.

•▪ Return westward along The Vineyard and cross to the south side.

Nos 29–23 are early 19C semi-detached houses.

On the opposite side, **Queen Elizabeth's Almshouses** were built in 1958. They replaced earlier almshouses of 1767, a plaque from which is inserted in the wall. Originally the almshouses were founded in 1600 and stood further north in what is now Paradise Road.

Immediately opposite, on the north side, **No 11** is an early 19C villa.

Next to Queen Elizabeth's Almshouses are Bishop Duppa's Almshouses.

Bishop Duppa's Almshouses. A legacy from Bishop Brian Duppa founded these originally on Richmond Hill in 1661 as a thanks offering for his deliverance from Oliver Cromwell. They were rebuilt here by *Little* in 1851. Some of the stonework and the gateway may have come from the earlier building.

Above the gate is an inscription, presumably composed by Duppa, 'I will pay the vows which I made to God in my troubles.'

Opposite, facing the street called The Hermitage, is an attractive villa **No 9**, **Newark House**, *c.*1750 with modern extensions.

Michel's Place, an early 19C terrace, follows.

Michel's Almshouses were founded on the same site in 1695, and rebuilt in 1811. The south range R was added in 1858.

No 2 Clarence House by *Rawlins*, *c.*1696, faces Michel's Almshouses. This is the grandest house in The Vineyard and is set back behind a courtyard surrounded by a high wall. It was, until recently, the home of actor Brian Blessed.

➥ *First L Lancaster Park.*

Vine Row 2–3 Lancaster Park. These two cottages, *c.*1700, are some of Richmond's oldest and most picturesque.

➥ *Return to The Vineyard L. Cross the road to St Elizabeth's.*

St Elizabeth of Portugal. This Roman Catholic Church was built in 1824, its tower, chancel and presbytery were rebuilt by *F. A. Walters* in 1903.

➥ *Continue ahead. First L Richmond Hill. First R Compass Hill. The footpath R leads to Petersham Rd R. First L follow the path to the riverside walk L.*

Location 17	**RIVERSIDE, RICHMOND BRIDGE TO THE TERRACE GARDENS**

Many 18C mansions, with their riverside gardens front the Petersham Road but their river facades have always been more important. Most are now converted to hotels.

Seen in the following order from the bridge is a terrace of late Victorian houses.

Nos 35 and **37** are early 19C.

No 39, **Bellevue**, with a pediment is late 18C.

No 42 is mid Victorian.

Nos 43–47, the **Hobart Hall Hotel**, was built in 1690 and has many 18C additions including castellations. William IV resided here, briefly, in 1789 while Duke of Clarence.

No 49 is a Victorian villa.

The adjoining public garden was once the site of another large house.

No 55, *c.*1720, has a Regency bay.

No 57–61, **The Paragon**, are also *c.*1720.

No 63, the **Bingham House Hotel**, is *c.*1760.

☛ Continue to the Raj Tavern (for many years the Three Pigeons). Take the path L, cross Petersham Rd and continue ahead through the Terrace Gardens. Follow any path up the hill to Richmond Hill.

Location 18 | **TERRACE GARDENS**

These gardens were created in the mid 19C by *Walter Montagu-Douglas-Scott*. They then formed the grounds of his residence, Buccleuch House, which, together with the adjoining Lansdowne House, was demolished and the grounds acquired by the local authority for public gardens in 1886.

☛ At Richmond Hill turn R and cross the road.

Location 19 | **RICHMOND HILL**

Many fine 18C residences on the brow of Richmond Hill enjoy one of England's most famous views.

Passed immediately is a mid-19C terrace, formerly the Stuart Hotel, but converted to flats in 1984.

No 114, **Norfolk House**, is mid 18C but its front was remodelled in the 19C.

No 116, **Downe House**, *c.*1771, was leased by the playright Sheridan early in the 19C.

No 118, **Ashburton**, is partly 18C but was remodelled in the 19C.

☛ Cross to the terrace opposite for the famous view.

Many British artists, including J. M. W. Turner, have painted the view from Richmond Hill. On a clear day, Windsor Castle can be seen. It is claimed that Richmond, Virginia, USA, was so named because it possessed a similar view.

☛ Return to Richmond Hill R.

Nos 120–122 are mid Victorian.

Nos 124–6 are early 19C.

No 128 is mid 19C.

The Roebuck inn was built in 1749 but its ground floor front has been altered.

Nos 1A, 1 and **2 The Terrace** are mid Victorian.

Location 20	**NO 3 THE TERRACE** *Taylor (?) 1769*
Richmond Hill	Built in 1769 for a playing-card manufacturer, Christopher Blanchard. Mrs Fitzherbert lived here in the late 18C. She was secretly married by the vicar of Twickenham to the Prince of Wales, later George IV, in 1785 and it is alleged that they spent their honeymoon in this house.

Due to its style the house is believed to be the work of *Sir Robert Taylor* the designer of Asgill House (Location 14). Its stone facade is one of Richmond's finest.

•• *Continue southward.*

No 4 The Terrace is mid 18C.

Although **Doughty House** was built in the 18C its front was remodelled in 1915 for Francis Cook. A rear extension housed his large collection of old master paintings, since dispersed. The house is now divided into flats.

•• *First R Nightingale Lane. Proceed to the Petersham Hotel.*

Location 21	**THE PETERSHAM HOTEL** *Giles 1865*
Nightingale Lane	The Petersham Hotel was built on the site of Sir Charles Nightingale's early 19C mansion, Nightingale Hall. Originally the hotel was called the Richmond Hill Hotel but changed its name to the Star and Garter Hotel in 1924 and adopted its present name in 1978.

It is believed to possess the largest unsupported staircase in England.

•• *Return to Richmond Hill R. On the corner R is The Wick.*

Location 22	**THE WICK** *Mylne 1775*
Richmond Hill	The house, little altered, was built for Lady St Aubyn on the site of the Bull's Head inn. It was for many years the home of the actor Sir John Mills and his family.

Location 23	**WICK HOUSE** *Chambers 1772*
Richmond Hill	Sir Joshua Reynolds built this as his weekend residence. It was remodelled in the late 19C and again, internally, in 1950 to provide residental accommodation for nurses at the Royal Star and Garter Home.

•• *Cross the road to the Richmond Hill Hotel opposite.*

Location 24	**RICHMOND HILL HOTEL**
Richmond Hill	The hotel consists of 18C houses linked by later extensions. Its core is the recently renovated red brick building R. This was built *c.*1725 for the Countess of Mansfield.
	Wings were added on either side in the mid 19C and in 1875 the building became the Queen's Hotel.
	Buildings west of this are mainly mid 18C, some with Regency additions.
	An unfortunate extension, L of the ballroom entrance, is modern.
	The hotel adopted its present name just before the First World War.
	●● *Continue southward.*

Location 25	**RICHMOND GATE HOTEL**
Richmond Hill	Two cottages built in 1728, and two larger residences *c.*1784 were converted in the 1930s to form the Moorshead Hotel. It was extended to the rear and renamed in 1974.
	●● *Cross Richmond Hill and proceed to the Royal Star and Garter Home.*

Location 26	**THE ROYAL STAR AND GARTER HOME** *Cooper 1924*
Richmond Hill	This enormous edifice was constructed as a home and hospital for two hundred disabled war veterans. Most of the present residents fought in the Second World War. It was built on the site of the fashionable Star and Garter inn which stood from 1732 until it burnt down in 1870. A Victorian replacement proved to be too large and uneconomical. During the First World War disabled servicemen had been lodged there, but the building was demolished and replaced by the present structure.
	The home is not directly associated with the British Legion's poppy factory which stands at the base of the hill in Petersham Road.
	●● *Exit R. Cross Richmond Hill.*
	Immediately L is Ancaster House.

Location 27	**ANCASTER HOUSE** *R. Adam (?) 1772*
Queen's Road	Queen Charlotte granted the property, then within Richmond Park, to Peregrine, Duke of Ancaster. It had been the site of a hunting lodge. The house is now the official residence of the Commandant of the Royal Star and Garter Home.
	●● *Enter Richmond Park through the gate and cross the road to the entrance lodge.*
	The gate and its adjoining lodge were designed by *Capability Brown* in 1798.
	●● *Proceed through the park following the footpath R of the lodge.*

Location 28   **RICHMOND PARK**

Always open to pedestrians.

Open to motorists from dawn to dusk.

This 2000-acre royal park was once a royal hunting chase. Charles I purchased additional common land, walled in the area and named the enclosure New Park in 1637. Public access was for long permitted, but in the 18C Prime Minister Sir Robert Walpole became Ranger, and only allowed token holders to enter. Admittance became even more restricted under the rangership of George II's daughter, Princess Amelia. Eventually an outcry led to the reassertion of the public's rights and the gates were reopened.

Richmond Park is encircled, anti-clockwise from the north, by Richmond, East Sheen, Roehampton, Putney Vale, Coombe, Kingston, Ham and Petersham. Red and fallow deer roam the park freely; they can be dangerous if approached too closely when with their young.

The park is mainly flat and thinly wooded; it is at its most picturesque around the central Pen Ponds and in the Isabella Plantation, towards Kingston, where in May there is a famous display of azaleas and rhododendrons. There are only a few buildings within the park.

White House Lodge. Built for George I by *Morris* in 1729. This was the birthplace of Edward VIII (later the Duke of Windsor). It now accommodates the Royal Ballet School.

The lodge is an early example of the Palladian revival.

Pavilions were added by *S. Wright* in 1752.

Thatched House Lodge *Kent* (?) *c.*1727. The residence of Princess Alexandra. This was built for Prime Minister Robert Walpole and was named for the thatched summerhouse that stands in the garden.

A car is necessary to explore the park fully, but a short walk to Petersham Gate gives a representative impression of the park.

•● *From Richmond Gate take the path R, parallel with the road, following the west edge of the park. Enter the first gate R and follow the path ahead to Pembroke Lodge.*

Pembroke Lodge. Built in the mid 18C and once the home of philosopher Bertrand Russell. It is now a municipal tea house.

•● *Descend the steps from the centre of the terrace that runs west of the house. The path R leads to a small gate. Descend the hill. The path R leads to Petersham Gate. Exit from Richmond Park and cross Petersham Rd. Take bus 65 to Richmond Station (BR) and District Line.*

•● *Alternatively, if continuing to Ham and Petersham (page 55) exit L Petersham Rd. Cross the road. The second path R leads to St Peter's Church.*

Twickenham

Old Twickenham, bordering the Thames, retains the most nautical feel of all London's riverside villages. Many of its great 18C mansions survive and some may be entered. Although spoilt by small, indiscreetly placed car parks, much of the ancient core of Twickenham, huddled around Church Street, survives. Horace Walpole's house, Strawberry Hill, that inspired the Neo-Gothic style, is well preserved and may be visited, albeit with limitations. Ham House, described in this book as part of the visit to Ham and Petersham may, alternatively, be included in a visit to Twickenham if preferred.

Timing Fine weather is essential. Orleans House does not open until 13.00 and closes Monday. Marble Hill House closes Friday. Ham House, if included, also closes Monday. The ferry from Twickenham to Ham House operates daily Easter–October and weekends only mid-November–Easter (depending on weather). The service ceases between 13.00–14.00.

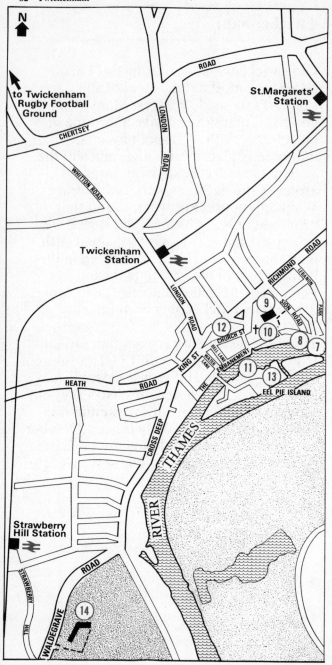

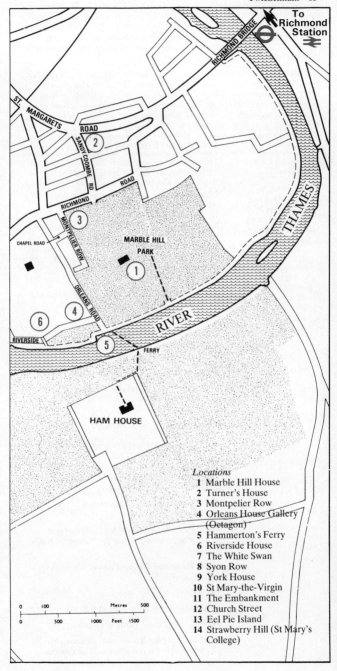

To
Richmond
Station

RICHMOND BRIDGE

ST. MARGARETS ROAD

SANDY COOMBE RD

ROAD

②

THAMES

RICHMOND

MONTPELIER ROW

ROAD

③

CHAPEL ROAD

MARBLE HILL
PARK

①

ORLEANS ROAD

⑥ ④

RIVER

RIVERSIDE

⑤

FERRY

HAM HOUSE

Locations
 1 Marble Hill House
 2 Turner's House
 3 Montpelier Row
 4 Orleans House Gallery
   (Octagon)
 5 Hammerton's Ferry
 6 Riverside House
 7 The White Swan
 8 Syon Row
 9 York House
10 St Mary-the-Virgin
11 The Embankment
12 Church Street
13 Eel Pie Island
14 Strawberry Hill (St Mary's
   College)

0   100   Metres   500
0   500   1000   Feet   1500

Start *Richmond Station, District Line or BR from Waterloo Station. Exit from the station L and proceed ahead to Richmond Bridge. Cross the bridge and descend the steps L to the towpath R. Proceed towards the gate R to Marble Hill Park. Enter the grounds and continue ahead to the house which lies in the west part of the grounds.*

Alternatively, Twickenham may be approached by river, Easter–September, from Westminster Pier (930 2062) to Richmond Pier. Cross Richmond Bridge and continue as indicated above. The earliest boat (10.30) arrives at 13.00, too late to complete the itinerary if Strawberry Hill is to be seen. If a river trip is preferred it is better to return to London by boat from Richmond, but check the time of the last boat (940 2244).

Location 1	**MARBLE HILL HOUSE** *1729*

Marble Hill Park
(892 5115)

*Open Saturday–
Thursday 10.00–
17.00. Sunday 14.00–
17.00. Closes 16.00
November–January.
Admission free.*

The grounds are now rather different from those designed by *Alexander Pope* and laid out by *Bridgeman* when the house was built. Marble Hill House was commissioned for Henrietta Howard, later Countess of Suffolk. She was a Maid of Honour to Caroline, Princess of Wales, and the house was paid for by Henrietta's 'close friend' the Prince of Wales, later George II. It was built by *Roger Morris*, to a design by *Colen Campbell*, based on original sketches by *Henry Herbert*. Mrs Fitzherbert occupied the house in 1795. Restoration was completed in 1966.

The building, which played an important part in the Palladian revival, is stuccoed and painted cream with stone dressings.

•➤ Enter from the north door.

The furnishings throughout are contemporary with, although not from, the house.

•➤ Ascend the stairs R to the first floor.

The Great Room. This takes the form of a 24 ft cube and was influenced by the work of Inigo Jones.

The carving is by *James Richards*.

Displayed are copies of paintings by *Van Dyck*.

•➤ Turn L.

The Countess's Bedchamber. The Thames-side painting is by *Richard Wilson*.

The 18C chimney-piece was brought from elsewhere.

•➤ The cantilevered stairs lead to the second floor. When convenient, staff will show the rooms to visitors.

Green Room and **Wrought Room.** These were redecorated in 1985.

•➤ Descend to the ground floor.

On the south side is the central hall.

•➤ Proceed L to the Breakfast Parlour.

Breakfast Parlour. This retains its screen by *Herbert* which was possibly based on designs by *Inigo Jones*.

Dining Parlour. This room was created by

Brettingham in 1751, by combining two small rooms.

•● *Exit from the house L and proceed to the west side of the park.*

Stables. These ivy-clad, early-19C buildings have been converted to tea rooms.

The clock was fitted in 1830.

•● *Proceed northward across the lawns and exit from the grounds. Cross Richmond Rd immediately and continue ahead to Sandycombe Rd. Proceed to the end. R Turner's house.*

Location 2	**TURNER'S HOUSE** *J. M. W. Turner 1814*
Sandycombe Lodge, Sandycombe Road	This white, Italian-style house at the far end of Sandycombe Road, partly hidden by trees, was initially built as a country retreat for the great painter J. M. W. Turner and subsequently occupied by his father in retirement. It is *Turner*'s only known architectural work.

•● *Return to Richmond Rd R. First L Montpelier Row.*

Location 3	**MONTPELIER ROW** *c.1724*

Montpelier Row has been judged outer London's finest early Georgian terrace. Two famous poets lived here, Tennyson at No 15 and Walter de la Mare at No 30.

Nos 1–15 were built as a speculative development, their exteriors are similar apart from the door surrounds.

Towards the end R, following the Victorian additions, is **No 25**, designed for himself by architect *Geoffrey Darke* in 1967.

•● *Return northward. First L Chapel Rd. L Orleans Rd. Enter Orleans Park R. The path R leads to Orleans House (Location 4).*

•● *Alternatively, if Ham House (page 58) is to be visited from Twickenham, bear in mind that Orleans House does not open until 13.00 and it may, therefore, be preferable to visit Ham House at this stage. If so, continue to the end of Orleans Rd. Proceed through the gate L. Ahead Warren Footpath. Hammerton's Ferry (Location 5) to Ham House leaves from the jetty R. Return later to see Orleans House.*

Location 4	**ORLEANS HOUSE GALLERY (OCTAGON)** *Gibbs 1720*
Orleans Park (892 0221)	Orleans House was built for James Johnston, William III's Secretary of State for Scotland, by *John James* in 1692. It lay east of the existing gallery but was demolished by its owner, the shipping magnate William Cunard, in 1927.
Gardens open daily 09.00–sunset. House open Tuesday–Saturday 13.00–17.30. Sunday 14.00–17.30. Closes 16.30 October–March. Admission free.	'Orleans' was adopted for the name of the house following the residency of Louis-Philippe, Duc d'Orleans, from 1800 to 1817. Don Carlos of Spain also lived here in 1876.
	The gallery was added to the house by *Gibbs* in

1720, probably to accommodate a reception for Princess Caroline. Mrs Ionides bequeathed the estate to the local authority in 1962.

The octagonal design of the gallery was influenced by pavilions that were fashionable in the gardens of great German houses in the early 18C.

Urns originally stood on the pilasters above parapet level.

☛ *Enter the gallery.*

The Baroque plasterwork is by the Italians *Artari* and *Bagutti*, whom Gibbs employed for most of his major work.

Busts of Queen Caroline and George II are displayed.

Two of the medallions probably also represent the King and Queen, with the third possibly depicting Louis-Philippe.

Topographical paintings of the area are displayed in the adjoining south-west wing which was built to link the gallery with the house.

☛ *Exit and return to Riverside R. Continue ahead to Riverside House (Location 6) on the corner.*

☛ *Alternatively, continue to Hammerton's Ferry and proceed to Ham House.*

Location 5	**HAMMERTON'S FERRY**
Jetty off Warren Footpath (892 9620) *Operates daily Easter–October. Mid November–Easter Saturday and Sunday only. No service between 13.00–14.00.*	This, one of the few private ferries still operating on the Thames, is generally reliable but telephone first to confirm that it is operating. Hail the ferryman when he is on the opposite bank. Ask him to point out the concealed east entrance to Ham House grounds to avoid an unnecessary walk. If visiting Strawberry Hill later, book the return with the ferryman before 13.00. Ham House is described on pages 57–62.
Location 6	**RIVERSIDE HOUSE** c.*1810*
Riverside	This is, after York House, Twickenham's largest house in the Classical style. Riverside House possesses typical Regency bow windows but is difficult to see as it lies behind a high wall.

☛ *Continue ahead.*

Passed R are **Ferry House**, late 18C, and **Ferryside**, also 18C but now roughcast.

Location 7	**THE WHITE SWAN** *18C*
Riverside	Known to locals as 'The Dirty Duck', the pub possesses a first floor terrace and a riverside garden, separated from the building by the road. Balconies were added in the early 19C.

☛ *Exit R.*

Three houses with Regency fronts are passed.

Location 8	**SYON ROW** *1721*
Syon Road	Twelve houses make up this terrace (note the original spelling of 'SION' on the plaque). They were built only three years before Montpelier Row nearby (Location 3) but their overhanging eaves, breaking the 1707 Building Act, give them an earlier appearance. However, it is possible that work on the Row began earlier.

◄● Continue ahead. Proceed through the gate to York House L.

Location 9	**YORK HOUSE** c.*1650 (?)*
Richmond Road (892 0032) *The house is only open for guided tours during 'Twickenham Week' at the end of May. The gardens are open daily. Admission free.* 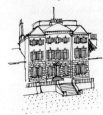	An old farmhouse, Yorke Farm, was replaced by the present house which retained the name. The mansion is believed to have been built by the Earl of Manchester. It became the summer residence of the Earl of Clarendon, Lord Chancellor to Charles II, in the late 17C. Allegedly, the house was occupied by James II when Duke of York; his first wife, Anne Hyde, was Clarendon's daughter. Like Orleans House nearby, York House was favoured as a residence by members of the French Royal Family early in the 19C. The last private owner was an Indian tycoon, Sir Ratan Tata, who installed the elaborate garden statuary. It now accommodates local authority offices.

York House was remodelled early in the 18C and most of the external detailing dates from this period.

Internally, only a mid-17C staircase in the north wing is of particular interest.

◄● Proceed L through the gardens to the rock garden on the south side with its pool and palm tree. Cross the ornate bridge ahead R.

In the south-west corner of the grounds is an amusingly vulgar fountain (1904) with nude Italianate maidens.

◄● Follow the river path R to the exit. L Riverside.

Passed R is **Dial House** (the vicarage) 1890. In its grounds is a sundial made in 1726 for a now demolished 18C Twickenham mansion designed by *James*, the architect of the parish church.

◄● First R Church Lane leads to Church St R and St Mary's.

Location 10	**ST MARY-THE-VIRGIN**
Church Street *Open infrequently apart from services.*	The earliest record of a church on the site is in 1332. St Mary's was rebuilt of Kentish ragstone towards the end of the 14C but its nave collapsed in 1713. This was rebuilt in brick by *James*, but the ancient tower was retained.

Externally, the fine quality of the brickwork is apparent.

◄● Enter from the north door.

Renovations in 1860 removed the box pews but the galleries, although altered, were retained.

The ceiling of the church and the sanctuary have recently been redesigned by *Richardson*.

The **north aisle**'s east window commemorates painter Sir Godfrey Kneller who is buried in the church. His monument, intended for St Mary's, is in Westminster Abbey.

Although the pulpit was made in 1714 its tester is modern.

In front of the chancel step L, a brass floor plate commemorates the burial in the church of the poet Alexander Pope, d.1744. The plate was presented by three American scholars. Pope lived nearby at Pope's Villa in Cross Deep, since demolished.

He lies beneath the adjoining stone inscribed with a 'P'.

The altar rails and reredos are original.

In the **sanctuary** is the monument to Sir W. Humble, d.1680, and his son, by *Bird* (?). This was brought from the earlier church.

On the east wall of the **south aisle**, beneath the gallery, a monument, also from the earlier church, commemorates Francis Poulton, d.1642, and his wife.

•➡ *Return to the west end of the church*.

Beneath the **tower** are two 17C monuments: Sir Joseph Ashe, from the studio of *Gibbons*; General Lord Berkeley of Stratton.

•➡ *Proceed L to the door in the south-west corner. A further door L leads to the south gallery. Unfortunately, this will be locked unless there is an attendant present, a rare occurrence.*

The monument to George and Anne Gostling is by *Bacon the Younger*, 1800.

Nathaniel Piggott, d.1737, is commemorated by a monument designed by *Scheemakers*.

•➡ *Proceed to the door in the north-west corner. A further door R leads to the north gallery – again probably locked!*

The monument to Admiral Sir Chaloner Ogle is by *Rysbrack*, 1751.

Alexander Pope is commemorated by a memorial commissioned by his friend Bishop Warburton in 1761.

At the east end, a further memorial to Alexander Pope commemorates, not the poet, but his father and mother, *Bird*.

Below this is a memorial to author Richard Owen Cambridge, d.1802.

•➡ *Exit from the church L. First L Church Lane. Second R The Embankment.*

Passed R is **The Riverside Tavern**, *c.*1720.

Location 11	**THE EMBANKMENT**

A passage separates the houses along The Embankment from their original riverside gardens – now car parks.

No 2 is early 18C.
No 3, **Strand House**, in Queen Anne style is probably earlier.
No 5 appears to be the oldest building. Its timber frame indicates early 17C (?).

At the end, R, the Mission Hall by *Edis*, 1871, has been converted to form the **Mary Wallace Theatre**.

First L Church Lane. L Church St.

Location 12	**CHURCH STREET**

This, the original village high street, is basically 18C and has been recently restored after years of neglect. At the north end, 18C cottages were demolished in the 1950s and their sites have unfortunately become car parks.

First L Bell Lane. R The Embankment. Cross the pedestrian bridge to Eel Pie Island.

Location 13	**EEL PIE ISLAND**

There is no road access, nor is the island linked with the opposite bank. The two main paths may be walked along in spite of 'Private' notices; both are cul de sacs. A hotel on the south side, now demolished to make way for housing, once sold eel pies to trippers – hence the name. Leafy alleyways link the various styles of dwelling; wooden chalets predominate.

Follow the main path ahead.

Hurley Cottage R is judged to be the island's most picturesque building.

Return and take the second path L just before the bridge. Return from this and cross the bridge to The Embankment R. First L Water Lane leads to King St L.

If visiting Strawberry Hill, take bus 33 to St Mary's College. From the bus stop continue northward to the porter's lodge L.

Alternatively, if not visiting Strawberry Hill, cross King St and take bus 33, 90B or 290 to Richmond Station (BR), District Line.

Location 14	**STRAWBERRY HILL (ST MARY'S COLLEGE)**

Waldegrave Road
(892 0051)

Open Wednesday and Saturday 14.30 by appointment only. Apply to the principal. Closed during term holidays at Christmas, Easter and mid-June–mid-October. Admission free.

Wealthy Horace Walpole, writer, dilettante and younger son of Prime Minister Sir Robert Walpole, leased a late-17C cottage at Strawberry Hill Shot in 1747 and purchased the estate two years later. Deciding it was too small for adaptation to Classical grandeur he transformed it in the Gothic style.

Although seeking to achieve a playful Gothic fantasy, Walpole insisted, for the first time, that the Gothic detailing should be reasonably accurate. *William Robinson* began the alterations in 1748, but his work was not regarded as Gothic enough and Walpole set up a 'committee on taste' to complete the work. This committee, made up from his personal friends, included *John Chute*, *Richard Bentley*, *Thomas Pitt* and the poet *Thomas Gray*. *Robert Adam* joined them later. To ensure authenticity, examples of Gothic design from great north European churches were copied. There was no objection, however, to a tomb becoming a fireplace or window tracery a ceiling. The house was ready by 1766, but Walpole's work was not finished until 1776 when the Beauclerk Turret was built.

Strawberry Hill was so influential in promoting the 18C Neo-Gothic style (as opposed to the 19C Gothic Revival) that this is often referred to as 'Strawberry Hill Gothic'.

In the 19C, Strawberry Hill was neglected until Lady Waldegrave inherited the property and restored it in 1856. It is now a residential Catholic training school.

● *Proceed with the guide to view the south facade.*

Immediately R, divided by a bay, is the original small house of 1698. Its south front was remodelled by *Chute* in 1752. The bay itself may have been an addition.

West of this is the **Long Gallery** by *Chute*, 1762.

In the 19C, Tudor-style chimneys replaced the original pinnacles and the towers were lengthened.

Pebbledash, added at a later stage, unfortunately replaced the earlier roughcast rendering.

The bay was recently heightened by one storey by *Richardson*.

Immediately L of the Long Gallery, running northward, is the wing added in 1862 on the site of Walpole's stables. It is believed that *Lady Waldegrave* designed the building herself.

South of this is the office wing designed by *James Essex* in 1779 but built under the direction of *Wyatt* in 1790. This was Walpole's 'Dairy and Coal Hole'.

Other buildings to the south, except for the Chapel in the Wood, described later, were built in the 20C.

The grounds of Strawberry Hill originally led eastward to the river, and views of the Thames were unobstructed by trees. Sheep grazed around the house adding to the rural ambience. Although the site of the house is raised slightly above river level, Walpole was certainly exaggerating when he christened it Strawberry Hill.

● *Entered immediately is the Little Parlour.*

It is known that Walpole preferred soft lighting and muted colours and much of the décor of the house would have been more sombre than it is today. Unfortunately, all of Walpole's furniture was disposed of in the 'Great Sale' of 1842. Some of it may be seen in the Lewis Walpole Library at Farmington, Connecticut, USA.

Walpole's unusual collection of antiquities was also dispersed at this sale. A contemporary jested that Walpole would have purchased 'the wart from Cromwell's nose, had it been available'.

Set in windows throughout the house are fragments of ancient stained glass. Most of it is 17C and several pieces are Dutch.

Little Parlour. Much of Walpole's collection was displayed here.

The chimney-piece by *Bentley*, 1753, was inspired by Bishop Ruthall's tomb in Westminster Abbey.

Visitors are usually shown rooms in the following order but changes may be made from time to time.

Walpole's Yellow Bedroom. This is sometimes called the 'Beauty Room' as reproductions of 'The Windsor Beauties' by *Lely* were hung here.

The chimney-piece, by *Bentley*, was originally painted black and yellow.

Staircase Hall. Formed by *Bentley* in 1754, the balustrade tracery is believed to have been inspired by work at Rouen Cathedral.

Lancet windows are post-war additions by *Richardson*.

Little Cloister. Built by *Chute* in 1761. Its Oratory was added in 1762.

Great Parlour or **Refectory**. Completed in 1754, the chimney-piece is by *Bentley*.

The window was enlarged in 1774.

➥ *Ascend to the first floor rooms.*

Blue Breakfast Room. This was remodelled for Lady Waldegrave as a 'Turkish boudoir' in 1858.

The lower part of the fireplace is the work of *Robinson*, 1748, who began the conversion of Strawberry Hill until he was demoted, by Walpole, to Clerk of Works.

Armoury or **Library Anteroom.** Here were displayed Walpole's collection of suits of armour.

Library. Work here by *Chute* includes bookcases based on drawings of the doors of the screen in Old St Paul's Cathedral and the chimney-piece inspired by John of Eltham's tomb in Westminster Abbey.

Walpole himself designed the ceiling, based on Jacobean work.

Star Chamber. This was completed in 1754. The window was recently rebuilt by *Richardson*.

Holbein Chamber. Holbein's drawings in the royal collection at Windsor were traced for Walpole and originally hung on the walls of this room, hence its name.

Bentley completed the chamber in 1758 as a guest room. The screen's inspiration was the choir gate of Rouen Cathedral.

Rouen's high altar supplied part of the design of the chimney-piece, and Archbishop Wareham's tomb in Canterbury Cathedral was copied for another section.

The ceiling is a replica of that in the Queen's Dressing Room in the State Apartments at Windsor Castle.

Long Gallery. Interior work was executed jointly by *Chute* and *Pitt* in 1763.

The ceiling vault is a copy of the fan vaulted aisles of the Henry VII Chapel at Westminster Abbey.

St Alban's Abbey's north door provided the design of the door. It has been renewed. Canopies and niches reproduce part of Archbishop Bouchier's tomb in Canterbury Cathedral.

Chapel or **Cabinet**. Completed by *Chute* in 1763, this was originally a cabinet but has since been consecrated

Its ceiling vault is based on York Minster's Chapter House.

Round Room. The ceiling design reproduces the tracery of Old St Paul's rose window.

Panelling in the bay window was inspired by Eleanor of Castile's tomb in Westminster Abbey.

The fireplace, by *Adam*, was based on Edward the Confessor's shrine at Westminster but 'improved' according to Walpole.

Visitors are generally conducted through the 19C wing, added by Lady Waldegrave.

Immediately south of the porter's lodge is the Chapel in the Wood. This was designed by *Chute* in 1772 but the work was executed by *Gayfere* in 1774.

•● *Exit from Strawberry Hill. Cross the road and take bus 33 to Richmond Station (BR), District Line.*

Osterley

Osterley Park is, like Syon, a Tudor residence, although a little later, dating from the Elizabethan period. It, similarly received the attention of Robert Adam who, in the late 18C, spent nineteen years redesigning the interiors. Due to one family's continuous ownership over many years, most of the furnishings and fittings designed by Adam, have uniquely survived.

Timing The house may be visited throughout the year, except for Monday when it is closed. If preceding with Syon, bear in mind that Syon House is also open in the afternoon (not winter) but closes Friday and Saturday.

Suggested connection Precede with Syon.

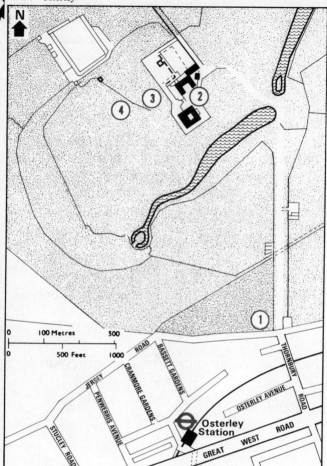

Locations
1 Osterley Park
2 Elizabethan Stables
3 Garden House
4 Temple of Pan

Start *Osterley Station, Piccadilly Line. Exit L Great West Road. First L Thornbury Avenue. Continue ahead to Osterley Park and follow the drive which bears L past the lake to the house.*

Alternatively, continue from Syon as indicated on page 104.

Location 1 | **OSTERLEY PARK**

Osterley (560 3918)

The grounds are open daily 10.00–dusk. Admission free. Osterley Park House is open Tuesday– Sunday 11.00–17.00. Also open Bank Holiday Mondays. Admission charge.

Sir Thomas Gresham, the Elizabethan founder of the City's Royal Exchange, acquired Osterley Manor a late 15C building, in 1562. Alongside this he built his new country house, Osterley Park, *c.*1577. Gresham then demolished the original manor house and no trace remains; it is believed to have stood just south of the present building. Banker Francis Child obtained the property in 1711, but never lived there. It was his grandson and namesake who made major changes to the house, commencing in 1756. *Chambers* was appointed as architect and completed some remodelling. However, the more fashionable *Robert Adam*, working nearby at Syon, took over in 1761 and his commission lasted for nineteen years. Adam supervised the design of practically everything, including the furnishings, down to the minutest detail. Although less extravagant than Syon, Osterley is of unique interest as the Child family, during their continuous ownership, have preserved practically all of Adam's work. Osterley was acquired by the nation in 1949.

Continue and follow the drive to the lake. Turn L, and proceed towards the house.

The fabric and format of the house, built around an open courtyard, remain from Gresham's building. Osterley's appearance, however, is radically changed. The four corner turrets, with ogee (onion-shaped) caps, are Jacobean in character and were probably part of alterations made early in the 17C.

The brickwork was renewed, and stone quoins added, by *Chambers*, who also constructed the hall and a continuous passageway on part of the central courtyard *c.*1757.

All the windows were converted from casement to sash in the 18C.

On the main east front, the Classical open portico, approached by steps, acts as a screen and this, together with the balustrade along the roof was added by *Adam*. The original Elizabethan house probably had an elaborate stone centrepiece with an archway to the courtyard.

Proceed behind the house to its west facade.

The horseshoe staircase with its decorative railings is typical of *Adam*'s work.

Return to the east facade and pass through the portico to the courtyard. Enter the house through the door ahead.

Only the gallery, the ceilings in the Drawing Room and Eating Room and probably the breakfast room, were designed by *Chambers*, the remainder is all the work of *Adam*. Most of the furniture throughout the house was also designed by *Adam* and each piece remains in its original position: even the dining chairs are still ranged formally against the walls in the 18C fashion.

Hall. This is entered immediately. Every item except the statues was designed by *Adam*.

The marble floor echoes the ceiling pattern.

➡ Proceed ahead.

Gallery. This was designed by *Chambers* in his more robust, Palladian style. Here, only the six large girandoles (mirrored candle brackets) the pier glasses and the two end sofas are by *Adam*.

➡ Turn R and L.

Small Turret Room. This was fitted out as a water closet in 1759.

➡ Turn R and enter the Eating Room.

Eating Room. Apart from the ceiling, which is attributed to *Chambers*, the work in this room is by *Adam*.

Staircase. The ceiling was once covered with an original painting by *Rubens*, on canvas. However, this was removed to another location where it was unfortunately destroyed in a fire. It has been replaced with a modern reproduction.

Library. The paintings above the bookshelves are by *Zucchi*. The surprisingly strong ceiling colours are not now believed to be an accurate representation of Adam's intentions.

Breakfast Room. This room is plainer in style and probably by *Chambers*. The ceiling is in rococo style and was recently painted white.

➡ Return to the end of the gallery and proceed to the suite of state rooms L.

Drawing Room. A theme of ostrich feathers and sunflowers on the ceiling is repeated on the carpet.

Tapestry Room. Gobelin tapestries 'The Loves of the Gods' were designed by *Boucher* in 1775.

State Bedchamber. The domed four-poster bed with the Child family crest is judged one of *Adam*'s finest pieces of furniture design.

The mirror, also incorporating the Child crest, above the fireplace was the earliest example of plate glass to be made in England.

Etruscan Dressing Room. The ceiling design includes Greek themes, although Adam believed them to be Etruscan, hence the name given to the room. It is an early example of this popular style.

➡ Exit and turn R.

Study (Demonstration Room). Drawings and photographs of Osterley are displayed. An explanatory slide presentation is given in an adjoining room.

➡ Return to the hall by the corridor. Exit from the house L and proceed to the old stables.

Location 2	**ELIZABETHAN STABLES**

The three-winged Elizabethan stable block north of the house has been converted to summer tea rooms.

Its clocktower was added in 1714.

← Exit R and follow the wall of the stable block.

Location 3	**GARDEN HOUSE**

This garden building was constructed in Palladian style by *Adam, c.*1770.

← Cross the west lawns facing the garden house.

Location 4	**TEMPLE OF PAN**

The garden temple was probably designed by *Chambers*. It is built of Portland stone.

Inside, the plasterwork is a 1930 reproduction of the original.

← Return towards the house, exit from the park and proceed to Osterley Station, Piccadilly Line.

Syon and Old Isleworth

Syon, built in the Tudor period, is outstanding for its late–18C interiors by Robert Adam, regarded by many as the great architect's *chef d'oeuvre*. The grounds of Syon Park include many entertaining displays and museums. Nearby, Old Isleworth is dominated by its famous riverside inn, The London Apprentice.

Timing Although Syon Park is open throughout the year, the house can only be entered afternoons from Good Friday to 28 September, Sunday to Thursday, and October, Sunday only.

Suggested connections Precede with Hampton Court. Continue to Osterley.

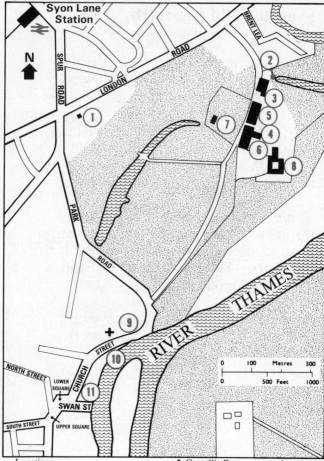

Locations

1　Crowther of Syon Lodge
2　Syon Park
3　The Heritage Collection Motor Museum
4　Great Conservatory and Formal Gardens
5　Camellia Restaurant and Banqueting Centre
6　Garden Centre
7　The London Butterfly Museum
8　Syon House
9　Old Isleworth
10　The London Apprentice
11　Blue School

Start　*Train from Waterloo Station (BR) to Syon Lane Station (BR). R Spur Road. L London Road. Cross the road.*

Alternatively, continue from Hampton Court as indicated on page 31.

Location 1	**CROWTHER OF SYON LODGE**
Busch Corner, London Road, Isleworth (560 7978). *Open daily 11.00–16.30. Admission free.*	The house, built by *R. Adam* in 1780, was once the residence of the Dowager Duchess of Northumberland. It was acquired by Crowther in 1929. Wrought iron gates, garden statuary and ornaments are displayed in the grounds. All are for sale and most are antique.

Inside the house, complete period rooms with chimney-pieces may be seen and purchased.

Crowther's offices occupy the old stables and are lined with Jacobean panelling and fireplaces – not for sale. George VI came personally to Crowther's to choose mantelpieces for Windsor Castle.

Exit R. Pass the main gate designed by Adam *(not open). First R follow the Brent Lea pedestrian entrance to Syon Park (just before the traffic lights). Continue ahead.*

Location 2	**SYON PARK**

London Road, Isleworth (560 0881)

The park is open throughout the year. Admission free. The car park is also free.

Protector Somerset brought mulberry trees here from abroad in the 16C, thus creating England's first horticultural garden. The grounds were landscaped by *Capability Brown* in the late 18C while Adam worked on Syon House.

Follow the path ahead to the forecourt. Take the first path L (signposted).

Location 3	**THE HERITAGE COLLECTION MOTOR MUSEUM**

Open daily March–October 10.00–17.30. Admission charge.

Here is displayed the world's largest collection of historic cars made by companies now within the British Leyland group. Many vehicles are in working order and may be hired (with chauffeur).

Exit L. Proceed to the Great Conservatory.

Location 4	**GREAT CONSERVATORY AND FORMAL GARDENS**

Open daily April–September 10.00–18.00 or dusk. Admission charge. A combined ticket also gives admission to Syon House.

Fowler built the conservatory in 1827, the same year as he constructed The Market at Covent Garden and ten years before the erection of the Palm House at Kew by *Burton* and *Turner*. It was designed, in Classical style, to look like a stone-built house topped with glass and ironwork.

Enter from the south side.

Within are an aviary and an aquarium.

Exit L. Proceed ahead to the restaurant, north of the formal gardens.

Location 5	**CAMELLIA RESTAURANT AND BANQUETING CENTRE**

(568 0778)

Lunches and dinners are served Monday–Friday and lunch at weekends.

This restaurant possesses a bar, the only one within the park but reserved for diners only. There is a lakeside cafeteria.

Continue southward.

Location 6	**GARDEN CENTRE**

Open Monday–Saturday 09.30–17.15. Sunday 10.00–17.15. Admission free.

All plants, seeds and garden equipment are for sale. Nearby is the Arts Centre which displays changing selections of works.

Exit ahead.

Location 7	**THE LONDON BUTTERFLY HOUSE**

Open March–
October 10.00–17.00.
November–February
10.00–15.30.
Admission charge.

This is one of the world's largest collections of live butterflies. Many exotic varieties, together with some moths, fly freely around the visitors. There are also live spiders and scorpions, etc., fortunately securely housed in glass display cases.

●● *Exit ahead and cross the car park to the main path R. Follow the first path L through the gate to Syon House.*

Location 8	**SYON HOUSE**

Open Good Friday or
1 April (whichever is
earlier)–28 September
Sunday–Thursday
12.00–17.00;
October, Sunday only
12.00–17.00. Last
admission 16.15.

Following the dissolution of the monasteries, the estate of Syon (named after Mount Zion), which had belonged to a nunnery, was presented to Edward Seymour, Lord Protector Somerset, by his young nephew Edward VI in 1547. Somerset built Syon House on the site in 1550, but two years later he was executed for conspiracy. The next owner, John Dudley, was soon also to be executed, by the new monarch, Mary I, in 1553, as he had promoted the rival claims to the throne of his daughter-in-law, Lady Jane Grey. On the accession of James I, Syon passed to the Percys, Earls of Northumberland, and remains in their possession today, in spite of the execution and imprisonment of several members of the family. Coincidentally, the blood of Syon's builder, Protector Somerset, flows in the present owners, as his descendant, Charles, sixth Duke of Somerset, married Elizabeth Percy in 1682. The Northumberland earldom ended for a period, due to lack of a male heir, but in the 18C a member of the family by marriage, Sir Hugh Smithson, became Earl of Northumberland and later, first Duke of Northumberland. He commissioned *Robert Adam* to remodel some of the interiors at Syon in 1761.

Although the house retains its Tudor format, it was built of red brick and not faced with stone until the 19C. Syon's austere appearance from outside gives no hint of the splendours within. The main east facade to the river, may be glimpsed from the rose garden but it can only be viewed satisfactorily from the north side of Kew Gardens, the river itself or the towpath on the south bank. It has a Classical 17C colonnade, possibly by *Inigo Jones*, and on the roof stands the great stone lion, a copy of a work by Michelangelo. This was brought here from the Percys' London residence, Northumberland House, a Jacobean mansion that was compulsorily purchased and demolished in 1874, for the construction of Northumberland Avenue. The family originally lived in the City and acquired Northumberland House by marriage in 1642.

●● *Enter Syon House from the west door.*

Adam planned to remodel most of the interior and designed a rotunda to cover the central courtyard. The duke, however, did not want to lose all of Syon's Tudor character, and in the event Adam redesigned only four rooms and the

hall. The result has been judged his *chef d'ouvre*, 'amongst the greatest works of art in England' (Sitwell). Most of the furnishings throughout were also made to Adam's designs.

Hall. The appearance is formal, with delicate plasterwork by Adam's favourite, *Joseph Rose*; much of the plasterwork in the Adam rooms is his work. Through a window ahead can be seen the Northumberland lion on the east facade.

← *Ascend the steps.*

Anteroom. Designed in Roman style, this is the most splendid room in the house.

The Ionic columns are clad with green marble and much of the plasterwork is gilded.

The floor is of scagliola (imitation marble).

State Dining Room. *Adam* began his work at Syon in this room. Although the columns are Corinthian it is more plainly decorated and there is less gilding of the plaster.

Red Drawing Room. The walls are covered with 18C red silk made at Spitalfields.

Paintings of the Stuarts include works by *Van Dyck* and *Lely*.

The carpet was made to Adam's own design by *Thomas Moore* in 1769.

The ceiling is painted in Etruscan style with medallions by *Cipriani*.

On the sideboards are mosaics, brought from the Baths of Titus in Rome.

Long Gallery. The gallery was planned for ladies to retire to after dinner. The structure remains Tudor. It is alleged that in this room Lady Jane Grey was offered the Crown of England in 1553.

Print Room. The room was decorated in the 19C by *Monterelli*.

The four-poster bed is 18C.

A painting of the first duke, Adam's patron, by *Gainsborough* is displayed.

The cabinets are rare late-17C examples.

The Oak Passage. Again, there is no work here by Adam.

Stairwell. This was also the 19C work of *Monterelli*. The painting of Diana is by *Rubens*.

← *Exit from the house L. Enter the rose garden L through the turnstile.*

Partial views can be obtained from here of the river facade of the house.

← *Exit and proceed southward through the grounds following the drive. Exit from the grounds to Park Road L. Continue ahead to the river. R Church St.*

Location 9	**OLD ISLEWORTH**

Much of Old Isleworth retains its appearance of an 18C Thames-side village.

All Saints. The medieval church was mostly burnt down in 1943, not by bombs, but by two schoolboys who destroyed three churches in one night. Only the 15C tower was saved but a modern church has been built amidst the ruins.

Church Street. The street was once Isleworth's main thoroughfare. Many 18C houses remain but the first building, **Butter Field House**, in Neo-Gothic style, was built, surprisingly, in 1971.

Location 10	**THE LONDON APPRENTICE**
Church Street	

This pub was built early in the 18C, on the site of an ancient inn. It was remodelled c.1905 and again in the early 1960s. The name allegedly commemorates the London apprentices who rowed here from the City on public holidays.

There is a large riverside terrace for summer drinking.

•● *Exit L. Proceed ahead to Lower Square.*

Location 11	**BLUE SCHOOL**
Lower Square	

This Neo-Gothic castellated building was built as a schoolhouse in the 18C. It was remodelled as offices in 1983.

•● *Proceed ahead to Swan St. L Upper Square leads to South St. Take bus 37 eastward to Richmond Station (BR), District Line.*

•● *Alternatively, if continuing to Osterley (page 93), take bus 37 westward to Kingsley Rd, Hounslow. Proceed to Hounslow East Station and train to Osterley Station, Piccadilly Line. Exit from the station L. First L Thornbury Rd leads to the entrance to Osterley Park. Follow the drive to the house.*

•● *Alternatively, and preferably, proceed to Osterley direct by taxi (telephone from Old Isleworth).*

Kew

Kew is, of course, mainly visited for its famous botanical gardens, still the most extensive in the world. However, due to its royal connections since the early 18C, many outstanding properties line its green and the north section of Kew Road. Within Kew Gardens, the smallest of England's royal palaces may be visited.

Timing Obviously, late spring and early summer are most spectacular at Kew Gardens but something of interest is always on view due to the extensive range of hot-houses that have been built.

Kew Palace can only be visited from April to mid-October.

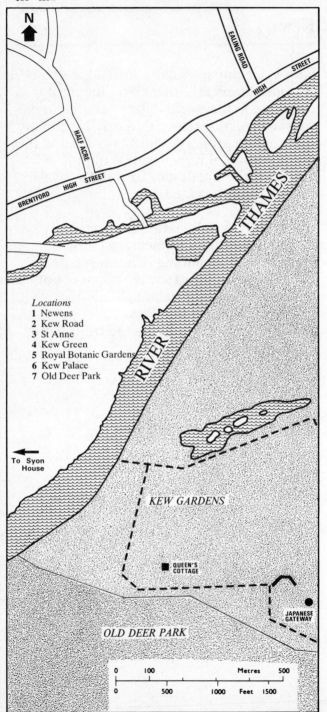

N

EALING ROAD

HIGH STREET

HALF ACRE

BRENTFORD HIGH STREET

THAMES

RIVER

Locations
1 Newens
2 Kew Road
3 St Anne
4 Kew Green
5 Royal Botanic Gardens
6 Kew Palace
7 Old Deer Park

To Syon
House

KEW GARDENS

QUEEN'S
COTTAGE

JAPANESE
GATEWAY

OLD DEER PARK

0   100   Metres   500

0   500   1000   Feet   1500

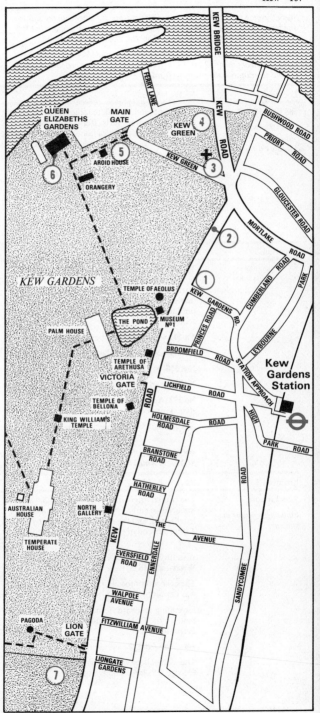

Start *From Kew Gardens Station, District Line, pass beneath the railway line by subway and exit from the station. Ahead Station Parade. First R Station Approach leads to Kew Gardens Rd. Second R Kew Road.*

Alternatively, boat from Westminster Pier, Easter–September. NB: the earliest arrival time is 12.00. From the landing stage proceed ahead to Kew Green. Continue to the south-west side.

Location 1	**NEWENS**
288 Kew Road *Open Tuesday–Saturday, also Monday a.m.*	This traditional English tea shop is famed for its 'Maids of Honour' tarts. Reputedly, Henry VIII saw the queen's maids of honour eating them; the King tried one and was so impressed that he decreed that henceforth they should be cooked only for the Royal Family. After Henry's death, the recipe was sold for £1000 to a Mr Billett whose chef was an ancestor of the Newens family, the present owners of the shop. 'Maids of Honour' may be eaten within or bought to take away. •● *Exit R.*

Location 2	**KEW ROAD**

The northern end of the road, towards Kew Green, has the properties of greatest interest. Further south, late Victorian villas and undistinguished blocks of modern flats predominate. Period houses are passed as follows:

No 294 with a Regency bow window.

Nos 300–302, Cumberland Place, dated 1831.

Nos 338–342, Hanover Place, *c.*1712.

No 350, early 18C with a Regency balcony.

No 352, **Adam House**, late 18C with an Adam-style doorcase.

Nos 356 and **358**, **Denmark House**, both early 18C.

•● *Cross Kew Rd. First L Kew Green. Proceed to St Anne's which stands in the green.*

Location 3	**ST ANNE** *1714*
Kew Green *Open afternoons in summer.*	The church originated as a simple chapel and replaced an early Tudor structure. Its nave was lengthened, and the north aisle added, by *J. J. Kirby*, a friend of the painter Gainsborough, in 1768.

A south aisle and the west facade, altered by *Wyatville* in 1838, were added in 1805.

The east end of the church, including the cupola, was rebuilt by *Stock* in 1884.

Extending eastward from this is the mausoleum built for the Duke and Duchess of Cambridge by *Ferrey* in 1851.

•● *Enter from the west portico.*

The west gallery was added to accommodate George III's large family in 1805.

At the east end of the south aisle is the only impressive monument in the church, to Dorothy, Lady Dowager Capell, d.1721.

← Exit L.

Buried in the churchyard are two famous painters. Gainsborough's tomb is L of the south porch and surrounded by railings.

Zoffany's tomb lies east of the church.

← Return to the south-east corner of Kew Green and proceed westward.

Location 4

KEW GREEN

Kew began around this triangular village green which is now divided by the approach road to Kew Bridge. Its name derived from Kayhough – low lying land with a quay. Kew Green has been a fashionable address since the 16C. Cricket is played here on summer weekends.

Most of the houses on this side were built, or remodelled, in the 18C when the Royal Family returned to the area.

Nos 17–19, **Gamley Cottage**, is early 18C.

No 33, early 18C, set back from the road, was used as a study by the Earl of Bute.

No 37, **Cambridge Cottage**, early 18C, has a porch, added in 1840, which stretches half-way across the road. The house was the residence of the Duke of Cambridge, one of George III's many sons. Later occupants included the Earl of Bute and the mother of George V's consort, Queen Mary.

Nos 39–45, **The Gables**, is a 17C house remodelled in the 18C.

No 51, **Royal Cottage**, is late 18C.

← Pass Kew Gardens' gate and continue along the north side of Kew Green.

Herbarium House consists of an 18C core, once known as Hunter House, and several extensions made between 1877 and 1969. Hunter House was the residence of another of George III's sons, the Duke of Cumberland, who later became King of Hanòver, but was better known as 'Butcher Cumberland of Culloden'.

More 18C houses follow.

← Return eastward and enter Kew Gardens.

Location 5

ROYAL BOTANIC GARDENS (KEW GARDENS)

Open 10.00–16.00. Admission charge. In summer the gardens close progressively later – up to 20.00 in July and August. Glass houses open 11.00–1600 and also close later in summer

Inside the gates, by *Burton* 1846, an information board immediately L lists items of seasonal and special interest which may be seen. The gardens must be viewed selectively as they cover 288 acres and have no internal transport. Blooms are most spectacular in spring and early summer.

In the 18C the gardens were divided and formed the private grounds of three royal residences.

*– up to 17.50. There is
no additional charge.*

Kew Palace and Kew House (the White House)
stood to the north and Ormond Lodge (later
Richmond Lodge) to the south, in what is now
the Old Deer Park. The grounds were linked in
1802 although part of the Old Deer Park is once
more a separate entity and serves as a golf course
and athletic ground. Of the royal residences only
Kew Palace survives.

Exotic trees and fruits were first planted here by
Sir Henry Capell in the late 17C. Augusta, widow
of Frederick, Prince of Wales, allocated an area
for experiment in 1759, thus founding the botanic
gardens. George III, 'Farmer George',
enthusiastically continued this work. Queen
Victoria presented Kew Gardens and its
buildings to the nation in 1841.

The following suggested tour covers the items of
greatest general interest.

•➡ Proceed ahead.

The first building passed R is the **Aroid House
No 1**. This was one of a pair designed by *Nash*
for Buckingham Palace and transferred here in 1836.
The other survives *in situ*.

*•➡ Exit R and proceed ahead. Kew Palace lies R
of the path.*

Location 6

KEW PALACE *1631*

Kew Gardens

*Open daily April–
mid-October 11.00–
17.30. Admission
charge.*

Kew Palace was built on the site of the Earl of
Dudley's Elizabethan house for Samuel Fortrey
in 1631. Fortrey was a merchant of Dutch descent
and named his residence the Dutch House. It was
acquired by George II *c*.1728 and served as a
nursery for his children. George IV, when Prince
of Wales, and his brother Frederick lived and
studied at the house in 1771.

Kew became the smallest royal palace in the
country when George III and Queen Charlotte
adopted the house as their temporary summer
residence in 1802 following the demolition of the
White House. Charlotte died here in 1818 and
Kew Palace was never to be occupied again.

The house was designed in the Flemish style,
fashionable during the Carolean period. Its
brickwork is outstanding.

Above the door is the date 1631 and the initials of
Samuel Fortrey, the builder of the house, and his
wife Catherine.

Each window was originally divided into four
lights by brick mullions and transoms but the
usual conversion to sash took place in the 18C.

*•➡ Enter the palace. From the hall turn R to the
King's Dining Room.*

Throughout Kew Palace, restoration work and
furnishings emphasize its character during the
early 19C occupancy of George III and Queen
Charlotte. However, *Kent* had remodelled the
interior *c*.1728 for its use as a royal nursery, and
much of his décor survives.

King's Dining Room. William IV, when Duke of Clarence, held his wedding breakfast in this room. 'Jacobean' plasterwork, above the door ahead, is now believed to be an 18C imitation of the style, possibly by *Kent*.

King's Breakfast Room. Original panelling survives.

Staircase. This is carved in typical mid-18C style.

●➡ *Ascend to the first floor.*

The lantern R is 18C.

George III is depicted in needlework by *Mary Knowles* based on a contemporary painting by *Zoffany*.

●➡ *Enter the Queen's Boudoir and proceed clockwise.*

Queen's Boudoir. The ceiling's plasterwork is original and a late example of the Jacobean style.

Queen's Drawing Room. In this room, the Duke of Clarence, later William IV, and the Duke of Kent, both married German princesses on the same day in July 1818. Although now laid out as a music room, royal guests frequently played cards here.

The chimney-piece is original.

Anteroom. Wigs belonging to the king were kept in the closet in this room.

King's Bedchamber. The unusual chimney-piece was fitted in 1802 as part of the refurbishing of the house when it became a temporary royal residence.

George III used the dressing table.

Queen's Bedchamber. It is alleged that Queen Charlotte died sitting in the chair ahead R, on 17 November 1818.

●➡ *Proceed through the anteroom and descend the stairs.*

Page's Waiting Room. Exhibits include a large model for a royal palace by *Kent* intended to replace the White House but never built.

●➡ *Proceed through the library to the anteroom.*

Anteroom. Linenfold panelling is 16C work, retained from the Elizabethan house that previously stood on the site.

●➡ *Exit R and proceed to the south side of the palace and Queen Elizabeth's Gardens.*

The south facade is similar to the north facade.

Queen Elizabeth's Gardens. These gardens, laid out in formal 17C style, were opened by Elizabeth II in 1969.

●➡ *Exit and proceed ahead to the sundial.*

This late 17C sundial, erected by William IV in 1832, stands in the centre of the site previously occupied by Kew House, or the White House as it was later called. This was commissioned by

Frederick, Prince of Wales (who died after being
struck by a cricket ball), and designed by *Kent* in
1735. It had replaced Sir Henry Capell's 17C
residence which was separated from the Kew
Palace estate by a road leading to Brentford
Ferry. The White House was demolished in 1801,
George III, an enthusiast of Gothic work, had
commissioned *J. Wyatt* to build a new country
mansion, overlooking the river behind Kew
Palace. This was designed in the style of a
medieval castle and known as the Castellated
Palace. Its interiors, however, were never
completed and the building was blown up by
George IV in 1828.

•● *Turn L and continue ahead to the Orangery.*

Orangery *Chambers* 1757 (but dated 1761). This
white stuccoed building is now used for
temporary exhibitions and also serves as a
bookshop.

•● *Exit and return to the west end of the
Orangery. Turn L and follow the main path ahead
to the pond.*

The tulips which bloom in May and June between
the pond and the Palm House are outstanding.

On the opposite side, L of the pond, is **Museum
No 1** by *Burton* 1857.

Ranged on the east side of the Palm House are
the **Queen's Beasts**. They are stone replicas of
plaster originals made by *James Woodford* in
1953 to front the Westminster Abbey annexe
erected for the coronation of Elizabeth II.

Palm House *Burton* and *Richard Turner*
(engineer) 1848. This iron and glass structure has
been judged to be even more successful
aesthetically than the old Crystal Palace which
was built in 1851, also by *Decimus Burton*.

Within, a gallery above the palm tops is reached
by spiral steps.

•● *Exit from the west side.*

Here is the famous rose garden that blooms
June–September.

•● *Proceed southward to the flagstaff.*

Flagstaff. This is the trunk of a Douglas Fir tree,
225 ft high, which was brought from British
Columbia and erected in 1959.

•● *Turn R and proceed westward.*

Temperate House *Burton* 1860. Known originally
as the Winter Garden, this is judged to be less
impressive than the same designer's Palm House.

The north and south wings were added in 1899.

During restoration in 1982 all the glazing was
renewed and the wooden frames replaced by
aluminium.

•● *Exit R and proceed in a north-west direction.*

Lake. Surrounded by weeping willow trees, the lake contains exotic wildfowl (which should not be fed).

Follow the lakeside path, on either side, westward.

At the west end is a view of the main facade of Syon House on the north bank (described on page 102).

Continue ahead towards the river and follow the path L. Take the first path L to the drinking fountain, then follow the path R to Queen's Cottage in the south-west of the gardens.

Open April–
September Saturday
and Sunday 11.00–
17.30. Admission
charge.

Queen's Cottage. The cottage was a summer house built for Queen Charlotte in 1770 and allegedly designed by her. In May the bluebells that surround the cottage are in bloom. The property was presented to the nation by Queen Victoria in 1898.

Prints by *Hogarth* are exhibited in the central ground floor room.

A room upstairs has been painted to represent a floral arbour.

Exit and return to the main path L. Take the first path R and the second path L. Proceed to the mound L.

Japanese Gateway. This is not a folly but a copy, four-fifths size, of a Buddhist temple gate known as Chokushi Mon – Gate of the Imperial Messenger. It was imported from Japan and first seen at the Japanese exhibition in 1910 before being presented to Kew.

Proceed eastward to the pagoda which faces the Lion Gate exit.

Not open to the
public.

Pagoda *Chambers* 1761. The 163 ft high pagoda was originally more decorative, with a total of eighty enamelled dragons protruding from the eaves which punctuate each storey. It is a survivor of the numerous mid-18C follies that once decorated the gardens. Most were the work of *Chambers* although he frequently used the designs of *Muntz*. Buildings lost include: a Moorish Alhambra, Turkish Mosque, Chinese House of Confucius, Gothic Cathedral, Theatre of Augustus and several Classical temples. Surviving elsewhere in the gardens, however, are three Classical temples and a ruined arch, all by *Chambers*, and King William's Temple, added by *Wyatville* in 1837 for William IV.

East of the pagoda, on the south side of the path, lies Old Deer Park.

Location 7

OLD DEER PARK

The park is shared by the Richmond Association Athletic Club and the Mid Surrey Golf Club. It was formerly the garden of Richmond Lodge which stood at its north end near the present Kew Gardens boundary.

Richmond Lodge was purchased by William III in the late 17C thus marking the first return of royalty to the area since Richmond Palace had been abandoned. William may have found it a convenient stopping-off point between his favourite residences at Kensington Palace and Hampton Court.

The Duke of Ormond leased the house *c.*1702, partly rebuilt it and renamed it Ormond Lodge. In 1719 the Prince of Wales acquired the property as a summer residence before moving to the White House. George III inherited both Ormond Lodge and the White House, and for a brief period their grounds, now Old Deer Park and Kew Gardens, were united. Ormond Lodge was demolished *c.*1775. Foundations were laid for a new royal palace but it was never built (a model for this by *Kent* is exhibited in Kew Palace). Garden buildings by *Kent*, including a Hermitage and Merlin's Cave, were demolished at the same time and the grounds laid out by *Capability Brown*.

•● *Leave Kew Gardens by the Lion Gate. Cross the road and take bus 27 or 65 to Richmond Station (BR).*

From the top of the bus, on the R side, can be viewed the old Kew Observatory which stands near the river in Old Deer Park (it is not open to visitors). This was built by *Chambers* in 1769 and had been commissioned, together with its great telescope, by George III for Herschel, the Astronomer Royal.

•● *Alternatively, if continuing to Richmond (page 65), cross The Quadrant immediately L. Take the footpath first R through the Oriel House archway. First L cross the railway bridge to Little Green (R).*

Chiswick and Hammersmith

Chiswick and Hammersmith, together with Strand-on-the-Green, possess London's most attractive riverside streets. Many Georgian houses and pubs overlook the water. Chiswick House is London's outstanding example of an 18C Palladian Revival villa.

Timing Any day is suitable, except in the winter when Chiswick House closes Monday and Tuesday and for one hour at lunchtime, and Hogarth's House closes Tuesday. Fine weather is a great advantage and the riverside is more attractive when the tide is in. NB: parts of the footpath are impassable if there is a high tide. All the locations may be seen in one day with a mid-morning start.

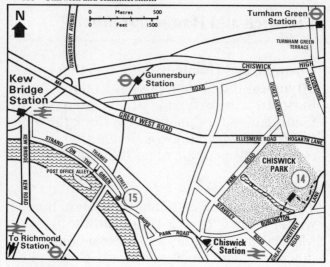

Locations

1 Hammersmith Bridge
2 Lower Mall
3 Furnival Gardens
4 The Dove
5 Upper Mall
6 St Peter
7 St Peter's Square
8 Hammersmith Terrace
9 Chiswick Mall
10 St Nicholas
11 Church Street
12 Hogarth's House
13 Chiswick Square
14 Chickwick Park and House
15 Strand-on-the-Green

Start *From Hammersmith Station, District and Piccadilly lines, leave by the King St exit ahead. Turn L. Take the pedestrian subway ahead indicated for King St. Exit L. Ahead King St.*

From Hammersmith Station, Metropolitan line, leave by the Beadon Rd exit ahead. Cross Beadon Rd immediately and continue ahead. First R King St.

At King St continue ahead (on R King's Mall shopping centre). First L Angel Walk. R Great West Rd. Cross this at the first pedestrian crossing and pass beneath the flyover. Ahead Bridge View. At the end, continue ahead to the river.

Location 1	**HAMMERSMITH BRIDGE** *Bazalgette, 1887*

The predecessor of this bridge, also a suspension bridge and the first of that type to cross the Thames, was erected in 1827. Bazalgette's superstructure has been judged to be excessively bulky.

Turn R and follow Lower Mall.

Location 2	**LOWER MALL**

Nos 6–9 are early 19C and some of the trellis work is original.

Kent House, *c*.1782, is now the premises of the Hammersmith Club.

Nos 11–12, originally 17C fishermen's cottages, are believed to be Hammersmith's oldest houses.

Two Victorian inns are passed; the **Blue Anchor** and the **Rutland**.

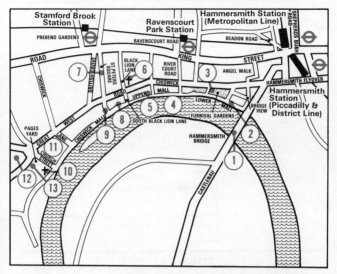

No 22, laying back as the last building before the
public gardens, is early 18C. Until recently it
accommodated the office of the Electoral
Register.

•► Proceed ahead to Furnival Gardens.

Location 3	**FURNIVAL GARDENS**

These gardens provide a surprising oasis of
greenery between the Lower and Upper Malls.
They were created just before the Second World
War, after a creek had been filled.

It was intended that the gardens would face a new
civic centre but due to the construction of the
Great West Road this scheme never
materialized.

*•► Continue ahead, following the riverside path.
At the Dove Marina turn R. First L Upper Mall.*

Immediately R **Sussex House** is early 18C.

Location 4	**THE DOVE**
Upper Mall (748 5405)	The 17C Dove was a popular coffee house in Georgian times and is now one of London's best-loved riverside pubs. Literary *habitués* have included A. P. Herbert, Graham Greene and Ernest Hemingway, the tavern appearing as 'The Pigeons', in Herbert's book *The Water Gypsies*. The words for 'Rule Britannia' were reputedly written by James Thomson in one of the inn's upper rooms.

When built, the property was combined with the
adjacent **No 17** as one house.

The sign, painted in 1948, replaced an earlier example almost 100 years old, which erroneously featured two doves.

● *Enter the pub.*

Immediately R a door leads to what is claimed to be London's smallest bar.

A small brass plate on the wall ahead marks the level of the highest tide ever recorded on the Thames, 7 January 1928.

The beamed front bar retains some Georgian features and the fireplace, although constructed in 1948, is made from Elizabethan bricks.

Above this is a Portland stone dove emblem, also modern.

The riverside terrace, remodelled in 1985, retains an ancient vine.

Moorings at Dove Marina may be hired from the landlord by arrangement.

● *Exit L.*

| Location 5 | **UPPER MALL** |

Apart from Sussex House, already passed, other outstanding 18C buildings survive in Upper Mall.

No 22 is early 18C.

No 26, Kelmscott House, 1780, was once the residence of the renowned 19C designer and manufacturer William Morris. He kept a tapestry loom in one of the bedrooms.

● *Continue ahead and pass River Court Rd (first R).*

The first house R, not named or numbered, is **No 36**, *c*.1810.

● *Proceed towards the Old Mill Lane corner (second R).*

Linden House, early 18C, is now occupied by the London Corinthian Sailing Club.

● *Pass beneath the arch ahead, still keeping to the river.*

The 18C **Old Ship** has been well renovated and possesses a good riverside terrace.

● *Exit R. Proceed ahead. First R South Black Lion Lane. Passed immediately R is the 18C* **Black Lion Tavern**. *L Great West Rd. Descend the steps to the subway and ascend to the north side. Immediately ahead is St Peter's.*

| Location 6 | **ST PETER** *Lapidge 1829* |

St Peter's, Hammersmith's oldest church, retains its original gallery.

● *Exit and proceed ahead to St Peter's Square R.*

| Location 7 | **ST PETER'S SQUARE** *c.1830* |

This square, and its adjoining streets, is Hammersmith's only planned Georgian area.

The central gardens are public.

Houses were originally rendered with undecorated stucco but are gradually being painted.

☛ Return by the subway to South Black Lion Lane. Proceed ahead. Second R Hammersmith Terrace.

| Location 8 | **HAMMERSMITH TERRACE** c.*1750* |

These sixteen identical houses were designed, unusually, with their fronts facing the river rather than the road. They are surprisingly urban in appearance as, when built, the terrace was surrounded by open country.

A. P. Herbert, lawyer, writer and river enthusiast, lived at No 12.

☛ Continue ahead to Chiswick Mall.

| Location 9 | **CHISWICK MALL** |

Chiswick Mall consists of grand houses separated from their private riverside gardens by the road.

Glass panels and high gates are flood protection measures.

In the centre are three adjoining residences, **Morton House**, 1730, **Strawberry House**, 1730, and **Walpole House**, part 17C. The last was the residence of Barbara Villiers, Duchess of Cleveland, who became the mistress of Charles II and immediately preceded Nell Gwynn in the King's affections. The house is believed to have been the model for Miss Pinkerton's Academy in *Vanity Fair* by Thackeray.

☛ Continue ahead passing Chiswick Lane South (first R).

Towards the end of Chiswick Mall are **Eynham House** and **Bedford House**. These originally formed one residence in the 18C, which was called Bedford House in honour of its landowner, the Duke of Bedford.

Adjoining is 18C **Woodroffe House** with a later bay window on the ground floor.

☛ R Church St. Cross the road.

| Location 10 | **ST NICHOLAS** |

Church Street

There has been a church on this site since the 12C. Although the bulk of the present building was constructed in 1884, its tower dates from 1436.

In the churchyard L is the tomb of artist William Hogarth. This is enclosed by railings and surmounted by an urn. Behind, west of the church, is the huge Chiswick Cemetery.

☛ Exit from the churchyard L. Pass the church and cross Church St.

The partly half-timbered house R is The Old Burlington.

Location 11	**CHURCH STREET**

Several Georgian properties remain but the most interesting is **The Old Burlington**. This 16C building originally served as an inn, and is one of the best examples of its type in the London area.

Latimer House opposite is early 18C and possesses outstanding cast-iron gates.

•● Continue to the end of Church St. Cross the road.

Pages Yard was created in the 17C. The two large dormer windows of Nos 1 and 3 are later additions.

•● Exit from the yard L. First L Great West Rd. Cross by the subway. Turn L at the first exit. Ascend the steps R. L Hogarth Lane.

Location 12	**HOGARTH'S HOUSE** *late 17C*
Hogarth Lane	This house was owned between 1749 and 1764 by the artist William Hogarth who used it as a summer country house. It was opened to the public in 1904. Although damaged by Second World War bombing, the house has been restored and within can be seen the largest existing permanent display of Hogarth's etchings.
Open April–September, Monday–Saturday 11.00–18.00. Sunday 14.00–18.00. October–March, closes 16.00 and Tuesday. Admission free.	

The artist's studio was in a room above the stables, now demolished.

•● Exit R. Return by the subway to Burlington Lane R. First L Chiswick Square.

Location 13	**CHISWICK SQUARE**

Houses L and R on this recently restored three-sided square were built *c.*1680.

Boston House, 1740, now subdivided, occupies the south side.

•● Exit L Burlington Lane. Continue ahead and cross the road at the pedestrian lights. Enter Chiswick Park at the first gate R. Turn L and follow the main path which leads to Chiswick House.

Location 14	**CHISWICK PARK AND HOUSE**
Burlington Lane	Chiswick House, designed by *Lord Burlington* with interiors by *Kent*, is London's finest example of a Palladian Revival villa.
Park open daily 08.00–dusk. Admission free. House open 15 March–15 October, daily 09.30–18.30. 16 October–14 March: Wednesday–Sunday 09.30–13.00 and 14.00–18.30. Admission charge.	The Chiswick Park estate, together with its Jacobean mansion, was purchased by the first Lord Burlington in 1682. Richard Boyle, the third earl, built an adjacent villa, the present Chiswick House, in 1729, basing his design on works by the Italian architect Palladio and his pupil Scamozzi. The Villa Capra, near Vicenza, was its chief inspiration. Burlington and his group were later to be known as the Palladians, due to their preference for Palladio's pure Classical style over that of the currently fashionable English Baroque.

The gardens were laid out and the interiors of the villa planned by *Kent*, who incorporated some designs by *Inigo Jones* which were in Burlington's possession.

It is now considered that the first floor of the villa was planned as two suites of rooms, on either side of the central drawing rooms, for Lord and Lady Burlington. It was also a 'temple of the arts'. Burlington's works of art and books were kept in the villa and his friends entertained there.

A building linking the villa with the summer parlour of the house was also constructed by *Burlington*, but the original Jacobean house was demolished in 1788, possibly following a fire. It was not rebuilt, but the villa survived and was extended to become a residence by the addition of north and south wings by *James Wyatt* in 1788. The north wing incorporated the link building. Similarly retained was the summer parlour by *Burlington* (?), which had also survived the fire. These extensions were made by the fifth Duke of Devonshire, whose wife, Georgina, was then regarded as the 'queen' of English society. Two tsars of Russia were entertained here in the 19C, and Edward VII, when Prince of Wales, frequently stayed with his family at Chiswick House in the summer.

In 1892 the works of art were removed, mostly to the eighth duke's principal country residence at Chatsworth. The house and its grounds then became the premises of a lunatic asylum. Threatened with building development, the local authority acquired the estate in 1929 and Chiswick Park was opened to the public. The house was restored and all post-Burlington additions, including *Wyatt*'s north and south wings, were removed in 1952. Chiswick House now appears little different from Burlington's time.

Ahead is the main east facade fronted by a courtyard. Until moved in 1828 to its present position, the Bath Road passed immediately in front of the courtyard gate piers.

Terms (Classical busts on shafts) surround the courtyard.

The two-storey villa has a low ground floor of rusticated Portland stone. This was private to Burlington and guests ascended the steps directly to the first floor.

Flanking the steps are statues of Palladio and Inigo Jones by *Rysbrack c.*1730.

The first floor is higher and accommodates the most important rooms.

Immediately R is the link building of Bath stone.

The flat-topped building R of this is the summer parlour. It was added to the old house, which stood to the north, before work on the villa began. It was also probably built by *Burlington*.

➡ *Turn L and proceed clockwise around the house.*

The south facade was entirely hidden by Wyatt's

extension until this was removed in 1952. The venetian window had been demolished and the present example is a reconstruction.

●● Continue to the west facade.

The three venetian windows on this facade are original, although much restored.

*●● Continue ahead, passing the west facades of the link building and summer parlour, to the **Inigo Jones gateway** ahead.*

The gateway by *Inigo Jones* was first erected in 1621 as the new entrance to what had been Sir Thomas More's old residence in Chelsea. When that house was demolished in 1736 the arch was brought here. Only the arch itself is original, the side pieces and urns being added by *Burlington*.

●● Return to the east facade of the house and enter by the small door on the ground floor.

The house is unfurnished, although selected paintings and mirrors are hung. Some fireplaces are based on designs by *Inigo Jones* including examples from Old Somerset House. Both floors were designed with an identical inter-connecting room layout.

Drawings by *Burlington* and his draughtsman *Flitcroft* are displayed on the ground floor.

*●● Proceed through the lobby and the **Octagonal Hall**.*

The room ahead is the central of three that once housed Burlington's library.

*●● Turn R and proceed through the link building and modern corridor to the **Summer Parlour**.*

Although an extension, probably the work of *Burlington*, this is all that survived of the old house. Its walls are painted in grisaille (grey monochrome), work commissioned by Alexander Pope, a great admirer of Burlington.

*●● Return to the first of the three library rooms. Turn L and descend the stairs to the old **wine cellar** in the basement. Return, turn L and proceed through the central library room to the room ahead. Turn L and ascend the spiral staircase to the upper floor.*

Immediately entered is the circular section of the Gallery (described later). Turn L.

The **Red Velvet Room** is one of three that have been lined with flock wall paper to represent their original appearance.

The ceiling is by *Kent*.

Chimney-pieces are dated 1729 and mark the completion of work at the villa begun four years earlier.

The **Blue Velvet Room**'s ceiling is considered to be the finest work at Chiswick by *Kent*.

Roundels above the doors represent the bearded Inigo Jones by *Dobson* and Alexander Pope by *Kent*. The subject of the third roundel is unknown.

A fine view of the courtyard is gained from the **Red Closet.**

•➡ Return to the circular section of the Gallery.

The **Gallery** comprises three interconnecting sections which give spaciousness to the whole.

The central room, which follows, has half-domed apses at both ends.

Niches contain statues. All are modern copies except for that of Apollo at the south end.

Original porphyry vases flank the window.

The third section of the gallery is octagonal.

•➡ Continue clockwise to the **Green Velvet Room** *and* **Bedchamber.**

The Bedchamber gained its name following the death in this room of the leader of the Whig party, Charles James Fox, in 1806.

Roundels above the doorways represent Alexander Pope by *Kent* and Lady Burlington and Lady Thanet, both by *Aikman.*

•➡ Return to the Green Velvet Room. Turn L and enter the **Domed Saloon.**

This is the most important room in the house. It is octagonal in shape and a picture hangs on each wall. These were removed to Chatsworth in the 19C but have now been returned for permanent display.

Classical busts stand on brackets between the doorways.

•➡ Cross to the Red Velvet Room ahead. Turn R to the circular section of the Gallery and descend the stairs. Exit from the house and proceed ahead between the two piers. Turn immediately R and follow the path that crosses the lake. Follow the lake until parallel with the house. Then take the path L to the obelisk ahead. Exit from Chiswick Park, R Burlington Lane. Continue ahead to Chiswick Station (BR) and cross the railway by the pedestrian foot bridge. Turn R, then L and continue ahead to Grove Park Rd. Follow its R fork to the river and Strand-on-the-Green's riverside footpath R.

•➡ Alternatively, from Chiswick Station (BR) return to Waterloo Station (BR).

Location 15	**STRAND-ON-THE-GREEN**

The 'Green' of the name is believed to refer to an old orchard which once stretched behind the houses. This is judged to be London's prettiest riverside village, even though there is now a distant view of Brentford's high-rise flats and a railway bridge carries regular, noisy trains. The towpath, instead of a road, though often impassable at high tide, enhances the charm. Interesting examples of flood protection are apparent.

Passed immediately R is **Strand-on-the-Green House**, late 16C.

Two riverside pubs follow. Just before the railway bridge, is the 17C **Bull's Head**, but with a much altered front.

The **City Barge** just after the bridge, was bombed during the Second World War and mostly rebuilt. It is claimed that the inn was founded in 1484. The Lord Mayor's state barge was moored here in the winter. The name of the pub was changed from the Navigator's Arms in the 19C.

Post Office Alley is locally called 'Beatles Alley' as it was featured in the Beatle's film *Help*.

The symmetrical terrace, **Nos 53–55**, is mid 18C.

Other properties of interest lie further west, including **No 64**, **Magnolia House**, late 18C. Three early 18C houses follow.

No 65, **Zoffany House**, where the painter Zoffany lived from 1790–1810.

Nos 66 and **67**, **Springfield House**.

No 70 is early 19C and retains a brick 17C (?) porch, possibly retained from an earlier house on the site.

●━ *Proceed to the Kew Bridge approach road. Turn R and cross the road to Kew Bridge Station (BR).*

●━ *Alternatively, take bus 27 or 65 from the bus stop immediately R to Richmond Station (BR).*

Barnes

Barnes retains one of London's most attractive village greens, complete with duck pond. The parish church of St Mary exhibits recently discovered examples of outstanding late 12C internal decoration.

Timing St Mary's Church is open Monday–Friday 10.30–12.30. Barnes Bridge Station is closed Sunday but the adjacent Barnes Station remains open.

Suggested connection Continue to Wimbledon.

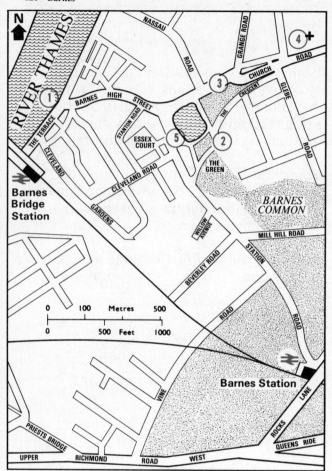

Locations
1 The Terrace
2 The Green
3 Church Road
4 St Mary
5 Station Road

Start *Barnes Bridge Station (BR) from Waterloo Station (BR). From the platform descend the steps and turn R. R The Terrace.*

Location 1	**THE TERRACE**

Houses were first built here in 1720, when the coach service from Barnes to London was inaugurated. Most are early 19C, but some original buildings survive, generally with early 19C additions such as balconies and bow windows. Flood defences, in the form of low walls, are still necessary in spite of the recently completed Thames Barrier.

Nos 14 and **13** are early 18C examples.

Gustav Holst, the composer, lived at **No 10** from 1908–13.

●➡ *Continue eastward to the end of The Terrace. R Barnes High St. Second L Church Rd and The Green. Immediately L is The Sun Inn.*

Location 2	**THE GREEN**

With its large duck pond, the original village green still gives Barnes a rural feel. Stocks stood here until 1835.

Overlooking The Green, the late 17C (?) **Sun Inn** retains its low, beamed interior and some Victorian woodwork.

Immediately R, the white Victorian Gothic lodge, built in 1850, stands on The Green, east of the pond. It was attached to the old village school which lies behind and is now a day centre for the elderly.

●➡ *Continue eastward along Church Rd.*

Location 3	**CHURCH ROAD**

This thoroughfare forms the north side of The Green. It leads to the parish church and includes some of the oldest and most important properties in Barnes.

No 43 is early 18C.

No 45 is an example of the Neo-Gothic style.

The Grange, an early 18C mansion, has a later porch and bow window.

On the Kitson Rd corner (second L), **Strawberry House** stands behind a high wall. This was originally built, early in the 18C, as the rectory.

●➡ *Continue ahead to the parish church of St Mary.*

Immediately L is the **lych gate** built in 1912.

Location 4	**ST MARY**
Church Road	
Open Monday–Friday 10.30–12.30.	

Although St Mary's was badly damaged by fire in 1978, with the loss of many important monuments, practically all of its ancient sections have been salvaged and incorporated in the rebuilt church. Restoration work, in fact, revealed some of the best examples of late 12C internal decoration that can be seen in the London area.

A chapel was built c.1100 and the Norman fabric of its south wall survives, immediately ahead, forming most of the present south wall.

● Proceed eastward following the path.

Both buttresses were erected *c*.1480.

The building was doubled in size *c*.1190, a date only recently established. A tradition that this building was consecrated on its completion by Stephen Langton when he returned to London from the Magna Carta ceremony in 1215, therefore, seems to be unjustified.

Surviving from the late–12C work are the south and east stone walls of the original chancel, now the Langton Chapel. This follows the second buttress.

In the east wall of the chapel are three late-12C lancet windows, blocked in 1777 but rediscovered and restored in 1852.

Most work north of this point is by *Cullinan* 1984.

The stone section of the clergy **vestry**, which protrudes eastward, immediately north of the Langton Chapel, survives from the extension of 1905.

● Return westward, passing the south porch.

Immediately west of the porch is a further short section of the late-12C wall which was extended westward in the 13C to the point where the tower now stands.

The **tower** was added *c*.1480. Its clock and sundial were made in 1792.

● Return eastward to the south entrance.

This entrance was formed *c*.1480 and the original Norman doorway, slightly further east, was then blocked.

The present porch was built in 1777.

At the same time the buttress R was erected at the point where the old doorway had stood.

● Enter the church.

Following the recent rebuilding, the high altar was re-sited to the north.

● Turn L.

The modern font was made of stones from the ruined part of the church.

On the wall, R of the window, is an example of the double line-block pattern with rosettes executed in the 13C(?) and discovered after the fire.

On the west wall are fragments of early 17C Black Letter script.

● Return eastward, passing the entrance door, and follow the south wall.

Within the filled early-12C doorway are traces of late-12C single line-block pattern decoration together with a more elaborate pattern.

Until it was destroyed in the fire, the Hoare family monument, the most imposing in the church, had stood in front of the blocked doorway. Banker Sir Richard Hoare, d.1787, was the owner of Barn Elms, a late–17C residence which had replaced an earlier mansion owned by Elizabeth I's Secretary of State, Sir Francis Walsingham. The house stood near the river but was demolished in 1954.

Just before the chancel arch is a curved recess, remains of the stairway to the rood screen's loft, probably blocked in 1566 when rood lofts were abolished.

The walls of the old chancel, now the Langton Chapel, are decorated with 14C angel bosses which came from the earlier roof. They bear the Downshire arms.

Between the last two east windows is the memorial to Rector John Squier, d.1662.

Fragments of a 14C frieze survive above the east wall's lancet windows.

On the north wall of the chapel, below the first window from the east, is the brass of the Wylde sisters, 1508. It was previously set in the chancel floor.

Proceed northward.

The old part of the church is linked by a short nave to the **sanctuary** with its transepts.

All this work is new, but some small windows, and the large window (1852) above the altar, were saved from the fire and re-used.

By 1777, the north wall of the medieval church had disappeared completely due to extensions, and there was further major rebuilding on this side in 1852 and 1906. Very little of the medieval St Mary's structure was, therefore, lost in the fire.

Exit from St Mary's and follow the path immediately L through the churchyard. Pass through the gate ahead.

East of the church is the early-18C **Homestead House**.

Return to The Green. Follow the footpath ahead passing the old village school and the south side of the pond to Station Rd R. Continue ahead to the Essex Court corner (first L) and Milbourne House.

Location 5	**STATION ROAD**

Milbourne House was built early in the 17C and internally retains some Jacobean features. Its front was remodelled in the 18C. Henry Fielding, author of *Tom Jones*, lived here.

Return southward along Station Rd.

Facing the green are **Nos 66** and **68**, early 18C but altered.

No 70 is Neo-Gothic.

Continue to the Mill Hill Rd corner (first L) and The Cedars.

The Cedars is a much altered late-18C house. The conservatory was added above the porch in the 19C and the brickwork has been rendered, unfortunately, with pebbledash.

•• *Continue ahead to Barnes Station (BR) and return to Waterloo Station (BR).*

•• *Alternatively, if continuing to Wimbledon (page 45), pass Barnes Station and ascend the steps L. R Rocks Lane. R Upper Richmond Rd. Take bus 37 eastbound to Putney Hill (request stop). From the bus stop continue ahead. First R Putney Hill. Cross the road and take bus 80 or 93 to Wimbledon High St (the stop after the Rose and Crown). Return westward. First R Church Rd.*

Pinner

Like Harrow-on-the-Hill, Pinner is another rare oasis in northern London's suburbia. It possesses a picturesque, gently rising High Street, proudly overlooked by the medieval parish church. Pinner's greatest attraction, however, is its group of timber-framed buildings dating from the early 15C. They are unique in the London area.

Timing Pinner can be seen in a few hours and may follow a visit to Harrow, nearby. If this is done, consult the timing advice for Harrow, otherwise any day is suitable.

Suggested connection Precede with Harrow-on-the-Hill.

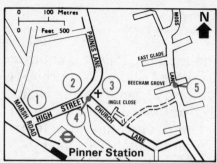

Locations
1 High Street
2 Church Farm
3 St John-the-Baptist
4 Church Lane
5 Moss Lane

Start *Pinner Station, Metropolitan Line (Amersham, Chesham or Watford direction). Exit from the station ahead. R Marsh Rd. First R High St.*

Alternatively, continue from Harrow as indicated on page 144.

Location 1	**HIGH STREET**

Pinner's High Street, with its many period houses, climbs up a low hill, at the top of which stands the parish church. Although definitely part of suburbia, Pinner retains much of its ancient appearance and its centre is known locally as 'the village'. A street fair has been held here annually since medieval times. Most properties of interest are on the east side.

The **Victory** tavern, dated 1580, has a beamed interior.

No 24 has a Regency bow window. Its 'half-timbering' is fake.

No 32, **Wakefield House** is 17C.

Nos 34–36, half-timbered, are probably early 17C.

•● *Cross to the west side of High St.*

Although the **Queen's Head** sign is dated 1705 the building appears to be much older. Possibly the date refers to the renaming of the inn in the year of Queen Anne's death.

•● *Follow the bend L where the road becomes Paine's Lane. Immediately L is Church Farm.*

Location 2	**CHURCH FARM**

Now no longer a farm, the house is part-17C and part-18C. Although built of brick the facade has, unfortunately, been rendered.

•● *Proceed immediately opposite to Church Lane.*

Preceding the church is **No 64**, **Hayward House**, mid-18C with later additions.

On the south corner, opposite, are two houses which now form the **Hilltop Wine Bar**. The facade is late 16C or early 17C, with later extensions.

Location 3	**ST JOHN-THE-BAPTIST**
Church Lane	The present church, consecrated in 1321, replaced a small 13C chapel that had stood on the site.

Its tower, added in the 15C, received new battlements as part of the 1978 restoration.

☛ Proceed clockwise.

The west wall of the nave's south aisle (and north aisle), with its lancet windows, is all that survives of the original massive west wall. The rest was demolished in the 15C, when an opening was made to provide a link with the new tower.

The south porch was rebuilt in the 15C.

Dormer windows were added to the nave's roof by *Pearson* in 1880.

Walls of the south transept are believed to incorporate fabric from the 13C chapel.

The chancel's south aisle was added in 1859. Its triple lancet window is a replica of the original window of the chancel's south wall that had to be demolished when the aisle was built.

☛ Return to the south porch and enter the church.

The roof was part of the major restoration by *Pearson* in 1880. It was decorated in 1958.

The floor was relaid in 1958.

☛ Proceed to the north aisle.

Internally, both windows in the north aisle are 14C (they have been rebuilt externally).

In front of this aisle's blocked north door is a 15C octagonal font, much restored. Its modern cover is by *Spooner*.

Like the south transept, the north transept's walls are believed to retain fabric from the 13C chapel. Its staircase and doorway were built in 1954.

The lower part of the chancel's north wall is also believed to incorporate 13C material at its east end.

The pulpit, L of the arch, was designed by *Pearson c.*1880.

Jacobean altar rails were recently brought forward.

The east window was formed in the 15C.

A black 17C marble tablet commemorates John Dey, vicar of the church.

The 16C altar, usually covered, came from St George, Hanover Square, Mayfair.

☛ Proceed to the Lady Chapel at the east end of the south aisle.

The chancel's south wall was demolished in 1859 when the south aisle was constructed to accommodate members of the Royal Commercial Travellers' School, which had recently opened nearby and needed additional space for worship. It was replaced by the present arcade.

The aisle was heightened and extended eastward in 1880 to house an organ that was finally dismantled in 1967. It was dedicated as a Lady Chapel in 1936.

Fixed to the wall on both sides of the south door are carved and decorated panels from the early 17C choir stalls which were replaced in 1937.

At the west end of the south chancel's wall is the monument to Sir Christopher Clitherow, *d.*1685. The skull at the base has no jaw bone, indicating that he was the last male member of the family.

The east arch of the south transept was formed in 1859 to provide a link with the chancel's new south aisle.

Exit from the church ahead to Church Lane.

Location 4	**CHURCH LANE**

Immediately facing the church is **Church Cottage** 18C.

Proceed eastward.

Next to the church is **Chestnut Cottage**; basically 17C with two bays added later.

Pinner House, 1721, is Pinner's grandest residence. It has been converted to an old people's home.

Proceed past Ingle Close (first L). First L the footpath leads to Moss Lane. Continue ahead passing L Beecham Grove and East Glade. At the bend, immediately L, is Tudor Cottage.

Location 5	**MOSS LANE**

Tudor Cottage, 1592, is the first of a rare group of ancient farmhouses and barns that have miraculously survived. They provide the finest examples in the London area.

Continue ahead. Turn L at the footpath.

East End House is early 17C but with a Georgian facade added.

East End Farm Cottage is a rare, early-15C hall-type house. Its chimney-stack is Elizabethan.

Opposite are two barns dating from the Elizabethan period, now unfortunately put to light industrial use.

Return to Church Lane by the same route. L High Street. Proceed to Pinner Station, Metropolitan Line.

Harrow

Perched on its hill top, the town is an oasis in a desert of suburbia. It is hard to believe that very few buildings existed southward between Harrow and Hampstead until the coming of the Metropolitan railway in the 19C. From a distance, Harrow is dominated by the spire of its ancient church. Although the northern part of the town consists mainly of grim Gothic Revival buildings owned by Harrow School, more attractive, older properties line its High Street and steep lanes to the west. Harrow School's early-17C classroom survives and may be visited. Mementoes of the school's most famous pupils, Byron, Churchill and Nehru are to be seen.

Timing Friday to Sunday is preferable as St Mary's Church is closed Monday, and Harrow School's art gallery/museum in the Old Speech Room is closed Tuesday, Wednesday and Thursday. However, much depends on arrangements made to visit the school buildings (apart from the Old Speech Room).

Suggested connection Continue to Pinner.

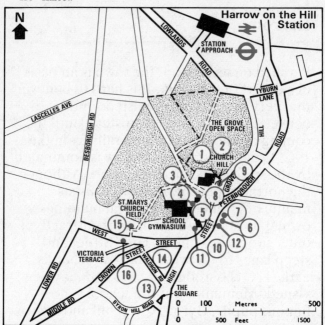

Harrow on the Hill Station

Locations

1 Peachey Stone
2 St Mary
3 Harrow School
4 Old School
5 Old Speech Room
6 Vaughan Library
7 Chapel
8 Memorial Building
9 New Speech Room
10 Headmaster's House
11 Druries
12 High Street
13 King's Head
14 Crown Street
15 Harrow Pie House
16 West Street

Start *Harrow-on-the-Hill Station, Metropolitan Line. At the barrier turn L and descend the steps. Ahead Station Approach. L Lowlands Rd. Follow the footpath uphill through the green R. At the end turn L and follow the path to the terrace. Immediately L is the 'Peachey Stone'.*

Location 1	**PEACHEY STONE**

The tomb of John Peachey is famous only
because of its association with Lord Byron, one
of Harrow School's most famous pupils. Here, at
'my favourite spot', Byron frequently sat
admiring the view which, in the early 19C, was
almost entirely pastoral.

An iron grille now protects the tomb from the
poet's many admirers who might wish to emulate
him. Inscribed on a marble plaque in front of the
tomb is a verse from Byron's 'Lines written,
beneath an elm in the churchyard of Harrow,
September 2 1807.'

*●● Return to the next path R and proceed through
the churchyard to the west tower of St Mary's.*

Location 2	**ST MARY**

Church Hill

*Closed Monday.
Apply in writing to
make brass rubbings.*

Although the 19C flint facing to the body of the
church gives St Mary's a Victorian appearance it
is basically a medieval structure and part of its
tower was built in the late 11C.

Harrow belonged to the Archbishops of
Canterbury from 825 until the estate was seized
by Henry VIII in 1545. Much of it was then
granted to Sir Edward North. The name Harrow
is believed to derive from the Saxon word *hergae*
meaning a temple or shrine. However, there is no
record of a church on the site in Saxon times.
Earliest information available refers to the
church consecrated by St Anselm in 1094.

The lower stages of the **tower** are all that survive
from the 11C building.

The upper stage, together with the spire, was
added in the mid 15C.

The tower's west portal, south window and north
windows (seen later) are Romanesque.

Above the west portal is a small lancet window.

South of the tower, an upright black stone
commemorates Thomas Port. Its inscription
refers to his death in 1838 after being struck by a
train.

*●● Proceed anti-clockwise following the south
side of the church.*

The **nave** was rebuilt *c*.1235. It was heightened in
the mid 15C when the clerestory was added in
Perpendicular style. At the same time the aisle
windows were remodelled.

Battlements were added and the body of the
church refaced in flint by *George Gilbert Scott* in
1849.

●● Continue towards the south porch.

A floor was added in the 14C, thus dividing
internally the high late-12C **south porch** to
provide an upper level **parvise** (priest's room or
chapel). At the same time the porch was
remodelled externally and gargoyles were added.

The outer doorway of the porch has been renewed.

● Continue eastward.

It is believed that the **south transept** was erected, like the north transept, when the nave was rebuilt in the 13C.

Although the **chancel** was built in the late 12C, only its south wall survives from this period as *Gilbert Scott* rebuilt the remainder in 1849 when he restored the church.

The lancet windows on this wall had been blocked but were opened up and restored in 1893.

Figure corbels and gargoyles, probably 14C, decorate much of the exterior of St Mary's.

● Continue anti-clockwise to the north side of the chancel.

The chancel's **north chapel** and the **north porch** were added by *Gilbert Scott* in 1849.

A north **vestry** was built in 1908.

The **north transept**, like the south, is believed to be late 13C.

Two further Romanesque windows survive on this side of the tower.

Although stonework is now exposed at the tower's lower level, it is believed that this part of the church has always been rendered.

● Enter the church from the south porch.

The tie beam roof was constructed in the mid 15C when the nave was heightened for the new clerestory.

Its twelve wall posts, carved to represent the apostles, are supported by grotesque head corbels.

Immediately L, the **south aisle** wall has been stripped of rendering to reveal its 13C stonework.

Steps L of the door lead to the parvise which may be viewed, with an attendant, when convenient.

When conversion took place in the 14C, probably to provide a chantry chapel, two round headed windows were blocked and the present 14C window added. The outline of the east window is clear.

On the east wall, a carved niche probably supported a statue of the Virgin.

Traces of 14C decoration survive.

● Return to the nave, south aisle L.

The early-13C Purbeck marble font, discarded in 1800, was retrieved from a local garden in 1846.

● Proceed to the tower.

From the tower it can be seen that some columns in the nave are set at angles, indicating settlement. As their capitals are horizontal, work may have been halted until the settlement ended.

In the tower's Romanesque south window L, modern stained glass depicts John Lyon, the founder of Harrow School.

Stained glass in the tower's Romanesque north window, also modern, depicts Archbishop Lanfranc.

●➡ *Proceed eastward following the north aisle.*

L of the north door is the monument to Lord North by *Hopper* 1831.

The late-12C north door was originally the external door of the south porch. It was presumably transferred here in the 14C following the remodelling of the south porch.

The most easterly arch of the north aisle arcade is incomplete; the reason for this is a mystery.

Figure corbels supporting the **north transept** arch from the crossing have been dated 1236. This may, therefore, be the approximate completion date of the present nave and transepts.

●➡ *Proceed to the north transept's west pier.*

On the south side is the brass commemorating John Lyon, d.1592, and his wife. It was taken from the original floor slab and fixed here in 1880.

Above is Lyon's monument by *Flaxman* 1813.

On the east wall of the north transept are alabaster fragments from the tomb of William Gerard, d.1609, and his sister.

In front of the lectern is the white floor slab made in 1880 to mark the burial place of John Lyon.

On the north wall of the **chancel**, L of the aisle, is the monument to James Edwards, d.1816. He was a bookseller and it is recorded that his coffin was made, at Edwards' request, from his library shelves.

The reredos is by *Webb c.*1908.

Glass in the east window was designed by *Comper*, also *c.*1908.

The pulpit, *c.*1675, was acquired in 1708. Its tester is of a later date.

Some of the splays (angled sides) of the lancet windows on the south wall of the chancel retain original, late-13C decorations. Chevrons are believed to be *c.*1400.

The stained glass was made in 1893 when the windows were unblocked.

The **south transept's aisle** is believed to be late 12C. If so, this would indicate that the earlier nave also had transepts.

To the L of the transept's east window are traces of an earlier window; possibly a double lancet.

On the west wall is the monument to Joseph Drury by *Westmacott*, 1835.

Just before the south door is a chest, *c.*1200.

●➡ *Exit from the church and proceed ahead through the lych gate. Descend Church Hill.*

Location 3

HARROW SCHOOL

Three of England's public schools are pre-eminent – Eton, Winchester and Harrow. Harrow's famous ex-scholars include Winston Churchill, Lord Byron and Pandit Nehru. Most public schools were originally formed expressly for the education of local children but are now privately funded, apart from a limited number of scholarships, and 'public' has, therefore, become a misnomer.

Elizabeth I granted John Lyon, a yeoman farmer, a charter to refound the school at Harrow in 1572. The schoolhouse of an earlier, probably pre-Reformation, school had stood in the churchyard of St Mary's. Work began on its successor in 1609 and was completed in 1619.

Although primarily intended for local boys, few were attracted by the Classical curriculum, and fee-paying pupils from further afield have always been taken. All Harrow scholars now pay fees.

As the school prospered in the mid 19C, boarding houses were built specifically for the boys' accommodation. Most of them are mid- or late-19C dark brick 'piles', designed in an uncompromisingly High Victorian Gothic style. Whether intentional or not, their appearance must have instilled fear and gloom into many youngsters.

●▬ *Immediately R is Old School. Proceed through the gate and ascend the steps to await the guide in Bill Yard.*

The steps and terrace were laid out by *H. Baker* in 1929.

Boys answer here to their names on the master's 'bill' – hence the yard's name.

Visitors are shown some of the buildings which are grouped around Old School and form what is virtually a 'Forum Scholasticum'. They will probably include Old School, Memorial Building, Speech Room, Vaughan's Library and the Chapel. In spite of their apparent age only part of Old School pre-dates the 19C.

Location 4

OLD SCHOOL

Open by appointment only. Apply to the Bursar.

The oldest section, L, was completed in 1615. However, the apparently early-17C details of its main facade – gables, bay windows, porch and cupola – were all constructed by *S. P.* and *C. Cockerell* when they added an east wing in 1820.

Fourth Form Classroom. This was the only classroom at Harrow until the 19C. Its 17C oak panelling is covered with graffiti, most of it featuring the names of schoolboys. The guide will point out those of Byron, Robert Peel, Sheridan, Trollope and Churchill. (It is not certain if the Byron carving was made by the poet or his brother.)

The oak benches and fireplace are also 17C.

The bay window was added as part of the remodelling in 1820.

At the end of the room is the headmaster's throne.

Other rooms in this, the oldest part of the building, provide small classrooms, storerooms and caretaker's offices.

•➥ Proceed to the Old Speech Room which lies east of the block.'

Location 5	**OLD SPEECH ROOM** *S. P. and C. Cockerell*

Open Monday, Friday, Saturday and Sunday 14.30–16.00. Tuesday and Thursday 16.30– 18.00. Admission free.

This room represented the major part of the 19C extension.

Although built for speeches, it became the examination room when a new larger speech room was completed in 1877. It was here that Churchill took his exams. The room was remodelled in 1976 to accommodate the school's art gallery and museum.

Exhibits include a painting of Lord Byron, ancient Egyptian and Greek works of art and one of the world's largest collections of mounted butterflies.

Temporary exhibitions are held throughout the year.

A wall plaque L commemorates where, from this room, the seventh Earl of Shaftsbury witnessed a pauper's funeral which so disturbed him that he became a philanthropic reformer.

•➥ Exit and descend the steps to the yard. Descend the flight of steps R. Cross the road. Immediately ahead is the Vaughan Library.

Location 6	**VAUGHAN LIBRARY** *George Gilbert Scott 1863*

Open by appointment only.

This is the school's most important library. Its name commemorates Dr Vaughan, a headmaster of the school.

•➥ Exit R and proceed to the chapel.

Location 7	**CHAPEL** *George Gilbert Scott 1863*

Open by appointment only.

Transepts were added to the chapel in 1902.

The memorial to Dr Vaughan is by *Onslow Ford*.

•➥ Cross the road to the Memorial Building opposite.

Location 8	**MEMORIAL BUILDING** *H. Baker 1921*

Open by appointment only.

This was built to commemorate Harrow boys killed in the First World War.

On the wall of the New Speech Room's corner tower, R of the entrance, is a statue of Elizabeth I, in whose reign the school was founded. It was brought from Ashridge Park, Herts, in 1925.

•➥ Enter the building with the guide.

The **Fitch Room** was provided by Sir Cecil and Lady Fitch as a memorial to their son,

Lieutendant Alex Fitch, who was killed in action in 1918. His portrait is perpetually illuminated.

In addition to souvenirs of Fitch the room contains outstanding furnishings.

Elizabethan carved oak panelling lines the walls. It was brought from Brooke House, Hackney, East London, where Elizabeth I held court in 1587.

The 15C fireplace, from the reign of Henry V, incorporates later carvings added in the reign of Henry VII.

The refectory table is Cromwellian.

At the east end of the room is a Jacobean table.

● Exit L and proceed to the New Speech Room.

| Location 9 | **NEW SPEECH ROOM** *Burgess 1877* |

This replaced the function of the Speech Room in Old School. It is here that the school songs are sung, an annual event inaugurated in 1869. The entire school and Old Harrovians attend the occasion, to which Winston Churchill came every year after the Second World War until his death in 1963. Tears of sentiment rolled down his cheeks as he joined in the school song, 'Forty Years On'.

Stained glass windows bear the coats of arms of seven Harrovian prime ministers.

A painting of India's first prime minister, Pandit Nehru, also a Harrovian, is exhibited.

● Exit L.

A wall plaque on the Grove Hill–Peterborough Road corner, fixed in 1969, records the first fatal motor accident in Great Britain which occurred nearby on 25 February 1899.

Another plaque, on the pillar at the end of the wall facing Grove Hill, marks the position of 'King Charles's Well'. Here, by tradition, Charles I watered his horse, on 27 April 1646, before surrendering to the Scottish army at Southwell. The spring still runs below.

● Return southward. First R High St. Cross the road to the first house south of the Vaughan Library.

| Location 10 | **HEADMASTER'S HOUSE** *Burton 1845* |

1 High Street

The house was built on the site of the earlier headmaster's residence but not in Burton's preferred Classical style. Gothic, albeit with some Tudor-style features, was adopted for this, like Harrow's other 19C buildings.

On the opposite side of the road (unnecessary to cross) is Druries.

Location 11	**DRURIES** *Hayward 1868*
High Street	This is one of eleven boarding houses which now accommodate 750 pupils. There are no dormitories and every Harrovian has a separate room.

This building replaced an earlier Druries which the school acquired in the 18C as its first dormitory building. It is a typical example of the school buildings with its great height and Gothic gables.

In the grounds is a late-17C house, partly weather-boarded.

●● Cross the road to the east side of High Street and continue southward.

Location 12	**HIGH STREET**

High Street represents the 'town' rather than the 'gown'. Here, on the east side, the school's Gothic Revival buildings are replaced by shops and houses, mostly in the more restrained Georgian style.

No 5, **The Old House**, early 17C (?), is gabled and retains some exposed half-timbering at upper level.

No 7, **Harrow School Bookshop**, is early 18C.

No 9, **Moretons**, 1826.

No 13, **Flambards**, is late 18C. The Flambard's were a noted Harrow family who lived in the town during the 14C.

No 15, **The Park**, was built for Lord Northwick, in three stages between 1795 and *c.*1803. On the south range above the door is a statue of a lion, probably in Coade stone.

●● Continue ahead to The Square and cross to the King's Head Hotel.

Location 13	**KING'S HEAD** *part 1750*
The Square	By tradition this tavern was founded in 1535 in a building that had served as a hunting lodge for Henry VIII.

A dining room, where both lunches and dinner are provided, is popular with parents visiting their straw-hatted offspring. Attractive pastoral views may be enjoyed from the rear garden.

●● Return northward. First L Waldron Rd. First R Crown St.

Location 14	**CROWN STREET**

Crown Street was originally called Hog Lane. Much has recently been rebuilt but some period cottages survive.

A market and fair were held in Crown Street and Middle Road, with which it connects further south, from the 13C to the 16C.

●● First L West St. Cross the road to SRM Plastics. Here request to see Harrow Pie House. This building lies L of the path between the plastics factory and No 69 West St.

Location 15	**HARROW PIE HOUSE** *16C*

<table>
<tr>
<td>Off West Street

Open by appointment only.
Admission free.</td>
<td>This small Elizabeth building once accommodated the Pie Powder Court which was set up to deal with misbehaviour at the Crown Street–Middle Road fair nearby. The name referred to the speed with which justice was dispensed, i.e. before the accused's dusty feet (in French pieds poudreux) could be cleaned.</td>
</tr>
</table>

Externally, the timbered side wall and gable survive. The interior originally consisted of one high room; its dividing floor was added later.

•● *Continue along the path which bends R, and then L.*

At this point a better view of the exterior of Harrow Pie House may be gained.

The path leads to a field now known as St Mary's Church Field but for long called 'High Capers' due to the jollifications that took place here whilst the nearby fair was held.

•● *Return to West St L.*

Location 16	**WEST STREET**

Houses of most interest are on the north side.

No 13, timber-framed, was built *c.*1640 and is Harrow's most picturesque building. It was formerly two properties, a shop and an ale house called the Sugarloaf. Although now a private dwelling, the Victorian shop front has been retained.

•● *Continue uphill towards the east end of the street.*

Nos 17–15, **Penny Stone Cottages**, are dated 1740.

•● *L High St. First L Church Hill. Proceed L through the churchyard passing the west tower of the church. Follow the path R and the next path R. Descend through the green ahead to Lowlands Rd L. First R Station Approach and Harrow-on-the-Hill Station, Metropolitan Line.*

•● *Alternatively, if continuing to Pinner (page 131), take the northbound train in the direction of Amersham, Chesham or Watford not Uxbridge. Exit from the station ahead. R Marsh Rd. First R High St.*

Enfield

Although Enfield retains its medieval parish church with many fine monuments, visitors are chiefly attracted to the town by Gentleman's Row. This is one of London's most picturesque streets, comprising houses from many periods, chiefly the 18C. It is partly fronted by the New River which adds to the rural charm.

Timing Any day is suitable but the town is liveliest on Saturday when the market is held.

Suggested connection A visit to Enfield is ideally followed by Waltham Cross and Waltham Abbey nearby, thus making a full day's itinerary.

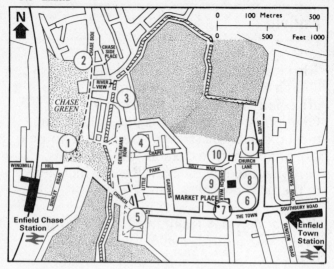

Start *Enfield Chase Station (BR) from Moorgate Station East (BR) (direction Hertford North). Exit from the station R Windmill Hill. L Chase Green.*

Location 1	**CHASE GREEN**

The green once stood on the eastern edge of Enfield Chase, a royal hunting forest particularly favoured by Elizabeth I and James I. Henry VIII owned Elsynge Hall, later Enfield Hall, which lay nearby, a little to the north of the town, until demolished in 1629. Both Elizabeth I and Edward VI stayed there as children. This small park is all that survives.

➻ *Continue through the park following the main path directly ahead. L Chase Side. Cross the road.*

Location 2	**CHASE SIDE**

Most properties are early 19C, but some Georgian examples, all on the east side, survive.

Nos 39–41 and **43–45** are early 19C. Their porches were added later.

Nos 59, **61**, **63** and **63A** are Georgian.

Nos 77–83 form a Regency terrace.

No 85, weather-boarded, is early 18C.

No 87, early 19C, is where the writers Charles and Mary Lamb lived from 1827 until moving next door in 1829.

No 89, **Westwood Cottage**, is early 19C. Here the

Lambs stayed with the Westwoods, who helped
to care for Mary during her periods of mental
disturbance. They left for Edmonton in 1833.

•• *At Westwood Cottage return southward.*
Follow the footpath L to Chase Side Place ahead.
Turn L. First R River View and New River.

Location 3	**NEW RIVER**

This man-made stream, completed in 1613,
flowed from the Chadwell Springs, between
Hertford and Ware, to Islington. Sir Hugh
Myddleton, who lived in Enfield, was the
instigator of the scheme which brought a new
fresh water supply to London. Here the river
follows its original course, but in 1860 much of it
was straightened. The New River is no longer
used for the water supply at this point and most
of it has been filled.

On the opposite side of the river, just before the
third bridge, is the main facade of Brecon House.

•• *Cross the bridge to Gentleman's Row.*

Location 4	**GENTLEMAN'S ROW**

Gentleman's Row has been fashionable since the
16C although most residences that survive were
either remodelled or rebuilt in the 18C. It is one
of the most picturesque streets in the London
area.

No 55, **Brecon House**, is mid 18C. It was restored
in 1985.

•• *Continue ahead, passing 19C terraces, to*
where the road branches. Keep to the L path.
Immediately R is No 32, Rivulet House, mid 18C.

Nos 33–27 form an early 19C terrace.

Lying back on the west side is **No 16**, **The Haven**,
an early-18C residence.

•• *Continue ahead on the east side.*

No 23, *c.*1730, was originally a tavern. Its
archway now leads to Chapel Street.

Nos 21 and **19** are early 18C.

No 17, **Clarendon Cottage**, is the 17C house
where Charles and Mary Lamb stayed with the
Alsopp family in 1825 and 1827.

Nos 15 and **13** are mid 19C.
Coach House was adapted from a 16C barn.

No 11, **Fortescue Lodge**, is early 18C.

No 9, **Elm House**, also early 18C, possesses an
elaborate crested gate.

No 1, a late 18C residence, originally called Little
Park, now provides offices for the local authority.
It was remodelled in 1985 and restored externally.

•• *Cross Little Park Gardens and follow the*
footpath immediately ahead to Church St L.

| Location 5 | **CHURCH STREET** |

Church Street, together with The Town, which it joins further east, forms Enfield's shopping centre. Although an ancient thoroughfare, little survives that pre-dates the late 19C.

On the south side of Church St R is Enfield Green. Here, until it was demolished in 1928, stood a Tudor mansion, Eltham Manor House or 'Palace'.

●▶ Continue ahead to The Town which begins at the Market Place. Proceed to No 22 on the north side.

| Location 6 | **NO 22 THE TOWN** |

This building, polygonal at ground floor level, was erected in the early 19C to provide an office for the beadle. It later became a police station and 'cages' were added on either side where criminals were held pending trial. Later the building was used as vestry offices for the parish church. It is now a solicitors' office.

Immediately opposite, the weather-boarded 18C house is The Town's only other building of architectural interest.

●▶ Return westward. First R Market Place.

| Location 7 | **MARKET PLACE** |

Market day is Saturday.

This has been the venue of the weekly market since permission was granted by Edward I in 1303. A licence for two fairs to be held here annually was acquired in 1869.

●▶ Proceed ahead to St Andrew's on the north side.

| Location 8 | **ST ANDREW** |

Market Place

When closed telephone the caretaker (363 7491).

St Andrew's was first recorded in 1136 and some Norman foundations survive. A church probably stood here in Saxon times. St Andrew's was completely rebuilt in Early English style in the 13C and almost completely rebuilt again in the 14C.

Immediately ahead, the 14C **south aisle** of the church was rebuilt of brick in 1824. It had been much lower than the late-15C north aisle and was heightened to match this and to accommodate a gallery.

●▶ Turn L and proceed clockwise around the church.

The **tower** is late 14C with most windows renewed.

Adjoining the tower L is the west wall of the **north aisle**. A modern doorway has been inserted in its wall.

●▶ Proceed to the north side.

The north aisle was rebuilt and probably heightened in the late 15C.

The clerestory of the nave wall behind may have been added at the same time but the windows were not glazed until 1522.

Between the first two windows of the aisle's north wall are traces of an earlier doorway, now blocked.

The tower's lower window on this side is an original 14C example, all others are relatively modern.

The **east turret** was built to accommodate a staircase which led to the rood screen's loft.

Immediately past the turret, the **north aisle** of the **chancel** was rebuilt in 1530 to link with and match the recently rebuilt north aisle of the nave.

The **north porch** and **choir vestry** attached to it were added in 1867.

Forming the oldest external wall of the church is the central section of the **chancel east wall**. It is 13C and, together with the chancel's south wall, was retained during the 14C rebuilding. Its present window was formed in 1873.

•● *Proceed to the south porch and enter the church.*

Both aisle arcades are 14C.

•● *Turn L and proceed R to the centre of the nave*.

Carved alternately between the clerestory windows are 16C rosettes and wings, the emblems of Sir Thomas Lovell, minister of Henry VII and Henry VIII. Lovell, a benefactor of the church, provided the original glass for the clerestory windows.

•● *Proceed to the north wall of the* **north aisle**.

Above the entrance to the **north chapel** is a door which originally gave access from the outer staircase turret to the rood screen loft. These lofts and their superstructure were removed by order of Elizabeth I in 1561. Although the parishioners were permitted to keep the rood screens with the beam above, most were eventually demolished to improve visibility between the nave and chancel.

The doorway to the north chapel is believed to date from the rebuilding of 1531 and is therefore the oldest still in use in the church.

Visitors may be shown the north chapel if convenient. Here a chantry chapel was founded at Enfield by Agnes Myddleton in 1471 for her parents, four husbands and herself. This was rebuilt in 1531, but the chantry was abolished, like all others, in 1547. It was later used as a vestry and is generally closed.

•● *Exit and continue eastward.*

The wall monument commemorates Robert Delcrowe, d. 1586.

The monument to Martha Palmere by *Stone*, 1617, is on the north wall of the **sanctuary**.

In the north-east corner of the sanctuary stands the monument to Sir Nicholas Raynton, d.1646, and his family. Raynton was a lord mayor of

London and built Forty Hall which survives north of Enfield. It stands on the site of Henry VIII's Elsynge Hall which was demolished for it.

On the east wall is a breadshelf c.1630.

The altar tomb of Lady Jacosa Tiptoft, d.1446, on the south wall, is the most important monument in St Andrew's. Its brass is outstanding and well-preserved. The canopy was added c.1530, probably to commemorate her grandchildren, Edmund and Isabel. Their father was Sir Thomas Lovell.

The 13C south wall of the chancel is contemporary with the east wall. It was originally an outer wall and its lancet window survives, although now unglazed. Traces of the sockets for the iron glazing bars can be seen.

The sedilia has recently been rebuilt.

All woodwork in the sanctuary is 19C.

•● *Proceed to the* **nave**.

The pulpit is 19C.

The chancel arch, enlarged in 1777, incorporates much 14C stonework. Around the arch, the Crucifixion scene was painted in 1923 as a First World War memorial.

Traces of a blocked doorway to the rood screen loft remain by the north side of the arch, below St George.

•● *Enter the* **Memorial Chapel** *in the south aisle of the chancel.*

A chantry chapel, dedicated to St James, was founded here by Baldwyn de Radington in 1398.

Ancient door jambs, recently discovered built into the 19C south wall of the south aisle, immediately R of the screen, probably formed part of the late-14C outer doorway to the chapel.

The blocked recess, below the lancet window in the north wall, may have been a 'squint', from where the high altar could be observed. Its angle, however, has led many to dispute this.

L of the screen is the font.

Immediately R of the 'squint' is the Italian marble monument to Thomas Stringer, d.1706, by *Guelfi*, 1731.

Three 14C angel roof corbels survive on the north wall of the south aisle.

Two adjacent early 17C monuments in the south-east corner commemorate Francis Evington, d.1614, and Henry Middlemore, Groom of the Privy Chambers to Elizabeth I.

•● *Proceed westward along the* **south aisle** *of the nave.*

The third window from the east in the south aisle incorporates the oldest stained glass in the church. Arms of Thomas Roos, with T. R. and 1530, commemorate the first Earl of Rutland.

Below this, additional fragments of 16C stained glass, depicting 'eight nuns', are the remains of a window commemorating Sir Thomas Lovell.

The organ in the west gallery was built in 1753. Its carved case is original.

All the earlier galleries have now been removed.

•● Exit from the church R. Proceed through the churchyard and leave by the gate L. R Church Walk. Proceed to the point opposite the church tower. Immediately L is the Old Grammar School.

Location 9	**OLD GRAMMAR SCHOOL** *1586*

Church Walk

The school was founded in 1548 and paid for by revenues obtained from the suppressed Radyngton Chantry Chapel in the parish church. There was originally one large ground floor classroom in the present building which, although now subdivided, is still used for teaching purposes.

The three dormer windows each retain some original sections.

•● Continue ahead towards Holly Walk L.

Uvedale House is Elizabethan.

•● First L Holly Walk.

Location 10	**UVEDALE COTTAGE** *16C*

1 Holly Walk

This house, also Elizabethan, was much remodelled in the 18C. Dr Robert Uvedale lived here while headmaster of the Grammar School from 1664 to 1676. Uvedale was a keen gardener and introduced the sweet pea to this country from Sicily.

Externally, some timber is original.

•● Return to Church Walk. Follow the path L. Exit from the churchyard. R Church Lane, L. Silver St.

No 58 Silver St is mid 18C.

Location 11	**WHITAKER HOUSE**

68 Silver Street

This 18C weather-boarded residence was occupied from 1862 to 1895 by Joseph Whitaker, creator of *Whitaker's Almanac*, which is still revised and published annually.

•● Return southward.

No 36 is the Enfield Vicarage. It was built in the 17C.

•● First L Southbury Rd. Cross to Enfield Town Station (BR).

•● Alternatively, first R The Town, leads to Church St and Windmill Hill. L Enfield Chase Station (BR).

•● Alternatively, if continuing to Waltham Abbey or Waltham Cross (page 153), first L Southbury Rd. From the second bus stop take bus 217B, 310, 360 or 735 to Waltham Cross. From the bus stop

*continue ahead to view the Cross. NB: bus 217B
continues to Waltham Abbey and, to shorten the
itinerary, Waltham Cross may be viewed from the
top of the bus. Otherwise, after viewing the Cross,
proceed to the second bus stop on the north side of
Eleanor Cross Rd and take any eastbound bus to
Waltham Abbey. From the bus stop return
westward along Quaker Lane. Second R
Stewardstone St leads to Market Place. L Church
St. Cross the road to Waltham Abbey Church
(page 155).*

Waltham Abbey and Waltham Cross

The only Eleanor Cross in the London area is at Waltham Cross; Charing Cross has a 19C monument to the original but not the cross itself. Further east lies Waltham Abbey which, although only a third of the great pre-Reformation monastic church, is one of the country's most important examples of Norman architecture. Nearby is the ancient Market Place which, together with Sun Street, provides a treasure-trove for the enthusiast of ancient pubs.

Timing The Epping Forest District Museum is closed Wednesday and Thursday. Market days at Waltham Abbey are Tuesday and Saturday.

Suggested connection A visit to Waltham may be followed, but preferably preceded, by Enfield.

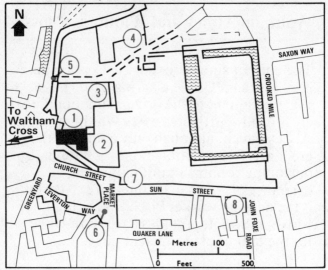

Locations
1 Waltham Abbey Church
2 King Harold's burial place
3 Cloister Passage
4 Stoney Bridge
5 Gatehouse
6 Market Place
7 Sun Street
8 Epping Forest District Museum

Start *Waltham Cross Station (BR) from Liverpool Street Station (BR). Exit from the station, cross Eleanor Cross Road and take any eastbound bus to Waltham Abbey. From the bus stop return westward along Quaker Lane. Second R Stewardstone St leads to Market Place. L Church St. Cross the road to Waltham Abbey Church.*

Alternatively, continue from Enfield as indicated on page 151. If this is done, Waltham Cross (Location 9) will be seen first, either from the bus or, for a closer inspection, at the cross itself.

Location 1	**WALTHAM ABBEY CHURCH** c.*1120*
Church Street	Waltham Abbey Church possesses what has been described as 'the noblest Norman nave in southern England'. Although almost 108 ft long, the church represents less than one third of the great monastic building which stood here in the 16C prior to the Reformation. Its size would have been similar to that of Canterbury Cathedral but its appearance, with two crossing towers, would probably have been unique in England.
	A church at Waltham is first recorded *c.*1030 when a stone crucifix was installed there by Tovi the Proud, a courtier of King Canute. The crucifix had been discovered on his land at Montacute, Somerset, and reputedly worked miracles.
	A new, larger church was commissioned by Harold Godwinson, later to become King Harold II, who was defeated by William the Conqueror at the Battle of Hastings. This was consecrated, probably in 1057 on 3 May, the day on which St Helen's discovery of 'the True Cross' was

celebrated and the church was dedicated, therefore, to the Holy Cross. Its earlier dedication is unknown.

Harold's building probably consisted of an aisled nave, north and south transepts, a central tower and a chancel. Nothing of this building appears to survive above ground.

A college of twelve secular canons and a dean was founded at Waltham by Harold. It is likely that, even at this early period, the nave served as the parish church whilst the remainder was reserved for the canons.

Rebuilding of the nave took place again from *c*.1100 onwards and this, apparently the third nave on the site, is the building that survives today.

Henry II founded three monastic establishments, probably as part of his penance for the murder of Thomas à Becket. Waltham Church was one of these, becoming a priory in 1177 when the king replaced the thirteen secular canons with sixteen Augustinian canons, later increased to twenty-four.

Work soon began on rebuilding and extending the church from the tower eastward. It is known that Harold's transepts were kept, and his crossing and tower may have survived; however, his chancel (canon's choir) was certainly rebuilt. William de Vere was responsible for this new building but only fragments survive and its appearance is uncertain. It appears to have been Early English in spite of its early date. The bulk of this work was probably completed *c*.1183 when Henry II's last payment is recorded but the south-east transept was not finished for another fifty years. The establishment was elevated to the status of an abbey in 1184 and became a 'Royal Peculiar' (directly responsible to the Crown), remaining so until 1857.

The existing nave was dedicated (possibly rededicated?), separately, to St Lawrence *c*.1242. St Lawrence was a Roman deacon, martyred on a grid iron in 258 for refusing to surrender church treasures to the authorities. The joint dedication to Waltham Holy Cross and St Lawrence remains the official name of the church although it is still generally referred to as Waltham Abbey.

It was almost certainly in the canon's part of the church that the body of Queen Eleanor rested, for one night in 1290, on her journey to Westminster. The body of her husband, Edward I, lay there for much longer – three months – while funeral arrangements were made, also at Westminster, in 1307.

Soon after 1286, the west front was rebuilt in Decorated style and internal modifications made at the west end of the nave. The south chapel, with its undercroft, was built *c*.1345.

Waltham was the last abbey to be dissolved by Henry VIII and the property was acquired by the Crown in 1540. The choir, second tower, together with its transepts, and east end were demolished, but the 12C nave and its south chapel were retained for parish use.

At the east end of the nave stood the earlier crossing and tower and these were also retained, probably for structural reasons. The parishioners were required to purchase the church bells. It is probable that the transepts were demolished at this time, apart from the west wall of the south transept.

The ancient tower collapsed in 1552 and its remnants were demolished. A new tower, the present structure, was then built at the opposite end of the church.

●● *Proceed from the tower anti-clockwise around the church.*

Tower. The present tower was the first to be built at the west end. It served as a buttress to the building, as some of the late-13C alterations were structurally unsound and a westward lean had developed. Rubble from the collapsed east tower was used for its construction and certain features came from parts of the late-12C building that Henry VIII had demolished. The tower, which was completed in 1558, was the only one to be built during the reign of Mary I. Its upper part was rebuilt for the third time in 1904.

The 13C doorway was re-used from the old building but remodelled on its installation in 1558.

Immediately above is a 13C lancet window, also re-used, but the other windows in the tower are contemporary with its construction.

The clock face was made in 1887 when a new mechanism was installed.

West front. Much of the late-13C Decorated west front disappeared when the tower was built. Its wings project on either side behind the tower. Other surviving elements are seen later when the porch is entered.

Nave – south aisle wall. Brickwork at clerestory level denotes renovations made between the 17C and the 19C; money was not available for stone.

Gothic windows in the first bay, at aisle and clerestory level, were part of the late-13C alterations.

Virtually all external detailing was renewed during the 1860 renovations.

South doorway. Although basically Norman, the exterior was largely renewed in the 19C. It originally had a porch which, considering its position, indicates that the nave was always parochial.

South chapel. This was added to the church *c.*1345. Originally its external doorway was probably the only entrance to the chapel.

Its east wall, *c.*1100, originally formed the west wall of the south transept and is probably the oldest surviving part of the church. At the lower level is herring-bone masonry.

A blocked round-headed window survives.

East wall. The present east wall of the church was remodelled in 1860.

Infilling closed, L to R, the west arch of the south transept from the south aisle, the crossing from the nave and the west arch of the north aisle from the north transept. The infill of the crossing arch incorporates the back of a stone screen, possibly late 13C, with evidence of two doorways for processional purposes.

The demolished abbey church. From this point eastward stood the crossing with its tower and transepts of the 12C church. All this was demolished after the tower had collapsed in 1552.

Harold's chancel (canon's choir) had originally extended east of the tower but was rebuilt as part of the late 12C extensions. A second tower, with its own wider transepts, was added at the east end of the new choir and a retrochoir stretched beyond this. The new choir was almost the same length as the Norman nave. All that survives above ground of this great building is one buttress of the south-east transept (seen later from the Sun Street car park), and probably the doorway and lancet window that were re-used in the west tower.

•● *Return to the west tower and enter the porch. Turn around to face the inner side of the tower's west wall.*

Porch. Above the door, L of the lancet window, is half of the monument to Francis Wollaston; the remainder is seen later.

On the north wall are traces of diapering (lozenge pattern) which came from a tomb *c.*1300.

Elements of the late-13C Decorated west front survive on the west wall, but most was destroyed, including a huge window, when the west tower was added in the 16C.

The doorway is original from that structure but its doors are 19C.

Above are the arms of Charles II, 1662

On the doorway's pediment is a bust of St Lawrence.

Capitals of the doorway's columns retain outstanding carvings which include an owl, a dog, a pelican and a foliated head.

Dragons on either side of the doorway are original apart from the large one that has been restored.

•● *Proceed through the inner doorway.*

It can be seen that the west wall is almost six feet thick, probably for structural reasons.

•● *Enter the nave.*

Nave. Much of the internal carving, especially at lower level, was restored, generally sensitively, in the mid 19C.

Above the massive piers, which alternate between circular and composite, are, as is usual in an English church of this period, a gallery and an arcaded clerestory with a vaulted wall passage.

The overall effect is evocative of a scaled-down simpler version of Durham Cathedral.

The nave was rebuilt from east to west as was usual. In order to support the crossing tower the first two bays would have been completed c.1110–20. The remainder was probably built c.1130.

It was the custom to decorate Norman churches internally with zigzag patterns, usually painted in yellow and red, but at Waltham there are indications that the zigzags were formed, at least partly, by strips of metal, probably gilded bronze. Waltham Abbey's nave would, therefore, have originally presented a highly decorated, even gaudy, appearance, very different from today. Later decorations included wall paintings and a vine leaf pattern in red, green and black. Much of the interior was whitewashed and painted with red lines to imitate the joins between ashlar (large stones). This work was possibly executed in the late 12C to harmonize with the interior of the recently completed canons' section of the church.

Major restoration work on the nave was completed by *William Burges* in 1860. He designed the present ceiling, based on the 13C work at Peterborough Cathedral. The main panels were painted by *Edward Poynter*.

•• *Turn L and proceed towards the north aisle.*

North aisle. The first two arches of the aisle arcade, immediately ahead, and the first and second aisle windows were remodelled in the new Decorated Gothic style in the late 13C. Similar remodelling took place on the south side. It was this work which weakened the structure and caused the nave to lean westward. The new west front probably received its 6-ft wall to help remedy this, but it was not until the west tower was built in the 16C and acted as a buttress that the problem was finally solved.

On the sill of the first window is displayed the mechanism of the clock which was installed in the tower in 1627.

•• *Proceed eastwards.*

Diamond-shaped wooden panels bearing arms are displayed on the walls of both aisles. They are funeral hatchments which were hung outside a house where a person had recently died, and then transferred to the church as a memorial. This custom lasted from the 16C to the early 19C.

Immediately above, it can be seen that the gallery floor has been removed at some period.

The 12C north doorway L was largely renewed in the 19C and appears to have come from elsewhere in the church.

Just past the door, the wall monument commemorates James Spilman, a director of the Bank of England, d.1763, and his wife, Esther, d.1761.

The pulpit R, initially a three-decker, was made in 1658. Its sounding board is original.

The last two aisle windows have been converted to Gothic, the most westerly is Decorated and the other Perpendicular. Both have been restored.

Before the aisle screen is the bust of Francis Wollaston. He died of smallpox aged sixteen in 1684. This is believed to have originally stood elsewhere on the north aisle wall, forming the top section of his monument. The lower section has already been seen in the porch. This monument was divided and its separate parts moved in the 18C when a gallery was constructed.

Below stands a 17C chest. All chests in the church were domestic and bought in 1870.

● *Proceed through the 14C oak screen.*

Against the wall, the urn inscribed 'Caroline' is a monument to Caroline Chinnery, d.1812 and her brother Walter, d.1802.

Above this, a monument commemorates Thomas Leverton, d.1824. He was a fashionable architect and is believed to have been responsible for Bedford Square in Bloomsbury, London's least altered Georgian square.

Robert Smith, a sea captain, d.1697, is commemorated by a carved tomb chest. It has been claimed, without evidence, that the side panel is the work of *Gibbons*.

R of this, a brass floor slab commemorates Henry Austen, d.1638. He was Gentleman of Horse to the Earl of Carlisle.

In the floor in front of this, are the remains of a late-13C tomb, found east of the nave during excavations many years ago. It is believed to be the only part of a Waltham abbot's tomb to survive and possibly commemorates Abbot Reginald de Maidenhyth, d.1289. Its brass has been lost.

Nearby is another 17C chest.

The adjoining floor stone R, with a cross, was brought from elsewhere in the church and originally formed the lid of a 13C coffin.

Before the door stands a 16C chest.

The east wall ahead, probably first built when the tower collapsed in the 16C, was rebuilt c.1860, and marks where this aisle originally continued into the north transept. A low wall was built right across the church at this point in the late 13C to divide the nave, used by the parish, from the remainder of the building, used by the canons.

● *Turn R and enter the nave. Immediately L is the sanctuary.*

Sanctuary. Most furnishings in the sanctuary, including the choir stalls, reredos, altar and altar rails are relatively modern.

Above the altar are the east windows designed by *Burne Jones*, 1861. The carvings around them were designed by *Burges*.

On the east wall, the Romanesque arch was also

filled following the collapse of the tower. The present infilling is 19C.

On both walls, at upper level, are carved imps, 'the imps of Waltham'.

•➤ Proceed to the east wall of the south aisle.

South aisle. This originally led to the south transept. Its east wall was similarly blocked in the 16C and, like the remainder of the east end of the church, rebuilt *c.*1860.

The window was formed in the 19C but the late 13C (?) figure corbel, came from a destroyed section of the church and was probably external.

A 16C alabaster effigy depicts Elizabeth Grey, cousin of Lady Jane Grey the 'Queen of nine days'. This originally lay on a four-poster tomb, demolished in the 18C for the construction of a gallery. It was originally painted.

Below are fragments from a set of late-13C (?) carved mourners which once decorated a tomb chest. They were discovered buried in the churchyard.

•➤ Continue to the south wall.

The large monument commemorates Sir Edward Denny, d.1599, and his wife, Margaret. The Denny family were Lords of the Manor of Waltham. Edward was brother-in-law of Elizabeth Grey, whose effigy has just been seen. His children are also represented below the tomb.

•➤ Proceed westward to the second pillar R.

This pillar was possibly erected over a burial pit as it sank nine inches, thus distorting the bays on either side. It was rebuilt *c.*1860 using a darker stone.

On the north side of the south gallery wall, the projecting piece of timber (and a similar section opposite) forms all that remains of the rood beam.

•➤ Proceed to the wooden screen of the Lady Chapel L.

Lady Chapel. The screen to the Lady Chapel was made in 1876. It is believed that the south wall of the church originally continued here and the chapel could only then be entered externally.

•➤ Ascend the steps, enter the chapel and turn L.

This chapel, together with its undercroft, was probably added to the church *c.*1345. It is believed to have belonged to the Guild of Our Lady which was abolished in 1548 by Edward VI. The chapel was then used as a school and later a storeroom. Much remodelling took place but the chapel was restored by *Burges* in 1875.

Immediately L, in the arch of the chapel's north wall, stands a damaged late-14C stone Virgin, discovered nearby during recent excavations behind Sun Street. The statue was originally painted and may have stood in the Lady Chapel.

•➤ Continue to the east wall.

The east wall formed the entire south wall of the south transept built *c.*1100. Only a trace of its blocked window, already viewed from the exterior, can be seen internally.

The 'Last Judgement' wall painting, probably *c.*1500, shows evidence of an earlier work.

Two angel corbels are below.

In the corner R is a piscina.

Windows on the south wall had been blocked but were restored in 1875. However, as there were no remains of the original tracery, *Burges* designed this completely.

The window in the west wall is original. On either side are figure corbels.

The painting, R of the door, is by *Henry Holliday*, *c.*1860. It formerly occupied the window in the corner R, facing the nave.

•● *Exit from the chapel L.*

South aisle. Behind the organ console R, a tablet commemorates Thomas Tallis, the 16C 'father of English church music'. He was organist at Waltham from 1538 until 1540 and later became Henry VIII's Master of the Chapel Royal.

Rivet holes on the pier, third from the east, are probably remnants of the fixing of the gilt metal zigzag decoration.

•● *The door L leads to the undercroft. Descend the steps.*

Undercroft. The vaulted undercroft of the Lady Chapel was probably the chapel of the guild of the church. In it were deposited parishioners' bones from the churchyard which had been disturbed by grave digging and masses were said for their souls.

Local Quakers were imprisoned here in the 17C following the Restoration.

Display panels relate the history of Waltham.

South aisle continued. Carvings of beasts on the south doorway L are original.

The west gallery, which houses the organ, was reconstructed *c.*1860. Fixed to this are the arms of Elizabeth I. All other galleries were removed in the 19C.

Part of the organ, presented in 1819, survives, but it has been much remade and repositioned.

•● *Proceed towards the west wall.*

At this end of the church are further examples of late 13C alterations from Romanesque to Gothic.

The late-13C Purbeck marble font, L of the door, was remodelled in the 19C and its present cover was made at the same time. It was originally square and decorated with plain arches.

•● *Exit from the church L and follow its south facade to the east end. Continue eastward to the stone marking Harold's alleged burial place.*

Location 2	**KING HAROLD'S BURIAL PLACE**

By tradition, the body of Harold II was brought to Waltham Abbey after his death at the Battle of Hastings in 1066 and buried behind the high altar of the church which he had founded. A stone has been erected at the point where this is believed to have stood.

•• Turn L and proceed diagonally to the north-east corner of the green.

Location 3	**CLOISTER PASSAGE** *late 12C*

Two bays survive of this passage that originally led northward from the north-east corner of the cloister, no trace of which survives.

The east cloister fitted against the west wall of the north-east transept and the south cloister against the choir. The south part of the west cloister was built against the east wall of the north-west transept and its north part then continued against a domestic building, possibly a storehouse, later part of the abbot's residence. The north cloister would almost certainly have been built against the south wall of another domestic building, probably the refectory.

•• Ascend the steps immediately R of the passage entrance. Turn L and proceed diagonally ahead to

Location 4	**STONEY BRIDGE**

This was built in the late 14C to facilitate access to the abbey's farm buildings which lay to the east. It is sometimes erroneously referred to as 'Harold's Bridge'.

•• Return southward and follow the path to the remnants of the gatehouse.

Location 5	**GATEHOUSE**

This was built *c.* 1369 when the abbey was granted a licence to defend itself.

Large red bricks on the adjoining 14C south wall L are a very early example of the use of this material in medieval England.

On the south side of the gatehouse, part of an angle turret survives. Foundations of a corresponding north turret remain under the water.

•• Follow the path L towards the church.

The late-17C vicarage stands L of the tower.

•• Pass the church and follow Church St ahead.

No 4, *c.* 1500, is timber-framed but was stuccoed later.

Lychgate House, L through the archway, has a *c.* 1400 core but the remainder is 17C.

•• Continue ahead to the pedestrianized Market Place.

Location 7	**MARKET PLACE**

Market Place was probably laid out *c*. 1200 by the abbey, which had acquired control of the area. by grant of Richard I in 1189. The Romans and Saxons had also been active in the vicinity.

Although the south side was unsympathically redeveloped in the 1960s, much of interest remains, particularly for the pub enthusiast.

On the north side, the section of the **Welsh Harp** L including the archway is 16C, the remainder is 17C.

•● Continue clockwise around Market Place.

The **Queens Arms** may be 16C.

A plaque on the wall of the **Green Dragon** describes the Moot Hall that stood in the centre of Market Place from *c*. 1200 until 1670. This functioned chiefly as a courthouse. From 1670 until 1852 it was replaced by the Market House. In the centre of Market Place, dark bricks outline the position of the **Moot Hall**.

•● At the north side of Market Place turn R and continue ahead to the pedestrianized Sun Street.

Location 7	**SUN STREET**

Like Market Place, Sun Street was laid out *c*. 1200. Much of it, especially the south side and its passageways, consist of houses built between the 16C and 19C.

•● Follow the first passage L to the car park. Turn L.

The wall R at the far end follows the line of the south wall of Waltham Abbey Church's south-east transept. One of its 10ft-high buttresses remains. Nothing else survives above ground from the canons' part of the church.

•● Return to Sun Street L.

The Sun R, part *c*. 1500 and part 17C, gave its name to this street, previously called East Street.

•● Continue ahead to the end of the street and the Epping Forest District Museum R.

Location 8	**EPPING FOREST DISTRICT MUSEUM**

39–41 Sun Street (Lea Valley 716882)

The two houses were converted in 1981 to accommodate the museum.

No 41 was built *c*. 1520. It originally possessed a jetty (projecting upper floor) on its street front. The roof was raised by half a storey *c*. 1634 to provide attics.

No 39 was built in the 18C but much altered and 'Tudorized' *c*. 1900 at the same time as **No 41**.

•● Enter the museum.

Exhibits include outstanding 16C oak panelling, probably from the Waltham abbot's house. It is carved with the pomegranate emblem of Catherine of Aragon and devices connected with Waltham's last abbot.

The 14C stone head may represent Edward III.

The skeleton of an abbot is exhibited.

Old farming implements from various farms in Epping Forest district are displayed.

Temporary exhibitions are frequently held.

Return westward. First L South Place.

Nos 2 and **3** were constructed as one building *c.* 1600.

Return to Sun St L and continue ahead through Market Place to Church St. L Leverton Way. Cross the road to the bus stop and take any westbound bus to Waltham Cross.

Alternatively, if not viewing the medieval cross, alight from the same bus, but earlier, at Waltham Cross Station (BR).

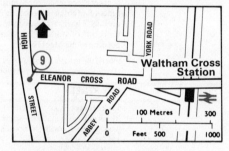

Location 9   **WALTHAM CROSS**

Eleanor, beloved Queen of Edward I, died at Harby, near Lincoln, in 1290. Her body was brought to Westminster Abbey for burial and the sorrowing King ordered crosses to be erected wherever her body had rested on its journey southward. Twelve crosses were made but only three survive, outside Northampton, Geddington and here at Waltham.

The master masons of Waltham Cross were *Nicholas Dymenge* and *Roger Crundale*, some of the carving being by *Robert de Corfe*. The original effigies of Eleanor, which stood beneath canopies, were carved by *Alexander of Abingdon*.

The cross has been carefully restored several times since 1830 and no 13C work appears to have survived. The three original statues of Eleanor are now in the Victoria and Albert Museum; they have been replaced by replicas.

Eleanor's body actually rested in Waltham Abbey's church, one mile distant, not where the cross stands.

Cross to the south side of Eleanor Cross Rd. Turn L and continue to Waltham Cross Station (BR).

Hampstead

Due to its narrow, winding streets lined with 18C cottages, a hilltop position and the bucolic heath, Hampstead has the strongest rural feel of all London's villages. The early 19C residence of poet John Keats and Fenton House, an outstanding William and Mary mansion, may be visited.

Timing Any day is suitable but Fenton House closes Tuesday and Friday and throughout the winter. Hampstead is the best place to be after one of London's infrequent snow falls. Due to its height and distance from the river the snow keeps crisper and cleaner longer than elsewhere in the capital and the 'village' becomes a living Christmas card. Tobogganers and skiers take over the heath and ice skaters replace the ducks on the ponds.

Suggested connection Continue to Highgate. It should be possible to add Ken Wood to the Hampstead itinerary but more will prove tiring.

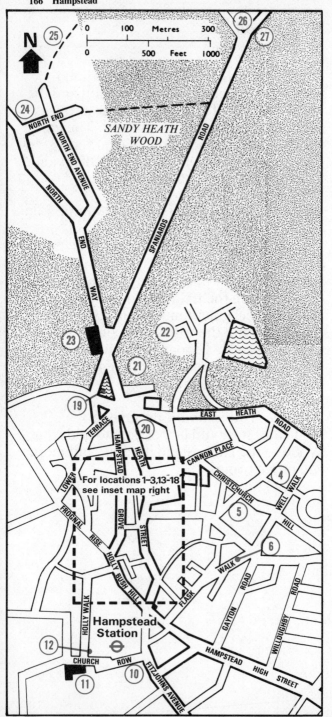

For locations 1–3, 13–18 see inset map right

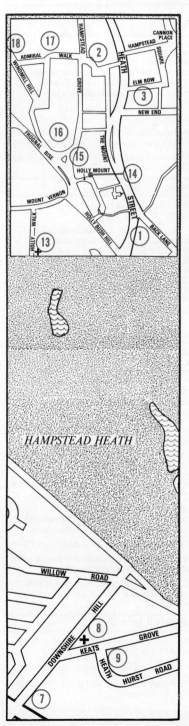

Locations

 1 Heath Street
 2 Mount Square
 3 Elm Row
 4 Well Walk
 5 Burgh House
 6 Flask Walk
 7 Downshire Hill
 8 St John's Chapel
 9 Keats' House
10 Church Row
11 St John
12 St John's Cemetery
13 St Mary
14 Holly Bush
15 Romney's House
16 Fenton House
17 Admiral's House
18 Grove Lodge
19 Whitestone Pond
20 Heath Street Art Exhibition
21 Hampstead Heath
22 The Vale of Health
23 Jack Straw's Castle
24 Old Bull and Bush
25 Old Wyldes
26 The Spaniards
27 Tollhouse

Start *Hampstead Station, Northern Line (London's deepest at 180 ft). Exit R Heath St.*

Location 1	**HEATH STREET**

Heath Street serves as the High Street of Hampstead village. Most properties at the southern end are late 19C and 20C; more picturesque 18C examples are seen later.

•● Second L Hollybush Steps. First L Golden Yard.

A wall plaque on the wall of **No 7**, L, explains how the yard's name derived from the Goulding family.

•● Return to Heath St L. First L The Mount leads to Mount Square.

Location 2	**MOUNT SQUARE**

This is a typical small Hampstead square of 18C cottages.

•● The path, first R, leads to Heath St. Cross the road immediately. Ahead Hampstead Square. The path first R leads to Elm Row, a short terrace of cottages.

Location 3	**ELM ROW** *c.1720*

These cottages make up one of Hampstead's oldest terraces.

•● Return to Hampstead Square. First R Cannon Place. First R Christchurch Hill. Second L Well Walk. Proceed ahead to No 13.

Location 4	**WELL WALK**

The springs that made Hampstead a popular health spa in the 18C were discovered here *c.*1700 but now a memorial fountain outside No 13 is the only reminder.

*•● Cross the road, turn R and proceed to **No 40**.*

This was one of the many Hampstead homes of the painter John Constable. An ever expanding family was the chief reason for his frequent moves. Constable's paintings of early-19C Hampstead are mostly displayed at the Victoria and Albert Museum and the Tate Gallery.

Before moving to Downshire Hill, Keats lived with his brother in a house, now demolished, which stood by the side of the Wells tavern.

•● Return northward. First L East Heath Road.

Immediately L is the entrance to Foley House, built in 1698 for the proprietor of the spa.

•● Follow the southern continuation of Well Walk. Third R New End Square. Proceed to the first house R.

Location 5	**BURGH HOUSE** *1703*

New End Square

Open Wednesday– Sunday 12.00–17.00. Admission free.

Burgh House was named after a local vicar who resided here in the 19C.

•● Enter the house.

Immediately R, the panelled music room displays works of local artists.

*◗ Return to Well Walk. First R Flask Walk.
Follow the upper walkway.*

Location 6	**FLASK WALK**

This street is so-named because the Well Walk
spa water was bottled here in flasks for sale in
London.

Nos 19–27 form a Victorian terrace with Regency
style porches and bow windows added later.

The **Flask Tavern**, 1873, is built on the site of the
old Thatch'd House inn where the spa water was
bottled.

*◗ Continue to the end of the paved section, L
Hampstead High St. Eighth L Downshire Hill.*

Location 7	**DOWNSHIRE HILL**

Begun in 1815, the houses are designed in a wide
variety of styles.

Location 8	**ST JOHN'S CHAPEL** *S. P. Cockerell (?) 1818*
Downshire Hill	The chapel retains its original galleries, box pews and pulpit.

*◗ Exit L Keats Grove. Proceed towards the end
and cross the road.*

Location 9	**KEATS' HOUSE 1816**

Keats Grove
(435 2062)

*Open Monday–
Saturday 10.00–13.00
and 14.00–18.00.
Sunday 14.00–17.00.
Admission free.*

This was built as two semi-detached residences.
Poet John Keats moved into the house L in 1818
and stayed there with his friend Charles Brown
for two years. Meanwhile, Fanny Brawne came
to live in the adjoining house and they became
engaged. 'Ode to a Nightingale' was written in
Charles Brown's garden.

Keats memorabilia and some furniture,
contemporary with his period although not
original to the house, are displayed.

*◗ Exit R. First L South End. First L Willow Rd.
First L Downshire Hill. R Hampstead High St.
Fourth L Perrins Lane leads to Fitzjohns Avenue
R. First L Church Row.*

Location 10	**CHURCH ROW** *1720*

This, one of Hampstead's oldest existing streets,
is little altered apart from the block of mansion
flats on the north side.

◗ Continue ahead to St John's.

Location 11	**ST JOHN** *Sanderson 1745*
Church Row	The church, which was built later than the present houses in Church Row, replaced an earlier building.

Its chancel and transepts were added by *Hesketh*
in 1843.

Unusually, the tower is at the east end.

◗ Enter from the north transept.

The interior, with the altar at the west end, was
remodelled by *F. P. Cockerell* in 1873.

The pulpit is original but the altar and reredos are late 19C.

•▶ Exit R and return to the east end of the church. Turn R. The path ahead is signposted to the tomb of John Constable, at the end sited behind railings. Exit from the churchyard L by the main gate facing Church Row. Cross the road to St John's Cemetery.

Location 12	**ST JOHN'S CEMETERY**

This cemetery was laid out in 1811 as an additional burial ground for the parish. Tombs of several famous residents in the south-east corner, may be seen from Church Row R to L as follows: Anton Walbrook the actor, George du Maurier the cartoonist, Hugh Gaitskell, leader of the Labour party 1955–63 and Kay Kendall, actress wife of Rex Harrison.

•▶ Continue westward. First R Holly Walk follows the west side of the cemetery. Pass Benham's Place, dated 1813, and continue ahead to Holly Place.

Location 13	**ST MARY** *1816*
Holly Place	

St Mary's was one of the earliest post-Reformation Catholic churches to be built in London. The church originally served French immigrants who had escaped from the revolution. General de Gaulle worshipped here while in exile during the Second World War. Its front was remodelled and stuccoed in 1830.

•▶ Continue ahead. Second R Mount Vernon. First R and first L the path leads to Holly Bush Hill. Cross the road immediately where the railing ends. Proceed ahead to Holly Mount. In the corner L is the Holly Bush.

Location 14	**HOLLY BUSH**
Holly Mount	

This Georgian pub was originally built as the stables to Romney's House nearby. It still has a village atmosphere.

•▶ Exit R and return to Holly Bush Hill R. First R Hampstead Grove.

Location 15	**ROMNEY'S HOUSE** *1797*
5 Hampstead Grove	

The house was built as a studio for the painter, George Romney.

•▶ Continue ahead. On the corner L are the gates of Fenton House.

Location 16	**FENTON HOUSE** *1693*
Hampstead Grove (435 3471)	

Fenton House is the oldest and most important building in Hampstead and typical of the William and Mary period. It is administered by the

The house and grounds are open April–October, Saturday–Wednesday 11.00–18.00. March Saturday and Sunday only 14.00–18.00. Admission charge to the house; the grounds are free. Occasional concerts are held at Fenton House and Shakespeare is performed in midsummer.

National Trust. The architect and first owner of the property are both unknown and its present name commemorates the merchant's family that owned the house in the late 18C.

The gates facing Romney's House are designed in the style of *Tijou* and led to the original main entrance.

☛ *Proceed ahead following Hampstead Grove to the present main entrance.*

The colonnade was built early in the 19C to link the two wings and the door on this side then became the main entrance.

Flanking the door are statues of a shepherd and shepherdess by *Cheere*.

Early in the 18C a clock had stood above this door and the property was then known as the Clock House.

Internally, many rooms were enlarged in the 18C by removing the partition walls. Fenton House, together with its 18C furniture and porcelain, was bequeathed to the nation in 1952. Displayed in several rooms are pieces from the Benton Fletcher collection of keyboard instruments which were brought here in 1952. Harpsichord students may play them by prior arrangement.

☛ *Exit L. First L Admirals Walk.*

| Location 17 | **ADMIRAL'S HOUSE** |

Admiral's Walk

This early 18C house, once the residence of the Victorian architect George Gilbert Scott, has been much altered. For many years it was alleged that an eccentric admiral, Matthew Benson, had retired here in the late 18C and fired a cannon from the flat roof on public occasions. It has recently been confirmed, however, that he lived elsewhere in Hampstead.

☛ *Proceed to the next house.*

| Location 18 | **GROVE LODGE** |

Admiral's Walk

Galsworthy wrote most of the 'Forsyte Saga' in this house where he lived from 1918 to 1935.

☛ *Continue ahead. First R Windmill Hill. Cross Lower Terrace and Upper Terrace and proceed to the heath. The footpath ahead crosses the heath to Whitestone Pond.*

| Location 19 | **WHITESTONE POND** |

Once a horse pond, this is now a popular venue for children's boats in summer and a skating rink in winter.

North-west of the pond, Harrow's church can still be seen, as in Constable's day, perched on its distant hill.

☛ *Proceed clockwise around the pond to Heath St R.*

Location 20	**HEATH STREET ART EXHIBITION**

During the summer, an open-air art exhibition is held in this part of Heath Street; all items are for sale. It has been recorded that in the early 1930s one stall specialized in original watercolours by *Paul Klee* at 15 shillings (75p) each. They are now, of course, worth many thousands of pounds.

•● After viewing the exhibits return northward to Hampstead Heath R. Descend the steps opposite Jack Straw's Castle. First R enter Hampstead Heath.

Location 21	**HAMPSTEAD HEATH**
The heath is always open to the public.	

Many fresh water springs surface on the heath, and this led to Hampstead's popularity with washerwomen in the 16C. Most of London's forgotten rivers, now subterranean, have their sources here, including the Tyburn, Westbourne and Fleet. A long battle took place throughout the 19C to protect the 800 acres of parkland and woods from development; fortunately the conservationists won. Hampstead Heath merges with Parliament Hill Fields to the south, Golden Hill Park to the west and Ken Wood to the north. There are comprehensive views south-eastward to the City.

•● Follow the path R and descend the hill. At the end of the path through the heath turn L. The Vale of Health village lies ahead.

Location 22	**THE VALE OF HEALTH**
Hampstead Heath	

This small village is situated like an oasis in the heath. Until the 18C its site was a swampy area known as Hatches Bottom. It was then drained so that houses could be built and renamed to reassure would-be developers. A legend that it gained its name because the inhabitants survived the 1665 plague is untrue. Some lanes are just four feet wide.

•● Follow the path first R (L of Chestnut Cottage). Turn L at the next path. At the road turn R. First L Byron Villas. Proceed ahead to the fairground.

This small fairground is permanent. The famous Hampstead Heath fair which takes place on August Bank Holiday is sited further north.

•● Follow the path R to the pond.

The Vale of Health pond is one of three large ponds in Hampstead Heath.

•● Return to Byron Villas. At the end turn L. First R Villas on the Heath. Follow the path R and the first path L. The path ahead leads to Jack Straw's Castle.

Opposite the inn is **Heath House**, a detached 18C mansion.

Location 23	**JACK STRAW'S CASTLE**

Although an 18C inn, the building was remodelled and castellations added in 1964. Its name commemorates Wat Tyler's henchman Jack Straw who led a riotous mob that allegedly assembled nearby in 1381.

•• *Continue ahead to the Old Bull and Bush inn, a ten minute walk.*

•• *Alternatively, and preferably, take any westbound bus to the inn.*

•• *Alternatively, to shorten the itinerary, second L Spaniards Rd. Take bus 210 northward to either the Spaniards (Location 26) or the Iveagh Bequest, Ken Wood (page 176).*

Location 24	**OLD BULL AND BUSH**
North End Way	

'Come, come, come and make eyes at me, down at the Old Bull and Bush' was a popular Victorian music hall song which is still well known and maintains the fame of this low-ceilinged 18C inn.

It was originally a farm and, although remodelled in the 1920s, many interesting features remain.

Photographs of theatrical artists decorate the walls.

•• *Exit L. First L North End. First L North End Avenue. Follow the bridle path at the end. Old Wyldes lies to the L.*

Location 25	**OLD WYLDES** c.*1588*

Until the 1970s, Wylde's was a farmhouse, the last in the area to operate. It is Hampstead's oldest property but was heavily restored following a fire in 1982.

•• *Return to North End. Turn L at Breed Cottage. Continue ahead to the path which leads through Sandy Heath Woods to Spaniards Rd L. Proceed to the Spaniards inn.*

Location 26	**THE SPANIARDS**
Spaniards Row	

Allegedly, the name of this 18C inn commemorates a Spanish ambassador who lived here when it was a private house.

There is a rear garden for summer drinks and snacks.

•• *Continue ahead.*

Location 27	**TOLLHOUSE**
Spaniards Road	This was one of three toll points between Hampstead and Highgate, making this an expensive route. No toll is now requested but the picturesque 18C house is preserved.

●● *Cross the road and return by bus 210 to Jack Straw's Castle. Descend Heath St ahead to Hampstead Station, Northern Line.*

●● *Alternatively, if continuing to Highgate, take bus 210 outside The Spaniards to the Iveagh Bequest, Ken Wood (page 177). Ask for the request stop before the main entrance. Cross Spaniards Rd and enter the grounds. The second path L, between the piers, leads to the house.*

Highgate

The Iveagh Bequest of Ken Wood includes the house remodelled by Robert Adam for Lord Mansfield in the late 18C. Outstanding old master paintings are displayed in what are regarded as some of the finest rooms in England. Highgate, like Hampstead nearby, retains many period properties in picturesque streets, including Cromwell House, a rare Carolean survivor, built during the Civil War. Highgate's old cemetery contains what is regarded as the country's finest collection of Victorian necrophilia and can once again be visited.

Timing Any day is suitable, but if preceding with Hampstead bear in mind that Fenton House closes Thursday and Friday.

Suggested connections Precede with a brief visit to Hampstead.

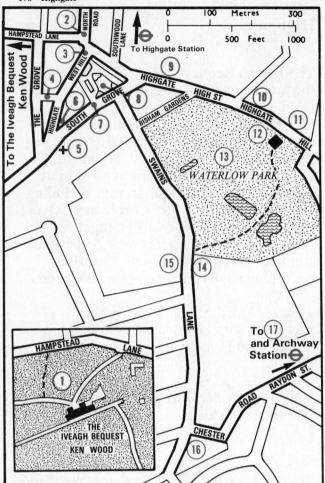

Locations
1 The Iveagh Bequest
2 North Road
3 Highgate West Hill
4 The Grove
5 St Michael
6 The Flask
7 South Grove
8 Pond Square
9 Highgate High Street
10 Highgate Hill
11 Cromwell House
12 Lauderdale House
13 Waterlow Park
14 Highgate East Cemetery
15 Highgate West Cemetery
16 Holly Village
17 Whittington Stone.

Start *Archway Station, Northern Line. Exit L and take bus 210 to Ken Wood. Ask for the request stop which follows the stop for the main entrance.*

Alternatively, continue from Hampstead as indicated on page 174.

| Location 1 | **THE IVEAGH BEQUEST** |

Ken Wood

*Open daily, April–
September, 10.00–
19.00. February–
March and October,
10.00–17.00.
November–January,
10.00–16.00. House
and grounds
admission free.*

*Temporary
exhibitions are
occasionally held in
the first floor rooms.
Admission charge.*

*Open air concerts are
held in the grounds
during summer
evenings. Admission
charge.*

London is fortunate to possess, in Osterley, Syon
and Kenwood, three great houses which retain
late 18C decor, little altered, by one of Europe's
greatest interior designers, *Robert Adam*.
Kenwood's library is regarded as particularly
outstanding. Lord Iveagh bequeathed the
grounds and house together with his art
collection to the nation in 1928.

Kenwood replaced an earlier house *c.*1730 and
was enlarged and altered for Lord Mansfield by
Adam between 1765 and 1775. It seems that the
new owner wanted the house to be known as
Mansfield House but the name Ken Wood, which
strictly applies to the grounds (originally Caen
Wood), has always been more popular although
when applied to the house the spelling is
Kenwood.

The portico and top storey were added to the
north facade by *Adam* but both wings were
extensions built by *George Saunders* in 1793,
following the Adam style.

•● *Turn R and proceed around the house anti-
clockwise to the south facade.*

The design of the south facade is entirely the
work of *Adam*.

Immediately L, the Orangery was first built as a
separate structure. Adam linked it with the
house, but it can be seen that it lies slightly at an
angle.

At the east end, this elevation was made
symmetrical by the addition of a library, entirely
the work of *Adam*.

•● *Return to the north facade and enter the
house.*

Some contemporary furniture is seen, but most of
the original pieces designed by Adam have been
dispersed.

Entrance Hall. The ceiling painting is by *Zucchi*.

Paintings by *Romney* and *Reynolds* are
displayed.

•● *Turn L and proceed through the* **East Hall**
which incorporates the main stairway.

Marble Hall. This was part of the additions by
Saunders in Adam style.

•● *Turn L to the dining room.*

Dining Room. Outstanding paintings include:
'Guitar Player', *Vermeer,* 'Self Portrait',
Rembrandt, 'Madonna and Child', *Rubens* and
'Man with Cane', *Hals*.

•● *Return to the Marble Hall and continue
ahead.*

Vestibule. This was built by *Adam* to connect the
Library with the house.

There are paintings by *Angelica Kauffmann*.

Library. This is regarded as the greatest room at Kenwood, and one of *Adam's* finest interiors.

Sofas and armchairs in the Library were originally designed for Spencer House, St James's, by *James 'Athenian' Stuart c.*1760.

The paintings are by *Zucchi*.

● Return to the Vestibule and continue ahead.

Lord Mansfield's Dressing Room and **Parlour.** The Parlour was originally two rooms which were linked early in the 19C. British paintings displayed include 'View of Dordrecht' by *Cuyp* and 'Fishermen on a Lee Shore' by *Turner*.

● Continue ahead.

Lady Mansfield's Dressing Room. Adam's furniture designs are exhibited.

Housekeeper's Room. This was added by *Adam* to connect the Orangery with the house. Displayed are Italian landscapes.

The Orangery. Originally an out-house this may have served later as an orangery. *Adam* connected it with the house. It is at a slightly different angle to the rest of the south facade.

Works by *Gainsborough* and *Van Dyck* are displayed

● Turn L.

Lobby. The painting 'Miss Murray' is by *Lawrence*.

Music Room. This room was added by *Saunders*.

Exhibited are paintings by the English school.

● Return to the Lobby. Turn L and proceed to the bookshop and hall. Continue to the East Hall and ascend the stairs to the exhibition rooms (not always open).

The first room possesses a fireplace by *Adam* in the Chinese style.

Generally exhibited in the rooms are 18C and 19C jewellery from the Hull Grundy collection and Lady Maufe's collection of antique shoe buckles. Temporary exhibitions replace this in the summer.

● Return to the entrance hall and exit L. The second path L is signposted to Dr Johnson's Summerhouse on the west side of the garden.

Dr Johnson's Summerhouse. The summerhouse was brought here in 1962. It had originally been erected in the grounds of Streatham Park, the residence of Dr Johnson's friends the Thrales, where the doctor often stayed.

● Exit L.

The grounds of Ken Wood were laid out with the advice of *Humphrey Repton c.*1796.

● Cross the lawn to the path L.

The lake below is crossed by a Palladian style bridge designed by *Adam*.

An open air concert bowl overlooks the lake.

Passed L are outbuildings constructed in purple bricks by *Saunders*. They now house a cafeteria.

Continue ahead and exit to Hampstead Lane. Cross the road and take Bus 210 to North Road, Highgate Village. From the bus stop return towards Hampstead Lane.

| Location 2 | **NORTH ROAD** |

Late Georgian houses occupy much of the west side.

A. E. Housman wrote 'A Shropshire Lad' at **No 17**.

Continue ahead. L Highgate High St.

The High Gate stood outside Ye Olde Gate House inn and, at 400ft, was London's highest tollgate. It was erected in the 14C by the Bishop of London but demolished in 1769.

Continue ahead.

| Location 3 | **HIGHGATE WEST HILL** |

Nos 47 and **46**, after Ye Olde Gate House, are notable early Georgian houses, built in 1729.

Opposite, **Nos 51–53** are early 19C.
No 54, late 17C, was formerly a farmhouse.

First R, opposite The Flask, follow the short road to The Grove.

| Location 4 | **THE GROVE** |

Nos 6–1 were built in 1700 and are judged to be Highgate's finest row of period houses.

The poet Samuel Taylor Coleridge lived at **No 3** from 1823 until his death in 1834.

At the end of The Grove R, an arched gatehouse (No 4) leads to Witenhurst. The west wing of the mansion R is late 17C but the remainder is a modern pastiche of the William and Mary style.

Cross The Grove to Highgate West Hill L.

| Location 5 | **ST MICHAEL** *Vulliamy 1830* |
| Highgate West Hill | |

The chancel was added by *Street* in 1881.

A tablet on the floor of the nave marks where Coleridge is buried.

Exit and cross the road.

| Location 6 | **THE FLASK** |
| Highgate West Hill | |

Part of this village-type pub with its small garden dates from 1767. It was founded in 1663 and the manor's court once sat here.

Exit L to South Grove.

| Location 7 | **SOUTH GROVE** |

Many distinguished houses are built on the south side R.

No 17, **Old Hall**, was built in 1671 on the site of an earlier building. It has been refronted.

No 14, **Moreton House**, was built in 1715.

No 10, **Church House**, *c*.1750.

No 9, **Russell House**, *c*.1730. Its stucco was added later.

●▶ Cross the road to Pond Square opposite.

| Location 8 | **POND SQUARE** |

Two village ponds that once stood here surrounded by grass were filled in 1864.

On the west side, **Nos 5** and **4**, of red brick, are late 17C.

●▶ Return to South Grove L. L Highgate High St. Cross the road to the east side.

| Location 9 | **HIGHGATE HIGH STREET** |

No 82 retains its Georgian wooden arcade.

●▶ Return southward down the hill.

No 62 also retains its arcade.

No 46 with a bowed shop front was built in 1729.

No 42 is mid 18C.

Outstanding houses on the opposite side are **No 23**, **Englefield House**, *c*.1730, and **Nos 17–21**, 1733.

●▶ Continue ahead to Highgate Hill remaining on the east side.

| Location 10 | **HIGHGATE HILL** |

On the east side, **No 130**, **North Gate House**, and **No 128**, **Ivy House**, are late 17C.

●▶ Continue ahead. Follow the upper walkway.

The Bank is a terrace of four outstanding houses.

No 110 is early 18C.

Nos 108, **Lyndale House**, and **106**, **Ireton House**, were originally one residence also built early in the 18C.

●▶ Proceed to No 104, Cromwell House.

| Location 11 | **CROMWELL HOUSE** *c.1638* |

104 Highgate Hill

Admission situation unknown due to change of ownership.

This is a rare example of a Carolean house, built during the Civil War. Cromwell House, which has no known connection with Cromwell, was commissioned by a merchant named Springell. Its brickwork is influenced by the Flemish style.

●● *Enter the house.*

The balustrade is of pierced panels carved with military trophies.

Some contemporary doorcases, panelling, fireplaces and ceilings remain although much restored.

The upper rooms were destroyed by a fire in 1865.

●● *Exit and cross Highgate Hill to Lauderdale House in Waterlow Park immediately ahead.*

Location 12	**LAUDERDALE HOUSE** *c.1580*

Waterlow Park

Open Tuesday–Friday, 11.00–16.00. Sunday, 12.00–17.00. Admission free.

Lauderdale House was built in the 16C but remodelled *c.*1800. It now serves as a local authority tea house. The building was named to commemorate its 17C owner, the Earl of Lauderdale, who was Charles II's Scottish Secretary and a member of the ruling cabal. He also owned Ham House.

It was allegedly here that Nell Gwyn threatened Charles II that unless he gave their illegitimate son a title she would drop him from the window. The King replied 'Save the Earl of Burford'.

●● *Enter the house.*

In the hall R is a 17C niche referred to as 'Nell Gwyn's Bath'.

The main south-east room retains some 17C woodwork.

Fire in 1963 badly damaged the late-17C staircase but it has been well restored. Above, the 18C lantern is a reproduction.

●● *Exit from the rear of the house via the cafeteria and proceed to the walled garden. Leave this garden from the south-west corner R. Follow the path L. The next path R leads downhill through the park to Swains Lane.*

Location 13	**WATERLOW PARK**

The park was presented to the local authority, together with Lauderdale House, by Sir Sydney Waterlow in 1889 to provide a 'garden for the gardenless'. It incorporates the grounds of three properties: Lauderdale House, Hertford House and Fairmont; the last two were demolished.

From the east side, the huge bust of Karl Marx may be seen in the adjacent cemetery.

●● *Continue southward through the park. Pass the ponds and proceed to the Swains Lane exit L. The entrance gate to the Highgate East Cemetery is L. Proceed ahead.*

Location 14	**HIGHGATE EAST CEMETERY**

Swains Lane

*Open daily, 09.00–
16.30.
Admission free.*

This, the new cemetery was opened as an extension to the existing Highgate Cemetery opposite, in 1854. In both sections, totalling 37 acres, approximately 166,000 people are buried in 51,000 tombs. Graves of the famous on the east side include the father of Communism, Karl Marx, d.1883, (bust by *Laurence Bradshaw*, 1956), writer George Eliot, d.1880, pioneer cinematographer William Friese-Greene, d.1921 and actor Sir Ralph Richardson, d.1984.

●● *Exit R and cross Swains Lane to the old cemetery.*

Location 15	**HIGHGATE WEST CEMETERY**

Swains Lane
(348 0808)

Open daily for guided tours only, on the hour April–September, 10.00–16.00. October–March last tour at 15.00. Groups by arrangement only. Admission free but donations are welcome.

This, the oldest section of Highgate Cemetery, opened in 1839. It was privately owned and run for a profit in the grounds of what had been Lord Ashurst's manor house. The area was laid out by *Geary* and *Bunstone Bunning* and contains what is considered to be the finest collection of Victorian necrophilia in the country.

Outstanding buildings include the Egyptian Avenue, Lebanon Circle and Terrace Catacombs.

After the Second World War maintenance ceased, nature took over, and the old cemetery was closed to the public. Due to the efforts of the Friends of Highgate Cemetery, visits can once again be made and a long campaign of rehabilitation has begun.

Michael Faraday, the scientist, and Dr Jacob Bronowski, famous for 'The Ascent of Man' television series, are buried here.

●● *Exit R and proceed down Swains Lane to the Chester Road corner L. Cross to Holly Village and proceed through the gatehouse.*

Location 16	**HOLLY VILLAGE** *Darbishire 1865*

Swains Lane

The Gothic Revival gatehouse leads to a green surrounded by eight detached residences designed in similar style. The village was built by Baroness Burlett Coutts for her retainers. Its pastoral setting just fails to overcome the horrors that High Victorian Gothic gives to many people.

●● *Exit R Swains Lane. First R Chester Rd. Where the road bends R, turn L Raydon St. L Dartmouth Park Hill, First R Highgate Hill. Proceed to the Whittington Stone at the bottom of the hill R.*

Location 17	**WHITTINGTON STONE**

Highgate Hill

The statue of a cat commemorates the spot where, tradition has it, Dick Whittington turned back towards London. He was Lord Mayor in 1397, 1406 and 1420. The stone was laid in 1821, and restored with a new bronze cat in 1935.

●● *Continue ahead to Archway Station, Northern Line.*

Islington

Islington is a mixed area with many Georgian streets and squares, a sylvan stream and part of a Tudor manor house. It was once a holiday village for City dwellers due to its supposedly health-giving springs. Islington was particularly fashionable in the Elizabethan period and again during the 18C spa boom.

Timing Any day is suitable. The Camden Passage flea market operates Wednesday and Saturday. A return visit would be necessary Saturday night to view the Elizabethan interiors of Canonbury Tower.

Suggested connections Islington may be preceded or followed by any itinerary described in *London Step by Step*.

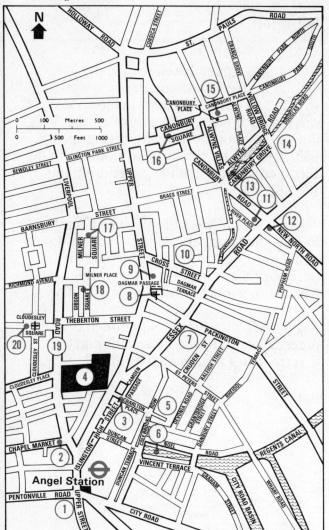

N

Metres
0 100 500
0 500 Feet 1000

Locations

1 The Angel
2 Chapel Market
3 Camden Passage
4 Business Design Centre
5 Colebrook Row
6 Regent's Canal
7 Old Queen's Head
8 St Mary
9 Little Angel Marionette
   Theatre
10 Cross Street
11 Mecca Bingo Hall
12 The Three Brewers
13 New River
14 Marquess Tavern
15 Canonbury House
16 Canonbury Square
17 Milner Square
18 Gibson Square
19 Liverpool Road
20 Cloudesley Square

Start *Angel Station, Northern Line. Exit R City Rd. Second R Islington High St. Cross the road.*

Location 1	**THE ANGEL**
Islington High Street	The area known as The Angel commemorates an ancient inn, first recorded in the late 16C and rebuilt several times, which stood on the corner of Pentonville Road and Islington High Street. As the inn occupied land owned by the knights of St John it probably began as a monastic hospice.

The present building was developed in 1899 as a Lyon's Corner House but is now a bank. Note the angel theme on the external tiles.

Much of the surrounding area is being redeveloped.

● *Proceed northward to Upper St. Second L Liverpool Rd. First L Chapel Market.*

Location 2	**CHAPEL MARKET**
Market operates Monday–Saturday.	A lively fruit and vegetable market is held in the street. Unfortunately, its eel and pie restaurant, a rare survivor, closed in 1985.

● *Return to Liverpool Rd R. First L Upper St. Cross the road where the pedestrian barrier ends and proceed to The Mall antique arcade. Turn R and L following Islington High St to Camden Passage.*

● *Alternatively, proceed through the arcade (open Tuesday–Saturday). Exit R. First L Islington High St. Continue ahead to Camden Passage.*

Location 3	**CAMDEN PASSAGE**
Flea market operates Wednesday and Saturday.	This alleyway is now lined with antique shops; most were built in the early 19C. Robert Carrier's gourmet restaurant did much to bring Camden Passage to prominence in 1966; it closed in 1984.

At the north end of the passage, 'Georgian Village' consists of Georgian-style antique shops located within a Victorian building.

● *Return southward along Camden Passage. Second R Charlton Place leads to Upper St.*

From Charlton Place can be seen the rear of the Business Design Centre.

Location 4	**BUSINESS DESIGN CENTRE**
Upper Street	The building was designed by *Peck* in 1862, as the Royal Agricultural Hall, specifically to house the annual Smithfield livestock show which took place here until 1938. It was also the first venue of the Motor Show, in 1898, and before the Second World War the hall was the venue for Crufts dog show.

Long derelict, the vast glass-roofed building with its 150ft clear span was converted to its present purpose in 1986, with showroom, conference and exhibition facilities.

● *Return along Charlton Place, cross Camden Passage and continue ahead. R Colebrooke Row. First R Duncan Terrace. Proceed ahead.*

Location 5	**COLEBROOKE ROW**

Colebrooke Row was completed in 1768 and Duncan Terrace in 1799. The New River once flowed between them but was covered over in 1861 and replaced by gardens.

Nos 56 and **57** Colebrook Row are little changed.

•➡ First L Vincent Terrace. Descend the steps L to the towpath and continue to the end. Cross the Danbury St bridge L. First R descend again to the towpath.

Location 6	**REGENT'S CANAL** *1874*

This extension of the Grand Union Canal runs eastward above ground from here to the Thames at Limehouse. The City Road Basin lies R, with views to the City. In the other direction, the canal runs underground through a tunnel westward as far as Caledonian Road, before emerging at Little Venice where it joins the main canal to the Midlands. Boat trips are available on the western section.

•➡ Return along the towpath beneath the bridge (ignore the 'No right of way' notice). At the tunnel,the path R leads to Colebrooke Row R. Third R St Peter's St. First L Cruden St. Second L Packington St. First L Essex Rd.

Location 7	**OLD QUEEN'S HEAD**
Essex Road	

This undistinguished pub has some very exceptional features. Its predecessor, the Queen's Head, was an ancient inn that stood on the site of Lord Burleigh's house. It was allegedly patronized by Elizabeth I, Essex and Ralegh, who was responsible for the licencing of taverns. When the inn was rebuilt in 1829 its rare Elizabethan stone fireplace, with carved overmantel and surrounding panelling, was kept and incorporated in the rear bar. The design features dogs attacking a man.

In the main bar, the ceiling, plastered in 1830, incorporates the Prince of Wales's feathers in its design.

•➡ Exit and cross Essex Rd R. Second L Dagmar Terrace. Cross to Dagmar Plassage which runs parallel with it. Immediately before the Little Angel Marionette Theatre, enter the gate and proceed through the churchyard to St Mary's.

Location 8	**ST MARY**
Upper Street	

The church was probably first built in the Elizabethan period. It was rebuilt by *Dowbiggin* in 1754 – a rare period for churches. The nave was rebuilt following Second World War bomb damage.

•➡ Return to Dagmar Passage L. Immediately L is the Little Angel Marionette Theatre.

Location 9	**LITTLE ANGEL MARIONETTE THEATRE**

14 Dagmar Passage
(226 1787)

*Performances
Saturday and Sunday
15.00.*

This is London's only puppet theatre. It was opened in 1961 in what had been a temperance hall. Some of the fittings, including the tip-up seats, came from the famous Collins Music Hall that stood nearby from 1897 until it closed in 1958.

•● *Continue ahead and bear R to Cross St.*

Location 10	**CROSS STREET**

Most of the south side R was built *c.*1760 and forms one long terrace. The doorways of **Nos 35** and **33** are designed in Adam style.

Opposite, on the north side, **No 24**, **The Pattern House**, was built as a warehouse in the Regency period and its crane and pulley are original.

•● *Second L Essex Rd. Proceed to the River Place junction (first L). On the corner is the Mecca Bingo Hall.*

Location 11	**MECCA BINGO HALL** *1930*

Essex Road

This was built as the Carlton cinema with its exterior design incorporating ancient Egyptian themes.

The interior has ancient Roman motifs and can be visited if convenient.

•● *Cross Essex Rd L. Proceed to the New North Rd corner (first R).*

Location 12	**THE THREE BREWERS**

Essex Road

This Victorian tavern possesses exceptional green majolica ceramics and a fine chimney-piece of carved mahogany.

•● *Exit and cross Essex Rd. Ahead Canonbury Rd. First R Canonbury Grove. Pass through the gate L to New River Gardens. Follow the path R.*

Location 13	**NEW RIVER**

This artificial river was created in 1613 by Sir Hugh Myddelton to provide London with an alternative fresh water supply to the Thames. The New River originally ran from Hertfordshire to Clerkenwell but most of its southern course was covered over *c.*1860 when a conduit was formed. The use of the conduit was discontinued in 1946 but the river still supplies London north of Stoke Newington.

Decorative ponds at this point occupy part of the rivers' original course but the water is now pumped in. Public gardens, rare in Islington, border them and they run northward almost to St Paul's Road.

•● *Continue to the second exit. Ahead Willow Bridge Rd and the Marquess Tavern.*

Location 14	**MARQUESS TAVERN**
Willow Bridge Road	This Victorian inn, one of Islington's more genteel, possesses some contemporary furnishings, fireplaces and pine wainscotting. *•● Exit to Willow Bridge Rd R. Cross the bridge. Second L Canonbury Place.*

Location 15	**CANONBURY HOUSE (TOWER THEATRE)**

Canonbury Place
(226 5111)

The tower is open for viewing at the end of Saturday evening theatre performances. Admission free.

These remnants of a Tudor manor house are the only pre-Georgian buildings to survive in Islington and the tower itself contains London's best domestic Elizabeth interiors.

The estate was granted by Ralph de Berners to St Bartholomew's Priory in 1253 and became known as Canon's Burgh, hence the name of Canonbury. Prior Bolton built a mansion here early in the 16C, designed as a three-sided rectangle with a central courtyard open to the north. Canonbury Tower stood at its north-west corner and the garden lay to the south.

After the Dissolution the estate was acquired by the Crown and Canonbury House was occupied briefly by Thomas Cromwell. It was purchased by John Spencer, a Lord Mayor and City cloth merchant, in 1570. He carried out much rebuilding and left it to his daughter in 1610, after finally forgiving her for marrying Lord Compton against his wishes. It is alleged that Elizabeth I herself arranged the reconciliation by tricking Spencer into becoming godfather to an 'unfortunate infant', his own grandchild.

Coincidentally, not only does this part of Spencer's country house survive, but also his town house, Crosby Hall, which has been re-erected at Chelsea. Compton was later created Earl of Northampton and his descendants still own the freehold of Canonbury House although none have lived here since the 17C.

Tenants included Francis Bacon in 1616, Oliver Goldsmith in 1762, and Washington Irving early in the 19C. Ephraim Chambers, creator of *Chambers Dictionary* also lodged here.

Sir Edmund Halley had an observatory in Islington in the late 17C from where he made observations of the comet that now bears his name. It may well have been situated in this tower, which would, as Islington's highest building, have been eminently suitable for that purpose. Unfortunately, however, the Northampton family cannot locate the tenancy records for the period. Halley headed his letters simply 'Islington' or 'London' and verification will probably never be obtained.

John Dawes leased the property in 1770, demolishing most of the south range and building houses in their place. They faced a new street, which is also confusingly called Canonbury Place, and one of the houses that he built is called, equally confusingly, Canonbury House.

Existing from the Tudor period are: the tower, two garden houses and part of the east range.

Canonbury Tower. Only this section of the house is open to the public. It is at present leased to the Tavistock Repertory Company.

•► Enter L of the tower through the attached early-19C house.

The adjoining house, R, is 18C.

Interiors of the two main rooms, the **Spencer Room** 1570, on the first floor and the even grander **Compton Room** 1599, on the second floor, both possess richly carved Elizabethan panelling and chimney-pieces.

There is a mysterious bullet hole in the Compton Room wall, possibly made during the Gordon Riots.

Above is the **Inscription Room** with a list of kings and queens of England from William I to Charles I painted on the wall, *c.* 1625. This is believed to have been a schoolroom.

In the summer visitors are taken to the roof with its fine views over London. The roof was flattened comparatively recently.

•► Exit L.

A circular tour of the area occupied by the original house and its garden now follows.

•► First L Alwyne Villas. First L Canonbury Place.

On the corner is the 18C Canonbury House.

The other houses, built in 1780, are an early London example of stucco work.

•► Continue to the end of Canonbury Place.

From here can be seen the old east range of Canonbury House.

East Range West Side. The gables denote a Tudor origin.

•► Return to Alwyne Villas L. Proceed to No 4.

South-west Summer House. Attached to No 4, Alwyne Villas, is a three-storey octagonal Tudor building which stood in the south-west corner of the garden of Canonbury House. Above the door can be seen Prior Bolton's rebus (punning pictorial representation of a name) of a bolt and a barrel (tun).

•► First L Alwyne Rd. Proceed to the Alwyne Place corner.

South-east Summer House. This building stood in the south-east corner of the garden. One storey has been added and the summer house possesses little of its original Tudor appearance.

•► First L Alwyne Place.

East Range East Side. Unlike the rear, seen previously, the front of this range is not gabled. It is partly used by a children's play group.

There are some Tudor ceilings and fireplaces which visitors may be shown if convenient.

•● First L Canonbury Place, second L Canonbury Square.

Location 16   **CANONBURY SQUARE**   *Leroux c.1800*

The square is little altered although rather spoilt by traffic. It is pleasanter to walk through the central garden. Canonbury's long established literary associations were continued in this square by Evelyn Waugh, author of *Brideshead Revisited*, who lived at **No 17A**, and George Orwell, author of *1984* and *Animal Farm*, at **No 27B**.

•● Continue ahead. Cross Canonbury Rd and proceed through the central gardens to Canonbury Lane. Second L Upper St. First R Barnsbury St. First L Milner Square.

Location 17   **MILNER SQUARE**   *Roumieu and Gough c.1840*

The architecture here marks a half-hearted break with the Classical style and the effect is strangely sinister. Milner Square lies in Barnsbury, an area roughly half a mile square, which was laid out by *Cubitt, c.*1820. Its name commemorates Ralph de Berners who granted the manor to St Bartholomew's Priory.

•● Ahead Milner Place leads to Gibson Square.

Location 18   **GIBSON SQUARE**   *c.1840*

Although contemporary with Milner Square, Gibson Square remains entirely Classical in style.

•● At the end R Theberton St. Cross Liverpool Rd.

Location 19   **LIVERPOOL ROAD**

The road was originally called Islington Back Road but renamed in 1826 to honour Prime Minister Lord Liverpool. Many terraces date from 1818 and 1834, and provide some of London's longest stretches of late Georgian architecture. Some side streets also date from the same period.

•● Immediately ahead is Cloudesley Square.

Location 20   **CLOUDESLEY SQUARE**   *c.1825*

The houses are late Georgian, but in the centre is a Gothic Revival church, Holy Trinity, built by *C. Barry* in 1826. It was one of the earliest designs in this style by the future architect of the Houses of Parliament.

•● First L Cloudesley St. L Cloudesley Place. R Liverpool Rd. Fourth R Upper St. First L City Rd. L Angel Station, Northern Line.

The East End

Since the arrival of the Huguenots in the 17C, much of London's 'East End' has provided a haven for ethnic groups, each of which has moved on and been replaced, in turn, by others. All have left their mark on the area. Much of the East End has a rundown, even derelict, appearance, and its charms are for those with catholic tastes. By the end of the century redevelopment of the old docklands will have completely changed the East End along most of its riverside. Highlights are the Sunday street markets, riverside pubs, three great Hawksmoor churches and two unusual museums.

Timing All the major street markets are in full swing on Sunday morning. The Bethnal Green Museum of Childhood closes Friday. The Whitechapel Art Gallery closes Saturday.

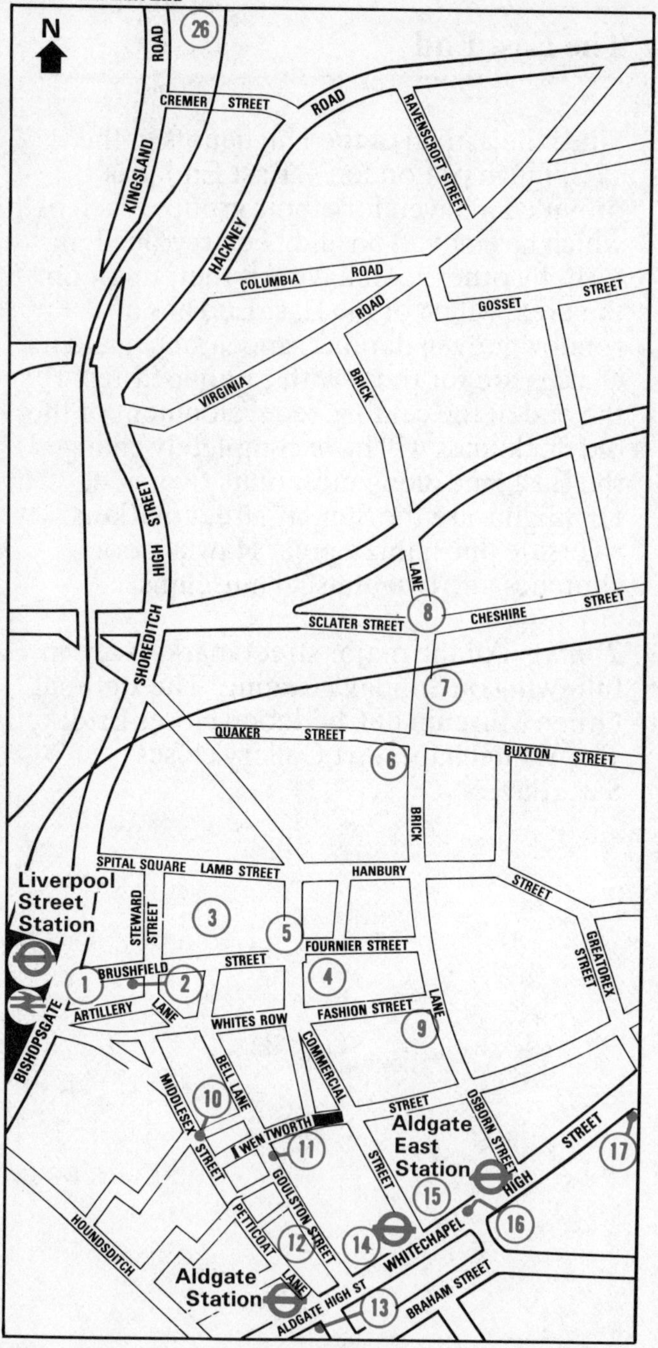

N

26

KINGSLAND ROAD

CREMER STREET

RAVENSCROFT STREET

HACKNEY ROAD

COLUMBIA ROAD

GOSSET STREET

VIRGINIA ROAD

BRICK LANE

SHOREDITCH HIGH STREET

SCLATER STREET

8

CHESHIRE STREET

7

QUAKER STREET

BUXTON STREET

6

BRICK

SPITAL SQUARE

LAMB STREET

HANBURY

STREET

Liverpool Street Station

STEWARD STREET

3

5

FOURNIER STREET

GREATOREX STREET

BRUSHFIELD

1

2

STREET

4

BISHOPSGATE

ARTILLERY LANE

WHITES ROW

FASHION STREET

9

LANE

COMMERCIAL

BELL LANE

MIDDLESEX STREET

10

STREET

WENTWORTH

11

Aldgate East Station

15

OSBORN STREET

17

HIGH STREET

HOUNDSDITCH

PETTICOAT LANE

GOULSTON STREET

12

14

WHITECHAPEL

16

Aldgate Station

13

ALDGATE HIGH ST

BRAHAM STREET

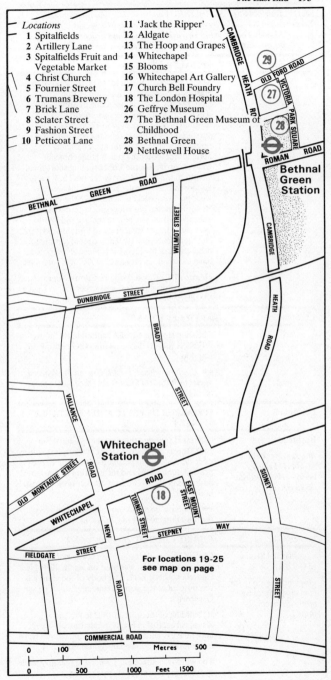

Locations
1 Spitalfields
2 Artillery Lane
3 Spitalfields Fruit and Vegetable Market
4 Christ Church
5 Fournier Street
6 Trumans Brewery
7 Brick Lane
8 Sclater Street
9 Fashion Street
10 Petticoat Lane
11 'Jack the Ripper'
12 Aldgate
13 The Hoop and Grapes
14 Whitechapel
15 Blooms
16 Whitechapel Art Gallery
17 Church Bell Foundry
18 The London Hospital
26 Geffrye Museum
27 The Bethnal Green Museum of Childhood
28 Bethnal Green
29 Nettleswell House

For locations 19-25 see map on page

Start   *Liverpool Street Station (BR), Central, Circle and Metropolitan Lines. Leave the station by the Bishopsgate exit. L Bishopsgate. Third R Artillery Lane. Turn R at the Steward St junction and proceed to No 56A Artillery Lane ahead. The area known as Spitalfields has now been entered.*

Location 1	**SPITALFIELDS**

Many consider Spitalfields to be the heart of the East End. St Mary's Priory and Hospital at Lollesworth, the original name of Spitalfields, was founded in 1197. It was refounded as the hospital of St Mary Spital in 1235 and the surrounding meadows then became known as Spitalfields. The area remained basically agricultural until the French Huguenot silk weavers arrived in the 17C, bringing short-lived wealth to the area. Wages were low, however, and by 1807 the employees of the silk weavers were poverty-stricken. After 1825 the industry slowly dwindled but a few specialized weavers existed until shortly before the Second World War. Jews began to migrate to Spitalfields from Northern Europe *c.*1880 and spread rapidly to other parts of the East End. They, in their turn, have mostly been replaced by Asian immigrants.

Henry VIII's Royal Artillery Company practised at Spitalfields in the 16C and street names such as 'Artillery' and 'Gun' commemorate this.

Location 2	**ARTILLERY LANE**

The shop front of No 56A, added to the house *c.*1757, is judged the finest mid-18C example in London.

•➤ Continue ahead. First L Crispin St. Proceed ahead to Bushfield St and cross the road to the market.

Location 3	**SPITALFIELDS FRUIT AND VEGETABLE MARKET**

Bushfield Street

Market operates Monday–Friday, 06.00–1100; Saturday 0600–09.30.

Charles II founded this market by Charter in 1682. It was originally a street market, but houses were demolished to permit its extension to the present dimensions and the erection of market buildings in 1922. The fruit market is the largest in Britain.

•➤ Continue ahead to Commercial St and cross the road immediately to Christ Church.

Location 4	**CHRIST CHURCH** *Hawksmoor 1727*

Commercial Street (247 7202)

Open occasionally for concerts, otherwise apply at the crypt door L.

Christ Church, the largest of Hawksmoor's three East End churches, was built under the Fifty New Churches Act of 1711. The body of the church is reminiscent of the same architect's St Alfege at Greenwich.

Rebuilding of the spire in 1822 led to the disappearance of many of its decorative appendages. Other alterations to the church were made following damage by lightning in 1841.

The windows, altered in 1866, have recently been restored to their original appearance.

•➤ Enter the church.

Because of dilapidation, and the restoration work being carried out, the church is only open on special occasions. It is intended that Christ Church will eventually match its original internal appearance with the restoration of north and south galleries and box pews.

The church retains its original font and lectern, together with a pulpit converted from the 18C reader's desk. These will be relocated in the church when building work is completed. Unfortunately, the reredos disappeared many years ago and its design is unknown.

Although Christ Church is virtually an empty shell, Hawksmoor's skilful handling of special elements is, as usual, immediately apparent.

The flat coffered ceiling of 1729 has been restored.

On the north wall of the chancel is the monument to Sir Robert Ladbroke, Lord Mayor of London, by *Flaxman*.

Facing this, on the south wall, is the Edmund Peck monument by *Dunn*, 1737.

Exit R. First R Fournier St.

Location 5	**FOURNIER STREET**

Fournier Street, built 1718–28 as Church Street, became a fashionable address for merchants and Huguenot silk weavers. Some of the houses, with their original carved doorways, are under restoration. Most retain their weaving attics with deep rear windows.

No 2 was designed by *Hawksmoor* as the Christ Church rectory.

The large building at the end of the street L is a measure of the changing nature of the East End. Built as a church for French Protestants in 1743, it later became a Wesleyan chapel, then a synagogue, and is now a mosque serving the Asian community (London Jamme Masjid).

The sundial beneath the pediment is dated 1743.

 If it is Sunday continue ahead. L Brick Lane.

 Alternatively, R Brick Lane. First R Fashion St (Location 9).

Location 6	**TRUMANS BREWERY**
Brick Lane	A brewery has stood on the site since the 16C.

Trumans buildings now combine 18C warehouses with a modern office block.

Horse-drawn drays have been reintroduced for local deliveries from the brewery.

Location 7	**BRICK LANE**
Street market operates Sunday 09.00–14.00	Although short, the Sunday street market in Brick Lane is one of London's liveliest. It begins with fruit and vegetables after the railway bridge and then becomes a general market.

Indian shops and restaurants proliferate on either side.

In the 17C the lane was used by carts transporting bricks to Whitechapel from the nearby kilns.

At the Bethnal Green Road end the Beigel Bakery sells beigels with various fillings – a Jewish speciality popular in the United States, though rare in London.

← Return along Brick Lane. Second R Sclater St.

Location 8	**SCLATER STREET**

This extension of Brick Lane market has even more variety. At the far end caged birds and animals have been sold for many years. Megaphone-wielding animal lovers are protesting against the conditions here and the trade is diminishing.

← Return to Brick Lane and cross to Cheshire St ahead where the market continues. Return to Brick Lane L. Proceed to the railway bridge. Fifth R (after the bridge) Fashion St.

Location 9	**FASHION STREET**

A unique factory, known as the Fashion Street Arcade, occupies the south side. It was built as a bazaar and designed with Islamic features by *Abraham Davis* in 1905. This was prophetic, considering the later influx of Asian immigrants to the area. On a sunny day a photographer could 'prove' he had returned from an area much further east than London's East End.

← Cross Commercial St and proceed ahead to White's Row.

No 5 White's Row, L, is early 18C. Its original carved door surround survives, but the ground floor and basement windows have been altered.

← Cross Crispin St. Ahead Artillery Lane. Where the road bends R continue ahead following Artillery Passage. L Sandys Row leads to Middlesex St.

Location 10	**PETTICOAT LANE (MIDDLESEX STREET)**

Market operates daily but is extended on Sunday.

The market in this street is less varied than it once was and tends to be dominated by new clothing. Most stallholders are still Jewish and many give an amusing 'spiel'.

The street was first recorded as Hog Lane, but the name Petticoat Lane was established by the 17C due to the Spitalfields silk industry. It was renamed Middlesex Street in 1832.

← Third L Wentworth St. First R Goulston St.

Location 11	**'JACK THE RIPPER'**

Five prostitutes were brutally murdered in Whitechapel between 31 August and 9 November 1888. Their killer wrote to the police, signing himself 'Jack the Ripper'. The Whitechapel Murders were never solved and no one was ever charged. Many theories have been, and still are, confidently propounded. 'Suspects' have included Montague Druitt, Sir William Gull, Thomas Cream, Frank Miller, George Chapman, Sir Robert Anderson, Assistant Commissioner of

Police, painter Walter Sickert and the future
Edward VII's eldest son, the Duke of Clarence.
Also implicated have been Queen Victoria
herself, Prime Minister Lord Salisbury and Sir
Charles Warren, Commissioner of Police. Most
of the victims lived in the streets of Spitalfields,
around Christ Church, but their mutilated bodies
were found between Aldgate and Whitechapel
Road.

Apart from his letters, the only clues left by The
Ripper were in a block of tenement flats that
stood, until 1986, on the east side of Goulston
Street, known as Goulston Street Buildings (later
Wentworth Dwellings). An apron, stained with
the blood of Catherine Eddowes, was placed at
the foot of the stairs to Nos 118–119. Above it, on
the wall, were the words 'The Juwes are the men
who will not be blamed for nothing'.
Surprisingly, Police Commissioner Warren
ordered the immediate removal of the writing
before it could be examined.

None of the streets where the bodies were found
are of particular interest but some devoted
'Ripperologists' still like to seek them out. The
victims, with the dates and locations of the
murders, are as follows.

Mary Nicholls 31/8	Durrard Street (behind Whitechapel Station), then Bucks Row.
Annie Chapman 8/9	29 Hanbury Street, in the backyard.
Elizabeth Stride 30/9	Henriques Street (off Commercial Road), then Duffield's Yard, Berner Street.
Catherine Eddowes 30/9	Mitre Square (Aldgate).
Marie Jane Kelly 9/11	Millers Court, Dorset Street; demolished for the Fruit and Wool Exchange.

Some believe that the first victim was Martha
Tabrum, alias Turner, whose body was
discovered on 7 August 1888 on the first floor of
George Yard Buildings off Whitechapel Road.
As suddenly as they began, the Ripper murders
ended. Their fascination for criminologists is as
strong as ever.

●● *Return to Wentworth St L. L Middlesex St. At
the end cross Middlesex St by subway to the south
side of Aldgate High St. Cross to the Hoop and
Grapes opposite.*

Location 12	**ALDGATE**

The name of the area is derived from an ancient
gate, one of six that punctuated London's wall.
First built by the Romans, it was named
Ealdgate, i.e. old gate, by the Saxons. The gate
was rebuilt in the 12C and Geoffrey Chaucer
leased a room in it from 1374–85. It was again
rebuilt in 1609 but, with the other city gates,
dismantled in 1761. The structure was re-erected
at Bethnal Green but only stood for a short time.
Its original site was at the junction of Aldgate
(the street) and Duke's Place. No trace of the
gate survives.

Location 13	**THE HOOP AND GRAPES**
Aldgate High Street	This late-17C inn was dismantled and reconstructed in 1983 but, in spite of good intentions, little of interest survives internally. The legend of a tunnel leading directly to the Tower of London has not been confirmed. It is reputedly the oldest licensed house in the City and was probably founded in the 12C.
	Exit and return to the west side of Middlesex St. L Whitechapel High St.

Location 14	**WHITECHAPEL**
	The parish of St Mary Whitechapel was established *c*.1338. Its name derives from a chapel built in the 13C. 'Nuisance' trades, such as metal working, were transferred here from the City in the 17C. When East European Jews migrated to the area 1880–1914 the second-hand clothing trade developed.
	Continue eastward passing Aldgate East Station's west entrance and proceed to Blooms restaurant.

Location 15	**BLOOMS**
90 Whitechapel High Street (247 6001)	London's best known kosher restaurant was opened in Brick Lane in 1920 by Morris Bloom, who developed a new method of pickling salt beef. There is a take-away counter and a restaurant. Blooms is packed Sunday lunchtime, so arrive early if dining. It opens at 11.30.
	Exit L. Continue ahead towards Aldgate East Station's east entrance. The Whitechapel Art Gallery stands immediately before this.

Location 16	**WHITECHAPEL ART GALLERY** *Townsend 1899*
Whitechapel High Street *Open Sunday–Friday 11.00–17.50. Admission generally free but there is occasionally an entrance charge.*	The art gallery was specifically built to house avant-garde exhibitions. The Art Nouveau-style building, with arts and crafts reliefs, is reminiscent of Townsend's Horniman Museum at Forest Hill. Above the door is a mosaic 'The Sphere and Message of Art' by *Walter Crane*.
	Exit L and proceed to the public library immediately past the station entrance.
	On the wall L ceramic tiles illustrate a haymarket in the High Street in 1786. This market remained until 1927.
	Cross the road. Turn L and proceed eastward to the Fieldgate St junction (third R).

Location 17	**CHURCH BELL FOUNDRY**
34 Whitechapel Road	This was the world's most famous bell foundry, probably established *c*.1420. Records go back to the 16C when the company moved from Houndsditch to Whitechapel; it transferred to the present site in 1738. The offices and shop were originally built in 1670 as the Artichoke Inn and its cellars survive. There was a coachyard at the rear which has now been taken up by the foundry. Big Ben and Philadelphia's Liberty Bell were both cast here.

Inside the shop, above the door, is the original template of Big Ben.

●● Exit R and continue ahead.

Passed R is the East London Mosque, built in 1984.

Location 18	**THE LONDON HOSPITAL**

Whitechapel Road

The hospital was founded in 1740 by John Harrison, a surgeon, and transferred here *c*.1751 when fields still remained in Whitechapel. Part of the original building, by *Mainwaring*, is incorporated in the present structure.

●● Cross to Whitechapel Station, East London Line, and train to Wapping.

●● Alternatively, taxi to St George-in-the-East (Location 19), pausing to view its exterior, then continue in the taxi to the Prospect of Whitby (Location 21).

The church exterior can be seen later in the middle distance from Shadwell Basin.

Location 19	**ST GEORGE-IN-THE-EAST** *Hawksmoor 1726*

Cannon Street Road

The church was bombed in the Second World War and only the exterior has been restored to its original appearance.

The tower is judged to be Hawksmoor's most distinctive.

Internally, the church is modern and dates from the 1964 restoration by *Bailey*.

●● Continue by taxi to The Prospect of Whitby.

●● Alternatively, from Wapping Station exit R Wapping High St. First R Wapping Wall.

Location 20	**WAPPING**

Founded by the Saxons, initially on the north side of the river, Wapping derives its name from Waeppa's people. Wapping High Street was built up in the 16C but the area was essentially fields and market gardens until the London docks were formed in the 19C. Boat building and allied trades became established and later the warehouses, which still dominate the area, were built. It was at the Red Cow tavern in Wapping High Street that Judge Jeffrey, 'the hanging judge' was captured in 1688 attempting to escape to France. No trace of this building survives.

Oliver's Wharf, Wapping High Street, became, in 1973, the first warehouse to be converted into apartments. It marked the beginning of the extensive London dockyards redevelopment programme, due for completion by the turn of the century.

Location 21	**THE PROSPECT OF WHITBY**

57 Wapping Wall

The inn was founded in 1520 but its present facade is Victorian. The famous waterside terrace has views eastward to St Anne, Limehouse.

Formerly known as the Devil's Tavern, the Prospect of Whitby gained its present name in 1777, as a ship from Whitby, ferrying coal from

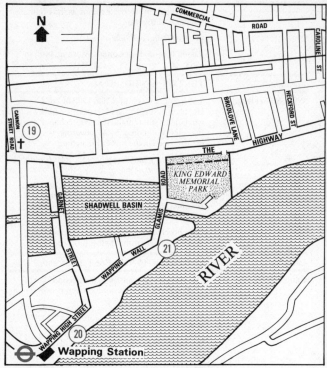

19 St George-in-the-East
20 Wapping
21 The Prospect of Whitby
22 Limehouse

23 Limehouse Basin
24 The Grapes
25 St Anne

the North, was frequently moored outside the inn. This pub specializes in live entertainment and has a first floor restaurant.

The main bar has a low beamed ceiling and the flag stone floor survives.

To the west, exact location uncertain, lay Execution Dock where condemned pirates were hanged and their bodies chained while three tides washed over them. Captain Kidd, the notorious 18C pirate, was executed there.

•• *Exit R. Wapping Wall. Continue ahead to Shadwell Basin.*

Canoeing facilities are provided free of charge on the basin.

The exterior of St George-in-the-East (Location 19) may be seen L with a backdrop of City skyscrapers.

•• *Proceed along Glamis Rd. R. King Edward Memorial Park. Enter and proceed through the park to The Highway. Passed R is Free Trade Wharf, an important part of the London*

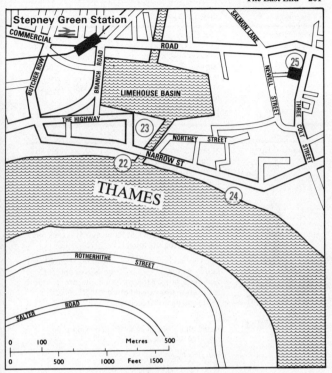

dockyards redevelopment. *Conversion to apartments and offices is underway, First R Narrow St.*

| Location 22 | **LIMEHOUSE** |

The name of this area derives from the lime kilns which functioned in the 14C. Seamen resided here in the 16C and Limehouse later became a shipbuilding centre. London's first Chinatown was established here around the riverside when Chinese sailors began to settle *c.*1880. Although only about four hundred of them ever lived here, their gambling and opium smoking became notorious. Some Chinese restaurants remain, but following the Second World War the Chinese population became centred around the southern section of Soho.

| Location 23 | **LIMEHOUSE BASIN** |

Here the Regent's Canal enters the Thames. The basin was created in the mid 19C but ceased operation in 1969. One quay is now reserved for pleasure craft. The docks R and the basin L provide picturesque views. North-east of the basin, the tower of St Anne's protrudes from a surprising number of trees.

Continue along Narrow St.

Location 24	**THE GRAPES**

| Narrow Street, Limehouse | This Georgian riverside inn was featured by Charles Dickens in *Our Mutual Friend* as the Six Jolly Fellowship Porters. Unfortunately the river bar was 'Tudorized' in the 1960s. The first floor restaurant is open weekdays and gives good views; more important, however, is the riverside terrace. |

Exit R. Third L Three Colt St. L Commercial Rd.

Location 25	**ST ANNE** *Hawksmoor 1724*

Commercial Road

Open for Sunday services only at 10.30 and 18.30

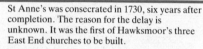

St Anne's was consecrated in 1730, six years after completion. The reason for the delay is unknown. It was the first of Hawksmoor's three East End churches to be built.

St Anne's possesses London's highest church clock.

The interior, with its Greek cross plan, was influenced by Wren's St Anne and St Agnes but the nave is slightly longer.

The roof and most fittings, including the font and pulpit, were renewed by *John Morris* and *P.C. Hardwick* in 1857 following a major fire. Further restoration was carried out by *A. Blomfield* in 1891, and again after Second World War damage.

In the churchard is an unusual pyramid, the origin of which is unknown.

Exit L.

West of the church is Newell St, formerly Church Row. Many 18C houses survive.

Turn R and continue to Commercial Rd. Take bus 5 to Liverpool Street Station. Outside the station, in Bishopsgate, take bus 22, 22A, 48, 149 or 243A to the Geffrye Museum, Kingsland Rd. Cross the road.

Alternatively, and preferably, take a taxi direct.

Location 26	**GEFFRYE MUSEUM**

Kingsland Road (739 8368)

Open Tuesday– Saturday 10.00– 17.00. Sunday 14.00– 17.00. Admission free.

This museum of English decor and furniture opened in 1914, and covers the period from the Tudors to the 1930s.

The buildings were founded as almshouses for the Ironmongers Company with a bequest by a former Lord Mayor, Sir Robert Geffrye, in 1716. Originally, there were fourteen separate houses, each with its own front door; the central section was a chapel.

Shoreditch was an apt choice for the museum as it was, in the 18C, the centre of London's furniture industry.

Exit L. Return by any bus to Liverpool Street Station then train to Bethnal Green Station, Central Line. Exit R Cambridge Heath Rd.

Alternatively, and again preferably, take a taxi direct.

Location 27

THE BETHNAL GREEN MUSEUM OF CHILDHOOD

Cambridge Heath Road (980 2415)

Open Monday–Thursday and Saturday 10.00–18.00. Sunday 14.30–18.00. Admission free.

The building's iron roof, by *Cubitt*, was originally erected as part of the South Kensington Museum, 'The Brompton Boiler', in 1856, on the site of the present Victoria and Albert Museum. It was re-erected here in 1872, encased externally with brickwork, and is now operated by the V & A as their doll and toy department. Exhibits include costumes, dolls' houses, toys, model theatres and puppets.

On the top floor 19C continental furniture, sculpture and decorative art are displayed.

●▶ Exit L. Cambridge Heath Rd. First L a footpath leads through Bethnal Green Gardens.

Location 28

BETHNAL GREEN

'Blida's corner' is believed to be the Saxon origin of Bethnal. Bethnal Green Gardens were the original village green. In the 18C weavers and dyers resided in the area which soon became the poorest in London. Furniture, shoe and clothing manufacturers later took over in Bethnal Green.

●▶ Victoria Park Square

Nos 18–16, immediately ahead, were built *c*.1700

●▶ Proceed to the rear of the museum. Enter the courtyard and turn R to view Netteswell House.

Location 29

NETTESWELL HOUSE *c.1660*

Old Ford Road

This is the oldest surviving property in Bethnal Green. Much restoration and alteration has taken place. The windows were changed from casement to sash in the mid 18C.

●▶ Return to Victoria Park Square L. First L Old Ford Rd.

Nos 21–15 are mid 18C.

●▶ L Cambridge Heath Rd. Continue ahead to Bethnal Green Station, Central Line.

Greenwich

The town is visited mainly for its complex of 17C royal buildings which, viewed from the river, provides one of England's best known vistas. The National Maritime Museum, Old Royal Observatory and the Painted Hall and Chapel of the Royal Naval College now occupy much of this complex and can be visited daily throughout the year.

Timing Monday to Saturday is preferable, allowing a whole day to see the town and its museums. The Royal Naval College does not open until 14.30.

Suggested connections Continue to Blackheath, Charlton or Woolwich if time permits.

Special buses connect Greenwich Pier with the Thames Barrier at Woolwich.

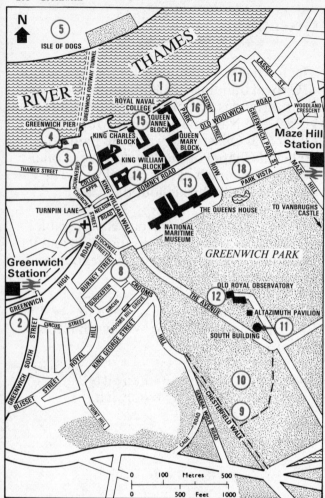

Locations
1 Greenwich from the river
2 Queen Elizabeth's College
3 *Cutty Sark*
4 *Gipsy Moth IV*
5 The Isle of Dogs
6 Greenwich Town Centre
7 St Alfege
8 Crooms Hill
9 Ranger's House
10 Greenwich Park
11 Greenwich Planetarium
12 Old Royal Observatory
13 The Queen's House and National Maritime Museum
14 Royal Naval College
15 George II Monument
16 The Trafalgar Tavern
17 Trinity Hospital
18 Park Vista

Start *Greenwich Station (BR) from Charing Cross Station (BR).*

Alternatively, Greenwich can be reached by river boat, most of which are now almost completely covered. Much of the journey is through London's dockland but when the tide is right it ends with the world famous riverside view of the royal buildings of Greenwich, 'The Queen's View'.

Boats leave Charing Cross Pier (opposite Embankment Station, Bakerloo, Northern, Circle and District Lines) from 10.00 and from Westminster Pier (south of Westminster Station, Circle and District Lines) from 10.30. Calls are made at the Festival Pier and the Tower Pier. Check the time of the last boat if returning by river.

Location 1	**GREENWICH FROM THE RIVER** **'THE QUEEN'S VIEW'**

If a view of the royal buildings is provided from the boat, they are seen as follows:

The buildings, which originally formed the Royal Naval Hospital, but which now house the Royal Naval College (Location 14), are grouped in the foreground.

Directly overlooking the river R is **King Charles Block**.

Behind this lies **King William Block**.

Directly overlooking the river L is **Queen Anne Block**.

Behind this lies **Queen Mary Block**.

The white villa, situated behind this complex in Greenwich Park, is the **Queen's House** which, with its wings linked by the colonnade, houses most of the National Maritime Museum (Location 13).

On the hill, behind R, is the **Old Royal Observatory** (Location 12), now also part of the Maritime Museum.

The large boat R is *Cutty Sark* (Location 3).

The small ketch further R is *Gypsy Moth IV* (Location 4).

From Greenwich Pier proceed ahead to Cutty Sark (Location 3).

Alternatively, if arriving at Greenwich Station, exit to Greenwich High Street and cross the road to Queen Elizabeth's College.

Location 2	**QUEEN ELIZABETH'S COLLEGE** *James Gibson (?) 1817*
Greenwich High Road	The almshouses were founded during the reign of Elizabeth I, *c.*1574, by the historian William Lambarde. They were rebuilt on the same site. *Continue ahead to Greenwich Church St and proceed to the river. Turn L to* Cutty Sark.

Location 3 **CUTTY SARK**

Open Monday–
Saturday 10.30–
17.00. Sunday 12.00–
17.00. April–
September closes at
18.00. Admission
charge.

The *Cutty Sark*, which has lain here in dry dock
since 1954, is the last surviving clipper ship. It
was designed in 1869 specifically for the China tea
trade, which required speedy transport, as higher
prices were paid for early deliveries of each new
season's crop. Later, the boat served the
Australian wool trade and remained at sea until
1922. A crew of twenty were needed to control its
30,000 sq ft of rigging. The name *Cutty Sark* was
inspired by the cutty sark (Scottish for a short
linen nightshirt) worn by Nannie the witch in
Robert Burns's 'Tam O'Shanter'. Nannie is
represented by *Cutty Sark*'s figurehead.

The boat's history is described within, and part of
the world's largest collection of figureheads from
ships' prows is displayed.

•● Exit and proceed ahead to Gipsy Moth IV.

Location 4 **GIPSY MOTH IV**

Open April–October
Monday–Saturday
11.00–18.00. Sunday
14.30–18.00. October
closes at 17.00.
Admission charge.

This 54 ft vessel is the ketch in which Sir Francis
Chichester became, at the age of sixty-six, the
first man to sail around the world single-handed.
Chichester commissioned the boat which was
completed in 1966. He took 226 days to complete
the 29,630 mile journey, landing at Greenwich in
1967. Here he was knighted by Elizabeth II with
the same sword that Elizabeth I had used in the
16C to knight Sir Francis Drake, also at
Greenwich.

•● Exit L to the domed building. This houses the
lift to the Greenwich Foot Tunnel which leads to
the Isle of Dogs on the north bank of the Thames.

•● Alternatively, proceed southward along King
William Walk to Greenwich town centre,
(Location 6). First R College Approach.

Location 5 **THE ISLE OF DOGS**

The tunnel entails a ¼-mile walk in each
direction. A ferry service has been proposed, due
to the new housing developments, and this would
be a great improvement as the walk is tedious and
the tunnel always cold, even on the hottest day.
However, unless visitors by boat have been
lucky, it is the only way of seeing 'The Queen's
View' during a visit to Greenwich.

At the Isle of Dogs proceed to the public gardens
which overlook the river. The view is described in
Location 1.

It is not certain how the Isle of Dogs gained its
strange name. In the Middle Ages the area was
known as Stepney Marsh. The first known
mention of the Isle of Dogs was made in 1588 and
probably referred to the hunting hounds that
Henry VIII kept on 'the island'.

•● Return to Greenwich and proceed past Cutty
Sark *to Greenwich Pier. R King William Walk.*
First R College Approach.

Location 6	**GREENWICH TOWN CENTRE**

Much of the town centre dates from the improvement scheme designed by *Joseph Kay* in the 1830s. The stucco facades of King William Walk, College Approach, Greenwich Church Street and Nelson Road were part of this scheme. The area that they cover was once the site of the 15C monastic establishment of the Observant Friars, dissolved at the Reformation.

●● *Continue along College Approach. First L enter the market.*

The right to hold a market was granted to the hospital in 1700. Fruit and vegetables have been sold here, wholesale only, since 1737. The present covered market was built by *Kay* in 1831. Inscribed above the entrance arch within the market is the motto 'A false balance is abomination to the Lord but a just weight is his delight.'

●● *Return to College Approach L. L Greenwich Church Street. Second L (through the arch) Turnpin Lane. Second R King William Walk. First R Nelson Rd. L Greenwich Church. Cross to St Alfege's Church.*

Location 7	**ST ALFEGE** *Hawksmoor 1714*

Greenwich Church Street

Generally open by appointment only apart from services.

St Alfege's is regarded as one of Hawksmoor's finest churches, however, little survives internally from his time; the steeple is by *James*.

St Alfege was a Saxon Archbishop of Canterbury who was kidnapped by the Danes from his cathedral. A rescue bid failed and he was martyred at sea for refusing to request a ransom in 1012. A 12C church is the first to be recorded here. The roof of the St Alfege that preceded the present building collapsed during a storm in 1710. In that church, Henry VIII had been baptised and Thomas Tallis, the Tudor organist and composer, buried.

The rebuilt body of St Alfege's was the first to be paid for with money allocated under the Fifty New Churches Act of 1711. Initially, the medieval west tower was retained but eventually it was encased by *James* in 1730. His steeple was completely rebuilt in 1813 as a replica.

At the east end, the original railings are punctuated by stone piers, surmounted by urns decorated with cherubs, now rather faded.

●● *Proceed to the west end and, if open, enter the church.*

St Alfege's was gutted by bombs in the Second World War and much was lost.

Little of the original monochrome painting by *Thornhill* in the apse survived apart from that on the pilasters. The remainder has been repainted.

The wrought ironwork is original.

The pulpit is a reproduction.

Undoubtedly the greatest loss was the woodwork by *Gibbons*. However, the carved supports of the Royal Pew in the south aisle survived the conflagration.

Wolfe of Quebec is buried in the crypt.

•➡ Exit to Greenwich High Rd R. First L Stockwell St leads to Crooms Hill.

Location 8	**CROOMS HILL**

Crooms Hill is one of London's oldest known roads, 'crom' being a Celtic word for crooked – the road winds uphill around the park. It has always been the most fashionable street in Greenwich and the west side is lined with 17C and 18C houses, some of which incorporate elements from even earlier buildings.

Most of the east side of Crooms Hill is bordered by Greenwich Park. Noteworthy houses, all on the west side, are passed as follows:

Nos 6–12, 1721.

No 14 is mid 18C.

Nos 16–18, 1656.

Nos 22–24 are late 18C.

•➡ R Gloucester Circus. Continue ahead and turn L.

Gloucester Circus was built by *Searles* in 1791 but only its southern section was completed.

The north side was added, to a different design, in 1840 but much of this was destroyed by Second World War bombing.

•➡ Return to Crooms Hill R.

No 26 is late 18C.

No 32 is early 18C with a late-18C south wing.

Nos 34 and **36** are mid 18C.

*•➡ R **Crooms Hill Grove**.*

The street was developed in 1838. Many ground floor windows have been altered.

•➡ Return to Crooms Hill R.

Nos 42–46, 1818 (Nos 44 and 46, unusually, share a porch).

The **gazebo**, which directly overlooks the pavement, was built in 1672, probably by Wren's assistant *Hooke*. It stands in the garden of The Grange and was commissioned by the Lord Mayor of London Sir William Hooker. The building is much restored.

No 52, **The Grange**, behind its high wall, was built in the mid 17C but fragments of much earlier buildings exist internally. It was formerly known as Paternoster Croft. The west wing was added in the 18C.

Mays Court, **Nos 54–60**, *c.*1770, have recently been converted into flats.

No 66, **Heath Gate House**, *c.*1630, was known until

recently as The Presbytery. It is an early London example of the Dutch style.

Past the 19C church, Our Lady Star of the Sea, **No 68**, now the **Presbytery**, is late 17C.

Park Hall was built by *James* in 1724 and intended for his own occupancy, but the architect eventually decided to live elsewhere. James Thornhill stayed here for a short time while he completed decorating the Painted Hall at the Royal Naval Hospital nearby.

The north wing was added in 1802 and conversion to flats took place in 1932.

Opposite Park Hall, on the west side of Crooms Hill, lies the **Manor House** built *c*.1695 for Sir Robert Robinson, Lieutenant General of the Royal Naval Hospital.

●● *Continue ahead following the footpath.*

Here Croom Hill becomes Chesterfield Walk which overlooks Blackheath. Passed L is the **White House** built in 1694 but its front was remodelled in the 18C. It was occupied by Elizabeth Lawson, the girl courted unsuccessfully by James Wolfe of Quebec, whose parents lived next door in Macartney House.

The main part of **Macartney House**, directly fronting the path R, is late 17C but this was extended on both sides by *Soane* in 1802. Additional extensions were made later in the 19C. The house is now subdivided into flats.

●● *Proceed to the next building, Ranger's House.*

Location 9	**RANGER'S HOUSE**

Chesterfield Walk

Open daily February–October 10.00–17.00. November–January 10.00–16.00. Admission free.

This late-17C residence, previously known as Chesterfield House, was occupied by Philip, 4th Lord Chesterfield and it was probably here that he wrote the famous letters to his son.

Wings were added, to the south by *Ware* (?) in 1750, and to the north in the late 18C.

The house became the residence of the Ranger of Greenwich Park in 1815.

●● *Enter the hall. Turn R.*

Paintings, mainly by the English School, are exhibited in the first room and the south wing's gallery. The Suffolk Collection of family portraits from Charlton Park, Wiltshire, include a famous series of Jacobean portraits by *William Larkin*.

●● *Return to the hall and ascend the stairs.*

On the first floor, the Dolmetsch Collection of Musical Instruments is displayed.

●● *From the rear of Ranger's House enter its grounds and proceed directly to Greenwich Park.*

●● *Alternatively, if visiting Blackheath, exit and follow the path immediately ahead across the heath. Cross General Wolfe Rd and continue ahead to Shooters Hill Rd R. First L Wat Tylers Rd. First R Dartmouth Hill. The Blackheath itinerary may now be joined at location 7 (page 229).*

Location 10	**GREENWICH PARK**

Open dawn–dusk.

This, the oldest of London's ten royal parks, was first enclosed by Humphrey, Duke of Gloucester, in 1427 and later formed the grounds of Greenwich Palace. Deer were introduced in 1515 and remain in the south-east section. The famous French landscape gardener *Le Notre* laid out the grounds for Charles II in 1662. However, his work was not entirely successful, mainly due to the fact that he never came to England and could not, therefore, survey the area. The park was walled-in by James I in 1619 and part of this wall survives. Greenwich Park was opened to the public *c*.1705.

•• Proceed ahead through the rose garden. Bear L and continue north of the tennis courts. Cross the road and proceed to the Greenwich Planetarium which lies ahead behind the trees.

Location 11	**GREENWICH PLANETARIUM** *1899*

South Building
Greenwich Park
(858 4422)

Open during school holidays Monday, Tuesday, Thursday and Friday 15.00. Also some Saturdays in summer 14.30 and 15.30. Planetarium programmes are changed regularly, telephone for details. Admission charge.

The planetarium is situated in the South Building which is part of the Old Royal Observatory. This was built for astrophysics – the study of the structure and lifecycle of stars and planets. Originally, the building housed two large telescopes which are still in use at the Royal Observatory's present home in Sussex. Surmounting the building is the Thompson Dome, named to commemorate the donor of the telescopes. Famous astronomers and instrument makers are recorded on the exterior of the building.

•• Continue northward.

Passed L is the **Altazimuth Pavilion** added to the observatory in 1898.

•• Continue ahead to the Old Royal Observatory enclosure L. Enter and turn L to the Great Equatorial Building.

Location 12	**OLD ROYAL OBSERVATORY**

Greenwich Park
(858 4422)

Open Monday–Saturday 10.00–18.00; Sunday 14.00–17.00. April–October closes Sunday–Friday 17.00; Saturday 17.30. Admission charge. A combined ticket also giving entry to the main building is available.

The Royal Observatory was founded at Greenwich by Charles II in 1675 for astronomical study expressly intended to aid marine navigation. A by-product of this work was the positioning at Greenwich of zero longitude, or the Prime Meridian, which gained universal acceptance in 1884 as the basis for the measurement of time throughout the world. Visitors may straddle the brass strip which represents the Prime Meridian, and thus stand with one foot in the Eastern hemisphere and the other in the Western hemisphere.

Buildings were added to the complex from time to time, until the late 19C, but as the Royal Observatory was moved to the cleaner air of Herstmonceux, Sussex, in 1948, their practical function has almost ended. The Old Royal Observatory now forms an important part of the National Maritime Museum and its historic buildings accommodate many ancient and beautiful instruments which illustrate the development of astronomy and the measurement of time. All exhibits are explained and only a selection are, therefore, described in this book.

Proceed northward.

The buildings are passed from south-east to north-west in reverse chronological order of construction. East of the entrance is the domed Great Equatorial Building.

Great Equatorial Building *1857.* The building was designed to house the observatory's first large telescope (12¾ in). This was replaced by a 28 in model in 1893 and a new, larger dome was built to accommodate it. Second World War bomb damage led to this dome's demolition but it was rebuilt in 1971 when the original telescope was returned from Herstmonceux. The book shop now occupies part of the ground floor.

Exit L and proceed ahead to the Meridian Building. The exterior of this range is passed on the way to Flamsteed House. Its interior is entered and described later.

Meridian Building. Although this long range appears to be entirely mid-18C work, it was extended or remodelled a number of times over a two-hundred-year period from 1676.

The first short, pedimented section passed was completed in 1855, the second section in 1813 and the central section, through which the Greenwich Meridian now passes, was first built in 1809 although remodelled in 1850.

The position of the Prime Meridian is indicated by a brass strip in the courtyard's floor.

Continue ahead.

The final section of the Meridian Building is the oldest and was completed in 1749 as Bradley's New Observatory. At its western extremity it replaced a small Quadrant House constructed in 1725 for Edmund Halley, the second Astronomer Royal and best remembered for predicting the return of the comet that now bears his name.

Turn R and proceed towards the entrance to Flamsteed House.

Flamsteed House *Wren 1675.* The house, together with part of its twin east and west pavilions, marked the commencement of the scheme; ancillary buildings are later additions. It was built to accommodate the first Astronomer Royal, the Rev. Dr John Flamsteed. Previously, Flamsteed had made his astronomical observations from the White Tower in the Tower of London. Wren designed the house 'for the observators' habitation and a little for pompe', but his budget was strictly limited. The foundations of a watch tower, built for Humphrey, Duke of Gloucester, in the 15C, were re-used together with second-hand bricks from Tilbury Fort and wood and metal from the Tower of London.

Externally, the house has changed little.

Amusing examples of economy are the 'stone' dressings that decorate the angles; many are really of wood.

A 17C plaque is inserted in the wall L of the entrance.

Surmounting the north-east turret is a pole supporting a red ball. This was erected in 1833 as the world's first visual time signal. Since that year the ball has been hoisted half-way up the pole at 12.55, raised to the top at 12.58 and dropped precisely at 13.00. Thereby, all passing vessels have been able to set and verify the accuracy of their chronometers. Modern time-keeping equipment, of course, now makes this redundant but the tradition is maintained.

●● *Proceed to the north-east* **Summer House,** *immediately R of the door.*

This summer house was built in 1676 and used by Flamsteed as his Solar Observatory. It was enlarged and remodelled in 1773. Set in the wall, R of the entrance, is Halley's tombstone.

The extension to Flamsteed House, facing its entrance, was added in 1794.

●● *Enter* **Flamsteed House.**

The small building that accommodates the entrance and stairwell is original to the house.

●● *Ascend the staircase to the Octagon Room.*

Octagon Room. *Wren*, who was himself an astronomer, designed this, then known as the Great Room, for observation purposes, and it was used in this way until 1830. The room, which was opened to the public in 1953 is little changed apart from the painting of the woodwork which was originally undecorated.

Flanking the entrance are replicas of the Tompion 17C clocks used by Flamsteed. Early telescopes are also displayed.

Flamsteed had been required to provide his own instruments and after he died his widow insisted on disposing of them. Unfortunately, all that have been traced are three Tompion clocks.

Paintings of Charles II and James II were hung in this room in the 17C but their whereabouts are now unknown. The painting of James II is modern and based on an illustration of the original. That of Charles II, however, is contemporary.

●● *Descend the west stairs ahead and proceed anti-clockwise.*

Halley Gallery. This section was added in 1836 to provide three additional living rooms for George Airy, the seventh Astronomer Royal. Representations of the heavens in the form of spheres, globes, and astrolabes, etc. are exhibited.

Maskelyne Gallery. This, together with the adjoining room, was added *c.*1790 to provide two drawing rooms and a library for the fifth Astronomer Royal, Nevil Maskelyne.

Nocturnal time-keeping instruments and hourglasses are exhibited, together with non-mechanical instruments for measuring time. These include a collection of sundials.

Nathaniel Bliss Gallery. Here is displayed the Harrison Chronometer.

Return to the Halley Gallery and descend the stairs.

Spencer Jones Gallery. This basement room was created in 1911. Exhibits relating to mechanical time-keeping are displayed.

Ascend the stairs. Turn L and proceed first L to the ground floor of Flamsteed House.

Seventeenth-century living rooms. The furniture, although not original, is contemporary with Flamsteed's period. These rooms provided domestic accommodation for the Astronomer Royal until 1948.

Exit from Flamsteed House R. Follow the railings and proceed through the Upper Garden to Flamsteed's Observatory L.

Flamsteed's Observatory. This was originally built by *Wren* in 1676 at the same time as Flamsteed House. Some original brickwork survives but most has been rebuilt.

From here Flamsteed measured the position of the stars and planets – regarded as his most important work.

Enter the building which is now divided into two rooms.

Quadrant House. A contemporary engraving of Flamsteed's 7 ft mural arc, his fundamental measuring instrument, is displayed.

Sextant House. Flamsteed's 7 ft equatorial sextant is represented by a full-size working model.

Proceed from Flamsteed's Observatory to the Meridian Building with which it links.

Quadrant Room. First built by Halley in 1725, this was rebuilt and incorporated in Bradley's New Observatory in 1749. The remainder of this observatory now forms the next two rooms. Two 18C quadrants and Bradley's zenith sector telescope are displayed.

Middle Room. This was designed as a work room, with bedroom above (now an office), for Bradley's assistant. Halley's and Bradley's 18C transit instruments are mounted in this room. The latter was brought from Bradley's Transit Room, seen next, where it had been used to define the Greenwich Meridian from 1750 to 1816.

Bradley's Transit Room. Troughton's instrument, which replaced Bradley's in 1816, is displayed. It was used to define the Greenwich Meridian which continued to pass through this room until 1850.

Airy's Transit Circle Room. The room was built in 1809 but remodelled in 1850 to accommodate Airy's transit circle which, in 1852, replaced Bradley's transit instrument. The Greenwich Meridian was immediately moved 19 ft eastward to pass, as it still does, through this room.

The Greenwich Meridian, or zero degrees longitude, was established by defining an imaginary north–south line across the earth's surface.

Although seamen had used the Greenwich Meridian since 1767 to establish longitudinal positions, the measurement of time varied throughout the world in a haphazard manner. The railways led to the acceptance throughout Great Britain, of Greenwich Mean Time in the 1840s and local British variations then disappeared.

In 1884 the Greenwich Meridian was chosen as the world's Prime Meridian, mainly because most shipping was using charts with Greenwich measurements, and the North American railways based their time zones on Greenwich Mean Time. From 1884, therefore, longitudinal positions were fixed from Greenwich and time zones established throughout the world.

Airy's transit circle is still mounted in this room, although the last of more than 750,000 regular observations was made on it in 1954.

●● *Descend the stairs and return to the Middle Room. Leave the Meridian Building. Turn R and exit from the Old Royal Observatory opposite the Equatorial Building. Turn L and proceed to the gate in the wall. The Shepherd Clock is fixed R.*

Shepherd Clock. This 24-hour clock is permanently fixed at Greenwich Mean Time and is, therefore, one hour different from the time used throughout Britain in summer. It was erected in 1851 and was an early example of an electrically operated public clock.

Standards of Length. Below the clock are standard measurements of Imperial lengths. They were fixed here for public use in 1866.

●● *Return eastward and proceed ahead to the Avenue.*

The statue of Wolfe by *Tait McKenzie*, 1930, was presented to Greenwich by the Canadian government.

Overlooking the east side of the park, in Maze Hill, is Vanbrugh Castle. Its green spire may be seen above the trees. Architect and playwright *Sir John Vanbrugh* designed this house in 1719 in the style of a medieval castle for his own occupancy and lived there until 1726. He also built other 'medieval' dwellings for his family on the same 12-acre site but none of these has survived. The house, now subdivided and with later southern extensions, may be approached more closely, if wished, at the end of the Greenwich itinerary (page 224).

*◗◗ Descend the hill R of Queen's House to Park
Row. Enter L the East Wing of the National
Maritime Museum.*

Location 13

**THE QUEEN'S HOUSE AND THE
NATIONAL MARITIME MUSEUM**

Greenwich Park
(858 4422)

*Open Monday–
Saturday 10.00–
18.00, Sunday 14.00–
17.00. April–October
closes Sunday–Friday
17.00, Saturday
17.30. Admission
charge.*

*NB: The Queen's
House is closed for
renovation until 1987
at the earliest.*

The Queen's House, designed for Anne of
Denmark by *Inigo Jones* in 1616, was England's
first Classical building. It forms part of the
National Maritime Museum, the world's largest
and most important naval museum. Not only the
Royal Navy but the entire shipping industry is
dealt with.

East Wing. This, together with the west wing,
seen later, was built by *Alexander* in 1807 to
provide a naval boarding school. Almost 1000
boys and girls were accommodated. The school
moved in 1933 and this wing became part of the
National Maritime Museum when it opened in
1937.

On the ground floor are 19C and 20C exhibits
describing the emigration of Europeans to
America.

◗◗ Ascend to the first floor, Rooms 18–23.

*◗◗ From Room 17 descend to the ground floor.
Exit from the East Wing R and proceed beneath
the colonnade towards the Queen's House.*

The colonnade was built by *Alexander* in 1811 to
link both wings with the Queen's House.

The Queen's House was England's first building
to be designed entirely in the Classical style and
is, therefore, of major architectural importance.
It occupies the site of a lodge gate that straddled
the main east to west public road, which
originally bisected the grounds of Greenwich
Palace. Traditionally, it was at this lodge gate
that Walter Ralegh gained a knighthood by
laying his cloak on the muddy road for Elizabeth
I to walk on.

James I gave Greenwich to his consort, Anne of
Denmark, in 1613, possibly as some
compensation for his perpetual mistreatment of
her, and *Inigo Jones* was commissioned to design
a new house for the Queen in 1616. The architect
had recently returned from his second visit to
Italy, where he had been greatly impressed by the
work of Palladio, and was determined to
produce, for the first time in England, a Classical
Italian villa in Palladian style.

Strangely, he designed two parallel blocks, north
and south of the road, which were connected at
first floor level by a bridge room, thus repeating
the function of the old lodge gate which had
linked both sections of the royal estate in a
similar way. Anne of Denmark died in 1619, and
work ceased with only the ground floor built. The
structure was covered with thatch for weather
protection until 1629 when Charles I asked Jones
to complete the Queen's House for his consort,
Henrietta Maria. She became its first occupant
*c.*1637.

The visual contrast between the Gothic buildings of the royal palace on the riverside below and the new Classical villa was enormous. The Queen's House soon became known as the White House and later, House of Delight. On her return to England following the Restoration, Henrietta Maria, now the Dowager Queen, once more occupied the Queen's House. Accommodation was increased for her by adding two further bridge rooms on either side of the first, *Webb* 1662, and this is why the house now appears, externally, to be a square villa.

From 1688 the residence was occupied, at various times, by the Ranger of Greenwich Park and the Governor of The Royal Hospital. The main road bisecting the house was diverted further north to its present position in 1699 by Lord Romney who was the Ranger at the time. It is still called the Romney Road. Staff of the naval school occupied the house from 1816 until the school moved elsewhere in 1933. The Queen's House was restored and opened to the public as the centrepiece of the National Maritime Museum in 1937.

Externally, the entire upper floor was initially of painted brick, cement rendering being added later.

All the windows were originally casement, but in the 18C the usual conversion to sash took place and those on the ground floor were deepened.

The south facade has a first floor loggia which evokes Washington's White House.

The main feature of the north river facade is the dual staircase which leads, via a terrace, to the original main entrance from the palace, now a window.

The Queen's House was closed in 1985 for lengthy renovation and its contents will be changed. None of the original furnishings have survived, nor do any of Inigo Jones's chimney-pieces remain *in situ*.

The house will be entered from basement level.

Great Hall. The hall is designed as a 40 ft cube, a favourite device of the Palladians. The carved and gilded ceiling beams originally enclosed nine panels painted by *Orazio Gentileschi,* possibly assisted by his daughter, *Artemesia*. These were eventually cut down and erected at Marlborough House, where they remain, for Sarah, Duchess of Marlborough. Apparently, Queen Anne,then still the Duchess's great friend, as the famous quarrel was still to come, gave permission for this vandalism.

The marble floor, designed by *Stone* in 1637, repeats the ceiling pattern.

• Leave the hall by the door immediately R of the entrance and ascend the staircase.

'Tulip' Staircase. Designed by *Inigo Jones,* this was Britain's first cantilevered spiral staircase. Its balustrade's pattern, in fact, represents fleur-de-

lys, not tulips, probably as a compliment to
Henrietta Maria who was French.

•➡ *At the first floor turn R. The first door R leads
to the North-east Cabinet.*

Room 6 North-east Cabinet. This became the
King's Presence Chamber for Charles II at the
Restoration in 1660.

The ceiling frieze is original and incorporates the
monogram of Charles I and Henrietta Maria.

•➡ *Exit R and follow the gallery to the first door R
which leads to the second most important room,
the Queen's Bedroom, Room 18.*

Room 18 Queen's Bedroom. The bedroom, the
most richly decorated room in the house, was
converted to provide the Queen's Presence
Chamber in 1660. Its ceiling's cove retains the
original painting although the main section was
repainted. The original work had been removed
during the Commonwealth.

Rooms 8, east side, and **10**, west side, are the new
bridge rooms added by *Webb* in 1662. Their
plaster ceilings are the work of *John Groves*.

•➡ *Descend the stairs to the ground floor's south
range. Proceed through the Orangery to the* **'Van
de Velde's Room'.**

Charles II provided a room for use as a studio by
the great Dutch maritime painters, father and
son, between 1675–8. It is not certain that this
was the room assigned to them.

•➡ *Exit from the Queen's House L and follow the
colonnade to the west central wing.*

Like the east wing, already seen, the west central
wing was added to accommodate the naval school
by *Alexander c.*1816. Situated immediately R is
the main bookshop of the museum.

•➡ *Continue ahead to the display of seals L and
medals R. Return through the bookshop, turn R
and proceed to the west wings. Descend the stairs
ahead R to the* **Neptune Hall** *(Room 7).*

This was built to provide the school's gymnasium
and assembly hall in 1874.

Development of the steamship is the theme. The
tug *Reliant*, built in 1907 and operational until
1968, is kept in working order and is believed to
be the largest item of industrial history exhibited
under cover in a European museum.

A cabin from the luxury liner *Empress of Canada*
has been reconstructed.

•➡ *Descend the steps L to the* **Barge House**
(Room 8).

Two royal barges are exhibited including the
state barge of Frederick, Prince of Wales,
designed by *Kent* in 1732. Beneath its roof is the
Prince's coat of arms. This barge was last used by
Prince Albert in 1849.

•➡ *Continue ahead and turn L.*

Rooms A–F display the development of wooden ships.

•▶ Return to the main staircase and ascend to the first floor.

Rooms 3–5 will reopen with new displays in July 1986 as follows:

Room 3: Britain Becomes a World Power 1485–1700.

Room 4: Trade War and Europe 1700–63.

Room 5: The Basis of Sea Power 1714–1815.

•▶ Descend to the ground floor and proceed to Rooms 6–10.

Captain Cook's discovery of New Zealand is featured in **Room 6**.

Nelson's naval career is dealt with in **Rooms 9** and **10**. Displayed is 'The Battle of Trafalgar' painted by *Turner*.

Opposite this is the coat worn by Nelson at Trafalgar, clearly showing the hole made by the fatal bullet.

*•▶ Return to Room 9 and proceed to the **south-west wing**.*

This building was added by *Pasley* in 1876. It will house the Spaceworks exhibition throughout 1986.

•▶ Leave the museum from the north side of the west wing. L Romney Rd. First R King William Walk. Enter the Royal Naval College R.

Location 14	**ROYAL NAVAL COLLEGE**

King William Walk (858 2154)

Open Friday–Wednesday 14.30–17.00. Thursday closes at 16.45. Admission free.

The buildings that now form the college provide England's most important complex in the Classical style. Although mainly designed by *Wren* for William and Mary as a naval hospital, it was the earlier design by *Webb* of King Charles Block, part of a projected palace for Charles II, that set the style for the whole scheme.

The college covers much of the site once occupied by Greenwich Palace. Internally, only the Painted Hall and Chapel may be visited.

The Plantagenet and Tudor Palace. Bella Court, a medieval manor house, was erected on the site of an abbot's residence built in Saxon times. It was inherited by Humphrey, Duke of Gloucester in 1426, who transformed it into a fortified castle.

Margaret of Anjou, consort of Henry VI, acquired the property in 1447. She embellished the house which was renamed Pleasaunce and later Placentia. It became the favourite residence of the Tudors, being much rebuilt by Henry VII and extended by Henry VIII who married Catherine of Aragon and Anne of Cleves within its chapel. Henry VIII, Mary I and Elizabeth I were born at the palace. Only a fragment of the complex remains. (see Location 18, The Chantry).

Stuart Buildings. James I is believed to have constructed the undercroft beneath the Great Hall *c*.1605 and this is the oldest part of the actual palace to survive. It is no longer open to the public.

Greenwich Palace was vandalized by Cromwell, and at the Restoration Charles II instigated a grand rebuilding scheme. As a first step, the east section of King's House (now King Charles Block) was constructed by *Webb* in 1664. However, the King lost interest, money ran out and work ceased. James II, during his brief reign, carried out no further work. William and Mary preferred to reside at Kensington Palace or Hampton Court and the concept of a new Greenwich Palace was doomed.

Following the naval victory over the French in 1692, Mary II ordered building to recommence and *Wren* was commissioned in 1694 to provide, not a palace, but the Royal Naval Hospital for elderly and wounded seamen, a plan first conceived by Mary's father, James II. A Royal Hospital had opened at Chelsea in 1692, also designed by *Wren*, to serve the needs of soldiers in a similar way.

At Greenwich, as at Chelsea, Wren wanted to provide an unbroken river facade, but Mary would not allow the recently opened-up view of the river from the Queen's House to be obstructed again, nor would she allow the existing King's House, built for her uncle, Charles II, to be altered. This is why the small and rather distant Queen's House surprisingly forms the axis of this grand Baroque design. During the construction of the hospital all the existing palace buildings, apart from King's House and an undercroft, were demolished. Although the first pensioners were accommodated by 1705, construction work continued for another fifty years with *Hawksmoor*, and later *Vanbrugh*, as surveyors. By 1869 the number of pensioners had decreased from the original 30,000 to 15,000 and it was then decided to provide them with funds to support themselves. The Royal Naval College transferred here from Portsmouth in 1873 and still occupies the building.

●➡ *Proceed ahead passing L an early 19C single storey range.*

Ahead L is the **King Charles Block**. Its west facade was rebuilt by *Yenn* in 1814 following a fire.

Only the eastern half of the south facade is by *Webb*.

Wren built the western half mirroring Webb's design. This section, however, was rebuilt as a replica by *J. Stuart* in 1769.

The **King William Block**'s west facade R was built, mainly for economic reasons, in red brick, probably by *Hawksmoor* in 1702. Such a flamboyant design is unlikely to have been the work of Wren.

Its north facade was completed by *Wren* in 1705.

Immediately L is the long east facade of the **King Charles Block**, all the work of *Webb*. This set the style for the whole scheme when it was built in 1629 as the first stage of Charles II's royal palace that was never to materialize.

Opposite, stands the **Queen Anne Block**, designed by *Wren* as a replica of the King Charles Block. This was completed in 1725.

●➡ *Ascend the steps.*

The **Queen Mary Block** ahead was also designed by *Wren* but not completed until 1751.

●➡ *Turn R and enter the King Williams Block's Painted Hall R.*

Painted Hall. This is divided into three sections: vestibule, great hall and upper hall. Its interior decoration was completed by *Hawksmoor* in 1707. *Thornhill* began the painting of the ceiling and walls in 1708 but he did not complete the work until 1727. During the building of this block William III, Anne and George I reigned successively and they are all featured in the paintings.

Vestibule. Situated directly beneath the cupola, this was the last part of the hall to be decorated. Paintings on the dome represent the four winds.

Names of the hospital's benefactors are featured on the walls.

●➡ *Ascend the steps.*

Great Hall. Nelson lay in state here in 1805 prior to his funeral in St Paul's Cathedral. The allegorical ceiling, completed in 1713, depicts William and Mary providing Europe with its freedom. It is judged to be the greatest Baroque painting by a British artist.

Mirrors on trolleys assist viewing of the ceiling.

●➡ *Ascend the steps to the Upper Hall.*

Upper Hall. The ceiling painting features Queen Anne and her consort, Prince George of Denmark.

On the wall immediately ahead George I is depicted with his family. Much of this painting is the work of *Andre,* Thornhill's collaborator. In the foreground *Thornhill* has painted himself beckoning to the onlooker.

The monochrome side walls illustrate the landing at Greenwich of William III (R) and George I (L).

From the windows can be seen the only view permitted of the east facade of this block. It is the most idiosyncratic work at Greenwich and again probably by *Hawksmoor.*

●➡ *Exit from the Painted Hall and cross the courtyard ahead to the Queen Mary Block. Enter the Chapel.*

Chapel. The interior, completed in 1742, was almost entirely destroyed by fire in 1779 and rebuilt ten years later by *James (Athenian) Stuart* in the Greek style. Much of the detail, however, was designed by the clerk of works *William Newton*.

The carving above the doorway is by *Bacon*.

●● *Enter the vestibule.*

The four Coade stone statues were designed by *West*. Originally, the pulpit formed the top section of a three-decker. Its medallions by *West* illustrate scenes from the life of St Paul.

The present altar rail was made in 1787.

Above the altar, is a painting of St Paul's shipwreck by *West*.

●● *Exit from the chapel and return to King William Walk R. At Greenwich Pier follow the riverside path R.*

If the 'Queen's View' of the royal buildings has not been seen the nearest equivalent can be viewed from this path as described in Location 1.

●● *Continue ahead. Behind the railings is the central lawn of the college with its statue of George II.*

Location 15	**GEORGE II MONUMENT** *Rysbrack 1735*

The King is fashionably depicted wearing a Roman toga. Marble used for the monument was allegedly discovered in a captured French ship.

●● *Proceed ahead and pass the college buildings.*

Location 16	**THE TRAFALGAR TAVERN**

Built in Regency style by *Kay* in 1837, the tavern replaced the Old George, an 18C inn. The Trafalgar was once famed for its dinners of whitebait, a small fish caught in the Thames during summer. These dinners were favoured by members of Parliament, and the entire Cabinet boated regularly to the Trafalgar for the feast. Names of those who participated in the more notable dinners are listed on boards which line the walls of the upper banqueting room. River pollution ended the catches and the whitebait dinners. The inn went into decline and closed in 1915. Although earmarked for redevelopment, the Trafalgar survived, and was refurbished and re-opened in 1968.

Whitebait dinners have been resumed, but the catch is no longer fresh from the Thames.

●● *Exit L. Follow the path first L (Crane St) and continue ahead passing the Yacht Tavern L. Immediately R is Trinity Hospital. (If an appointment has been made, the chapel is entered by ringing the entry bell R of the first gate R.)*

Location 17	**TRINITY HOSPITAL**
Ballast Quay	The hospital was founded as almshouses by
	Henry Howard, Earl of Northampton in 1613. As
Open free by	the Earl was born in Norfolk it was stipulated
appointment only.	that eight of the pensioners accommodated
Apply to the Warden.	

should always come from that county and the hospital became known as Norfolk College. It was much restored *c.*1812 when battlements and the rendering were added. The chapel, was completely rebuilt in 1812.

Outside the chapel stand figures of the Virtues, allegedly the earliest known English reproductions of antique originals.

•● *Enter the* **chapel**.

Above the altar is an early-16C Flemish stained glass window.

Below the south window R is the monument to Henry Howard by *Stone*, *c.*1696. Its tracery is a notably early example of Neo-Gothic work. The effigy was brought here from Dover Castle by the Mercers Company in 1696 but the original canopy has been lost.

•● *Exit R and proceed to the* **Cutty Sark** *inn*.

This was built in 1804 and its huge bow window is original.

•● *Exit L. First L Lassell St. Continue ahead and cross the main road to Woodland Crescent. L Maze Hill. First R Park Vista.*

Location 18	**PARK VISTA**

The road contains many properties of interest. Most of the south side fronts Greenwich Park.

Nos 1–11 are early 19C.

No 13, **Manor House**, has an early 18C front with a later Gazebo on the roof.

No 15, **Hamilton House**, is mid 18C.

Nos 16–18, **Park Place**, are dated 1791.

Of greatest interest is **The Chantry**, on the south side backing the park, as it retains vestiges of an outbuilding of Greenwich Palace. Lying back, at upper level, is some 16C brickwork to which is fixed a modern stone replica of Tudor arms.

•● *Return to Maze Hill R and proceed southward to view Vanbrugh's Castle more closely. It is described on page 216.*

•● *Alternatively, return to Maze Hill L. First R Tom Smith Close and Maze Hill Station (BR) to Charing Cross Station (BR).*

•● *Alternatively, if continuing to Charlton (page 231), train to Charlton Station (BR).*

•● *Alternatively, if continuing to Woolwich (page 237), train to Woolwich Arsenal Station (BR).*

Blackheath

Blackheath grew around its heath and the 'village', which lies to the south, was a later development. Many outstanding period houses survive, including The Paragon, one of the country's finest late-18C crescents, and Pagoda House, probably the most eccentric residence in the London area.

Timing Any day is suitable, but fine weather is essential as only Morden College may be entered (by appointment).

Suggested connections Precede with Greenwich (part). Continue to Charlton or Greenwich (part).

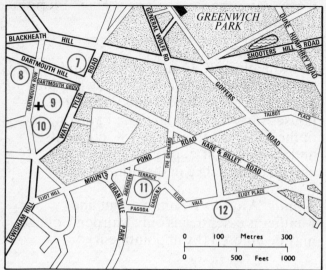

Locations
1 Blackheath 'Village'
2 Montpelier Row
3 Blackheath
4 South Row
5 The Paragon
6 Morden College
7 Dartmouth Hill
8 Dartmouth Row
9 Church of the Ascension
10 Dartmouth House
11 Pagoda House
12 Eliot Place
13 Grotes Buildings
14 Lloyds Place
15 Tranquil Vale

Start *Blackheath Station (BR) from Charing Cross Station (BR). Exit from the station L Tranquil Vale.*

Alternatively, continue from Greenwich as indicated on page 211, beginning at Dartmouth Hill, location 7.

Location 1	**BLACKHEATH 'VILLAGE'**

Tranquil Vale, together with its southern extension, named Blackheath Village, forms the centre of what is now referred to as 'the village', but the importance of this southern end of the thoroughfare was only established in the 19C with the coming of the railway. Blackheath first developed further north, around the heath, and this is where the oldest buildings survive.

•● First R Montpelier Vale leads to Montpelier Row.

Location 2	**MONTPELIER ROW**

Montpelier Row, which leads to the heath, was developed in the late 18C and early 19C.

•● First R South Row. Immediately L is Blackheath.

Location 3	**BLACKHEATH**

The heath has long been public, but is now traversed by numerous roads, many of which were laid out in the 19C and 20C.

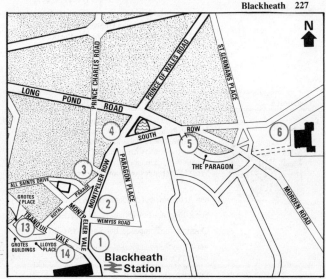

It has witnessed many historic events. Wat
Tyler's rebels assembled here in 1381, prior to
their march on London. The triumphant Henry V
was received on the heath by rejoicing Londoners
in 1415, following the battle of Agincourt. Jack
Cade's revolutionaries met on the heath in 1450.
Henry VII fought the Cornish rebels here in 1497
and it was at Blackheath that his son, Henry
VIII, first met the plain Anne of Cleves who was
to become his fourth wife. Inspired by Holbein's
flattering portrait of 'the mare of Flanders', the
King had agreed to marry her before seeing her.

Golf was introduced from Scotland by James I and
the game was initially played in England on the
heath. The Royal Blackheath Golf Club was the
first to be formed in England and its members
played here from 1608 until their amalgamation
with Eltham in 1932.

It is uncertain how Blackheath gained its name.
There are three possible sources: victims of the
medieval Black Death were buried here; many
robberies took place on the heath until the 19C;
black gorse covered the area until it was burnt to
amuse George IV's consort, Caroline of
Brunswick.

Hollows in the heath, some of which now form
ponds, were made for the excavation of gravel
which was permitted until 1866. Others were
filled with rubble from buildings destroyed during
the bombing of London in the Second World War.

🔊 *Continue ahead along South Row.*

Location 4	**SOUTH ROW**

Colonnade House was rebuilt in 1804, possibly by
Searles.

🔊 *Continue ahead. First R Pond Rd.*

The entrance to **Paragon House**, *Searles* 1794, from Pond Road has been embellished by the present doorway, which came from the Adelphi, the late-18C riverside development by the *Adam* brothers in central London, below Strand.

•● *Continue ahead to The Paragon.*

| Location 5 | **THE PARAGON** *Searles 1794–1807* |

This crescent is judged one of the finest in the London area. Part of the colonnade is believed to have come from a Palladian villa built on the site early in the 18C by *James* for Sir Gregory Page. The houses were damaged by bombs during the Second World War but restored and converted into flats in 1951.

•● *At the east end of The Paragon R Morden Rd.*

Some Regency houses survive in Morden Road.

Gounod, the composer, lived at **No 15** in 1870.

•● *Cross the road immediately to Morden College. Enter the gate and follow the path ahead.*

| Location 6 | **MORDEN COLLEGE** *Wren (?) 1695* |

Open by appointment only. Admission free. (If no appointment has been made the grounds may generally be entered to afford a closer view of the exterior of the building.)

Sir John Morden, a merchant who shipped goods to and from Turkey, commissioned the college to provide almshouses for 'decayed Turkey merchants'. They now accommodate pensioners.

Above the entrance porch are statues of the founder and his wife, probably added some time after the building was completed.

The windows are original and represent one of London's earliest examples of the sash method of opening.

•● *Pass through the central doorway to the cloistered quadrangle and await the guide.*

In the centre of the courtyard are the remains of two wells and an unusual lamp standard.

Each doorway from the cloister leads to individual dwellings.

The chapel door faces the courtyard's entrance.

•● *Enter the* **chapel** *with the guide.*

The carved reredos is allegedly by *Gibbons*. Small stained glass figures in the east window were made c.1600.

Morden, the founder, is buried within the chapel.

•● *Exit from Morden College and cross Morden Rd to the heath. Continue to the north side of the pond which lies immediately opposite The Paragon. Proceed diagonally north-westward across the heath towards the white painted block of two semi-detached houses on the extreme west side. When these are reached, cross Wat Tyler Rd to Dartmouth Hill.*

•● *Alternatively, if continuing at this point with the Greenwich itinerary, R Wat Tyler Rd. First R Shooters Hill. First L General Wolfe Rd. Continue ahead and then proceed R to Ranger's House (page 211).*

Location 7	**DARTMOUTH HILL**

Immediately L the two white-painted, semi-detached Palladian-style properties, **Sherwell House** and **Lydia House**, were built in 1776.

Nos 22 and **20** are late 18C. They originally formed one house which became the residence of the pioneer weather forecaster James Glaisher.

•● First L Dartmouth Row. Cross to the west side and continue southward.

Location 8	**DARTMOUTH ROW**

The name of this street commemorates an adviser to James II, Admiral Legge, later Lord Dartmouth, who purchased the entire Blackheath estate. He was granted a charter in 1683 for the Blackheath Fair, which is still held annually.

Dartmouth Row includes some of Blackheath's oldest properties which are passed as follows:

On the west side **Nos 20** and **22**, *c*. 1700.

No 28, 1794.

Nos 30 and 30A, mid 18C.

Nos 32–36A mid to late 18C.

•● Cross to the east side.

Nos 21 and **23**, **Perceval House** and **Spencer House**, were built in 1689 as one property, which was purchased by Prime Minister Spencer Perceval in 1812. Later that year he was shot by a bankrupt Liverpool broker whilst standing in the House of Commons lobby. Perceval is the only British prime minister to have been assassinated.

Above the windows are outstanding Coade stone figure keystones.

•● Enter the church next to Spencer House.

Location 9	**CHURCH OF THE ASCENSION**

The church was founded *c*. 1695 as the Blackheath Chapel. Its nave was rebuilt in 1834 but the original 17C east apse survives.

•● Exit L and proceed to the adjoining house.

Location 10	**DARTMOUTH HOUSE** *c.1750*
Dartmouth Row	The house was acquired for residential purposes in the late 19C by the College of Greyladies whose services were held in the adjoining church.

•● Continue ahead to St Austell Rd. First L Eliot Hill. Fifth R The Orchard. L Eliot Vale. First R Pagoda Gardens. Immediately R is Pagoda House.

Location 11	**PAGODA HOUSE**
Pagoda Gardens	This residence, one of London's most bizarre, was probably built as a garden house for the fourth Earl of Cardigan *c*. 1760.

It is believed that the upper, oriental features were added later for the Duke of Buccleuch *c*. 1780.

The wing of the house was built in the early 19C.

→ Return to Eliot Vale R.

Passed R on the south side are **Eliot Vale House** and **No 9**. Both were built in 1805.

→ Continue ahead to Eliot Place.

Location 12   **ELIOT PLACE**

Much of the street is composed of late 18C and early 19C properties which are passed as follows:

No 1, **Heathfield House**, 1795.

Nos 4–5, 1793.

No 6, 1797.

Nos 7 and **8** are dated 1792.

No 11, **St German's House**, and **Nos 12** and **13** are early 19C.

→ Continue ahead to the Hare and Billet pub. R Hare and Billet Rd. First R Grotes Place.

Immediately R are **Nos 1** and **2 Grotes Place**. They are early 19C and two of Blackheath's prettiest cottages.

→ The L fork in the road leads to Grotes Buildings R.

Location 13   **GROTES BUILDINGS**

These houses were developed 1766 by a German banker named Grote. The land is owned by Morden College, founded in 1695, hence the small wall plaque 'MC 1695'.

No 2 was stuccoed early in the 19C.

→ Continue ahead to Lloyds Place.

Location 14   **LLOYDS PLACE**

Immediately R is **No 4**, **Lindsey House**, 1774.

The last property, **Eastnor House**, is mid 18C.

→ At the end of Lloyds Place follow the footpath R (Camden Row) which leads to Tranquil Vale.

Location 15   **TRANQUIL VALE**

At this north end of the thoroughfare, behind modern shop fronts, are 18C and early 19C houses, passed, on the west side, as follows:

Weather-boarded, next to The Crown pub, is No 47, 18C.

→ First R Collins Square.

Nos 1–3 are picturesque mid-18C cottages.

→ Return to Tranquil Vale R.

Nos 25–27 were built as Vale House in 1798.

No 23 is mid 18C with a late Victorian shop front.

→ Continue ahead to Blackheath Station (BR) and return to Charing Cross (BR).

→ Alternatively, if continuing to Charlton (page 231), take bus 54 northbound from the station to The Village, Charlton. From the bus stop return northward to St Luke's.

Charlton

Technically, Charlton forms a large part of the Borough of Greenwich, but only its ancient centre, 'the village', on top of the hill, is of particular interest to the visitor. Here can be found a rare Carolean church and, even rarer, a little altered Jacobean mansion, Charlton House.

Timing Charlton House can be entered Monday–Friday and is best seen between 17.00–18.00 when few rooms are in use.

Suggested connections Precede with Blackheath or Woolwich.

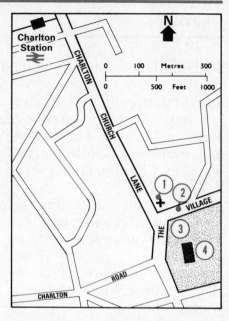

Locations
1 St Luke
2 The Village
3 Garden House
4 Charlton House

Start *Charlton Station (BR) from Charing Cross Station (BR). Exit from the station R Charlton Church Lane. Ascend the hill to The Village L (there is no bus service). Enter St Luke's churchyard.*

Alternatively, continue from Blackheath as indicated on page 230.

Location 1	**ST LUKE** c.*1630*

Charlton Church
Lane

St Luke's, constructed entirely of brick, is a rare London example of a church built in the reign of Charles I. Although still basically Gothic, some Renaissance features are apparent.

The manor of Charlton, named from a settlement of churls (free husbandmen), was given to Bishop Odo by William the Conqueror, his half-brother, in the 11C. Soon, however, it passed to the Priory of Bermondsey.

Charlton is mentioned in the Domesday Book and a Saxon church probably stood on the present site, although St Luke was first recorded in 1077. The present church was built with a legacy by Sir Adam Newton, who had purchased the manor from the Crown. Some of the fabric of the earlier walls was incorporated.

Above the first window is a sundial, a 1934 replica of the mid-17C original.

It is known that an earlier mid-15C legacy had led to some rebuilding of the chancel, and the existing south window may be a re-used survivor of this work. The chancel was extended in 1840.

The north aisle was added to the nave in 1639.

At the north-east corner of the church are vestries built in 1956.

The Dutch-style gabled porch is the only typically Carolean feature of the church. Its door is original.

•● *Enter the church from the south porch and turn L.*

The base of the **tower** serves as the baptistry. Its font is 17C.

Fixed to the roof, immediately above, is the sounding board of the 17C pulpit.

On the north wall of the tower is the large monument commemorating Grace, Viscountess of Ardmagh, d.1700.

The rounded arches of the **north aisle**'s arcade represent the most obvious Renaissance feature of St Luke.

Against the west wall of the aisle is the monument to Spencer Perceval. The bust is the work of *Chantrey*. Perceval, who is buried in the church, was the only British prime minister to be assassinated – in the House of Commons Lobby in 1812. (His house at Blackheath is described on page 00).

The north aisle's window includes 17C heraldic stained glass featuring the coats of arms of notable local families, including the Wilsons and Longhorns, owners of Charlton House.

A chapel was created in the north aisle in 1927. Its altar came from the chapel at Charlton House which had been consecrated and dedicated to St James in 1616.

The pulpit was made for the rebuilt church *c.*1630. It bears the arms of Sir David Cunningham.

On the south wall of the **south aisle**, just west of the chancel, is the monument to the Surveyor General of Ordnance to George I, Brigadier Michael Richards, d.1721 by *Guelfi* (?).

Past the door on the south wall is the wall plaque commemorating Edward Wilkinson, *d.*1567. He had been Master Cook to Elizabeth I and prior to this Yeoman of the Mouth to Henry VIII, Anne Boleyn and Edward VI.

Near the entrance is the monument to Sir Adam and Lady Newton by *Stone*. Sir Adam, d.1629, was not only the benefactor who made possible the building of the present church, but also the builder of Charlton House.

•● *Exit from the church.*

In the **churchyard** is a flagpole from which the British Ensign is flown twice annually, on St George's and St Luke's days. The privilege was granted to the church to commemorate when, in the early 18C, the flag was flown from the top of the tower as a navigational aid to Thames shipping.

◗ From the churchyard, cross The Village immediately to the Bugle Horn inn.

| Location 2 | **THE VILLAGE** |

Although little pre-dates the 19C, this quaintly named thoroughfare has preserved a village-like character.

The **Bugle Horn** inn retains some of its late-17C external appearance, but has mostly been rebuilt. Originally it was a two-storey cottage.

An internal staircase may be late 17C.

◗ Turn R and proceed westward. First L Charlton Rd. Immediately L are public toilets, once the garden house of Charlton House.

| Location 3 | **GARDEN HOUSE** *Inigo Jones (?) c.1630* |

This is England's most important public toilet – from an architectural viewpoint. It was erected in the grounds of Charlton House, serving as a garden house. Later the building became an armoury and an estate agent's office. Many believe it to be one of the few surviving works of *Inigo Jones*, partly due to the uncharacteristically simple design for that period. However, *Nicolas Stone* has also been suggested.

The building's most notable feature is its rare example of a saddleback roof, rebuilt after Second World War bomb damage.

Its original doorway has been filled and the windows altered.

◗ Follow the road southward and proceed to Charlton House.

In the grounds, facing the house, is a Classical archway built in the 17C but much altered. The front drive ran through this to the entrance.

| Location 4 | **CHARLTON HOUSE** *Thorpe (?) c.1612* |

Charlton Road
(856 3951)

Open Monday–Friday. Best visited 17.00–18.00 when most rooms are unoccupied. Admission free.

Charlton House is the least altered early-17C mansion in the London area. In 1923, following First World War use as a hospital, it was purchased by the local authority and now functions as a community centre. Although possessing no period furnishings, the house retains outstanding Jacobean woodwork, chimney-pieces and ceilings, some restored or remade as replicas. These features are preserved in reasonably good condition but appear rather incongruous amongst the general municipal drabness. Visitors must ponder on our cavalier treatment of such riches.

The manor of Charlton was acquired by Sir Adam Newton, Dean of Durham, after the dissolution of the monasteries. He demolished an existing manor house and commissioned the present building *c.*1612.

Charlton House originally overlooked the village green which was added to its grounds and enclosed in 1825.

The house was built in the usual H shape,

possibly by *John Thorpe*, the designer of Holland House at Kensington (mostly destroyed by Second World War bombing). The Wilson family owned the house from 1767 until 1915 and they made only minor changes to it, apart from restoration work (mostly by *Norman Shaw* in 1878).

Dominating the west facade is its exuberantly carved stone frontispiece. It has been recorded that this was reconstructed late in the 19C as a replica. The two coats of arms below the first floor window are 18C additions, those R being of Newton, the builder of Charlton, and those L of the Wilson family.

The north wing L with its tower was mostly rebuilt after war damage.

The south wing's tower is original but much restored. Its clock is dated 1784.

The bay on the south side has been rebuilt. Southern extensions were made in the late 18C, but the stable block is original, although somewhat altered.

All the Tudor style chimney-stacks are late 19C.

Enter the house from the central door.

It is possible to see most rooms, unguided, during an early evening visit. At other times, some may be occupied.

Most chimney-pieces and ceilings are 17C examples; many were installed by Sir William Ducie, a mid-17C owner.

The **hall**'s gallery was probably added early in the 18C.

The 17C-style panelling is apparently modern.

The ceiling and stained glass windows are reproductions of the originals.

Immediately L of the entrance is the **Jenkins Room**. This is fitted with a bar but was once the library. The original fireplace is intricately carved and dated 1612.

At the far end of the hall L is the entrance to the main stairway.

Ahead, the original doors of the **Wilson Room** and the **Chapel** are the best 17C examples in the house.

The richly carved **staircase** is original to the house and judged to be an outstanding example of Jacobean work. Decorative plasterwork around the stairwell was executed in the 19C.

Due to its height the hall occupies much of the first floor and, in consequence, the most important rooms are unusually on the second and not the first floor.

Ascend to the second floor.

The **Long Gallery** lies L of the stairs. Its panelling is not original, apart from the pilasters on each side of both windows.

Stained glass incorporates the arms of the Ducie family and is a post-war copy of 17C work.

Adjoining the gallery is the **White Room.** Its chimney-piece has, in its central panel, a plaster copy of the original carving depicting Perseus and Pegasus. The frieze above illustrates the triumphs of Christ and of Death (on horseback).

The **Grand Salon** which follows, lies directly above the hall and covers the same area. Its much restored pendant ceiling is a rare example.

Windows again feature the Ducie arms.

Inscribed in the west bay is 'JR' the monogram of James I (Jacobus Rex).

The east bay features the Prince of Wales's feathers and motto 'Ich dien' (I serve). This almost certainly commemorates Prince Henry, eldest son of James I, who had been tutored by Adam Newton until two years before his untimely death in 1612, aged eighteen. John Evelyn, the diarist, was a friend of the Newton's and enigmatically recorded in 1652 that the house had been 'intended for Prince Henry's use'.

Figures flanking the marble fireplace represent Venus and Vulcan.

The chimney-piece in the **Dutch Room** that follows is made of black marble and its later Classical design, c.1660, contrasts with most of the others in the house that are earlier.

Prince Henry's Room has an outstanding carved fireplace.

Exit from Charlton House R. Cross Charlton Rd and continue ahead to Charlton Church Lane and Charlton Station (BR).

Woolwich

For long one of London's most unjustly
neglected areas, Woolwich is now becoming
more widely appreciated by visitors
following the completion of its Thames
Barrier. At the same time, the historic
Royal Arsenal buildings have at last been
restored and can now be viewed by the
public. The Royal Artillery Barracks
presents a quarter-mile long unbroken
Classical facade, the longest in England,
and the regiment's Museum of Artillery is
housed in a massive tent, designed by Nash,
early in the 19C to mark Napoleon's
downfall.

Timing Monday to Friday is preferable, but
if preceding with Eltham choose Thursday
when Eltham Palace may be seen.

Suggested connections Precede with
Eltham. Continue with Charlton.

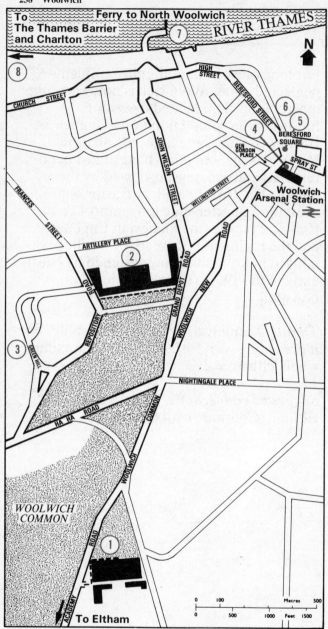

Locations
1 Royal Artillery Museum
2 Royal Artillery Barracks
3 The Rotunda
4 Simple Simon
5 Beresford Square
6 Old Royal Arsenal
7 Woolwich Ferry
8 Thames Barrier

Start *From Woolwich Arsenal Station (BR) from Charing Cross Station (BR). Exit L. If viewing the Royal Artillery Museum (Location 1) take bus 122 or 161 southbound to Academy Rd (request stop). Enter the main gate. Follow the first drive L to the end. Proceed R through the car park.*

Alternatively, if not viewing the museum, alight earlier from bus 122 or 161 at Grand Depot Rd. Cross the road to the Royal Artillery Barracks (Location 2).

Alternatively, continue from Eltham as indicated on page 249.

Location 1	**ROYAL ARTILLERY MUSEUM** J. Wyatt 1808

Academy Road
(856 5533)

*Open Monday–
Friday 10.00–12.30
and 14.00–16.00.
Admission free.*

The block accommodating the museum stands on the north side of the complex and overlooks Woolwich Common. It was built to house the Royal Military Academy which amalgamated with Sandhurst in 1964.

The chapel was added in 1902.

Much of the remainder, including the end pavilions, is late 19C.

The museum building has four corner turrets topped with cupolas in imitation of the White Tower at the Tower of London.

●● *Enter from the north side (past the library entrance).*

Exhibits relate to the history of the regiment since its foundation in 1716. Uniforms, badges, tableaux and photographs are displayed in three large rooms.

●● *Exit from the museum, return to Academy Rd and cross the road. Take bus 122 or 161 to Grand Depot Rd. Return southward, enter the grounds of the Royal Artillery Barracks through the gate R.*

Location 2	**ROYAL ARTILLERY BARRACKS**

Grand Depot Road

The grounds only may be entered. Admission free.

Ahead, the longest Classical facade in England stretches for approximately a quarter of a mile and, as Pevsner suggests, invites comparison with the palaces of Leningrad. It was mostly built 1775–82, by an unknown staff architect, but the western section was completed to match by *J. Wyatt* in 1802. The barracks can house 4000 troops.

●● *Cross the grounds passing the entire south facade and exit at the west gate. L Repository Rd. First R Green Hill. Continue ahead to The Rotunda.*

Location 3	**THE ROTUNDA (MUSEUM OF ARTILLERY)**

Green Hill (off Repository Road) (856 5533)

*Open November–
April Monday–
Friday 12.00–16.00
Saturday–Sunday
13.00–16.00. May–
October open until
17.00. Admission
free.*

The Rotunda began its life as a canvas tent and first stood in the garden of the Prince Regent's Carlton House, now part of St James's Park. It was one of six tents erected in 1814 to accommodate meetings between sovereign heads of state following the defeat of Napoleon. Their erection was premature. The tent was presented to the regiment by George IV in 1819 to house their museum. Three years later, the structure was made more permanent by *Nash*, who covered it with lead and lined the inside with timber. He raised the tent on to a brick wall, adding columns and a central pillar for strength.

The sandwiched canvas and ropes remain but cannot be seen.

Guns and ammunition from all periods and many countries are displayed. The oldest gun exhibited was fired at the battle of Crecy in 1346.

➡ Return to the Royal Artillery Barracks and proceed eastward. Exit L Grand Depot Rd. First R John Wilson St leads to Woolwich New Rd. Continue ahead, passing General Gordon Place to Simple Simon's R.

Location 4	**SIMPLE SIMON**

5 Woolwich New Road

This restaurant is a rare survivor of the Victorian eel and pie shops that once abounded to the east of London, specifically to serve the poor. Its speciality is stewed eels, served with a 'liquor', a pale green sauce to which vinegar is usually added. Until 1985 this establishment was called the Pie Mash and Eel shop and retained its Victorian decor, including outstanding tiling. It has now, sadly, been modernized and the atmosphere lost. However, the eels remain.

➡ Exit R. L Beresford Square.

Location 5	**BERESFORD SQUARE**

The market operates Monday–Saturday 09.00–17.00 but closes Thursday at 14.00.

A lively streeet market helps to give Woolwich the atmosphere of a separate town rather than a London suburb. In 1986 much of the square is undergoing major redevelopment, particularly the old Royal Arsenal buildings on its north side.

➡ Proceed to the north side of the square and the gatehouse of the old Royal Arsenal (now isolated).

Location 6	**OLD ROYAL ARSENAL**

Beresford Square
Opening details undecided.

Although the manufacture of armaments here ended in 1967, the public were not permitted to view the outstanding period buildings that stood within the grounds and it was feared that none would be preserved. However, restoration of the most outstanding was completed in 1986. It is believed that some of the buildings were the work of *Vanbrugh*, whose Castle Howard was the setting for the television adaptation of *Brideshead Revisited*. No other examples of Vanbrugh's English Baroque work are known to survive elsewhere in the London area.

The gatehouse, built in 1829, was remodelled and an upper section added in 1897. This is now cut off from the rest of the complex by a new highway.

➡ Cross the road to the wall ahead.

Behind the new wall lie the other Royal Arsenal Buildings that have survived.

The Royal Arsenal was founded as a military store in the 16C and was known as Woolwich Warre. It was situated near the Woolwich boatyard which closed in 1869. Here Henry VIII's *Great Harry* had been built in 1512 and

Charles I's *Royal Sovereign* in 1637.

A royal laboratory opened here in 1695 and two pavilions were built. Following an explosion at Moorfields, it was decided in 1717 to transfer the Royal Arsenal to Woolwich as this was sited further from the capital and less damage would be caused by any similar accidents.

A brass foundry, together with a gun-boring factory and smithy, which formed the entrance range to Dial Square, were built between c.1717 and 1720; these are the buildings attributed to *Vanbrugh*. Further ranges were added in the 18C and early 19C.

Immediately L is the **Old Brass Foundry**. Behind lies the **Guard House**.

Verbruggen House, c.1723, lies R and was built for the First Master of the Armouries.

Behind is a remnant of **Dial Square**. All post-mid-19C buildings have now been demolished.

'Royal' was added to the name of the Arsenal following a visit by George III in 1805. During the First World War 75,000 were employed on the 1200-acre site.

The famous Association Football Club, Arsenal, who now play at Highbury, were founded at Woolwich in 1886. They were first called Dial Square as it was in these buildings that most of the players worked. Some had played for Nottingham Forest, whose scarlet colours they adopted. The team first played on Woolwich Common and soon changed their name to Woolwich Arsenal. In 1913 they transferred to Highbury and became simply, Arsenal.

●● *Proceed to Beresford St, approached from the north-west side of Beresford Square. Take bus 177 or 180 westward to the Thames Barrier. Ask for Eastmoor St (request stop). Seen shortly R, from the upper floor of the bus, is the Woolwich Ferry.*

Location 7	**WOOLWICH FERRY**

This pedestrian and vehicle ferry is a curiosity because it is the only completely free ferry in the world and will remain so, in perpetuity, by Act of Parliament. Ferry boats cross the river to North Woolwich, where the King George V and Royal Albert docks, in operation until only recently, now form part of the dockland redevelopment scheme.

●● *From the bus stop return eastward. First L Eastmoor St. Proceed ahead to the Thames Barrier.*

Location 8	**THAMES BARRIER**

Riverside Walkway and Visitors Centre open. Admission free. Round the Barrier Cruises 11.00–16.30.

This barrier was completed in 1982 to protect low lying parts of London from abnormally high water levels. Its piers have been likened to a succession of mini Sydney opera houses. The barrier itself cannot be seen, except during operational tests, or in the event of a flood warning, when it is raised in sections from the

Also Woolwich to Westminster Pier Cruises.

river bed. A riverside path provides a good view, but a 'Round the Barrier Cruise', lasting thirty minutes, approaches more closely. These depart from the pier, as does the boat to Westminster Pier.

An exhibition of how and why the barrier was constructed is housed in the Thames Barrier Visitors Centre. There are two film shows.

●● *Return by boat from the pier to Westminster Pier.*

●● *Alternatively, take the limited stop bus to the centre of London.*

●● *Alternatively, return eastward by bus 177 or 180 to Beresford Rd, Woolwich, and proceed to Woolwich Arsenal Station (BR).*

●● *Alternatively, if continuing to Charlton, take bus 177 or 180 westbound to Charlton Church Lane. Ascend the hill to Charlton Village (page 231).*

Eltham

The moated, royal palace of Eltham, with its hammerbeamed Great Hall, is a unique London survivor from the Plantagenet period. Eltham Lodge, a Restoration mansion, was designed by Charles II's architect, Hugh May, and is his only known work to remain in its original form. The Tudor 'Barn', and Elizabethan bridge that crosses its moat, are remnants from the estate of Well Hall, the home of Sir Thomas More's daughter, Margaret Roper.

Timing Sunday or Thursday are preferable as only then can Eltham Palace be visited. Eltham may be thoroughly explored in half a day.

Suggested connections Precede with Dulwich. Continue to Woolwich.

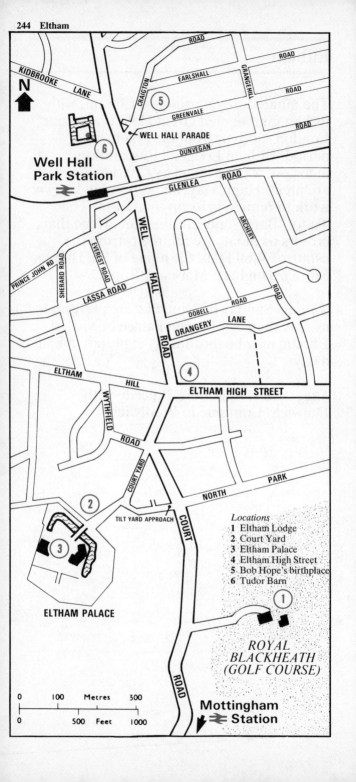

ROAD

KIDBROOKE LANE

N

EARLSHALL ROAD

CRAIGTON

GRANGEHILL

ROAD

(5)

GREENVALE

ROAD

WELL HALL PARADE

DUNVEGAN

(6)

Well Hall Park Station

GLENLEA ROAD

ARCHERY

WELL

HALL

PRINCE JOHN RD

SHERARD ROAD

EVEREST ROAD

LASSA ROAD

ROAD

DOBELL ROAD

ORANGERY LANE

(4)

ELTHAM HILL

WYTHFIELD

ROAD

ELTHAM HIGH STREET

PARK

COURT YARD

NORTH

(2)

TILT YARD APPROACH

COURT

Locations
1 Eltham Lodge
2 Court Yard
3 Eltham Palace
4 Eltham High Street
5 Bob Hope's birthplace
6 Tudor Barn

(3)

(1)

ELTHAM PALACE

ROYAL BLACKHEATH (GOLF COURSE)

ROAD

0   100   Metres   300

0   500   Feet   1000

Mottingham Station

Start *Mottingham Station (BR) is reached from Charing Cross Station (BR). Exit from the station L. First L cross the railway bridge to Court Road. Continue ahead and cross to the east side of Court Road at the entrance to the Royal Blackheath Golf Club. Follow the short drive to the club house.*

Alternatively, continue from Dulwich as indicated on page 257.

Alternatively, continue from Dulwich as indicated on page 257.

| Location 1 | **ELTHAM LODGE (ROYAL BLACKHEATH GOLF CLUB)** *May 1664* |

Court Road
(850 1795)

Open by appointment only. Admission free.

The north facade may be viewed at any time.

Eltham Lodge was built, at the Restoration, for banker Sir John Shaw in the Dutch style on Crown Land. Shaw had acquired the entire Eltham estate in 1663 but assigned the surviving buildings of Eltham Palace to agricultural use. The lodge remained a private residence until 1880. It became the clubhouse of Eltham Golf Club in 1891. (The club merged with Blackheath Golf Club in 1932.)

Enter from the north front and await the guide.

Columns screening the **Staircase Hall** from the entrance hall were a later addition. The banisters are sumptuously carved with cherubs and foliage but have unfortunately been painted.

The **Morning Room,** L of the entrance, has rococo plasterwork framing portraits of Roman emperors.

Visitors are shown the first floor **Dining Room** when convenient. The ceiling and chimney-piece are original.

Exit and return to Court Rd R. First L Tilt Yard Approach.

The brick wall L, with its arch at the far end, originally enclosed the Tudor tiltyard where knights jousted.

Continue ahead. L Court Yard.

| Location 2 | **COURT YARD** |

This street originally formed one side of Green Court that stood outside Eltham Palace.

The first house seen R, **No 32**, is timber-framed but was re-fronted in the 18C.

Nos 34–38 are half-timbered and were built in the 16C as the Lord Chancellor's Lodgings. Wolsey resided here as Lord Chancellor when visiting Henry VIII at Eltham. The buildings were remodelled in the 18C.

Continue to the entrance to Eltham Palace. Immediately ahead lies the bridge.

| Location 3 | **ELTHAM PALACE** |

Court Yard
(859 2112)

Open Thursday and Sunday 11.00–17.00. Closes 19.00 April–September., Admission free.

Eltham's royal connections go back to the 11C, when Bishop Odo, half-brother of William the Conqueror, acquired the manor house. A moated house was built on the site for Bishop Bek of Durham in 1296, and in 1305 he presented the estate to the Prince of Wales, later Edward II. Both Edward III and Richard II occupied the castle but only fragments of this building remain.

Richard II's Clerk of Works at Eltham was Geoffrey Chaucer. It has been alleged that Edward III founded the Order of the Garter here.

Eltham Palace was largely rebuilt for Edward IV in 1480, with a new Great Hall as its centrepiece. It was then known as Eltham Court and remained popular with successive monarchs until the early part of Henry VIII's reign. After this, the palace was only used as a hunting lodge. Greenwich Palace, situated more attractively on the river, was preferred by Henry VIII, who rarely came to Eltham after 1529. The last sovereign to visit the palace was Charles I and he is only known to have come once.

At its height, Eltham was a large complex of many buildings grouped around courtyards but when, during the Commonwealth, it was sold by Parliament to Colonel Rich who demolished most of it c.1650. Sir John Shaw became the new tenant in 1663 but lived nearby, in Eltham Lodge, which he had commissioned to be built in the fashionable new Dutch style. The palace then functioned merely as a farm. The Great Hall, moat and bridge have been restored and the foundations of the chapel and royal apartments excavated.

Eltham Palace is now used by the Army for educational purposes, although the Crown retains the freehold.

Bridge. This was probably rebuilt at the same time as the hall and much of the late-15C masonry survives.

Moat. The walls were first built c.1300 but replaced by the present moat walls for Edward III in the 14C and subsequently much altered and rebuilt, mainly in brick. Some of the lower sections of the inner walls, are, however, c.1300. Ahead, L of the bridge, the window in the wall was originally a sewage outlet. Flanking this are a 19C lion and unicorn by *Pugin* which were brought from the Houses of Parliament in 1936. Originally, the moat's water level was much higher.

At the end of the bridge L is a low brick structure, the remains of a **gatehouse**.

●● *Proceed ahead.*

Immediately L, linked to the Great Hall, is the house built for Sir Stephen Courtauld, who leased the estate in 1936. Standing behind and above can be seen timber gables of the lodgings c.1500.

●● *Proceed to the north facade of the Great Hall.*

Great Hall. This, the focal point of Edward IV's new palace, was completed c.1479 by master mason *Thomas Jordan*. During Sir James Shaw's 17C ownership the building functioned as a barn and continued to do so until it was partially restored c.1830.

The roof was rebuilt and most of the external stone facing above window sill level renewed c.1914.

The window tracery and the grotesque heads at parapet level have been restored.

The southern part of the palace grounds is not open to the public but the hall's facade on that side is similar.

•● *Enter the hall.*

The hammerbeam roof was designed by *Edward Graveley*. Westminster Hall and the Great Hall of Hampton Court are the only larger buildings known to have been built with with this type of structure. Eltham's hall possesses the earliest known example of hammerbeams with pendants (renewed *c.*1936 when the roof was restored).

The east gallery L was constructed from the screen *c.*1936.

Windows on the north and south walls are placed high to allow for the then fashionable display of tapestries beneath them.

•● *Proceed to the west end.*

The dais and reredos were made *c.*1936.

To the north and south are bay windows. The design of their fan vaults incorporates Edward IV's emblem – a falcon and fetterlock. Originally, their bosses were of stone but these were replaced by plaster replicas *c.*1936.

•● *Exit from the hall.*

The hall formed the south side of Great Court. To the west, running north and south of the Great Hall, were the Royal Apartments. Part of this range formed the west side of Great Court.

Immediately ahead, running parallel with the Great Hall, stood the Chapel which provided the north range of Great Court.

•● *Turn L and proceed northward following the excavated foundations of the Royal Apartments.*

Royal Apartments. Excavations in the 1930s revealed the footings of this three-storey building that overlooked the Great Court. Outlines of bay windows, added for Henry VII in the late 15C, can be seen. The king's private apartments lay south of the chapel, whilst the queen's lay immediately to the north.

•● *Turn R and proceed towards the moat bridge. Parallel with the Great Hall stood the Chapel.*

Chapel. Excavations were made in 1977 revealing extensive remains which have now been covered again.

Henry VIII rebuilt an existing chapel *c.*1515, and it was in this building that he appointed Wolsey Lord Chancellor of England in 1518. Two polygonal turrets at the west end led to the private apartments of the king and the queen.

•● *Exit from Eltham Palace grounds. Ahead Court Yard. Continue to Court Rd L. First R Eltham High St. Immediately R is The Greyhound inn.*

Location 4	**ELTHAM HIGH STREET**

The Greyhound is a 17C inn with, in its front bar R, a carved mid-16C stone fireplace, reputed to have come from Eltham Palace.

There is an attractive rear patio.

Next to the inn is **No 90**, **Mellins Wine Bar**, c.1700, with a later bow front.

•• *Cross to the north side and continue eastward.*

Nos 97–100, **Clifden House**, early 18C, originally formed one residence.

•• *Follow the path, first L, to the rear of the car park and the remains of an orangery.*

The early-18C brick-built **orangery**, with stone detailing is to be restored. It is all that remains from the Eltham House estate. Originally the Baroque building had a high centrepiece and a parapet.

•• *Turn L and follow Orangery Lane westward. R Well Hall Rd. Continue ahead beneath the railway bridge.*

•• *If viewing Bob Hope's birthplace: second R Well Hall Parade. Ahead, Craigton Rd. Continue to No 44 on the south side.*

•• *Alternatively, continue to the Tudor Barn, location 6.*

Location 5	**BOB HOPES'S BIRTHPLACE**
No 44 Craigton Road	Here was born, on 29 May 1903, Leslie Townes Hope, now better known as Bob Hope. The infant lived here for three years before his parents moved to Bristol. One year later the family emigrated to Cleveland, Ohio, where their son later achieved fame and fortune as one of the country's most popular comedians. Bob Hope has since made return visits to Eltham.

•• *Return to Well Hall Rd R. Cross the road and continue ahead to the Tudor Barn (its grounds are entered L, immediately after the public toilets).*

Location 6	**TUDOR BARN (WELL HALL PLESAUNCE)**
Well Hall Road	A mansion named Well Hall is recorded as early as the 11C. The property was inhabited in 1524 by William Roper, husband of Sir Thomas More's only daughter, Margaret. Following her father's execution, Margaret Roper allegedly retrieved his head from Old London Bridge where it had been displayed on a pike, and kept it at Well Hall. More's head is now buried in the Roper Chapel at St Dunstan's, Canterbury.
Open daily 10.30– 16.00. (Upper floor closed Saturday and some lunchtimes for private functions.) Admission free.	

The mansion itself was demolished in 1733 but the present 'barn', moat and a bridge survive. These, together with part of the grounds, were acquired by the local authority in 1936.

There were originally two complete moats encircling the mansion. First seen L is the Elizabethan bridge that crosses the inner moat.

•• *Cross the wooden bridge R. The 'barn' lies L.*

The building was unlikely to have been used as a barn as its chimney-stack and fireplaces on both floors are original. A simple barn would have had no need of these.

At the east end, immediately ahead, are restored turrets. Beneath their corbels are William Roper's monogram.

●● *Proceed ahead to the north facade.*

Most windows have been restored. The blind ground floor windows were originally plastered and painted.

In the centre of the north facade, at first floor level, is the coat of arms of the Tattersall family, dated 1568. They had been earlier occupants and the date was almost certainly a later addition.

●● *Enter the building.*

The ground floor has been converted to a restaurant.

Above, the first floor room is used as an art gallery or hired for private functions. Its beams and stone Tudor fireplace have been restored.

●● *Return to Well Hall Road R. Proceed to Well Hall Park Station (BR) R and train to Charing Cross Station (BR).*

●● *Alternatively, if continuing to Woolwich (page 237), take bus 161 (request stop) to the Royal Artillery Museum, Academy Rd. (Also a request stop.)*

Dulwich

A visit to Dulwich is generally motivated by
a desire to view its Picture Gallery, where
outstanding old masters are displayed.
However, the semi-rural ambience of the
town with its period houses and college
buildings is a further attraction. Though not
situated in Dulwich, the eclectic Horniman
Museum at Forest Hill is easily reached.

Timing Tuesday to Saturday is preferable
as the Dulwich Picture Gallery is closed
Sunday morning and all day on Monday. It
always closes 13.00–14.00. If continuing to
Eltham, bear in mind that Eltham Palace
can only be visited Sunday and Thursday.

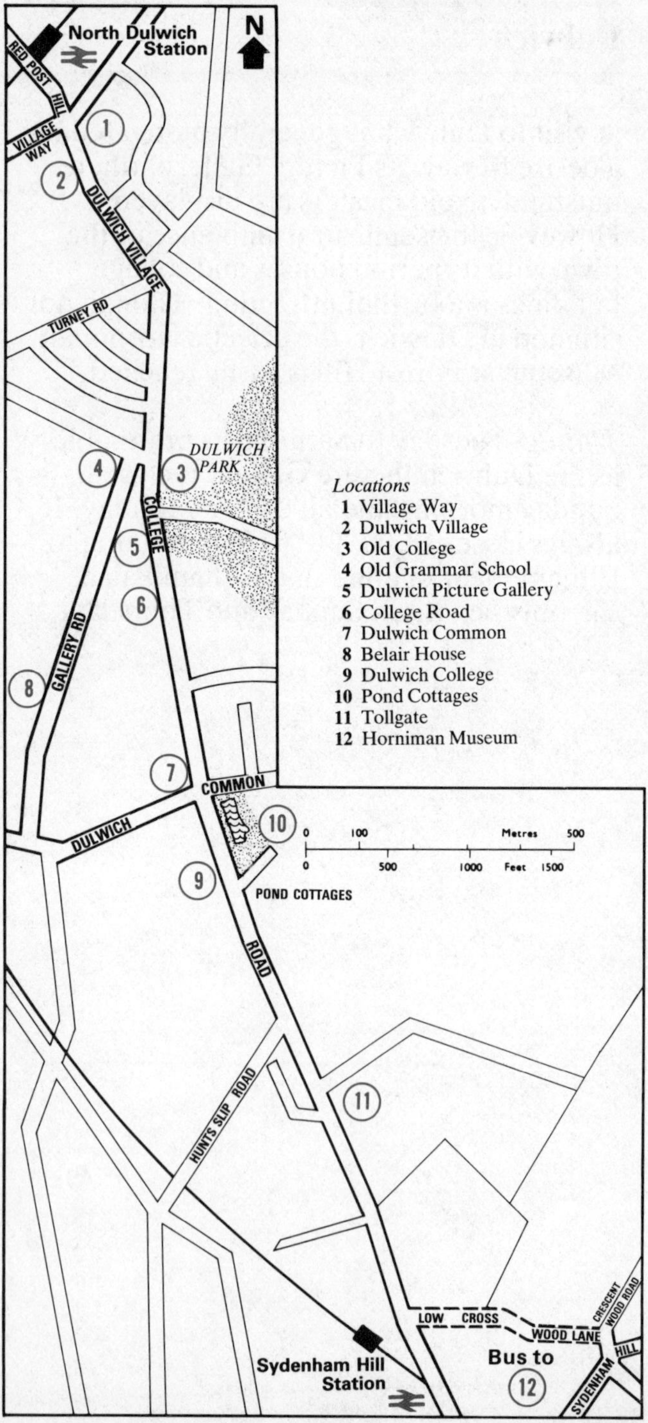

N

North Dulwich
Station

RED POST HILL

VILLAGE WAY

① Village Way

② Dulwich Village

DULWICH VILLAGE

TURNEY RD

DULWICH PARK

④ ③

COLLEGE

⑤

⑥

GALLERY RD

⑧

⑦

COMMON

DULWICH

⑩

⑨ P0ND COTTAGES

POND COTTAGES

ROAD

HUNTS SLIP ROAD

⑪

Locations

1 Village Way
2 Dulwich Village
3 Old College
4 Old Grammar School
5 Dulwich Picture Gallery
6 College Road
7 Dulwich Common
8 Belair House
9 Dulwich College
10 Pond Cottages
11 Tollgate
12 Horniman Museum

0	100			Metres	500
0	500	1000	1500	Feet	

LOW CROSS

WOOD LANE

CRESCENT WOOD ROAD

Bus to
⑫

SYDENHAM HILL

Sydenham Hill
Station

Start *Buy a single ticket to North Dulwich Station (BR) from Charing Cross Station (BR). Change at London Bridge Station (BR). Exit L Red Post Hill. First R Village Way.*

Location 1	**VILLAGE WAY**

Two detached 18C villas, **Lyndenhurst** and, next but one, **Pond House**, with venetian windows were built in 1759. A horse pond once stood in front of Pond House, hence its name.

•• Return eastward. First R Dulwich Village (the street). Cross the road and remain on the east side. Proceed to the Turney Rd junction (first R).

Location 2	**DULWICH VILLAGE**

This thoroughfare was called High Street until *c.*1912. The change of name probably reflects, even at this relatively early period, the desire of suburbanites to regain a semblance of rural life.

On the corner R, **Nos 52** and **54** are early 19C. Opposite, on the corner L, are **Nos 57**, 1793, and **59**, late 18C.

•• Continue ahead. NB: odd numbers are on the east side, even numbers on the west side.

Nos 60, **The Laurels**, and **62**, **The Hollies**, were originally built as one house in 1767. The bays are 19C additions. From this point on the east side many of the 'Georgian' houses are high quality fakes.

No 70 is early 19C.

No 72 is late 18C, but altered.

Nos 74, **76** and **78** are early Georgian.

A Georgian shop, **No 94**, retains its colonnade and balcony.

Nos 93 and **95** are 20C reproductions.

Nos 97–105 are genuine 18C houses with parts of the last two, *c.*1700, amongst the earliest in Dulwich.

•• Continue ahead to the roundabout and cross College Rd to Old College which occupies the corner site ahead.

The iron gates by *Buncker*, 1728, were brought here in 1866.

•• Enter the grounds and proceed ahead.

Location 3	**OLD COLLEGE**

College Road.

Courtyard open. Chapel open for services only. Admission free.

This was where Dulwich College of God's Gift, with its almshouses, was founded in 1619, for twelve poor scholars and twelve poor men. Boys drew lots for a place at the school; those who were successful drew a piece of paper bearing the words 'God's Gift'. Although the school has moved, the almshouses remain.

Its benefactor was the Elizabethan actor-manager and impresario, Edward Alleyn, who had purchased the manor of Dulwich in 1605. The builder was *John Benson*.

Old College's stone tower and cloisters date from 1870.

The **chapel** itself was remodelled in 1823. This is Christ's Chapel of Alleyn's College of God's Gift and still serves the college. Alleyn's original, 17C tomb, discovered in the yard of an inn, is displayed in the cloister, but he is buried within the chapel in front of the altar.

The chapel's font is by *Gibbs*, 1729.

The east wing, now Edward Alleyn House, accommodated the boys' dormitory and the almshouses. It was rebuilt in 1740 and again in 1821, this time purely as almshouses.

Pupils were taught in the west wing which now houses Dulwich College's Estate's offices. This was built in 1619, extended in 1820, and again more recently. It is only here that anything survives of the original Jacobean complex.

●● *Exit from the main gate L and cross Gallery Rd to the Old Grammar School.*

Location 4	**OLD GRAMMAR SCHOOL** *C. Barry 1842*

Gallery Road

This was built as an additional school to educate local boys because Dulwich College, which was intended for them, had become filled by fee-paying scholars from further afield. Its function as a school was short-lived, ending in 1858. The building now accommodates a playgroup.

●● *Cross Gallery Rd and pass the gates of Old College. First R College Rd.*

Immediately opposite is the entrance to Dulwich Park.

●● *Continue ahead to Dulwich Picture Gallery.*

Location 5	**DULWICH PICTURE GALLERY** *Soane 1814*

College Road
(693 5254)

*Open Tuesday–
Saturday 10.00–13.00
and 14.00–17.00.
Sunday 14.00–17.00.*

*Admission charge.
Guided tours are
available on Saturday
and Sunday at no
extra charge.*

Edward Alleyn bequeathed to the school his 16C collection of Tudor portraits; William Cartwright's collection, which included theatrical paintings, was added in 1686. Both bequests were of historic rather than artistic value.

King Stanislaus of Poland commissioned picture dealer Noel Desenfans to buy paintings for a projected Polish National Gallery in 1790. Many were purchased but the King was deposed in 1795, before he had paid Desenfans. The money was provided by Margaret Desenfans, the dealer's wife, who was, fortunately, a wealthy woman as no compensation was offered.

Desenfans tried to sell the pictures to the British Government for a national gallery but was unsuccessful. When he died he left the paintings to his wife but specified that his close friend, the painter and collector Francis Bourgeois, should be entrusted with their care. It was decided that they should be added to the existing Dulwich collection and a new gallery was sought for their display.

Following the death of Bourgeois, Margaret Desenfans commissioned an art gallery to be built at Dulwich, incorporating a mausoleum at the rear for herself, her husband and Bourgeois, an eternal *menage à trois*. This was to be flanked by almshouses. The new building by *Soane*, 1814, was opened in 1817 and is the oldest public picture gallery in England. In the late 19C the almshouses were converted to provide more galleries.

Dulwich Picture Gallery was partly destroyed by a rocket in the Second World War and only the front section survived; most of this had been built as an extension in Soane pastiche style in 1910. The damaged area of the gallery and the mausoleum were rebuilt to Soane's original designs, but very little of his original work survives.

●▬ *Enter the gallery*.

The following selection of the many important paintings is given, however, in order to raise funds, some works are on temporary loan and may not be displayed.

●▬ *From the hall turn L and proceed ahead to room I*.

I Linley family paintings *Gainsborough*.
II 'Samson & Delilah' *Van Dyck*. 'Mrs Siddons' *Reynolds*.
III 'Flower girl' *Murillo*.
IV 'St John the Baptist' *Reni*.
V Peasant children (two paintings) *Murillo*.
VI Landscapes *Cuyp*.
VIII 'Young Man' *Piero di Cosimo*.
X (off Room I) 'Venus' *Rubens*.
XI (off Room II) Two outstanding works by *Rembrandt* – 'Girl at the Window' and 'Titus'. Another Rembrandt, 'Jacob de Gheyn', has been repeatedly stolen and recovered. It may or may not be on view.

The rebuilt mausoleum, an exact replica of the original, lies at the rear of the building. Although part of the scheme, it retains a separate identity.

●▬ *Exit L and pass immediately through the garden door L*.

The west facade is a reproduction of Soane's original.

●▬ *Return to College Rd R and cross the road*.

Location 6	**COLLEGE ROAD**

On the east side, **Nos 13** and **15** are late 18C.

No 23, **Bell Cottage**, weather-boarded, is early 18C.

No 27, **Bell House**, 1767, has a white belfry; it now serves as a boarding house for the college.

No 31, **Pickwick Cottage**, is Regency and was formerly called Grove Cottage. Its change of name reflected the tradition that Dickens used this cottage as a model for Mr Pickwick's retirement residence at Dulwich.

●▬ *Continue ahead. First R Dulwich Common (the street)*.

Location 7	**DULWICH COMMON**

This thoroughfare is now part of the busy South Circular Road but was once a fashionable address; several Regency and Georgian villas remain.

On the west side, **No 48**, **Howletts Meade**, is early 19C.

No 41, **Oakfield**, on the east side, is also an early 19C villa.

The Willows and **Northcroft** were built by *Tappen*, the college surveyor, in 1810.

Old Blew House was built early in the 18C; its stucco was added later.

●● *First R Gallery Rd.*

Location 8	**BELAIR HOUSE** *1785*
Gallery Road	

Originally named College Place, this 18C mansion is a rare example in the locality. Designed in the Adam style, possibly by *Holland*, it was a private residence until 1938 but is now municipally owned.

●● *Return to Dulwich Common L. First R College Rd.*

Location 9	**DULWICH COLLEGE** *C. Barry jnr, 1870*
College Road	
The college and its grounds are not open to the public.	

This public school, which replaced Old College, now accommodates 1400 pupils, of which 140 are boarders. Designed in Northern Renaissance style, it is regarded as London's most ornate school building. The external decorative terracotta work is an early example of the extensive application of this material so favoured by the late Victorians.

Internally, the hall possesses an imitation hammerbeam roof.

●● *Cross the road.*

Location 10	**POND COTTAGES**

Overlooking the millpond, these 18C cottages provide the most picturesque scene in Dulwich.

●● *Continue southward along College Rd.*

Location 11	**TOLLGATE**

Constructed in 1789, this much altered, Neo-Gothic building is the last tollgate operating in London. Only drivers of vehicles are charged and it is completely free at night.

●● *Proceed ahead to Sydenham Hill Station. Immediately opposite, follow Low Cross Wood Lane to the end. R Crescent Wood Rd. R Sydenham Hill. Take bus 63 to Wood Vale (request stop). From the bus stop proceed to Lordship Lane R which leads to London Rd. Cross the road.*

●● *Alternatively, return from Sydenham Hill Station (BR) to Victoria Station (BR).*

Location 12

HORNIMAN MUSEUM
Harrison Townsend 1901

London Road, Forest
Hill

*Open Monday–
Saturday 10.30–
18.00. Sunday 14.00–
18.00. Admission
free.*

Here is displayed the esoteric collection of tea
magnate F. J. Horniman which is much enjoyed
by children. Exhibits include masks, African
buildings and carvings, weapons and shields,
butterflies, puppets, a torture chair (used by the
Spanish Inquisition) and a huge stuffed walrus.

*Exit L London Rd and descend the hill. L
Dartmouth Rd. Train from Forest Hill Station
(BR) to Charing Cross Station (BR).*

*Alternatively, if continuing to Eltham (page
243), descend the steps immediately R of the
station. R Perivale Rd. Cross to the bus stop and
take bus 124 to the Royal Blackheath Golf Club
(request stop). A taxi, however, is preferable as
the service is infrequent and a change of bus often
necessary.*

English architectural styles

Experts disagree on the precise definitions of some styles and periods, and as this affects their time spans, alternative dates are shown in brackets where applicable. It should be remembered that architectural styles always overlap by several years and no precise dividing line can generally be drawn. Dominant styles are shown in bold type.

Period ruled and rulers	Architectural style	Important outer London examples and their completion dates
Romans	**Roman** 43–410	
Anglo-Saxons and Danes	**Romanesque** 500–1200	
	Pre-Conquest Romanesque or Saxon 500–1066	Kingston: All Saints (cross)
Normans 1066 William I 1087 William II 1100 Henry I 1135 Stephen	Post-Conquest Romanesque or Norman 1066–1200	Harrow-on-the-Hill: St Mary, tower 1094 Waltham Abbey: Waltham Abbey Church *c.*1120 Kingston: Clattern Bridge late 12C Harrow-on-the-Hill: St Mary, porch late 12C
	Transitional 1145–90	
Angevins 1154 Henry II 1189 Richard I		
1199 John	**Gothic** 1190–1550 (or 1630) Early English 1190–1310	Barnes: St Mary, Langton Chapel 1190 Waltham Cross: Eleanor Cross *c.*1290 Harrow-on-the-Hill: St Mary, transepts late 13C
Plantagenets 1216 Henry III 1272 Edward I 1307 Edward II 1327 Edward III	Decorated 1290–1360	Kingston: Lovekyn Chapel 1309 Waltham Abbey: Waltham Abbey Church, Lady Chapel early 14C
	Perpendicular 1330–1550 (or 1630)	Kingston: All Saints, vestry mid 15C Eltham: Eltham Palace, Great Hall 1480
1377 Richard II *House of Lancaster* 1399 Henry IV 1413 Henry V 1422 Henry VI *House of York* 1461 Edward IV 1483 Edward V 1483 Richard III		Barnes: St Mary, tower *c.*1480 Richmond: Richmond Palace, gateway late 15C Islington: Canonbury House, tower and east wing 16C Richmond: St Mary, tower 1507 Hampton Court: Chapel Royal, Clock Court and Base Court *c.*1520

Tudors
1485 Henry VII
1509 Henry VIII

	English Renaissance 1528 (or 1550) –1650(or 1830)	Islington: Canonbury House, tower interiors 1570 and 1599 Petersham: Ham House 1610 Charlton: Charlton House *c.*1612 Greenwich: Trinity Hospital 1613

1547 Edward VI
1553 Lady Jane Grey
1553 Mary I
1558 Elizabeth I
Stuarts
1603 James I
(Jacobean period)

Dulwich: Old College, west wing 1616
Wimbledon: St Mary, Cecil Chapel *c.*1628
Greenwich: Heath Gate House *c.*1630
Charlton: St Luke *c.*1630
Highgate: Cromwell House *c.*1638

	Classical 1622–1847 Palladian 1622–1700	Greenwich: The Queen's House 1616–1629

1625 Charles I
(Carolean period)
1649 Cromwell
(Commonwealth period)

Dutch style 1630–1710

Kew: Kew Palace 1631
Eltham: Eltham Lodge 1664
Hampstead: Fenton House 1693
Petersham: Petersham House 1674
Wimbledon: Southside House 1687
Richmond: Richmond Green east side, early 18C

1660 Charles II
(Restoration period)

Wren Style 1660–1730

Greenwich: Flamsteed House 1675
Hampton Court: William and Mary ranges 1694
Blackheath: Morden College 1695
Greenwich: Royal Naval College *c.*1705

1685 James II
1689 William III/ Mary II (joint rulers)
1702 Anne

English Baroque 1705–31

Greenwich: Royal Naval College, King William Block (east and west facades) 1702
East End: St Anne Limehouse 1724
East End: St George-in-the-East 1726
Petersham: Sudbrook Park 1726
East End: Christ Church Spitalfields 1727

House of Hanover
1714 George I
1714 (or 1702) –1830
(Georgian period)

Neo-Gothic, or Georgian Gothic 1720 (or 1682) –1780

Twickenham: Strawberry Hill *c.*1766

Palladian Revival 1720–1830

Chiswick: Chiswick House 1729
Richmond: Asgill House 1758

1727 George II
1760 George III

Adam Style 1760–1790

Highgate: Kenwood, 1768
Syon: Syon House *c.*1770
Osterley: Osterley Park *c.*1780

	Greek Revival 1766–1847	
1811–20 Regency 1820 George IV		Greenwich: Royal Naval College, Chapel (interior) 1789 Dulwich: Dulwich Picture Gallery 1814 Hampstead: St Mary 1816 Hampstead: Keats' House 1816 Hampstead: St John's Chapel 1818
1830 William IV	Gothic Revival 1824–1900	Islington: Holy Trinity 1826 Harrow-on-the-Hill: School Chapel 1855 and Vaughan Library 1863 Highgate: Holly Village 1865 Richmond: Petersham Hotel 1865 Harrow-on-the-Hill: Druries 1868
	Tudor Revival 1800–1850	
	Italian Renaissance Revival 1830–50	
1837 Victoria		
	Romanesque Revival 1860–1900	Dulwich: Dulwich College 1870
	Neo-Wren (or Neo-Queen Anne or Neo-Georgian) 1880–1960	Harrow-on-the-Hill: Memorial Building 1921 Richmond: Royal Star and Garter Home 1924 Kingston: Guildhall 1935 Kingston: Bentalls 1935
	Art Nouveau 1900–1910	East End: Whitechapel Art Gallery 1899 Forest Hill: Horniman Museum 1901
House of Saxe Coburg and Gotha 1901 Edward VII (Edwardian period) *House of Windsor* 1910 George V 1936 Edward VIII 1936 George VI		
	Modernism (or *Functionalism*) 1950–82	
1952 Elizabeth II	*Brutalism* 1960–82	
	Post-Modernism from 1980	Barnes: St Mary, north section 1984

Vernacular architecture

Outer London's minor domestic buildings before the Classical period varied little with the prevailing architectural styles adopted for more important buildings and cannot, therefore, be tabulated with them. The oldest examples are as follows: *Pinner:* East End Farm Cottage early 15C. *Wimbledon:* Old Rectory House *c.*1500. *Eltham:* Tudor Barn, Well Hall 1520. *Eltham:* Lord Chamberlain's Lodgings early 16C. *Hampstead:* Old Wyldes *c.*1588. *Chiswick:* The Old Burlington 16C. *Waltham Abbey:* Queen's Arms 16C. *Pinner:* Tudor Cottage 1592. *Highgate:* Lauderdale House late 16C. *Kingston:* No 4 Market Place late 16C.

Architectural terms

Only the lesser-known terms in the book are generally included.

Abbey Monastic establishment under the authority of an abbot or abbess.

Altar (or *Communion*) *rail* Low structure enclosing the sanctuary.

Ambulatory Passageway in a church formed by continuing the aisles.

Apse Semi-circular or octagonal extension to a building.

Architrave Internal or external moulding surrounding an opening.

Ashlar Large blocks of smoothed stone laid in level courses.

Attic Low top storey of a building.

Baroque Exuberant continental development of the Classical style.

Barrel or tunnel vault A continuous arch forming a semi-circular roof.

Bay Compartment of a building divided by repeated elements.

Bay window A straight-sided window that projects from a building at ground floor level. The projection may continue at upper floor levels.

Blind A structure without openings.

Boss Ornamental projection covering the intersection of ribs in a roof.

Bow window Curved bay window.

Box pew Bench seat in a church or chapel enclosed by high partitions.

Buttress Structure attached to a wall to counter an outward thrust.

Capital Top section of a column or pilaster, usually carved in the distinctive style of a Classical order.

Cartouche Decorative panel painted or carved to resemble a scroll.

Casement window Window that is hinged and generally opens horizontally as opposed to a sash that slides and generally opens vertically.

Chancel Section of a church or chapel that houses the high altar and is reserved for the choir and clergy. It is an extension of the nave.

Chantry chapel Small chapel in or attached to a church. Built for the singing of mass for the soul of an individual, usually the benefactor.

Cladding Material added to a structure to provide an external surface.

Classical Styles following those of ancient Greece or Rome.

Clerestory Upper section of a wall, usually of the nave of a church, which is pierced with windows to provide additional light.

Coade stone Artificial, hard-wearing material resembling stone; cast in the 18C to provide statues or decorative features for buildings.

Coffering Recessed ceiling panelling.

Corbel Wall bracket, generally of stone, supporting e.g., a beam.

Corinthian Greek Classical order. Columns are slender and their capitals intricately decorated with carved leaves and small spiral scrolls (volutes).

Cornice A projecting decorative feature running horizontally at high level.

Coved Concave shaped ceiling.

Crossing Where the nave, transepts and chancel intersect in a church.

Cupola Small domed roof generally above a turret.

Curtain wall Non-loadbearing material providing an external surface.

Dais Raised platform at the end of a large room, generally a hall.

Decorated Second period of English Gothic *c.*1290–*c.*1360. Remarkable for ornate window tracery, pinnacles and porches.

Doric Classical order, the oldest and sturdiest. The capitals of Doric columns are virtually undecorated.

Dormer window Window protruding from a sloping roof.

Early English First phase of Gothic architecture in England *c*.1190–*c*.1310. Characterized by narrow pointed arches and windows (lancet).
Eave Horizontal edge of a roof overhanging the wall.

Fanlight Oblong or semi-circular window above a door.
Fan vaulting Ribs of the vault make a pattern resembling a fan.
Festoon Carved hanging garland of fruit and flowers.
Fluted Vertical grooving.
Flying buttress Semi-archlike structure that directly transfers the weight of the wall to a vertical pier.

Gable Upper section of wall at each end of a building.
Gallery Storey added to an upper level, always open on one side, and usually arcaded. Alternatively, a long room for displaying works of art.
Gothic Style of architecture from 12C–17C employing the pointed arch.
Gothic Revival Serious 19C attempt to reproduce the Gothic style.
Greek Revival Buildings designed *c*.1770–1840 in Greek style.
Groin vault Intersection of two tunnel (or barrel) vaults.

Hammerbeam roof Form of roof construction late 14C–16C.

Ionic Classical order. Columns are slenderer than those in the Doric order and capitals are decorated at corners with spiral scrolls (volutes).

Jamb Straight, vertical side of a door, arch or window.
Jetty The overhang of a building's upper storey or storeys that projects above its lower floor or floors.
Joinery Woodwork that is fitted in, but not structural to, a building.

Lady Chapel Chapel dedicated to the Virgin Mary.
Lancet window Slender window with a sharply pointed arch *c*.1190–*c*.1310.
Lantern Small turret pierced with openings and crowning a roof.
Light Section of a window filled with glass.

Majolica Glazed earthenware generally used as decorative tiling. Also known as faience.
Mansard roof A roof with two slopes, the lower being much the steeper. The name commemorates the 17C French architect François Mansart although its use pre-dates his period.
Moulding Decorative addition to a projecting feature such as a cornice, door frame, etc.
Mullions Vertical bars dividing a window into 'lights'.

Nave Body of the church housing the congregation.
Neo-Gothic Gothic features used in a light-hearted manner in the mid 18C.
Norman Romanesque architecture distinguished by semi-circular arches and massive walls *c*.1060–*c*.1200.

Order Classical architecture where the design and proportion of the columns and entablatures are standardized.
Oriel window Window projecting as a bay but at an upper level.

Palladian Style of architecture based on the 16C work of the Italian Andrea Palladio which itself derived from ancient Rome.
Parapet Low, solid wall surmounting a structure.
Pedestal Base between a column or statue and its plinth.
Pediment Low-pitched triangular gable above a portico, door or window.
Pendant Elongated, hanging feature decorating a roof or stairway.
Perpendicular Architectural style peculiar to England. The last and longest phase of Gothic, 1360–1550 (or 1660). Distinguished by large windows divided by horizontal transoms as well as mullions.
Pier Solid structure supporting a great load, frequently square in shape.
Pilaster Shallow, flat column attached to a wall.
Pinnacle Vertical decorative feature surmounting a Gothic structure.
Plinth Projecting base of a wall, column or statue.
Podium Lowest stage of a pedestal for a column or statue.
Portal Important doorway.
Portcullis Gate that can be raised and lowered vertically for defence.
Portico Classical porch of columns supporting a roof usually pedimented.
Priory Monastic establishment under the authority of a prior or prioress.

Putti Small, naked boys, usually cherubs.

Quoin stones Dressed stones fitted externally at the angles of a wall to give added strength. Popular in the late 17C and early 18C.

Refectory Dining hall, also known as a frater when situated in a monastery.
Reredos Decorative structure usually standing behind the altar in a church or chapel. Generally made of wood but occasionally stone.
Retable Raised shelf behind the altar in a church or chapel. Often decorated.
Retrochoir Section of a church behind the sanctuary.
Rib Protruding band supporting a vault. Occasionally purely decorative.
Rococo Last phase of the Baroque style in the mid 18C with widespread use of detailed ornamentation. Few examples are found in England.
Romanesque Style of architecture featuring semi-circular arches. Popular from the 9C to c.1200. Saxon and Norman buildings were Romanesque.
Rose window Circular window used in Gothic architecture. Its tracery pattern resembles a rose. Introduced in the mid 13C.
Rotunda Circular building, generally domed.
Roundel Circular decorative panel, e.g., of glass in a window.
Rustication Use of stonework on the exterior of a building to give an impression of strength. The jointing is always deep.

Sacristy Room in a church for storage or sacred vessels and vestments. Generally used for robing. Also known as a vestry.
Sanctuary Area behind the altar rail in which the high altar stands.
Sarcophagus Carved coffin.
Sash window A window of two separate panes that slides and generally opens vertically as opposed to a casement that is hinged and generally opens horizontally. Introduced into England c.1680.
Saxon English architecture in Romanesque style pre-dating the Norman Conquest of 1066.
Scissor beam Roof construction in which secondary beams cross each other diagonally in support of the main beams.
Sounding board Canopy above a pulpit. Also known as a tester. Introduced to improve acoustics.
Spire Tall pointed structure with flat or rounded sides surmounting a tower.
Steeple Tower together with its crowning structure e.g., lantern, spire.
Stoup Basin for holy water, usually of stone and situated near a door.
Stucco Plaster applied to the external face of a wall and painted.
Swag Carved representation of a piece of hanging cloth. Generally incorporates festoons of flowers, fruit, etc.

Terracotta Unglazed earthenware used as tiling.
Tessellated pavement Mosaic flooring.
Tie beam Horizontal main beam in a timber roof.
Tracery Intersecting bars that create a decorative pattern in Gothic architecture.
Transept The area that runs on either side of the nave of a large church forming the cruciform (cross) plan.
Transitional The merging of Gothic with Norman architecture c.1150–c.1200.
Transom The bar of stone or wood that divides a mullioned window horizontally.
Triforium Blind passage that runs above the roof of an aisle in a church.
Trophy Decorative sculptured arms or armour.
Tunnel vault Alternative name for barrel vault.
Tuscan Classical order. Roman adaptation of the Greek Doric order.

Undercroft Vaulted room or area at ground floor level.

Vault Underground room frequently reserved for internment. Alternatively, an arched structure forming a roof.
Venetian window Window of three openings. The central, large section having a semi-circular arch.
Vestibule Entrance hall or anteroom.
Vestry Alternative name for sacristy.

Wainscoting Timber-lining on the lower section of an internal wall.
Weatherboarding Timber strips fixed to an internal or external wall for
protection or decoration. Also known as clapboarding.

Designers

Outstanding architects, sculptors and decorators whose work is featured in
this book.

Adam, Robert 1728–92
Bacon, John the Younger 1778–
1859
Baker, Sir Herbert
1862–1946
Barry, Sir Charles
1795–1860
Bird, Francis 1667–1731
Blomfield, Sir Arthur William
1829–99
Blore, Edward 1787–1879
Boyle, Richard, Third Earl of
Burlington 1695–1753
Burne-Jones, Sir Edward Coley
1833–98
Burton, Decimus 1800–81
Campbell, Colen 1676(?)–1729
Chambers, Sir William 1723–96
Chantrey, Sir Francis
1781–1841
Cheere, Sir Henry 1703–81
Cibber, Caius Gabriel 1630–1700
Cockerell, Samuel Pepys 1754–
1827
Comper, Sir John Ninian 1864–
1960
Cure, William 1515–79
Flaxman, John 1755–1826
Fowler, Charles 1791–1867
Gibbons, Grinling
1648–1721
Gibbs, James 1682–1754
Hawksmoor, Nicholas 1661–1736
Hogarth, William
1697–1764
Holland, Henry 1745–1806
Hooke, Robert 1635–1703
James, John 1672–1746
Jones, Inigo 1573–1652
Kauffmann, Angelica
1741–1807
Kent, William 1685(?)–1748
Leoni, Giacomo 1686–1746
Lutyens, Sir Edwin
1869–1944
May, Hugh 1622–1684

Morris, Roger 1695–1749
Morris, William 1834–96
Mylne, Robert 1734–1811
Nash, John 1752–1835
Nemon, Oscar 1906–
Nollekens, Joseph
1737–1823
Paxton, Sir Joseph 1801-65
Pearce, Edward d. 1695
Pearson, John Loughborough
1817–97
Piper, John 1903–
Pugin, Augustus Welby Northmore
1812–52
Repton, Humphrey
1752–1818
Ricci, Sebastiano
1662–1734
Roubiliac, Louis François 1705(?)–
62
Rysbrack, John Michael
1693–1770
Scheemakers, Peter
1691–1781
Scott, Sir George Gilbert 1811–78
Soane, Sir John 1753–1837
Stone, Nicolas the Elder 1586–1647
Street, George Edmund 1824–81
Stuart, James 1713–88
Taylor, Sir Robert 1714–88
Teulon, Samuel Sanders 1812–1873
Thornhill, Sir James
1675–1734
Thorpe, John *c.* 1563–1655
Tite, Sir William 1798–1873
Vertue, William, d. 1527
Vulliamy, Lewis 1791–1871
Ware, Isaac, d. 1766
Webb, Sir Aston 1849–1930
Webb, John 1611–72
West, Benjamin 1738–1820
Westmacott, Sir Richard 1755–
1856
Wren, Sir Christopher 1632–1723
Wyatt, James 1746–1813
Zucchi, Antonio 1726–1795